MURDER IS A
FAMILY MATTER

For Andy.
- a long time friend
Hope you enjoy it.
Love Bev

Sept 06

MURDER IS A FAMILY MATTER

Beverley Armstrong-Rodman

iUniverse, Inc.
New York Lincoln Shanghai

Murder is a Family Matter

iUniverse books may be ordered through booksellers or by contacting:

iUniverse
2021 Pine Lake Road, Suite 100
Lincoln, NE 68512
www.iuniverse.com
1-800-Authors (1-800-288-4677)

ISBN-13: 978-0-595-38617-8 (pbk)
ISBN-13: 978-0-595-83527-0 (cloth)
ISBN-13: 978-0-595-82997-2 (ebk)
ISBN-10: 0-595-38617-2 (pbk)
ISBN-10: 0-595-83527-9 (cloth)
ISBN-10: 0-595-82997-X (ebk)

Printed in the United States of America

With heartfelt thanks to several important people in my life:

- my husband Ward for his unfailing love and patience

- my daughter and son, Heather and Greg, for their indefatigable efforts to drag me into this computer age

- my sister Jean Archer for her encouragement

- my life-long friend Marilyn Sutherland for her helpful hints and sense of humour

- my artistic friend Faith Amadio for her imaginative art work.

Without all of you, this book would never have seen the light of day

CHAPTER 1

▼

"Someone help me," she shouted, or had she only thought it? Where was she? Why wasn't Matt lying beside her? Thoughts were flying now like sparks from a campfire. The terror was incapacitating.

As the voices washed over her, she became more anxious, more bewildered. Trickles of fear oozed down her spine. Cruel daggers danced in her head as her heart pounded. Somehow the voices were familiar, and that set alarm bells clanging.

It felt as if someone was hammering a nail right into her forehead. Her tongue was crazy-glued to the roof of her mouth, and her lips were putty. Prudence Wainwright tried unsuccessfully to open her eyes. Was she blindfolded? Had she been kidnapped? Had she suffered a stroke? Panic taught her heart new tricks. It pounded and jumped as if trying to escape through her throat. Damn, what was it that she couldn't remember? It was as if a grey mesh screen had clanged down in her head, cutting her off from recent memories. She knew who she was, she just didn't know where she was. Rope-like tentacles of fear were strangling her. Surely everything would be all right if she could just calm down and open her eyes. In the darkness she saw tiny dots of light like fireflies whirling and twirling, coloured pinwheels against black velvet.

The sickly aroma of flowers was overpowering. Her heart lurched again. Oh God, please no. Please don't let this be a funeral parlour! I can't be in a coffin because I'm still alive. Who's doing this to me? "I'm alive" she tried to shout, but no sound came from her lips.

The voices were clearer now, the fragmented words bombarding her. She could make out bits and pieces — "old man dead — surprising that she survived

— should be dead — all that money — better for everyone." Were they talking about her? Was she going to die? No way José, not without a fight! Prudence, however, was in no shape to fight. At that moment a great lethargy seemed to wash over her, and she began a downward spiral back into the blackness.

Now she seemed to be floating in the boat, so gently, so peacefully. They were watching for the loons. Loons mate for life, just like she and Matt were supposed to. Voices intruded again — rippling and surging. The sounds ricocheted around in her head like pebbles in a can. Suddenly she recognized those voices, and with a shudder and a monumental effort of will, she struggled back up out of the viscous darkness. Now she realized where she was — not floating at the lake, and definitely not lying in a coffin. Thank God for that small mercy. With a mixture of relief and trepidation she understood that she was in a hospital bed.

The grey screen lifted then, and images started assailing her, like pictures in a movie preview, as she relived those last terrifying moments before the utter blackness. They had been in the car heading home. Matt and Jordan, father and son, had argued fiercely just before she and Matt went out in the boat for their evening cruise. When they returned to the cottage, Jordan was gone, and she and Matt packed up and headed back to Toronto. Matt was in a foul mood, Pru was in tears, and soon they were shouting at each other.

Suddenly he had been pumping the brakes in a frantic effort, as they hurtled down the steep hill past the blur of trees and rocks. She remembered pressing her knuckles to her mouth to keep from screaming. Even in the dark car she had seen the fear on his face. His hands were gripping the wheel — a death grip, she thought giddily. The car was careening from side to side as he tried to gain control.

"Pru, the brakes are gone. Someone's cut the brakes!" He seemed to be apologizing in those last few frantic moments. She had started to tell him that everything would be fine, but then came the curve, that hideous yawning curve through the rock cut. It was waiting for them. It had waited patiently all these years, waited and watched and bided its time. It embraced them with a terrible clamour — then had come blessed nothingness.

Matt, where are you? she silently cried. Oh please Matt, I'm sorry, just don't be dead. Don't leave me. They had been arguing furiously in the car. She was angry and hurt by his latest infidelity, but she didn't want him dead. He was her husband, and in spite of everything, she still loved him.

The voices again, those voices belonged to her kids! It was Jordan and Jenny talking so cavalierly and cruelly about her. This was too much to assimilate. She couldn't think any more just now. She had to let go and fall back into that peaceful darkness.

As the woman in the hospital bed drifted in and out of consciousness, she felt that she had been struggling for hours. In reality it was just a few moments in time. The man and woman standing by the window were totally unaware that she was in anything but a deep coma. If they had only bothered to look, they would have seen the tears on her face, and the slight movement of her hands.

An ambulance wailed importantly as it sped away to pick up some hapless victim. No one paid any attention to it, as the petite blond with the big brown eyes, stared into the small aquarium in the unusually well furnished hospital room. Jenny watched the vividly coloured fish swimming in desultory fashion, and wondered idly whether her mother would ever waken up and be able to enjoy them. Then she wondered how long it would be before she and Jordan were seeing tropical fish in Tahiti or some other exotic place. She fervently hoped it would be soon. The ineffable hospital smells permeated the room, and Jenny wrinkled her cute little nose in distaste. She couldn't stand this hospital with its noises and smells and terrifying machines.

Sighing deeply, she turned toward her brother, and gave him an appraising look as he gazed out the window. She was trying to gage his mood. Which approach would be better, gentle and adoring, or accusatory? Opting for the latter, she grabbed his arm and frowned up at him. "It's time we talked, Jordie. We haven't had a minute to ourselves since the crash, and you've been avoiding me. I've done a lot of thinking, and I have to get this straight in my head." Here she paused and glared at him with a belligerent intensity.

The tall dark haired man turned slowly, and stared at her with obsidian eyes. "Spit it out, Jen. What are you trying to say?"

"Jordie, you know you can trust me. Gawd, I've been covering for you all my life." She gave him a conspiratorial grin as she continued. "I know damn well that you did something to cause this crash. Dad's dead, and it won't be long for her." Here she nodded her head toward the woman lying immobile on the hospital bed, tubes and machines humming and hissing all around her like monstrous acolytes paying homage. "You've got to be honest with me now. I don't want to make any mistakes if I have to cover for you. What's the deal?" The harsh, straightforward words seemed out of place coming from that sweet, innocent face.

Jordan impaled her with his dark eyes, and replied in a low, viciously controlled voice. "Is this my baby sister accusing me of something? Is this the little sister who needs a few good belts of gin to get herself going in the morning?"

Grabbing her arms, he continued, hissing through clenched teeth. "Is this my little sister hallucinating again?"

"Horseshit" said Jenny, shaking off his hands. "Don't try to play games with me, brother dearest. I know you caused the accident. You know I love you, and I'll go along with anything you want. We're a team, Jordan and Jenny, the terrible twosome, so don't you dare try to shut me out. Talk to me. Don't play innocent, it doesn't suit you. Besides, it's too much of a coincidence. It was just last week that you were saying how great it would be to get our hands on all that money now instead of way in the future, when we'll be too old to enjoy it. You said that the folks would likely be stubborn and live forever, and - - -"

"Wow, slow down there, babe. As I recall, you agreed in your drunken state that there have been a few times when you felt like killing the old man yourself."

"True, but you knew damn well that it was just talk. You know I couldn't do anything like that." Her voice rose indignantly. "Anyway, I remember you said how easy it would be to stage an accident." Again there was a belligerent tone to her words. "Come on, Jordie, fess up. What did you do, and how did you do it? The more I know, the better I'll be able to help you. We're a team, dammit, and don't you forget it. I don't care what you've done, just let me in on it."

"That's enough. Don't say one more word of that trash. Now you listen and try to get it through that pretty little scheming head of yours. When I heard about the crash, I just figured that maybe you and Pete had done something to the car. You apparently thought I had done something. Let's forget the accusations and get on with things. I don't give a shit what really happened. As far as you know, it was an accident. As far as I know, it was an accident. More importantly, as far as the police know, it was an accident. The old man died, the old lady is going to die, and you and I are about to hit the jackpot — end of story." He glared at her as if daring her to contradict him.

Jenny knew that look, and she knew that it was time to back off. You could only push Jordan so far. Still, she had to make one more try. She had to know what had happened. "Jordie, come on. We both know what a good liar you are, but please don't lie to me. I don't want to hear all this shit. Don't shut me out."

Before she could say anything else, he grabbed her by both arms and began to shake her. "Get a grip" he hissed through clenched teeth. "From now on the subject is closed, so forget it. Just keep telling yourself that it was a tragic accident which just happens to be a piece of luck for us."

He was pinching her arms again, his face like a black cloud. Then like lightning, his mood changed. He smiled at her affectionately with an oily smile, and in a cajoling tone he said, "Now go wash your face and put on some lipstick. You fix yourself up all pretty and then we'll get out of here. Come on, I'll take you to lunch." He spoke as if to a child. "First we have to stop at the nursing station and talk to 'Miss finger-up-her-butt'." He laughed at his own humour. "As usual, you be quiet and look sweet and helpless. Leave the talking to me."

Kissing her on the forehead, he pushed her towards the washroom. Surprisingly, Jenny allowed herself to be manipulated. Jordan could always do that to her. She felt a cold little worm of fear thrashing around in her stomach, but she did as she was told. She usually did what Jordan told her to do, usually, but not always.

She was crying now. Tears had suddenly appeared in her big brown eyes, and were tracing their way down her cheeks in a very fetching way. Jenny always looked good when she cried. Was she crying because of the tragedy — her father dead, her mother in a coma? Possibly, but not likely. Were her tears for her beloved brother who would be in serious trouble if, indeed, he had caused the accident? That could certainly be the case. Was she crying for herself because she hated hospitals and sick rooms? That was a distinct possibility. Then, of course, anyone who knew Jenny well, and there were very few who fell into that category, would say that her tears were simply a little ploy to garner sympathy, and to make herself look helpless and forlorn. Only Jenny knew why she was crying, and she wasn't about to tell.

In spite of the long blue cotton dress and the open-toed spike heels, Jennifer Wainwright looked like a little girl. Her mother had always said that her unruly golden curls made her look like a dandelion. Jenny, however, didn't want to think about her mother right now.

While she obediently entered the washroom, Jordan stood gazing out the hospital window onto the parking lot below. It was old, full of potholes and loose chunks of asphalt. They had a nerve charging people to park there. Whether leaving the hospital happily or sadly, everyone had to stop and pay a reluctant ransom to the one-armed bandits guarding the exit. It seemed the final indignity.

He watched with cold eyes as a little bird wrestled with a piece of food lying on the ground. He wondered idly who had thrown food from a car window, probably some spoiled kid. Was it a cookie, or a French fry, or maybe a piece of fruit? At the moment it seemed to be the most important thing in the little bird's life. Jordan pictured himself squeezing it and wringing its tiny neck. Birds were such filthy things. A sudden gust of wind ruffled the bird's feathers, and an empty styrofoam cup rolled aimlessly along the pavement.

Hands in pockets, he stared unseeing at the cars coming and going. Some disgorged reluctant patients, fearful of what lay ahead, while others were picking up exuberant ones who had run the gauntlet of fear and pain, and had lived to tell the tale. His mother, he knew, would not be one of the lucky ones.

Eventually Jennifer returned, looking pale but calm. As they left the hospital room, neither the tall, dark, strangely handsome man, nor his slim, blond, pretty sister, bothered to glance at the pale figure on the bed. It was as if they had forgotten she was there.

If they had cared enough to look, they would have been shocked to see the fragile woman staring at them with wide, frightened eyes.

CHAPTER 2

▼

A hospital can be an unfriendly place where people come in hopes of being healed or in fear of dying. There is that certain dichotomy — the joy in the maternity ward juxtaposed beside the hopelessness of the chronic ward. It is a stage where doctors and nurses perform their magic on captive audiences.

This particular morning the large Toronto hospital was a madhouse. Some interns and residents raced around importantly, stethoscopes flying, while others lounged at the station, reading charts and flirting with the nurses. Of course, the female interns did their share of flirting too, so that there was always an underlying current of incipient or budding romance. At times the hospital seemed to be a hotbed of intrigue, a little Peyton Place of romance and entanglements.

As Jordan and his sister walked down the long hall towards the station, a nurse passed them, hurrying towards their mother's room. The monitors had suddenly alerted the nursing staff to a change in Mrs. Wainwright's vital signs. She was finally fighting her way out of the coma.

It was almost lunch time, and the rattling carts of lunch trays were emerging from the service elevator, lurching their way up the long crowded corridors, their unappetizing smells wafting ahead of them.

The occasional clergyman could be seen walking resolutely into some hapless patient's room, and emerging a few minutes later looking solemn and sad. The ubiquitous "pink ladies" were delivering flowers, and to add to the confusion, a technician with her cart full of blood samples, was jockeying for position amongst the wheel chairs, gurneys and staff. It was a chaotic scene of comings and goings.

Jennifer Wainwright hated hospitals, and the infrequent visits to her comatose mother these past few days had been a tour de force for her. Early as it was, she had needed a few good gulps of gin to steel herself for the ordeal. Surprisingly, her mother was out of that terrifying intensive care unit, and had been moved to a beautiful big private room, but Jenny still didn't want to be here. She wanted to be flying along the highway in a convertible, golden curls bouncing in the breeze. Better still, she would like to be at the cottage, sitting on the deck in her bikini, soaking up the sun, and sipping on a gin and tonic. Even sitting in the cool green park feeding the squirrels would be preferable to this. Of course, best of all would be lying on a Tahitian beach with Jordan.

It scared her to see her mother lying there so still and white, and pierced full of needles and tubes. There was no way she could recover from all her injuries, but she could hang on for a long time. Jenny shuddered at the thought of all those hospital visits. If Prudence Wainwright was going to die anyway, Jennifer, ever the pragmatist, hoped it would be sooner rather than later.

But what if her mother didn't die? What if she lived on and on as a hopeless, helpless invalid? What if she expected Jenny — her only daughter — to care for her? What then? There would be no easy access to the money, no wonderful life with Jordan. All her hopes and dreams would simply float away. The unthinkable idea made her gasp. There was no room in her life for nursing an invalid, even if that invalid happened to be her mother.

Jenny supposed that she had loved her folks when she was little, but way too much had happened in the intervening years. Now her dad was gone, and her mother, well, she was gone too for all practical purposes. Jenny didn't really care all that much as long as she had Jordan. She and Jordie were an unbeatable team. With a twenty million dollar cushion, they could live wherever they wanted, do whatever made them happy. And Jenny knew exactly what would make her happy.

At the nursing station Jordan Wainwright gave a pathetic and hopefully disarming smile, and murmured "Do you think our mother is any better today?"

Nurse Christina Marshall looked up from a chart, and frowned at these two tiresome people. The man was slim, and had an almost predatory look about him. He had an aquiline nose and sharply chiselled features. His black hair was thick and wavy, and his dark eyes, topped by thick black eyebrows, seemed bottomless. They were the blackest eyes Christina had ever seen. Some women would undoubtedly find his full lips sensuous, but Tina found them somehow repulsive. They always looked slightly wet. She was a good judge of character, and she knew in her heart that these two were totally insincere in their protestations of concern about their mother. He was definitely attractive, though, she admitted, as he stood there in grey casual slacks and a yellow cashmere sweater.

Unfortunately he reminded her of good old Uncle Freddy — the black sheep of the family. There had been a time when she had loved her Uncle Freddy as much or more than her own father, but that had been before he started casually groping her and rubbing himself against her, all under the guise of fun and games. When one tickling match went too far, she had been smart enough to tell her parents, and Uncle Freddy disappeared from her life. When she got older, she learned that he had molested another young girl and had been put away. She got the same uncomfortable feeling when she was around Jordan Wainwright. Yesterday she had noticed him staring at a cute little girl, and had kept an eye on him until the child was safely onto the elevator with her mother.

The blond sister was petite and childlike in appearance until you noticed the dark circles under her beautiful dark brown eyes, and the quick, nervous movements. She had a petulant but very kissable mouth. Christina could smell liquor wafting from her. After watching them come and go, she didn't believe for a moment that they really cared much one way or the other. They didn't even visit every day, and they stayed for only a few minutes. Tina just couldn't understand this. She would have thought that they would take turns sitting at their mother's bedside, talking to her and waiting for her to come out of the coma. Instead they sauntered in at their convenience with an overly casual attitude, and never stayed more than a couple of minutes. What was wrong with this picture? Christina felt that Jordan Wainwright was pretending a concern which was absolutely bogus. Jennifer might be more sincere, because at the moment her eyes were red and puffy as if she had been crying. Christina wasn't sure whether she was just a good little actress, or whether she really did care about her mom. If she did, she certainly had a strange way of showing it. As usual she was clinging to her brother's arm like a shy bride.

In the days since the dreadful car accident which had killed their father and left their mother in a coma, Christina had come to dread their infrequent visits. It had been almost a week, and she wondered idly when they were going to have the funeral for their father. What was the hold-up? She had heard via the hospital grape-vine that they were waiting for their mother to die so that they could have a joint funeral, but that seemed a bit bizarre. Anyway, Jordan's fawning and ingratiating ways gave her the willies. They both seemed to put their sad faces on and off like masks.

Jordan had dark penetrating eyes which bore holes in her, and sent shivers down her spine. This was a man she would not want to meet in a dark alley.

There was something indefinable about him. It was as if he knew all the dark and wicked secrets of the world. She suspected that he would take perverse pleasure in pulling wings off butterflies, and Christina admitted to herself that she was actually a little afraid of him. She recognized his type, and whether or not he was a pedophile, there was certainly something wrong with him.

Prudence Wainwright had been a gracious and well respected member of Toronto society. Her picture was often in the newspapers and on local television, showing her working with one charity or another. The story of the Wainwrights was well known. They had been independently wealthy because Matthew had been so successful in the stock market. Then just a year previously, they had the incredible luck of winning the super twenty million lottery jackpot. Tina couldn't help wondering how these seemingly decent people had managed to raise the strange pair standing before her now.

"Your mother's condition is stable" she declared in an icy tone. She wasn't prepared to say anything more at the moment.

"Well, we have great faith that she is going to waken up." He emphasized the "is". "It's just a matter of time. Now that our father is gone, she's all we have."

This last was uttered in a soft voice accompanied by a rictus of a smile, which Christina assumed was meant to imply great sadness. It was so phony that she couldn't help but grimace. Actually she felt like barfing. This man was absolutely loathsome.

Just then a bouncy red head with big green eyes, huge dimples which looked like craters in her cheeks when she chose to display them, and a luscious figure no nursing uniform could hide, hurried in behind the desk. "Sorry I'm late, Tina. I ran into an old friend at the door. Haven't seen him since high school days, and we just had to catch up a bit."

Relieved to have a reason to cut short her conversation, Christina Marshall said "Excuse me Mr. Wainwright. I have to go over these charts with Miss Connors."

Again he gave her that somewhat sinister smile. "Oh certainly, that's fine."

Bunny Connors gave him her most dazzling smile, showing off the deep dimples. Jennifer glowered at her, and gripped Jordan's arm a little tighter.

"I just wanted to tell you that we have to be away for a few days. We'll be going up to the family cottage in Muskoka. Here's the number. Please call us if there's any change in her condition. There's so much to be done since the accident, you know," he sighed.

Tina gave him a curt nod and turned to speak to Bunny — she of the big boobs and tiny waist. Without any further conversation, the two Wainwrights made their way toward the elevators.

"Those two are a pair of ghouls" said Christina, shaking her head in disgust. "There's something about them that just isn't right. I can barely be civil to them. I don't know, Bunny, but I feel somehow that they're trouble. What do you think?"

"Well," said Bunny slowly, smoothing her uniform skirt which was unprofessionally short. "She seems strange, but he's awfully cute in a funky sort of way. He'll have a pile of dough too when his mother dies," she sighed. "I don't think he's married, do you?"

"Bunny, don't take it for granted that she's going to die" chided Christina. "She isn't 'in extremis' yet, and I don't know or care whether he's married or not. All the money in the world wouldn't make me interested in that guy. I'd just as soon date Norman Bates."

Bunny giggled appreciatively. They had been down that conversational road several times during the past few days. Bunny was a nice girl, but a bit of a bubble-head. Christina often wondered how she had managed to pass her nursing exams. Still, she had to admit that in a way she was a bit jealous of Bunny. Most things seemed so easy for her. She floated through life seemingly without any cares, and she went through boyfriends like the proverbial hot knife through butter. Her figure was sensational, and the patients loved her. "Vivacious" should have been her middle name. She seemed so full of life and fun, and she treated everyone with the same zippy attitude. Thankfully, thought Christina wryly, she hadn't killed any of them yet!

Bunny had decided on nursing because she knew how good she would look in the uniform, and because it would give her access to all those rich doctors! She wished nurses still wore those wonderful red-lined navy capes, and the caps with the black stripe on them to signify that they were registered nurses. Things were too casual now, not as romantic as in the old days.

Failing her quest to marry a doctor, any rich guy would do. Recently, however, she had been dating Jimmy. He was poor, and he had no good prospects, but he was so sweet to her, and he loved animals the way she did. It would be just her luck to fall in love with someone who had no money.

Bunny was not overly bright, but she had surprised everyone by passing her nursing courses. Her dad had always teased her when she was little, saying she must have been in the garden the day that the I.Q. fairy came to call. Bunny didn't even get the joke until she was older, and then it really hurt. She knew it took her a while, but she eventually figured things out, and she had worked incredibly hard to pass her nursing exams. That had shown her dad! He was so proud of her now. Even though she was a red head, she had always been the quintessential dumb blond in the minds of most people, but she had shown them all. She was proud to be a nurse, and she would be even more proud if and when she became a doctor's wife. Jordan Wainwright wasn't a doctor, but he was going to be rich when his mother died. He was good looking too except for those scary eyes. He was a definite possibility, but she couldn't forget her dear sweet Jimmy. Well, she sighed, she would flirt with Jordan and see what happened.

Christina Marshall was a bit of a loner. She wore her loneliness like a comfortable old sweater. It was a familiar part of her. She had married young, and had become a young widow. It was an all too common story — a cliché really. Ronnie had been coming home with a pizza for their dinner when he was killed by a drunk driver. After six months of intense depression and grief, Christina came back to work. She had aged in that time, and some of her former vitality had disappeared. Nevertheless she was known around the hospital as an excellent nurse, caring and efficient, responsible and reliable.

As she turned back to the desk, two young and rather unkempt med students approached her, laughing and talking too loudly for a proper hospital atmosphere.

"Helllllllo Christina" called the chubby one in a familiar manner. "How's our Tina today, and how's Miss Bunny?" he leered in Bunny's direction. His hair was flying every which way, and it looked as if he had a pimple on his chin.

"Yuck" thought Bunny.

"Grow up George," said Christina, scowling at him.

"Tina, Tina, please don't be meana" sang chubby in a surprisingly mellow voice. The happy-go-lucky med student, blissfully unaware of what an unfortunate and unprofessional picture he presented to the world, edged his fat behind onto the corner of the desk and grinned at the nurses. His friend, a quiet, nervous looking chap, tall and skinny, distanced himself a bit and began looking at charts.

"Get your fat ass off the desk," said Christina crossly. "This is a hospital, not a school cafeteria."

"Wish it was a cafeteria, I'm starved" he replied good-naturedly. "Say, how's the zombie in 707? Has she opened her baby blues yet, or is she no longer in the land of the living?"

George fancied himself a bit of a comedian, but Christina was in no mood for jokes. She was more cross than she had intended, and by the time she had tartly reminded him of the respect medical people should show for every patient, he slunk away, momentarily chastened. He was always cheerful and ready with some clever witticism, and he would burst into song at the least provocation. His good humour seemed irrepressible, but today Tina felt guilty at how hurt he looked as he continued on down the hall.

"Now there's an immature twit who has a lot to learn," she muttered, knowing she had been a little too hard on him. She hated to be rude to anyone, but Mrs. Wainwright's fawning son and daughter had riled her. "Do you suppose he'll ever grow into a real live doctor, Bunny?"

"Sure, he's just a kid yet" pronounced Bunny from the lofty heights of her twenty-two years. "He's good natured, and he's nice to the patients — he makes them laugh." As she said this, she was taking a quick peek into the small mirror she always carried in her pocket. She was wearing a new lipstick, and wasn't sure whether she liked the colour or not. She had lushly extravagant lips — killer lips — thought Tina.

Bunny continued, "Betcha he'll be the kind of doctor everyone loves even if he isn't too smart" she added, smiling at her reflection just to check out her dimples.

"You know what's scary is that you're probably right" grinned Tina. She shook her head ruefully as she heard the buzzer for Mrs. Jackson's room.

Meanwhile, down the hall in room 707, Prudence Wainwright drifted back down into an all encompassing blackness.

CHAPTER 3

▼

The Toronto bus making its way to Niagara Falls was packed with tourists, mostly Japanese and Germans. Many were day trippers, heading over to see the wondrous falls, and to be entertained on Clifton Hill by the plethora of wax museums, souvenir shops and restaurants. Some had brought lunches to eat at the clean picnic tables situated along the green, grassy parkland. Some were coming strictly for the casinos, hoping to hit the big one and go home with a pocketful of money.

There was a holiday spirit in the air. Passengers laughed and chatted in their own languages as they peered out the windows at every interesting point along the crowded highway. Excitement mounted as they neared the famous city.

This morning, however, at least one of the passengers was not a tourist. His name was William Thomas Burton, aka "Willy the Weasel," and he was coming home. Well, at least he was returning to a place where he had once lived. Willy really had no home. Approaching the outskirts, he became more and more excited. It seemed that he had been dreaming of this day forever. He had served his time in the pen for rape, and now he was a free man — free to rape again. This time he had added a few killings to his agenda.

Willy was truly a weasel in looks, in thoughts and in actions. Never had a nickname been more suited. By the time he was twelve years old, he was an inveterate peeping Tom, as well as a thief and a bully. By his early teens he had graduated to rape. His hatred for women began at an early age and knew no bounds. His four sisters and his mother had abused and tormented him mercilessly. They laughed at his small stature, his ugly face, and his "little dickey" as they called it. He could remember them ganging up on him, pulling on it and pinching it, while he cried helplessly, the tears and snot running down his face in pathetic streams. His mother was as bad or worse than his sisters, telling him that no woman would ever want him, that he was useless, that he was too ugly to live. As a child, Willy believed them.

As he grew into his teens, however, his penis grew too, until it was a considerable size. In Willy's eyes it was a thing of beauty. He played with it constantly, and gradually began to realize that he could use it as a weapon against every woman who had ever ignored him, laughed at him or teased him. In Willy's world, that was just about every woman he had ever met.

His luck began to change too as he grew older. He was strong enough to fight back when his sisters attacked him. After raping two of them and breaking his mother's arm, they left him alone. They were too afraid of him to even call the cops. Willy was suddenly king in his own little world. The feeling of power was overwhelming. No matter how many times he broke into homes to rob or to rape, he never got caught. He began to feel invincible. Willy wasn't the sharpest tack on the wall, but with good luck he managed to stay free of the law for many years. Finally, however, everyone's luck runs out. The Niagara Regional Police had been trying to catch the rapist for a long time. Willy got a little too cocky, and when an elaborate undercover trap was set, he was caught. Finally William T. Burton was sent off to the pen.

What gnawed at William T. was the way the cops had humiliated him. They used a good-looking female to trap him, and he had fallen for it. What right did women have to be cops? It made no sense to Willy. He couldn't believe he had been trapped by a woman. The only good thing that happened on the day he was captured, was that he had managed to slash the face of one of the detectives. During his incarceration he nursed his grudge and his hatred for Detective Jack Willinger and his partner Detective Bud Lang. Willinger had been a tall good looking guy, but he wouldn't be so good looking now with that scar on his face, Willy told himself with satisfaction. What really rankled was the way they had treated him. After Willy slashed Willinger's face, the partner, a big bear of a man, shook Willy like a rag doll and handcuffed him to an inside railing while he and the female cop hustled Willinger to the hospital. It had seemed like hours before two other cops arrived to arrest Willy and cart him off to jail. They had laughed at him cuffed to the railing and shivering, his pants around his ankles. That was the final indignity. It seemed to Willy that people had been laughing at him all his life, and he vowed that someday he would get even.

The bitch of an undercover cop had died in a freak accident while Willy was doing his time in Kingston pen. Too bad about that. He had entertained serious plans for her. Then his shit-for-brains lawyer had died of a heart attack, so he focused all his need for revenge on Willinger and Lang.

One of his few friends on the outside had sent him a picture of Jack Willinger's wife, Darla. She was a foxy looking babe, and Willy had become obsessed with her. He vowed that when he got out he would do her six ways from Sunday, and then he'd have to kill her. He'd like to do it in front of Willinger, but it might not work out that way. He was scared of the detective with those piercing blue eyes, but that only made him more determined to kill him and his wife, and his damn partner too.

He peered excitedly out the window at all the changes which had taken place while he was doing his time. He hardly recognized anything, but that didn't matter, because he wasn't planning to stay long. He would finish his business here, and then head to Toronto or Vancouver. He could lose himself in a big city, and the pickings would be so much better.

Willy had a peculiar and annoying habit of sucking on his slightly protruding teeth. It was driving his seat partner crazy. She was an elderly woman returning from a visit to her grandchildren in Newmarket. She was trying to keep her mind on her book, but the continuous sucking and slurping sounds, coupled with the awful body odour wafting around Willy, were making her nauseous. Because the bus was packed with tourists on this bright summer day, she couldn't change her seat. People should have to pass a smell test before using public transit, she thought crossly. She was trying to breathe through her mouth so as to lessen the effect of the pernicious fumes emanating from her seatmate.

Willy was quite unaware of her discomfort. When he saw that she was elderly and unattractive, he dismissed her. Now his mind, which had been eroded by years of drug use, was full of hazy memories and unlikely plans.

As the bus finally pulled into the depot in an area known locally as "hooker haven", Willy hugged himself in anticipation, and began sucking his teeth even faster. Once he was settled in a room, he would get some beer, score a little coke, and look for a broad or maybe two. He'd screw them till their eyeballs popped and then beat the hell out of them. It had been a long time, too damn long. He was out of practice. After that he would finalize his plans for tracking down Willinger and Lang.

Niagara Falls was, is, and has always been a tourist mecca. Since the day in 1678 when Father Hennepin first gazed on the awesome wonder of nature, people have come from all over the world to view the incredible spectacle. The roaring, tumultuous falls hold a strange and compelling fascination, both for the first time viewer and the long term resident. There is something in the area for everyone, whether it is the falls themselves, or the miles of verdant parkland, or the myriad of entertainment spots. A multitude of new high rise hotels complement the casinos. The spectacular Festival of Lights draws thousands of tourists every winter. In the summer, the shops, streets, and hotels, along with the parks, are a teeming mass of humanity. Everywhere people are taking pictures, eating, spending money, and just generally having fun.

For the intrepid, the foolhardy, and the daredevils, there are innumerable attractions such as the Spanish Aero Car, which travels on cables across the gorge, the Maid of the Mist, which bravely makes its way to the foot of the falls, the mysterious caves behind the falls, and the jet boat which travels the rapids. There are even the fame seeking, death defying fools trying to tame the falls in a barrel or some other homemade contraption. The entire glitzy Clifton Hill tourist area of Niagara Falls is a hustling, bustling 24 hour Mardi Gras.

The official downtown area, however, is a different story. Old Queen Street has in essence gone the way of the dodo. It has been dying a slow, painful death for many years. Gasping and trying valiantly to hang on, it has fallen victim to the monolithic shopping centres and strip malls which have effectively sucked its life's blood. Store after store sits vacant, with boarded fronts or blank gaping windows, gazing in sullen despair at the meagre handful of shoppers.

The quiet Queen Street and the raucous Clifton Hill are joined by River Road, which proudly boasts an unbroken expanse of stately bed and breakfasts. These old mansions haughtily stand guard over the river which divides Canada from the United States.

Willy, however, didn't care about any of these things. Eschewing the bed and breakfasts on River Road, he grabbed a cab out to the west end of Lundy's Lane, where he knew he could get a cheap motel by the week. Aghast at the amount showing on the taxi meter, he paid it grudgingly from his small hoard of cash. Of course he didn't bother with a tip. He didn't notice, and wouldn't have cared about the finger the cabbie gave him as he gunned the motor and raced away.

He threw himself down on the tired looking bed, gazing at the mottled and cracked ceiling, totally oblivious to the sour, stale smell permeating the room. If truth be known, he smelled much worse than the room did. He once again went over in his fuzzy mind the grandiose schemes he had for killing the two detectives. Mostly his thoughts centered on Darla Willinger. He felt as if he knew her well. Her picture had been on the wall of his cell for several years now. He had stared at it night after night until he was so filled with rage that he wanted to punch that beautiful nose, pull out that luxuriant hair, bite that smooth skin. He would take care of her husband first, then turn all his attention to Darla. No, maybe he would tie up the husband, do what he wanted to do to Darla in front of him, then kill them both. That would be good. No, maybe he should kill both Willinger and his partner Bud Lang before he turned all his attention to Darla. He couldn't make up his mind just what he was going to do, but he snorted and sucked his teeth in anticipation.

William T. Burton was definitely one of God's mistakes. That's what his mother and four sisters had always told him. Not only was he ugly on the outside, but he was ugly on the inside, in his heart and soul and mind. He knew that women were good for one thing only. They had been put on this earth for men to use as punching bags, to use and abuse. It was as simple as that in the Weasel's simple mind. Women were whores, nothing more, nothing less. With this attitude Willy never experienced feelings of guilt or shame when he raped. He loved the feeling of control and power as he kissed them, screwed them, and slapped them around. He liked to torture them a bit with his trusty knife. He would run its fine point along their necks and between their breasts, and watch the thin red bloody line appear. Up to this point in his life he had never wanted to kill them, just scare them, and leave them realizing that he was in charge. Every woman took on the face of his hated mother or his bossy, cruel sisters.

Willy always wore a mask for two good reasons. First, he wasn't prepared to kill, at least he hadn't killed anyone yet. "Screw them and run" had always been his motto, so of course he couldn't let them see his face. Also, he knew very well just how ugly he was. His sisters and mother had told him often enough. His eyes were small and close together. With his prison pallor and pinched face, they looked like raisins stuck in an unbaked cookie. His pale skin was scabrous, and his nose — well his nose was nothing but a damn joke. His thin brown hair was stringy and greasy. He didn't have one redeeming feature. God had been sleeping the day Willy came off the assembly line.

He loved the power which raping gave him. The fear his victims experienced, excited him. He could rid himself of his anger and despair, and the loneliness for at least a little while, till the feelings built up again. It was a vicious circle, but William T. Burton didn't understand that. Rape was all he lived for. It was his "raison d'être." It was just what Willy did.

CHAPTER 4

▼

One week earlier, Cassandra Meredith was having a great day, that is right up until the wheels fell off and all hell broke loose. Certainly it had started out well. Getting up early, she had taken her tea and bagel out to the screened sun porch, along with her two cats, Muffin and Sugar Plum.

It was a sunny, perfect morning. "That old time rock and roll" was blasting from the stereo. The loud music didn't disturb anyone, since Cassie had a deaf neighbour on one side of the house, and a large wooded area on the other. Her feet were tapping as she munched on her bagel. She had just finished plumping the green and pink pillows on the white wicker furniture, and watering the many hanging plants. The little fountain with frolicking mermaids gave off a peaceful flowing sound as Muffy jumped onto her lap. The fountain had been Dave's idea. He had bought it in Florida, and Cass had to admit that it gave the sun-room a certain elegance.

As she gently petted Muff's soft fur, she laughed at the thought of how he gave new meaning to the term "lap cat". Nicknamed "Narcissy", he was an orange tabby, gentle and loving, and forever looking for a lap, when he wasn't admiring himself in the mirror. Sugar Plum, on the other hand, was always looking for another meal, and was sometimes called "Sugar Plump" for obvious reasons. She was a silvery tabby with a prima donna complex. At the moment she was intently watching the antics of two hummingbirds at the feeder.

Cassandra's husband David, aka "the rat" in Cassie's mind, had just left on an unexpected trip to Spain and Portugal. He owned a talent agency, and was look-ing for new, untapped talent in Europe. Although she had wanted to go with him, Dave had discouraged her. Actually he had given her a definite "no". They didn't always see eye to eye, and he could be a real pain in the ass, but they had worked through some tough times in the marriage, which now seemed to be pretty solid. Cass loved him, but was disappointed and thoroughly pissed off that she had been left behind. She felt resentful, and with their two kids away working as summer camp leaders, she found herself alone for the first time in years, except, of course, for the cats. Why the hell wasn't she there in Europe with Dave? Why hadn't she insisted on going with him?

She sighed as she watched a robin splash in the bird bath, while two gray squirrels frantically chased each other up and around the old maple tree. How was the garden going to survive without Dave, she wondered for the umpteenth time. He was the gardener with the green thumb. She was allergic to bees, one more sting could be lethal, so Dave did all the gardening, and Cassie enjoyed the fruits of his labours from the safety of the sun porch.

She was excited that her old friend Victoria Craig was flying in from Vancouver that afternoon to spend a few weeks with her. Vickie was taking the airport shuttle from Toronto to Niagara Falls, and would be there by dinnertime.

Cass and Vickie had been friends on and off since elementary school, and they had always felt that they were kindred spirits. As kids they had spent many happy hours playing "library" in the attic of Victoria's childhood home. Vickie's father had been an avid reader and collector all his life, and the attic was stuffed with books. The two young girls had revelled in the mystery and excitement of this eclectic collection. Cassie remembered those halcyon days with pleasure. They both shared a love of books which had lasted all their lives, and mysteries and suspense novels topped the list.

Even as kids, when they weren't reading mysteries, they were out looking for them. They had played at being Nancy Drew, and it often got them into trouble. With their over-active imaginations they could parlay any innocuous situation into a full blown crisis or mystery. They had fed off each other's creativity, and more than once had found themselves in hot water as a result of their wild imaginings. Cass smiled to herself as she remembered some of their scrapes and adventures. Now she wondered if perhaps they were more like Sue Grafton's heroine Kinsey Millhone, funny, intrepid and foolhardy. No, we're more like a pair of middle aged assholes, she told herself with a grin.

Going off to different universities, their lives had taken diverse paths, but they kept in touch by letter, phone and email. This would be the first time, however, that they would be together without husbands or kids.

Even though she was looking forward with great anticipation to seeing her friend, Cass had a niggling little frisson of doubt. What if they just couldn't get along together in close quarters for an entire month? What if they couldn't stand each other's idiosyncrasies? Maybe it only worked as a long distance friendship. Dave had almost insisted that she have Vickie come to stay for a few weeks. Come to think of it, that was very strange and somehow out of keeping with Dave's laid back personality. He had really pushed her into it, and now she was wondering whether it had been such a good idea. Could they live together for a month or more and still be friends? She heaved a sigh, and assured herself that it was going to be great. No use wasting her energies on foolish worries at this point. Only time would tell.

With her reddish gold hair and svelte dancer's figure, Cassandra Meredith was an attractively tall, willowy woman in her mid forties. Her friends had always called her "classy Cassie," and the nickname did fit. Cass looked better in a pair of tight jeans and a little tee shirt than most women did in their best finery.

Other than mysteries, her love had always been dancing, and in high school and university she had performed in every musical possible. She always regretted that she had been just a baby in the wild 60's when "go-go" dancers were all the rage. She could picture herself dressed in high boots and hot pants, dancing her buns off.

Early on in their marriage, Dave had encouraged her to open her own dance studio. What fun that had been! The studio was extremely successful, filling a need in the community. Her students loved her, and Cass was devoted to them. Two years ago, however, it had all come to a screeching halt when she broke her leg skiing in Switzerland. After months in a cumbersome cast, she had graduated to crutches, and after weeks of intensive physiotherapy, she was almost back to normal. It was only on rainy days, or after she had walked too far, climbed too many stairs, or danced too much, that the leg ached and throbbed.

Unfortunately while she was in the hospital and then in the cast, she was unable to teach, and her studio went all to hell. She couldn't find good instructors, and her students lost interest. It was a frustrating and demoralizing time. Finally she just said to hell with it, and selling the studio, she put it all behind her.

Vickie had never been much into music. She was always looking for excitement, and for years she taught English to inmates at Kingston Penitentiary. It was a program started by the government, and had had mixed results. Vickie loved the possible danger involved, even though the officials took every precaution for her safety. She had come to know some of the prisoners quite well, and even looked on a few of them as close acquaintances if not actual friends. Her husband, Brian, however, hated the fact that she worked at the prison, and was constantly nagging her to quit.

Eventually something occurred which scared her enough that she reluctantly gave up the job. Actually the government was about to cancel the program anyway, so the matter was taken out of her hands. Cass didn't know all the details, but she did recall that one of the prisoners had developed a crush on Vickie. When he was released, he found out where she lived, and showed up on her doorstep with flowers and candies. Vickie had tried to discourage him as gently as possible, but he was not to be deterred. Knowing that he had served time for armed robbery and aggravated assault, and that he had a hair-trigger temper, was not comforting. He stalked her for three months before the police finally caught him breaking into her home, and the would-be Don Juan found himself back in prison. Vickie and her family had moved to Vancouver shortly after that, and now she busied herself marking papers for the university and entering contests. She had won an amazing array of merchandise, and although it was a much safer way to spend her time, it was not nearly as exciting.

At this moment in time, Cassie felt in need of her old friend's companionship. She was angry and hurt that Dave hadn't wanted to take her along on his trip. Besides that, for several days now she had been feeling strange — fearful and edgy. Her scalp had that weird tingly feeling which usually presaged something bad. She felt with unease that something decidedly unpleasant was about to happen in her well ordered life. She couldn't put her finger on it yet, but the idea was there crouching in the back of her mind.

Unknown to Cassie, events relentless and unchallenged were building up around her, ready to shake the very solid foundation of her seemingly charmed life. Things would never be the same for Cassie or Vickie after the happenings of the next few weeks.

Looking slim and elegant in the sky blue short shorts and tank top, which just happened to match her blue eyes, she addressed the sleeping cat on her lap.

"Well, Muff, what do we do if Vickie turns out to be boring? She and I haven't been alone together for years and years you know. What if she's become an old "stick-in-the-mud?" She was petting Muffin between the ears, and his purrs were becoming deep rumbles. Looking over at Sugar Plum, she queried, "what if she just wants to sit around and watch TV all day, or listen to rap music, or sit in the garden and talk to the flowers? What if she's lost all her old zippadee-dooda? What if she doesn't even like to sit and drink wine at night?" Muff looked bored with these questions. He stretched, yawned, then curled up in a tighter ball. Sugie began licking her nether regions with enthusiasm.

Cass looked at the two of them fondly and then laughed. "Okay, maybe I'm getting a little carried away, but she has dogs you know. What if she hates cats?" she joked. Sugar looked up as if in total disbelief at this possibility, then grabbed her tail and started chewing. Muff didn't dignify the thought with any reaction. He was dreaming whatever little cats dream.

While Cassie prepared for her friend's arrival, Victoria Craig was making the most of this flight from Vancouver to Toronto. It was the first time she had flown by herself in many years, and it was exciting and exhilarating. In the last few years her life had become too quiet and predictable.

As Vickie closed her eyes and tried to relax, she thought about their childhood, and the few times she had met Cassie's older sister Prudence. There was a gap of fifteen years between the sisters, and Vickie had always thought that Pru was the epitome of glamour. There was some estrangement there, however, which Vickie didn't understand, but she knew that Cassie hadn't seen Pru for years. Maybe she could get Cass talking, and find out what had gone wrong in that relationship. All she knew was that sisters should be close, not live and act like total strangers.

Now with Brian in London doing research on a scholarly book, her kids away at summer jobs, and her two dogs being cared for by the next door neighbour, she felt a great sense of freedom. Brian was a dear, but he could be boring and stuffy. He really was not a fun guy. He wasn't the least bit like Dave, who was handsome and flirtatious, and always ready with a hug and a kiss. He often visited her and Brian on quick trips to Vancouver, and he and Vickie would stay up long after Brian went off to bed, laughing and talking. Brian had no sense of adventure, and she sometimes felt so confined and restless that she wanted to scream. Right now she was ripe for a change.

Victoria Craig was not quite as tall as her friend, Cassandra, but she was just as slim. She also had a very pretty face from which shone two mischievous brown eyes. Her naturally wavy auburn hair and peaches and cream complexion were the envy of all her friends.

Her euphoria at the moment was somewhat dampened by the fact that sitting beside her was a harried mother with screaming twins on her lap. The little darlings hadn't shut up since ten minutes before take-off. Victoria wished vehemently that she could push a button and have all three of them disappear into the cargo hold.

Across the aisle sat a portly fellow of undetermined age. He was enthusiastically working on his third scotch and water, and would likely have to be poured off the plane in Toronto, but at least he looked harmless. His seat partner, however, looked like the quintessential terrorist — swarthy, bearded, nervous. Vickie was keeping a close eye on him.

She smoothed the pants of her cream coloured suit. She didn't usually pay much attention to clothes, not like Cass who was a real clothes horse, and who looked great no matter what she wore. She did feel, however, that she looked very nice with her brown turtleneck and cream jacket, and she silently prayed that the twins would keep their sticky fingers to themselves. She wanted to look her best when she arrived in Niagara Falls. The very name had a magic sound to it.

She sighed as reality set in and she pictured herself with itchy, swollen eyes, a thick throat, and a red nose. She was very allergic to cats. She loved them though, and would just have to sneeze her way through the next few weeks. One of the first things she had packed was a good supply of antihistamines.

Frowning, she closed her eyes and thought about Cassie. She felt in the mood to gamble, to be reckless. Her plans were still unformed, but she knew without a doubt that her life and Cassie's would be changed irrevocably after this summer. With Brian and David not around to cramp their style, she would just have to play things by ear. She wondered fleetingly whether they would have any trouble getting along together. Dave had really pushed for her to make the trip at this time, so she would just have to be sure that things worked out.

C H A P T E R 5

▼

The two old friends chatted their way through the pot roast and lemon pie without really tasting them. They were excited to be together again with no encumbrances such as husbands or children. Cassie, however, felt that Vickie was holding something back. She seemed not as boisterous and ebullient as she always had been. There was something there, but Cass couldn't quite put her finger on it.

Sipping their postprandial tea in the sun porch, Victoria said, "This has worked out so perfectly with David in Spain and my Brian in jolly old England. To get this much time to ourselves after all these years is really priceless. Maybe we could dredge up a mystery to solve."

"That's not too likely. Niagara Falls is a pretty quiet city. There aren't many mysteries here, kiddo. Actually, though, I was thinking of hiring the Chippendale boys to greet you, but then I was afraid it would be just too much excitement for you," Cass added with a straight face.

"Well that's too bad. That's just the kind of excitement I wanted. I'm looking for a change of pace now that Brian's safely out of the way. Are there any male strip joints in town?"

"You're as bad as you ever were" laughed Cass. "You're going to get us into trouble, I just know it."

After a moment's thoughtful silence while they sipped their tea and munched on shortbread cookies, Cassandra said, "Now tell me about Brian's book."

"Not much to tell" said Vickie, shaking her head. "It seems to be going smoothly, and this research in England will finish it. He hopes to send it to the publisher by next spring."

"Good for him."

"Well, it's not exactly going to be a best seller, but it keeps him out of mischief" Vickie grinned. "He's an old dear, but honestly Cass, who the hell gives a rat's patootie about immigration in the 1800's. Boring!"

Cass laughed. "Vic, you haven't changed a bit. You're still as irreverent as ever."

"And I'm sure your irrepressible black humour is still intact" retorted her friend. "Anyway," she continued, "let's get to more interesting things. Do you ever hear from your sister Prudence?"

Cass looked at her in surprise. "Funny you should ask that. I had a call from her two days ago. Talk about a bolt from the blue! Prior to that I hadn't heard from her in a few years.

She was calling from the cottage, and said that she had been thinking about me a lot lately. That in itself was weird! What in the world would prompt her to call me after all this time? She sounded sad and really uptight. I suspect that those two kids of hers turned out to be total losers. I've heard things about them over the years from a mutual friend.

Anyway, Prudence was, I don't know, more friendly than I ever remember, and she seemed, — regretful or something, maybe closer to nervous. Honestly, Vic, it was a strange phone call. She went on and on about her husband Matt, and about some family barbecue they were having, and then she said that I was going to hear some very surprising news very soon, — news that will change my life, but she wouldn't elaborate. She also said that she and I have a lot to discuss, and she wants to talk to me when they get back from California. I don't know, maybe she'd been drinking, although she sounded sober. No kidding, it was quite a surprise to hear from her after all this time, and the more I think about it, the more I think that she sounded almost scared, but as I said, she was quite friendly. It was really just too weird."

"How long since you've actually seen her?" mumbled Victoria over the remains of another shortbread.

Cass laughed to herself, remembering how much Vickie had always loved to munch. She used to say that she had never met a butter tart she didn't like. That pretty well summed it up. If it was sweet, Vickie ate it. It was amazing that she didn't weigh two hundred pounds. Getting back to Vickie's question, Cass replied, "It's been ages since I've seen her, actually not since my — our — mom died. And of course I haven't seen the niece or nephew either. I think that Jordan was in the States or Mexico for a long time, probably hiding from the law, but he came hustling back after Pru and Matthew won the lottery."

"How about Jenny? I remember seeing her once when she was a little girl. She was a real beauty with that blond curly hair and those big brown eyes."

"All I know is that she has some kind of a drinking problem. I'm not sure just how bad it is. Pru has never talked about either one of them, but I know her neighbour at the cottage, Joanne Bailey. Apparently Jenny ran away and disappeared for a few years, but she turned up again shortly after they won the lottery. Joanne told me that Jenny seems okay when she's sober, but she's a totally different person when she drinks. I gather that she's a bit of a Jekyll and Hyde."

"What a shame" mused Vickie.

"You bet, but the real shame is that Pru and I have wasted all these years and I really don't know why. Fifteen years is a big age difference, but we could have been friends. We just never connected. I always felt that she didn't want anything to do with me. Now that I'm getting 'older,' here she rolled her eyes at her friend and shook her head, "it's a horrible thought isn't it? Well, anyway, I'm beginning to realize the importance of family in the grand scheme of things, and in a way I'd like to get closer to her, but I think it's too late."

"Au contraire mon amie" replied Vickie. "It's never too late for family. When I think of all those years that I spent wanting a sister, and here you have one you don't even know. It's ridiculous!"

Cass looked at her thoughtfully. "You know, you're right. Maybe we'll talk a bit when she gets back from this trip to California. Trouble is, she's always deflected any of my advances. Besides, I can't stand Matt, or 'Matthew' as he prefers. He's an arrogant snob."

"Well, shit, Cass, you don't have to talk to him, and all Pru can do is hang up on you, so what's the problem? You should definitely give her a call. Now how about some wine for your thirsty friend?"

"Okay, but first I want to hear about your kids, and then I have to give you a tour of the house. I want you to make yourself totally at home."

"Great. This is going to be so super" enthused Vickie with a big smile which seemed slightly false to Cassie. "Okay, now for my two brats. I think I told you, they're both performing in P.E.I. this summer in the "Anne of Green Gables" festival. You know that they've been acting in school plays for years, and this was a phenomenal piece of luck that they were both hired for the festival. They're having a great time, and couldn't be happier."

"What an opportunity for them" exclaimed Cass enthusiastically. "You must be so proud."

"You bet I am. As a matter of fact, I'm flying down the last week in August for a few days. I'll go to every performance, and act like a proud mama. Hopefully there'll be time for some sightseeing too. I've never had a real chance to see the island." Then, jumping up, she continued, "Now, let's have the grand tour. It's such a lovely house, Cass, so different and spacious. It's much bigger than it appears from the outside."

After a quick tour of the house, they sat down to have some more wine. After Muffy snuggled back onto Cassie's lap, she asked, "Now what do you want to do while you're here? Should we get tickets to the Shaw Festival and do the tourist bit like riding the Maid of the Mist? Or, we could go to the casinos and try our luck."

"You betcha, baby. Let's do it all, well, except for the Maid of the Mist. I'm not sure about that one, but anything else sounds great. I feel so free and young, no kids, no dogs, no husband. Honestly, Cass, I plan to reinvent myself this summer, maybe become the person I've always wanted to be."

"Oh, Vic, that's baloney. You're perfect the way you are. You're funny and smart and pretty and adventuresome. What more could you possibly want to be?" Cass wondered whether maybe her friend was having some marital problems.

"I'm not sure, but somehow I just feel that I'm going to be different by the time I go back to Vancouver. There's going to be some kind of drastic change — for the better I hope. I'm so darn restless these days. It's mid-life crisis I guess." She shrugged and rolled her eyes as Cass refilled their glasses.

"Maybe I'll have an affair while I'm here. Do you know any eligible candidates? Somebody like your Dave would be perfect." She grinned impishly, watching Cass for her reaction.

"Victoria Craig you are full of it. No wonder your eyes are such a deep brown. Listen, the day that you have an affair is the day that I'll find a pot of gold under my pillow" scoffed Cassie.

"Okay, maybe I won't go quite that far," laughed Vickie, "Let's just be teenagers again and have fun. We can shop, do movies, picnic along the parkway. Is it still as beautiful and picturesque?"

"Sure, it's still beautiful. I'm not too keen on picnics, though. Remember, I'm allergic to bees, and I guess I'm a bit paranoid about them."

"Hey, do I ever remember," Vickie replied with enthusiasm. "It was our Grade Five picnic at Bell Park, and you got into a fight with that awful Morlene O'Shea."

Cass laughed and cut in. "She was trying to hit a squirrel with a stick so I grabbed that long straggly hair of hers and yanked it as hard as I could. She was bigger than I was, and she shoved me against that old tree. Who would have guessed that it had a bee hive in it?" She shuddered at the memory.

Vickie took up the tale. "Those old bees came zooming out and started sting-ing you all around your head. You were screaming and dancing, and then you just fell down. That's when Miss Barclay picked you up and ran with you to the car. Lucky you were so skinny or she wouldn't have been able to carry you."

"All I can remember is not being able to breathe. I was gasping for air so hard that I thought my eyes would explode. Next thing I knew I woke up in the hospi-tal, covered with welts."

"Well, I went in the car with you. I was crying because I thought you were dead. It's lucky that Sudbury General was so close to the park. It only took five minutes to get you there. I can still remember some nurse saying that you were in anaphylactic shock. That was such a big word that I've never forgotten it. I was very impressed, and scared to death."

"Guess I was really lucky, but now I'm a total sissy about bees. I keep epi-kits all over the house. See, here's one in this drawer, and there's one in the kitchen, one in the bedroom, one in my purse, and one in the car. I don't take any chances" she said grimly.

"Anyway, enough about bees. I'm really happy that you're here, Miss Vickie. We can do anything you want. It will help get my mind off myself. What a pair! You're restless and looking for excitement, and I've had this weird feeling of impending doom lately. I just can't shake it. At first I was sure that Dave's plane was going to crash on the way to Spain, then I decided that your plane was going to go down in flames, and now I feel that something bad is waiting to pounce on me and the cats." Cassie hugged herself and shivered at this frightening confes-sion.

"Oh, oh, here we go. One of your precognitive experiences? Cassandra Meredith, you are absolutely delusional. You've had these forebodings all your life and they never come to pass. You are paranoia personified. Read my lips, girl. You do not have ESP, and you are not clairvoyant."

Cass smiled good naturedly as she stood up. "Guess you're right, kiddo, but if something happens — don't say I didn't warn you."

"Doo doo doo doo" hummed Vickie in a gloomy tone. "Listen, pal, while we're in this 'I can see into the future and things don't look too good' mood, I have just the thing for you. Come on up to my room while I unpack."

In the guest bedroom Vickie said, "Here you are, Cass. It's a little guardian angel pin. I want you to wear it all the time. Pin her on your shoulder, or even on your bra. Hopefully she'll watch over you and keep you safe. She might even scare away your premonitions."

"Oh, Vic, thank you. What a neat idea! I'll feel so much safer now" she added with a grin. Secretly she thought it was a rather dumb gift, but Vickie had also brought her a couple of books. One was "The Mysterious Ways of Cats", and the other was "Mysteries to Die For." Cass was delighted with them.

As the two women settled in for the night, neither of them suspected that it had been the last completely peaceful and carefree day they would have for quite a while, nor did they realize that Cassandra's forebodings were harbingers of things to come.

The ringing of the telephone didn't waken Cassie at first because it fit right in with her dream. Muffy, however, who had been curled at her feet, jumped up — offended at the interruption. This in turn wakened Cassandra. One glance at the bedside clock set her heart pounding. No one ever called with good news at 2:30 am.

"Hello" she whispered shakily.

"Hello, Cassandra, is that you?"

That scared her even more, because she had been hoping it was a wrong number. Her heart was now revved up to top speed.

"Yes, this is Cassandra" she croaked, clearing her throat.

"Oh, Cass, it's Joanne Bailey. I'm so sorry to waken you, but I didn't know whether you had heard the awful news."

Cassie's mind flew into overdrive. David had been mugged or stabbed, or his hotel had burned down. The kids had drowned at camp. But how could Joanne know all that before she did?

"News" she repeated stupidly, as she sat up and turned on the bedside lamp. "What are you talking about, Joanne?"

"Cassandra, I take it that the police haven't called you?"

"No, no one has called me" she parroted. "Why, what's happened?" she almost shouted.

"Is David there with you?"

"No, he's in Spain. What is it, Joanne?"

Cassie saw that Vickie had come to her open bedroom door with a worried look on her face, so she motioned her to come in and sit down. She noticed subconsciously that Vickie was wearing a tattered old plaid housecoat which looked too big for her, and which had definitely seen better days. It must have special significance, because she certainly wasn't wearing it for its beauty.

"Oh, Cass, I don't know how to tell you this." Joanne paused then, and seemed to take a big breath. Cassie waited impatiently, afraid of what she was going to hear.

"We left the cottage to head home just a few minutes behind Pru and Matthew. We always go down that same back route. It's a lovely clear night in Muskoka, and there wasn't another soul on the road. Going down that long hill they seemed to be swerving crazily, then we lost sight of them. Matt was going so fast, it wasn't like him at all. We couldn't keep up with him." Here Joanne started to cry, and Cassie's stomach did the old elevator drop.

"Go on, Joanne, what happened?"

"It was a nightmare. I'll never forget it. We were the first ones on the scene" she wailed.

"What do you mean — 'the scene' — ?" cried Cassie, somehow knowing what was to come.

"They crashed head on into that huge rock cut at the curve. We called 911 from the car phone, and we stayed with them till the ambulance arrived. The police got there first, but the ambulance seemed to take forever." Joanne was really sobbing now, and it was difficult to understand her words, but Cassie was getting the idea.

"Oh, God, we were just talking to them before dinner. They were so excited about this trip to California. Cass, Matt is dead, and they've air lifted your sister to Toronto."

CHAPTER 6

▼

The next morning the friends decided reluctantly that they probably should drive over to Toronto to visit Prudence in hospital. Cassandra was embarrassed to admit that she felt no great compulsion to race to her sister's side. After all, she was in a coma, and wouldn't know that Cass was there. On the other hand, there was no escaping the fact that Prudence was her sister. She should make the effort for decency's sake, and for her own sense of what was the right thing to do. Besides it would be interesting meeting Pru's kids after so many years.

Cassie made arrangements with her cat sitter, and by early afternoon they were on their way. They had decided that they would stay overnight and make it a bit of a holiday. No trip to Toronto should be wasted, and Cass felt guilty about spoiling Vickie's vacation, and here it was only the second day!

She called David in Spain before she left. Somewhat unwillingly, he offered to come home on the next flight. He knew very well that there was no love lost between Cassie and her much older sister. Cass was tempted to say "yes" to his half-hearted offer, but right now she had Victoria to lend moral support and a few much needed laughs. Besides, she feared that she might need him a lot more later on.

Her forebodings had come to fruition with that phone call, but Cass felt that there was another shoe to drop. She missed Dave terribly though, and he had only been gone a few days. She missed his wonderfully warm smile, his strong arms around her, and that "man" smell of him. It was a combination of wool, leather, and after-shave, with a little tooth paste thrown in. He always seemed to make sense too, and could calm her when she was about to shatter like crystal on a tile floor. He could be a bugger at times, but she loved him.

The trip to Toronto on the outdated and dangerous Queen Elizabeth Highway, known as the QEW by those who travelled it daily, was a nightmare in gray. It was wall to wall transport trucks and torrential rain. Driving this particular highway was not Cassie's favourite sport. She would rank it somewhere below white water rafting in a canoe without a paddle.

"Those damn truckers just won't give you a break" she complained, "no pun intended." As three more extra long double transports zoomed past, they threw up a curtain of water and mud. "This highway is an absolute disgrace. It should have been widened years ago."

"Are you sure there aren't any back roads we could be taking?" asked Vickie, only half joking.

"Not if we want to get there this week" laughed Cassandra. "Just stick with me, old girl, we're almost there."

There was silence then, as both women concentrated on the heavy rain, and the mud splashes on the windshield.

Something was clawing at the periphery of Cassie's mind. She couldn't quite grasp it, but it was bugging the hell out of her. Finally she said, "Vic, there's something that just doesn't make sense to me."

"Oh, what's that?"

"Well, you know by nature I'm a suspicious person. Maybe I've read too many mysteries, but I've got a feeling that there's something wrong here."

"Why, what are you getting at?" queried Vickie with renewed interest. "There aren't too many car accidents that do make sense, are there?"

"I suppose you're right. There's something bugging me though. I just feel uneasy. It's as if there's some little warning flag which I'm not quite getting. I told you that Pru called me a couple of days ago. She was talking about this trip to California they were planning. Actually they were leaving later this week I think. Well, anyway, in the course of the conversation she made a point of saying how safe she felt driving with Matt because he was so sensible and never exceeded the speed limit. She said he was an excellent driver, and it would be a very relaxing journey."

"So what?" Vickie was puzzled. She didn't know where the conversation was heading, but she was intrigued.

"Listen. This is the weird part. Pru said that Matt had just taken their new car in for its two month check-up. It was a Lexus I think, the only extravagant thing they had bought with their winnings. Anyway the day she called me, she said that it was in tip top shape and ready to make the long trip."

Vickie was trying hard to figure out where Cassandra was going with this. "Well, if that's the case, there wouldn't have been any mechanical problems" she mused, "and the brakes should have been good."

"Exactly" agreed Cass. "If the car was in perfect shape, and Matt was an excellent driver who didn't speed, and the driving conditions were good that night, then what the hell happened?"

"Maybe another car ran them off the road, or maybe good old Matthew had one cocktail too many before he set out" suggested Vickie, playing devil's advocate.

"Uh uh" Cass shook her head. "Joanne Bailey said that it was a clear night and they never saw another vehicle. I seem to recall that Matt wasn't much of a drinker, although I guess that could have changed over the years. I suppose it's possible that he suffered a heart attack at the wheel, an autopsy will show that. Or perhaps he swerved to avoid an animal, or," here she paused and glanced at her friend.

"Cut it out, Cass", Vickie interrupted. "You never change. You're always looking for trouble where there is none. What are you getting at — that it wasn't an accident — that it was somehow planned? That it was a double suicide, or a murder-suicide, or just plain old murder? It could have been caused by a thousand things — most likely Matt having a stroke or a heart attack. Don't go looking for trouble Cass. I'm sure that it was just a very sad accident."

"I don't know, but something doesn't feel right" answered Cass stubbornly as they wheeled into the hospital parking lot. Before they got out into the teeming rain, Cassie gave it one more shot. "Matt was an insufferable bore and a real son of a bitch. He was supposedly really ruthless in business, so it makes sense that he would have had a lot of enemies. I really hadn't thought about suicide, but why would he want to kill himself with Pru in the car? He wasn't the type. He liked himself too much." She sighed and frowned as she put her hand on Vickie's arm. "Pru told me that they were having a family barbecue at the cottage yesterday. She said that Matt and his brother Blake had been on the outs for ages and she wanted to get them together before she and Matt headed out west. She was having Blake and his wife and kids, along with Jordan and Jenny. That gave lots of people a chance to do something to the car didn't it?"

"You're a riot Alice" said Vickie, shaking her head as they dashed for the hospital. Still she was intrigued in spite of her scoffing. Wouldn't it be something if it really hadn't been an accident?

After finding out where the intensive care unit was located, they took the elevator. Walking down the hall, Cassie looked ahead and saw a lovely, petite blond approaching. "I think that's my niece Jenny" she said to Vickie as the young woman walked past them.

"Jenny?" asked Cassie.

Jenny looked up in surprise. "Oh, is it, yes it is, you're my Aunt Cassie. I haven't seen you in such a long time. What are you doing here?"

At this inane question, Cassie and Vickie glanced at each other in surprise. Jenny seemed to be swaying slightly, and Cass wondered whether she was going to faint. Quickly she put her arms around her niece and gave her a hug. "I'm so sorry about your dad, Jenny. What a tragedy. How's your mom doing? We've come over from Niagara Falls to visit her." She could now smell the distinct odour of gin wafting around this pretty little doll with the big brown eyes.

"Oh, she's just the same I guess" answered Jenny doubtfully. "It was just an accident you know. No one did anything. It just happened. It was just an accident."

"Yes of course it was" said Cass in surprise, trying to give her another soothing hug. "It was a dreadful accident." Why would Jenny say such an odd thing? Had someone suggested that it might not have been accidental?

"Thas right" agreed Jenny, nodding her head wisely. "Don't you listen to anyone who says it wasn't. It was just a stupid old accident. Nobody's to blame." Here she hiccupped and seemed to sway again.

"She's drunk" thought Cassie in disgust. She glanced at Vickie and raised her eyebrows. After introducing her to Jenny, she suggested that Jen might like to get a cup of coffee with them. Cassie couldn't picture her driving home in her condition.

"No, thas all right" Jenny slurred. "My friend's waiting. I hate hospitals you know" she said, as she wandered off towards the elevators, waving her hand in a vague way.

Vic and Cassie simply stared at each other. Cassie's scalp was tingling again. Why had Jenny insisted so vehemently that it was just an accident when no one had suggested anything to the contrary?

"Now do you believe me?" she asked. "Something doesn't smell right."

"Maybe she can't cope with seeing her mother in a coma, and her father being dead" suggested Vickie charitably. She was surprised at the girl's sodden condition in the middle of the day, and also very curious as to why Jenny kept insisting it was an accident. Maybe Cass hadn't been too far off the mark with her suspicions. Wouldn't that be something if there really had been foul play!

They continued on to the waiting room where Vickie began to shake water out of her hair. They were both bedraggled. Vic looked around in distaste, picturing gazillions of germs crawling over the few magazines. There were several other people in the room, some staring ahead gloomily, lost in their own thoughts, others flipping pages unseeingly. Vickie chose to sit here rather than in the tiny ICU waiting room down the hall. She knew that Cass wouldn't be very long.

Meanwhile Cassie, head up and shoulders back, adjusted her purse strap and reluctantly headed down the long corridor to the intensive care area. She was upset after seeing Jenny in such a state. What must the nurses have thought, and where was Jenny's brother? The other question of course was, what had Jenny been getting at?

At the nursing station she was told that only relatives were allowed in to see her sister, and that she could stay only a maximum of five minutes at a time. Cass wished fervently that Vickie could have come in with her. She needed the moral support.

She slowly approached Pru's bed. A snake-like tube came from behind her head, and fed oxygen up her nose. "Up your nose with a rubber hose" she thought giddily. There were so many tubes and monitors beeping and burping around her sister that it was like something from a science fiction thriller. Cassie half expected Prudence to rise up and come stalking toward her — arms outstretched like some demented female Frankenstein. She had a wild desire to laugh.

Pru, however, just lay there looking somehow diminished, like a corpse in a coffin. She looked small and so very vulnerable. Her sister had always been tall, but you couldn't tell that now. The bandages on her head, the ghoulish bruises on her face, and the tubes up her nose, along with all the other instruments of torture, made her appear totally inhuman and alien, and somehow very small.

Cass wanted to run. She felt embarrassed even looking at someone so defenceless, somewhat like a peeping Tom watching an innocent child bathing. She didn't even know what to say to this stranger. "I'm here, Prudence" she whispered. "It's Cassie. Hang in there, don't let go. You're going to be fine. Just keep fighting kiddo." What a crock, she thought to herself. It didn't look as if there was much fight left in Prudence Wainwright.

There was no response from Prudence whose machines wheezed and sighed for her. Cassie was relieved when the nurse signalled that she should go. Touching her sister's hand gently, she whispered, "I'll be back, Pru. See you in a while."

Just as she was leaving the room, a tall, good-looking raven haired woman was entering. She brushed past Cassie with only a nod. Cass smiled at her tentatively, wondering who she could be. She had been told that only relatives were allowed into the ICU.

Cass watched as the woman walked right over to Pru's bed. She stared in surprise as the elegantly dressed stranger took Pru's hand gently and began murmuring to her. She seemed to be taking a proprietary interest in the patient, patting her hand, straightening the covers which didn't need straightening, and checking the intravenous line as if she knew what she was doing. Cass was baffled as she made her way out to the waiting room. It had been shocking to see her sister this way, and she was confused by the dark haired woman.

"Maybe she's a private nurse" suggested Vickie as they hurried to the car.

"Yes, I suppose so" Cass replied doubtfully, "but it's odd that she wasn't wearing a uniform."

"Well, maybe she's just a friend who pretended to be a relative just so that she could sneak in and see her. Those nurses are probably pretty busy. They could easily be fooled."

"I don't know, Vic. My scalp is tingling again. There's something weird about that woman," said Cass warily, as they drove out of the hospital parking lot and headed to the hotel.

CHAPTER 7

▼

The next morning, back at the hospital, Cass was surprised to find the same dark haired woman sitting quietly by Pru's bed. She was sitting there with a rather arrogant and haughty manner, and when she turned and looked up at Cass, her big dark eyes seemed calm and self-assured. She acted as if she belonged there!

The nurses were all busy, and no one seemed to notice or care that Pru already had a visitor. No one stopped Cassie from walking right in. For some unknown reason she felt a bit intimidated by this stranger, yet she seemed friendly enough as she stood up and came towards Cass. She was staring at Cassie as if trying to memorize her features.

That's enough of this shit, thought Cassie to herself. "Excuse me, but may I ask who you are? Are you a special nurse?"

"Oh no" came the rather slow reply. It was as if the woman had to think about her answer for a moment. "I am Elena Santa Cruz. And may I ask who you are?"

Cass had the strange feeling that the woman already knew the answer to this question. She spoke with a low, gentle voice, very mellifluous. It flowed over Cass like golden honey. There was a decided accent too. She looks Italian or Greek, but her name sounds Spanish, Cass thought to herself as she tried to take control of the situation.

"I'm Pru's younger sister Cassandra Meredith," she said, putting on her loveliest smile. "Are you a close friend of Pru's?"

The woman had a beautiful smile too, and after a second's hesitation, she grasped Cassie's hand. "Oh my dear" she murmured in her low sultry voice. "This is so wonderful. Prudence has brought us together. I am your half-sister!"

Cass could only gasp and stare in disbelief at this elegant stranger. Was she crazed, possibly delusional? Cass had only one sister, and she was lying there in the bed in pretty bad shape. There was a moment of stunned silence.

"Pardon" she said, staring at this woman's face for any recognizable features. "What in the world do you mean? I don't have a half-sister!"

Here the stranger laughed a tinkling sort of laugh, which put Cassie on edge. Placing her hand on Cassie's arm in a familiar way, she answered. "Well, what I mean is that Joshua James Kiley was my father — and yours too of course. Juanita Elena Verdugo was my mother. I came to Toronto a couple of weeks ago to find you and Prudence. She didn't know about me either. I guess my mother and I were a very well kept secret. Prudence and I have become friends, and I was planning to contact you next." Here she seemed to stifle a sob. "But I never thought it would be under these awful circumstances."

Oh no, thought Cass. This is the surprise Pru talked about. Could it be possible? She was not going to blow her cool, but she was astounded and offended at this preposterous claim. Who the hell was this dame? No way was her beloved dad this creature's father too. She felt the room start to spin ever so slightly. If only she'd had more sleep she would be able to think more clearly. She wanted to say "get the hell out of here — whoever you are. I have only one sister, and it sure as heck isn't you." Taking a deep breath, however, she pasted a sickly smile on her face (always gracious in the face of disaster) she thought to herself. Then she stammered, "I don't understand. Could we go someplace and talk. There's obviously been a mistake here. My friend is waiting for me, perhaps we could go for coffee."

Elena agreed, and after meeting an astonished Vickie, the three women headed downstairs. Vickie rolled her eyes at Cass in total disbelief, and stared unabashedly. There was certainly no family resemblance that she could see.

As they left the hospital, they ran into Pru's brother-in-law Blake Wainwright, just arriving. Cassie remembered meeting him at her mother's funeral. He looked very much like Matthew, only better looking. He was suave and friendly, but obviously upset about Prudence. They chatted for a moment, exchanging pleasantries, and Cassie did not introduce Elena who had moved on ahead.

The three women found a coffee shop, and Cass and Victoria listened in absolute wonder at Elena's story. According to her, she had been born in Brazil, and her father J.J. (who of course was Cassie's father too — she was quick to point out), had sent her to a private school in Toronto when she was just eight years old. His wife Lizzie never knew about Elena or her mother Juanita, but J.J. visited her regularly in Toronto when he was home from Brazil. She had been sent to high school and university in Europe, and she had always longed to meet her half sisters.

The whole thing sounded very phony to Cass. The woman was, however, dressed elegantly, and she spoke beautifully, so maybe she had lived and studied in Europe. The part about longing to meet her half sisters sounded like a soap opera.

After the death of both her parents, and after Lizzie had also died, Elena, who was living in Europe, felt she needed to find her two half-sisters. Her father had told her all about them, but had made her promise never to try to contact them as long as Lizzie was alive. He didn't want to hurt his beloved Lizzie. She added this with grudging respect.

A bit too late to worry about hurting anyone, thought Cass angrily. She was having difficulty accepting this story which was more like a fairy tale than a family history.

Elena was forging ahead with her unbelievable narrative. When her husband Pablo Santa Cruz died, she had no one left. She was all alone in the world, so she came to Toronto to find Prudence and Cassandra.

It was such an unexpected and amazing tale that Cassie didn't have time to decide how she felt about it. This quiet, elegant woman was somehow mysterious and strange. Vickie was looking at her with cold distaste as if she smelled a bad smell. Cass almost had to laugh when she looked at her friend's face.

The entire story had to be a crock, and yet she — this Elena — seemed to have all her ducks in a row. She certainly knew a lot about all of them, but Cassie kept asking herself whether her beloved dad could have had a secret family all those years. Could he have done it without dropping any little clues or hints? Could he possibly have kept such a secret? Had he been that devious and deceitful? She was going to need some time to herself to figure this one out.

With a sinking heart, however, she knew that it could indeed be possible. Her dad J.J. had been a consulting engineer for a company which kept him building roads and bridges in northern Ontario six months of the year, and doing the same type of work in Brazil for the other six months. It was certainly conceivable that the lusty, fun-loving J.J. might have had a mistress in that lush, exotic country where he had spent so much time. It might have been conceivable, but it was odious.

Cassie wondered why she had never considered that possibility. Well, maybe she had, but she had always pushed the niggling doubts aside as too dreadful to contemplate. Not her dad, never her beloved dad. He couldn't have loved another family. She and Pru and their mom would have known, wouldn't they?

Cass remembered the tale her mom used to tell about her first visit to Brazil. She always told it with humour, but with an underlying tinge of sadness and regret.

J.J. had loved Brazil with its lush flora and fauna. He had exulted in the music of the jungle. The incessant singing of the exotic birds had always cheered him, filled his soul with joy. J.J. had a poetic streak in him, and the colours, the mystery, the ever-present danger had filled some inchoate void in his life. He was always happiest, most in touch with himself in his beloved jungles.

Her mom often told how, as a young bride, she had wanted to love Brazil the way J.J. did. The honeymoon, however, had turned out to be a nightmare. The oppressive heat and humidity had sapped her usual boundless energy. The dozens of flying, stinging insects attacked her mercilessly. They seemed big enough to carry her away. She was afraid of the snakes and the imagined head hunters.

At the hotel where she should have felt moderately safe, she saw a cockroach the size of a tea plate scurry across her foot, its long legs and antennae waving in a threatening fashion. As a little girl, Cass had always laughed and shuddered at this part. That had been it for Lizzie. Honeymoon or not, she threw in the towel. Lizzie Kiley was going home.

Cass remembered that her dad had been a man with lusty appetites. He had embraced life with gusto. Why had she ever supposed that he would live like a monk for six months out of every year? Her head had been in the sand. But what about her mother? Had Lizzie known about or suspected her husband's second family? Cass would never know, and she didn't even want to know. She wanted this awful Elena person to disappear and take her elegant, haughty manners with her. Still, Cass with her overdeveloped sense of curiosity, couldn't help but be intrigued by the tale. How amazing if this was indeed her half-sister. If, on the other hand, she was some scam artist, that would be intriguing too. She was pretty believable.

Cass and Vic would have to give this a lot of thought before they were taken in by some stranger. Her appearance at this particular time was just too coincidental with Matt dead and Pru lying in a coma. Was she somehow after a share of the Wainwright fortune, or was she just who she said she was?

Finally, after several coffee refills, Cass felt that her face was going to crack. She couldn't hear another word about her beloved dad — "their" dad, Elena kept saying. She knew that she had to get out of there before she did something foolish — something like punching this aristocratic snob in the mouth! Murmuring that she would be in touch, she pasted on a phony smile, and she and Vickie fled.

CHAPTER 8

▼

Pete Hoblonski was depressed. As he sprawled on a lounger in the tiny back yard of the dilapidated house, he munched on his cheeseburger and fries, and gazed around the cluttered yard with a jaded eye. He didn't notice that some mustard had oozed from the bun and was now perched proudly on his shirt.

Things were not going well in Pete's life, and he chided himself on being a bit of a screw-up. Actually, subconsciously he knew that he was a total screw-up, but he didn't like to admit it, even to himself.

He was a tall, big framed man, with a shock of blond hair always hanging in his eyes. He looked like a big Swede, but was in fact Polish. He hated all those stupid Polish jokes, so he let people think he was a Swede, until, of course, they heard his name.

Pete fancied himself quite a handsome hunk, but he had two big problems. The first was that one side of his face was pockmarked as though he had picked at his chicken pox when he was a kid. The truth was that he had fallen off his bike, and had slid on his right side, face first, on a cinder pathway. A beard would have helped cover the rough skin, but that was Pete's second problem. He couldn't grow a beard. Actually, except for his head, Pete couldn't grow any bodily hair at all. His back, legs, chest and arms were totally devoid of hair — not even a few blond ones. Just like a damn baby's bum, he had often thought to himself. Then one day, reading a magazine, the answer came to him — tattoos, lots of tattoos. So began Pete's entry into the sub-culture of tattoo parlours. He hadn't had his face done yet, but was still considering it.

First had come the requisite hula dancer, and she did perform beautifully when he flexed his muscles. She was a bit of an aberration though, because from then on Pete concentrated on boats. The first was a cigarette boat, long and sleek. Then came a cabin cruiser, and next came a power boat pulling a skier. The boats looked as if they were bobbing along on the tattooed blue water. Pete stood for hours admiring himself in the mirror. Gone was his shame about being hairless. He was now a walking work of art.

Today, however, he was really in the doldrums. He needed money, a lot of money, and he needed it now. He had many schemes and dreams, but one after another they had fallen apart and crumbled like stale bread.

Pete was a mechanic, and a good one. He knew he could have had his own business by now if he hadn't been so addicted to the "good life" — booze, horses, women and drugs. He had done a lot of things in his life which he didn't like to think about, but the day he met Jennifer Wainwright he was sure that his troubles were over. Shit, everyone knew her parents had won the big lottery. He couldn't even imagine having twenty million dollars. His mind couldn't cope with a number that big.

Jennifer had come to the garage where he was working. She needed her car serviced that day, and Pete had gladly obliged. When she came back to pick it up, he suggested that they test drive it. He knew everything was fine, but he wasn't going to let this opportunity fly out of his reach. They went for a long ride into the country, and were soon exchanging lies as if they were old friends.

He remembered that Jenny had looked very fetching that day in her tight blue jeans and yellow turtleneck. It matched her yellow hair, Pete thought, as he gave her his sexiest smile. He didn't know that Jennifer preferred dark sultry types like her brother, but that wouldn't have stopped him anyway. She was gorgeous, she came from money, and best of all, she seemed available. Pete grabbed onto her like a drowning man grasping at a life line. Unfortunately he had no way of knowing that there was an anchor tied to that life line, and it was going to sink him.

Before that fateful afternoon was over, they had stopped for drinks at a little bar north of Toronto. The more time they spent together, the better they liked each other. Jenny felt that she could easily handle this blond bozo, and Pete felt that she was an easy mark. For Jennifer it was an adventure, a walk on the wild side, a "stick it in your ear" salute to her parents, and someone to hold her at the end of the day. To Pete, Jennifer was a big dollar sign. The facts that she was cute and sexy, and appeared easy to manipulate were all pluses. Jennifer was going to be Pete's winning lottery ticket!

For their own reasons they dove head first into a wild affair. They fought, they drank, and they thought up crazy money-making schemes. When Pete lost one job he could usually get another. He was a great mechanic. There was nothing about car or boat motors that he didn't know.

At his urging, Jenny brought him up to the cottage to meet her parents. That was a disaster. Pete still got angry when he thought about it. He had told Matt Wainwright of his dream to go to Florida and open up a marina where he could work on the boats of the rich and famous. He would get himself one of those cigarette boats. They cost at least two hundred thousand dollars he imagined, and when he wasn't working, he would fly all over the Gulf of Mexico in his own beautiful boat. Those babies could do eighty miles an hour, maybe more. Matt Wainwright, however, did not seem impressed or even interested.

"Where do you intend to get the money for that?" he had asked sceptically, and Pete had felt a rage building up inside him. Here was this guy with all those millions which he hadn't even earned, he had won the goddamn money, yet he was looking down his nose at Pete.

Pete thought gloomily that someday he would show this idiot. He would find a way, and of course the way was going to be Jenny. It was then that he had realized he might have to marry her to get his hands on some of that pot of gold.

The disastrous meeting still rankled in Pete's soul. Wainwright could have given him half a million to start his marina, and he wouldn't have even missed it. Cheap bugger!

Soon after that, however, Pete and Jenny had a horrific argument. Of course it was about her parent's money. Why couldn't she coax some out of them? Didn't they care how badly she and Pete needed the dough? He had lost his temper and slapped her around a bit. He took all the money she had in her purse, and skipped out. That had been a mucho big mistake.

Maybe an even worse mistake had been going up to Muskoka and seeing Matt Wainwright again. Actually it had started innocently enough.

One of Pete's customers, Mr. Duncan, had a cottage on the lake near the Wainwrights. When he found out that Pete was good with boat engines as well as car motors, he asked him to come up to the lake and work on his boat. There was something wrong with the engine, and he told Pete he didn't trust the mechanic at the marina.

Pete had been happy to go, and he had a little idea floating around the back of his head. He worked on the engine all day, deliberately stretching it out until Mr. Duncan reluctantly suggested that he could stay overnight in the little guest cabin, and finish the engine the next day.

When the Duncans took their kids into town for a movie, Pete had hustled over to the Wainwright cottage, and found Matt working in the boathouse. No one else knew he was there, and he and Wainwright had quite a talk. Pete told him he was going to marry Jenny, and asked him outright for a loan — a big loan. Matt had not only refused, but he had laughed at Pete. They quarrelled. Pete was so angry that he felt like punching the guy out. He felt like pitching him into the black water.

Pete didn't want anyone to know that he had been at the Wainwright cottage that night. He was pretty sure that Matt wouldn't have mentioned it. It certainly wouldn't look good if certain people like the police or Jenny found out that he had been at the cottage, and had quarrelled with her father the fateful night of the car crash.

Now he had to make up with her and persuade her to marry him. The "accident" as people were calling it, hadn't worked out as beneficially for him as it could have or should have. Her father was dead, too bad the mother hadn't died too. He had it all figured out now though. He had to marry Jenny right away before the mother croaked. That way no one could say that he was just after her money. He had to convince her that he really loved her, but that wouldn't be a problem. Get a few stiff drinks into Jenny and he could talk her into anything. Besides, he did like her a lot, and all that money put her way ahead of the other dogs he had been dating.

As Pete finished his lunch and worked on his plans, the cute little teenager from next door came bouncing around the corner into his scruffy backyard. She was a nubile little doll, although Pete didn't know that word. He just knew that she turned him on with her bouncy boobs and luscious hips. Unfortunately she was jail bait, and Pete couldn't afford any trouble just now.

She was wearing tight short shorts which must have been hurting her crotch. No room to breathe there, thought Pete, staring unabashedly as she walked saucily towards him.

"Ola señorita" he cried, showing off one of his few Spanish phrases. Pete had once dated a Spanish-Mexican gal who taught him several Spanish words and phrases, most of which he had forgotten. Of course that wasn't all she had taught him. Anyway he liked to throw these Spanish words into conversations. He felt it made him sound smart — like a world traveller.

"Qué pasa" he continued, leering at the young girl.

"Oh Pete, you're so funny" giggled Samantha Greer. "Say some more" she begged, plopping down beside him.

That stumped Pete, so he quickly changed the subject. He really didn't want to waste time with Sammy today. He had too much on his mind.

They shared a beer and shot the breeze for a while, laughing and flirting. She was certainly a hot little pepper pot, but Pete's heart wasn't in it today. Luckily her father came home before the flirting went too far, and Samantha had to vamoose.

"Hasta la vista" called Pete, waving at her.

"And up yours too" she giggled, waggling her fingers and her bottom at him as she rounded the corner and disappeared from sight.

That left Pete free to go back to his plans for Jenny. He absently scratched his armpit, then ran his stubby fingers over the pockmarks on his face, as he realized that he would have to call her and make an appearance at her father's funeral. That should earn him a few brownie points. He wondered idly how to say Jenny in Spanish — Juanita maybe. He'd try that on Jen. She likely wouldn't know the difference.

"Muchas gracias, Juanita" he grinned slyly. Yes sir, Miss Jenny Big Bucks was about to become his ticket out of here. That Florida marina was getting closer every day.

CHAPTER 9

▼

It was a steamy, blistering hot afternoon, as Dr. Blake Wainright plodded wearily around the oversized yard, pushing a very heavy lawnmower. Sweat dripped off his chin as he cursed himself for cancelling the lawn service they had used for years. He had done it in a frenzy of money saving attempts, and now he realized how stupid and utterly unproductive the idea had been.

Just look at me, he thought in disgust, the big shot dentist cutting his own friggin' lawn. What a comedown!

Blake had debts right up the old kazoo, and he didn't know which way to turn. His credit cards were all maxed out, he was juggling three bank loans, and he had two big mortgages on the house. With three sons in university and his beloved Lindsay about to start in the fall, he was a man wearing concrete boots.

What was really driving him crazy as he trudged along, tearing up the lawn (this was damn hard work), was whether his brother Matt had really put him in his will as promised. With Matt dead, and Prudence hanging on by a thread, Blake could almost see light at the end of the tunnel. It wasn't that he really wanted Pru to die, he had always liked Pru. Still, if her death was inevitable, then he hoped it would be soon. That just might solve all his problems.

It had all been so bizarre. He and Matt hadn't gotten along for years, so the phone call and invitation to lunch had been a surprise. They had met at a very expensive restaurant, and Matt had proceeded to lecture him in his usual arrogant way, about his bad spending habits. How the hell did Matt know so much about his personal business? His snotty brother couldn't resist rubbing in the fact that he had won the twenty million dollars and had money to burn. Blake wished he had the nerve to ask Matt for some of that pot of gold, but of course he hadn't. He had far too much pride for that.

The bizarre part came when Matt disclosed that he was going to leave Blake a million dollars — Blake's heart had taken a leap at this news — but only after Matt and Pru were both dead! What possible good would that do me, Blake wondered. He would likely be dead long before they were. Matt was so damn superior in his attitude. He was dangling a carrot, a golden carrot at that, under Blake's nose, to tease him just as he always had when they were kids. It was so typical of their relationship.

Blake had been too stunned and angry to say anything, but he felt like stabbing a knife right into that smirking face. Then Matt got up, patted him on the shoulder, told him to have a nice day, and sauntered out, leaving Blake to pay the obscenely high lunch tab. Hell, with what that lunch cost, he could have paid off half his debts!

Many times since that day, Blake had gone over and over in his mind what would happen if Matt and Pru were to suddenly die, and whether Matt had really put him in the will. He never mentioned it to his wife Gloria, or to his four kids, but it haunted and taunted him constantly.

The two brothers had never been close as they grew up in Vancouver. Their mother died when they were young, and their father had always favoured Matthew, his first born. Matt seemed to take his father's love for granted. He was spoiled, arrogant and snobbish.

Blake was better looking than his brother, with his dark curly hair, big brown eyes, and cleft in his chin. He was taller than Matt too, and had many more friends. Still, Blake suffered from the lack of love from his father, and he grew up feeling envious and angry towards his older brother.

Matt may have had a lot of money and a lovely, charming wife, but his two kids were losers. Blake, on the other hand, had a sweet wife and four great kids. His daughter Lindsay was the light of his life. Sometimes he experienced a little shard of fear that they must have given him the wrong baby at the hospital. How else to explain Lindsay with her coppery red hair and cool green eyes? Actually, they were almost turquoise — like the aqua/blue of a tropical lagoon. Her complexion was luminous, and she had beautifully sculpted cheekbones. She certainly didn't look like anyone in his family, or in Gloria's, nor did she resemble her three brothers.

Not only was Lindsay beautiful enough to be a model, but she was smart too. She was going to med school. His daughter wanted to be a surgeon. Blake burst with pride when he thought about it. She was good in sports, she could play the piano, she was on the debating team. With her red hair and green eyes, and those long legs, she stood out in the gaggle of girls who were forever at the house. In Blake's proud mind she made them all seem like trolls in comparison.

Wearily pushing the mower, he thought about how his family spent money in such a carefree and profligate manner. Of course they had no idea that Blake was in a financial mess. He had never wanted to worry them, and he had been too ashamed to let them know just how badly he had botched things. He had always spared them the worries which gnawed at him constantly like giant rats.

Now, however, he didn't know where to turn. Lindsay wanted and expected a new car for school, and he didn't have the heart to tell her there was absolutely no money for it. He loved her so much that he would kill for her — yet he couldn't even buy her a little car. It was pathetic. He was pathetic.

He thought guiltily of the strange patient who had come to see him about a month ago. The guy was a loser, and Blake wasn't too surprised when his patient told him he couldn't afford to pay for the extractions. Instead, however, the weird little guy had asked if there was anything he could do for Blake, anything like "taking out" an enemy, or pressuring someone to back off, someone who might be dunning Blake for money. Blake wondered how in the world this little punk, Joey Tanofski, could possibly know about all the money he owed around town. The creep needed three more teeth pulled, and by the time he came back for his second appointment, Blake had pondered the offer, and had several questions for him.

Blake Wainwright had never really enjoyed being a dentist. His father had pushed him into it. He had actually always wanted to be an architect. To compensate for working in a profession which was totally anathema to him, Blake had poured all his money into a large and luxurious office. With a staff of ten, all the latest equipment, and soothing music, he could have been the most popular and successful dentist in town. Through attrition and lack of interest, however, the practice had dwindled over the years. Smelly breaths, foul mouths, and screaming kids faced him every morning. He liked to say that he had no patience with his patients! This little witticism pretty much said it all.

As Blake suffered in the sun, Gloria watched from the kitchen window. She knew there was something bothering him, but he wouldn't confide in her. Absently drying her hands on a pretty yellow and white towel, she took a bite of a cookie still warm from the oven. When she saw Blake stop and stare off into space, looking red faced and grim, she grabbed an ice cold beer from the frig, and hurried across the newly cut lawn with the strange ridges in it. Obviously Blake was new at this grass cutting game. She shook her head as she saw the poor job he was doing.

"Here you go, sweetheart, time for a break" she suggested, handing him the sweating beer bottle.

"Ah, ambrosia" murmured Blake, taking a huge gulp, then placing the cold bottle against his cheek and forehead.

"Don't wear yourself out, Dr. Wainwright" she commanded playfully, patting his bum. "I may have plans for you later tonight. You're no good to me if you're all tuckered out," she leered at him.

Laughing, he took another big satisfying swallow, and handed her the empty bottle. "Don't tempt me, harlot, I have work to do."

As Gloria returned to the house, a worried look on her face, Blake finished the mowing, then struggled with the sprinkler. As he bent over it, twisting and turning, it suddenly burst on with malicious energy, and drenched him. He didn't know whether to laugh or cry. "That's what I get for thinking about Pru dying" he told himself, as he waded to the back door.

CHAPTER 10

▼

Cass walked quietly down the upper hall, kicking a couple of dust bunnies under the armoire as she went. Vickie was still sleeping, and Cass didn't want to disturb her. House work was far down her list of priorities, and with Dave away, her cleaning attempts had been perfunctory, to say the least. Luckily good old Vic felt exactly the same. There were too many interesting pursuits in life to waste much time on mundane chores. Dust would wait, adventure would not.

It was only minutes later when Cassie laughed as she heard a series of gut-wrenching sneezes coming from Vickie's room. Muffin must have cosied up to her during the night, Cass thought guiltily as she called "Good morning to you too, and how is Miss Sneezy this beautiful morning?"

"Very funny" came the hoarse reply. As Vickie entered the kitchen, Cass could see that her eyes were red and swollen. "Oh you poor thing. Here, let me get you some cucumber slices." Deftly cutting two pieces of cucumber, she handed them to Vickie. "Sit there, and put them on your eyes," she ordered. "They'll take the heat and the itching away."

Her friend obediently held the cool slices to her eyes as Cass worked around her. "Sorry about that, Vic. Was it Muffy or Sugar?"

"It was Muff — the darling. He cuddled up right on my chest with his little face on my face. I couldn't push him away because I knew he was showing me that he loves me. I know that he sleeps that way with you sometimes. I knew it would kill me, but what the heck — he's such a sweetie. Oh these feel wonderful — they're so cool."

"Spoken like a true animal lover" laughed Cass. "People who don't love animals the way we do would never understand, would they?"

"No, I guess not. Anyway I know that you would be just as allergic to my dogs as I am to your cats, so it's a Mexican stand-off," laughed Vickie, as she settled back in the chair, holding the slices to her eyes.

Cass had been thinking about Prudence and her new-found half-sister. They seemed determined to invade her mind at odd moments. She was worried about Pru, and didn't know what to think about Elena. She knew that Vickie had disliked her from the start, and Vickie was usually a pretty good judge of character. Vic was positive that Elena was after Pru's money. Cass thought that was a good possibility, but had twinges of guilt at being so suspicious.

"Dammit, Vic, I've gone through life with one sister to whom I was never close, and one sister I never knew existed." Slamming down the tea pot she exclaimed, "Look at those wasted years!!"

"Yes, it's terrible" Vickie answered carefully. She didn't want to aggravate Cass. "I just think that you should ask for a lot of proof that Elena really is your sister before you get too involved. And, if she is who she says she is, don't you think she chose a very fortuitous time to come looking for you? She could have caused the crash so as to get her hands on some of the money. I don't trust her. She's hanging around Pru like fruit flies on a peach. Maybe she's working on Pru to change her will!"

"Victoria Craig, you are something else. Pru's comatose, for heaven's sake" laughed Cassie. "Just let me try to sort this out in my mind for a while. I should be happy at having a new sister, but I feel so resentful. I feel as if she has stolen from all of us. She stole our dad's love and his time. How could he have done this? Weren't we enough of a family for him? Oh, it makes me so angry! Anyway, right now I'm sick of looking for mysteries everywhere. She's obviously my half-sister even if I wish she weren't. I just have to deal with it."

"I don't care, you shouldn't trust her Cass. There's something that smells about this," said Vickie stubbornly, still holding the slices to her eyes.

"I feel as if I'm talking to Little Orphan Annie here," giggled Cassie, staring at Vic's cucumber eyes. "You should see yourself — you're straight from the comics. Anyway, let's drop the entire business about Elena. I don't want to talk about it anymore," she said more crossly than she had intended. The words floated on the air and filled the space between them.

Vickie removed the cucumbers and looked quizzically at her friend. "Okay, pal, I won't mention it again" she acquiesced regretfully. She really felt uneasy about this stranger who had burst upon the scene, but she had been wrong before, so she would drop it, at least for now.

As they worked around the kitchen, they turned again to their favourite subject — the crash. They kept thinking of what Jenny had mumbled in her inebriated state. Did she know something about what really happened, or had it just been drunken rambling? They couldn't make up their minds, but they were inclined to think that she knew something. If that were the case, how could they get it out of her?

"Pass me that thingamajig please" said Cass, pointing vaguely to an open cupboard, and leaving her friend to guess just what thingamajig she meant. Cass had always had a penchant for using a goofy word instead of the real one. Vickie had forgotten that little idiosyncrasy.

"Gosh that cheese sauce looks wonderful" she exclaimed, handing Cass a measuring cup. "You're a really good cook."

"Surely you jest," laughed Cass. "I've always thought that cooking was too much like chemistry lab, and you know how I loathed that! How many times did you and I almost burn down that stinking lab as we mixed a little bit of this and a whole lot of that? We drove that poor teacher crazy. I think his hair had turned white by the end of the year. Anyway, I can cook the basics, but I don't really enjoy it. If I had my way all homes would be built without kitchens. We could all just eat at Harvey's and Swiss Chalet. For years Dave and the kids referred to dinner as 'burnt offering time', but I forced myself to learn enough to get by. Now I can cook fairly well, I just don't want to." She sighed and laughed as they began reminiscing about adventures in the chemistry lab.

They worked happily together, preparing things for the evening meal. Then, as they were unloading the dishwasher, Cass suggested, "This would be a perfect opportunity to go down to the casino for a while. It shouldn't be too crowded at this time of day."

As usual, Vickie was totally enthusiastic, and the hurried trip to the new Fallsview casino was fun. The constant clanging of the bells, coupled with the shrieks of delight, created a cacophony which was both deafening and exhilarating. Vickie loved every minute of it, especially when, down to her last few coins, she hit a small jackpot of eight hundred dollars. She stared in disbelief as first one dancing Elvis, then a second one, then a "ten times" symbol appeared on the screen, all in a line. Cass was delighted for her friend. This would make her visit memorable in spite of what else might happen.

"Let's stay here for lunch — your treat" she laughed. "We'll take it easy the rest of the day because tomorrow's the funeral, and we might learn something interesting."

The next day, after a fairly decent sleep, the two friends found themselves once again headed for Toronto. "When you came to Niagara Falls for a visit you certainly didn't expect to be trekking back and forth on this loathsome highway so often, did you?" asked Cassie as she kept her eye on the ever present behemoths of the road — the transport trucks.

"That's for sure" laughed Victoria. "Don't worry about it though. I'm just enjoying being with you. It seems like old times, and I loved that casino trip yesterday. When can we go again? I'll have so much to tell Brian and the kids. I wish I had started keeping a diary while I've been here."

"We can go back anytime" grinned Cass. "You've got a nice cushion of money now. Honestly it's so great for me having you here for moral support. I might have wanted David to come back from Spain if I'd been all alone, and that would have upset me. I wouldn't want to admit to him that I needed him that much. I'm still pissed off that he wouldn't take me on this trip. The great thing that's come out of it, though, is that I have you all to myself for a few weeks."

"Do you think this will be a big affair" asked Victoria, waving at two little kids in the back seat of a convertible as it passed them.

"Oh, for sure. Matt wasn't well liked from what I hear, but everyone likes and respects Prudence. She's got the reputation of being gentle and kind, and having a great sense of humour. It's true that she's a bit of a snob too, but people seem to like her. Wonder what she ever saw in him? He was so arrogant — the very few times I met him I couldn't stand him. I've heard too, that he stepped on his fair share of toes and did a lot of back-stabbing over the years. Probably all his enemies will be there, and the rest will come out of respect for Prudence."

Both friends had dressed carefully for the funeral. Vickie was in an elegant royal blue suit with a creamy silk blouse. The colours were perfect with her auburn hair. Cass was wearing an ankle-length cranberry silk suit with a frilly pink jabot. "Thank heavens black is no longer 'de rigueur' for funerals" they had laughed earlier that morning as they got themselves ready for the long day ahead.

As they entered the hospital for a quick visit before the afternoon funeral, they ran into Jordan and Jenny just leaving. Her niece and nephew did not notice them approaching, and they were laughing heartily at some private joke. Jenny looked as cute and sassy as a bright red bow. She was not exactly mourning her father's demise.

"It's heart-warming to see that they're coping so well with their loss" remarked Cass dryly.

Vickie just grinned and shook her head.

Meeting on the hospital steps, Cassie tried to hug Jennifer, and was again assailed by the distinct aroma of gin. "God, this is déjà vu" she muttered. She felt like slapping the little twit, but then reminded herself that this might be the only way that Jenny could cope with the double tragedy. After all, she didn't really know the girl, but then, she didn't want to, she thought sourly. Jordan seemed friendly enough, but his dark deep eyes were unsettling. It was a very short encounter, and they watched as Jenny, clinging to her brother's arm, made her way gingerly down the stairs.

"God, I hope she sobers up before the funeral," she said, sighing. "Thank goodness Pru can't see her behaving this way. I hope she was asleep when they were visiting her."

The good news was that Prudence had been moved from intensive care to a beautiful private room. She was fully conscious now, and all her vital signs had stabilized. She was on the mend according to the nurse at the station.

Cass was surprised to see Blake Wainwright just coming out of the room as she approached. "She's asleep" he said. "She looks better today though. She's got some colour in her face." They stood and chatted quietly at the door for a few minutes, and then were startled to hear a weak, quavery voice say "Is that you Cassandra?"

They both rushed over to the bed where Pru was lying with her eyes open, and was trying feebly to raise her hand as if in greeting.

"We're here, Pru. It's Cass and Blake. How are you doing?" she asked inanely. She could only imagine how her bruised and battered sister was doing.

"Glad you're here" whispered Pru with some effort. "Please stay — sorry I'm so befuddled, it's the drugs, but we need to talk."

As Cass patted her hand, she continued, "There's an important secret, Cass. It's time for you to know, and I have to tell you about Matt." Here her voice trailed away, and she dozed off again.

Blake and Cassandra stood around for a few more minutes talking quietly, and waiting for her to open her eyes, but she seemed to have drifted into a deep, probably drug induced, sleep. They reluctantly left, and as they walked together down the long and seemingly endless hall, Cass wondered aloud about the "important secret." What in the world could Pru have meant? Blake suggested that it may have been nothing but delusional ramblings caused by her medication, but Cass wasn't sure. She felt uneasy, and wished fervently that Pru hadn't drifted back to sleep so quickly.

Passing one of the lunch carts loaded with trays, they noticed a nondescript gray mass probably masquerading as meat loaf. Along with it were the ever present red jello squares jiggling sullenly in their bowls. The sights and smells were almost nauseating.

"Looks like we're missing some gourmet dining here, Blake. Should we stay and partake?" Cass asked with a grin. He grinned right back at her and shaking his head, he took her arm. "Come on, lady, I've tried hospital fare, and I think I'd rather eat bugs. Let's get out of here."

They laughed as they walked along the crowded corridor, and as they parted company, they agreed that they would see each other again at the funeral. Cass went to rescue Vickie from the waiting room, and to tell her about Pru's ramblings.

CHAPTER 11

▼

As expected, the funeral for Matt Wainwright was a large affair. It seemed as if half of Toronto had shown up. Back at the house after the service, it annoyed Cassie to see the way Jordan seemed to have taken over, as if this beautiful mansion already belonged to him. He was playing the gracious host rather dramatically, and not showing any signs of mourning. Staring at the guests and accepting their condolences, he stood so straight and tall that Cassie wondered uncharitably whether he had an iron bar stuck up his ass. He had a generic "nice to see you" smile pasted on his face, but there was nothing behind it.

"He's a disgrace" she whispered in disgust to Victoria. "He can't even wait until his poor mother dies. He's playing lord of the manor. I don't think he cares a whit about anyone but himself." She had discovered that it was actually Blake who had made all the funeral arrangements, and his wife Gloria who had organized all the food and drinks. Jordan and Jenny, claiming to be too distraught, had done nothing.

It occurred to Vickie that survivors and friends tend to gather at funerals using the food and drink as the glue which holds them together. It was like an 'old boys club'. They were alive, and the guest of honour wasn't, so in a ghoulish way it was a kind of celebration.

Both women were surprised that Elena was there. She certainly wasn't losing any time in becoming part of the family. "I suppose she's just here to pay her respects" said Vickie grudgingly, "but she didn't know Matt did she?"

"Who knows? Maybe she's here representing Prudence" suggested Cass doubtfully.

They watched the tall, elegant woman as she moved quietly among the guests. Her dark, flashing eyes seemed to probe everything. It was as if she was studying the people and the surroundings. She seemed so intense.

I should give her a break, Cass scolded herself. She's in an awkward position — an illegitimate half-sister suddenly appearing in our lives. She admitted that she had mean spirited doubts about Elena. She just couldn't shake them, and Vickie was so openly hostile that it was certainly a touchy situation. Cass covertly studied Elena as she interacted with the funeral guests. What was it about her that rubbed her the wrong way, she wondered.

Tearing her eyes away from Elena, Cass thought that this might be an opportune time to tweak some noses, stir the pot as it were. If in fact Matt's death was no accident, and if the killer was here, she might be able to get a reaction. "Come on Vic, let's try something" she murmured, heading over to the family members who were standing in the shade of a big maple.

Grabbing a glass of wine on the way, she frowned, and began, "Isn't it dreadful to think that this might not have been an accident?" As she said this, she casually glanced from one to the other in the little group.

Jenny jumped as if someone had slapped her. Her eyes looked wide and frightened. Blake frowned and asked, "What do you mean?"

Pete just gave her a vacuous stare. Elena said nothing, but looked interested, and Jordan exclaimed, "What the hell are you blathering about?"

"Well" began Cassie, plunging right in, and wondering where she was going to go from here, "the police have indicated that there's something very suspicious about the entire matter," she figuratively crossed her fingers at this point, "and of course we won't want to rest until we get to the bottom of it. You must feel exactly the same. We can't let the killer get away with this" she added innocently, with the same worried frown.

"Actually, we're thinking of hiring a private investigator" jumped in Vickie, never one to be left out.

"That is absolutely absurd" spluttered Jordan coldly. "Don't you dare say anything like that in front of our mother, or anyone else. You keep your mouths shut and don't try to make trouble where there is none. You don't know what the hell you're talking about. This was an accident, a tragic accident."

Jenny simply nodded her head in agreement, as if she had been struck dumb.

Cass noticed that the only thing moving on Jordan's face was his mouth with those thick lips. His black eyes stared unblinking at her. She suddenly felt that this might have been a foolish mistake. His tone of voice was almost as murderous as the glare he was giving her. Jenny was still gaping in an alarmed way.

Before Cass could say anything else, however, she let out a squeal of alarm and spilled her glass of wine. "It's a bee — get it away" she shrieked, wildly flapping her arms.

"It's okay, it's gone" soothed a kindly old gentleman, picking up her wine glass. "What frightened you so, it was only a little bee."

"Thank you" said Cass, trying to smile. "I'm allergic to bees. I always carry an epi-kit in my purse and one in the glove compartment, because I've been told that one more sting could do me in. Sorry I made such a fuss. I feel very foolish." She looked around to see everyone staring at her in something akin to amusement. Even Vickie was trying hard not to laugh. She had seen Cass do this "dance of the bees" once or twice before.

Darn it, thought Cass, the timing was bad. They hadn't had a chance to get all the reactions to their lies about the police investigating the crash. If only they could have kept that conversation going instead of the interruption of the killer bee! She did notice, however, that Jordan was still glowering at her as if she was now on his permanent hit list, and Blake was looking at her with a quizzical expression.

Pru's cottage neighbour and friend, Joanne Bailey, was at the food table nibbling on a sandwich as Cass and Vickie approached. "Cass I can't believe that woman would show up here" she muttered indignantly. "And she's even got her husband in tow" she added in disgust.

"Why, who is she?" asked Cassie with interest.

"Who is she, huh, she's Matthew's girlfriend, that's who she is" declared Joanne angrily. "See that brunette in the green silk suit? She was Matt's sweetie until about two weeks ago, when her husband finally found out. See, that's her husband walking up to her now, the tall, heavyset guy with the moustache." Joanne had the grace to look guilty as she told this delicious piece of gossip. "Their names are Jim and Carol Sinclair. Apparently Matt met her in the bank just after he and Pru won the lottery last year. Jim has a fierce temper, and when he found out about the two of them, he went to Matt's house and punched him out. He knocked him down and gave him a black eye and a split lip."

Joanne paused here to relish the effect this little bombshell had on Vickie and Cassandra. "Jim said that he would kill Matt if he ever looked at Carol again. Pru was beside herself, she was so angry and hurt, and scared too. That's why they were going on this extended trip to California. Pru wanted to get him as far from Carol and her bully of a husband as she could."

All three women were now staring unabashedly at the Sinclairs. They all agreed that the pair had a great deal of nerve coming to Matt's funeral. "Matt was more of a louse than I thought" said Cassie in a low voice. "Poor Prudence. She had too lousy kids and a skunk for a husband. Her money and position certainly didn't buy her much happiness, did they?"

She eventually excused herself and wandered inside to seek asylum from any more bee attacks. To her dismay and annoyance, Elena followed her.

"Cassandra, could you spare me a few moments?" she asked, touching Cassie lightly on the shoulder.

"Sure, what's up?" queried Cassandra flippantly. She had no desire to talk to Elena.

"I'd like to speak with you" replied Elena, guiding Cassie into a small music room. It had wonderfully comfortable chairs, and soft indirect lighting which gave it a warm ambiance. As Cass sat down on the loveseat, Elena sat almost right beside her.

"Cassandra, I know you have many doubts and questions about me. Am I really your half-sister, or am I an impostor? I have felt the insecurity and doubt in your attitude." She spoke almost sadly, but with a gentle cadence which was very pleasant to the ear.

In all conscience, Cassie couldn't look into those large dark eyes and try to deny what Elena was saying.

"I have brought some things to show you. It is important that you believe me. Prudence does." She spoke in very careful English, and she said this in a quiet, regretful tone, as if Cassie had disappointed her somehow.

"Well, you see, Elena" Cassie began, but Elena put her finger to Cassie's lips and said firmly, "I have brought you proof. Please look at these."

She drew a birth certificate from the small carry-all which had been slung over her shoulder. "Here is the certificate which shows that J.J. was my father. Here is the baptism paper, and here are my first communion document and my passport." She slapped each one down in front of Cassie as if to say "Now what do you think?"

Cass looked at the pieces of paper without really seeing them. "I'm sorry, Elena, but documents can be forged" she said angrily. What the hell was she doing here with this stranger who was sitting too close to her, invading her space?

"I knew you would say that" cut in Elena, shaking her head. "Perhaps this will persuade you." With that she extracted a small photo album from the tote bag, and opened it. There on the first page was a picture of J.J. — Cassie's dad — his arms around a dark haired, dark-eyed beauty holding a baby. The woman looked a bit like Elena, and was undoubtedly her mother. The lush background was definitely South America. Cass gasped as she turned page after page, and saw pictures of the child at two and four and ten, always with her father or with the dark-eyed beauty. There was no doubt — J.J. was Elena's father. The pictures ended when Elena looked to be about twelve.

Cassandra was ready to hit someone by the time she finished looking at the album. If her dad were here she would punch him out. She felt anger and disbelief that he had perpetrated this great deception on his family, on Lizzie and Pru and Cass. Seeing these pictures of her beloved dad with that beautiful woman who was not her mother, broke her heart. How could he have done it? How did he get away with it all those years? Had her mom ever suspected? Cass doubted it. Her mom and dad had always seemed totally happy, totally in sync. Well, like it or not, she had a half-sister. Wait till she told Vickie! She grudgingly put her arms around Elena, but there was no warmth in the embrace. She secretly wished that she could push a button and have Elena disappear for good. All her doubts and misgivings had to be set aside, but she wasn't so sure about Vickie. Miss Doubting Thomas definitely would not like this development.

CHAPTER 12

▼

Since Vickie knew very few of the people at the funeral reception, and since her feet were hurting, she wandered into the den and began looking at the shelves of books. Finding an intriguing looking mystery which she hadn't read, she curled up in a high-backed wing chair facing the fireplace, and with her back to the door. No one could see her there, and she would wait until Cass was ready to leave.

She didn't know anyone had entered the room until she heard voices and realized that it was Jordan and Jennifer. Hoping to avoid them, she stayed quietly curled up in the chair, and prayed that they would leave quickly. After the little act she and Cass had staged in the garden, she was a bit leery of facing them. Her main fear was that she might start sneezing.

"Jen, you've had enough to drink. Don't have any more."

"Oh shut up. You can't boss me around. I'm not ten anymore you know. I'll drink as much as I want. This whole thing's been a nightmare, and now with Aunt Cassie stirring things up, I need something to calm my nerves."

"No you don't" he said in a vicious tone. "You can't do anything to screw things up. Don't you realize how close we are to all that lovely money?"

"Well, who pissed in your pocket" she asked belligerently. "How could I screw things up? I haven't done anything wrong." She emphasized the "I" as she glared at him.

"Jen, sometimes you are so stupid. You heard what Aunt Cass said. They're going to hire a private eye. I didn't realize the police were suspicious, but now I don't know. We sure as hell don't want to do anything to fuel the fire. We don't want an investigation, do we?"

Jenny's eyes narrowed as she stared up at him. "Oh, Jordie," she gasped, "you did do something to the car didn't you? I knew it! Why didn't you tell me?"

"Jen, look at me. You know it couldn't have been an accident," he hissed. "Think about it. It was a clear night. The old man was a great driver, he knew every inch of that road, he could have driven it blindfolded, and the car was in perfect condition. He never drank if he was going to drive. The Baileys said that there was no other car involved, and the autopsy showed that he hadn't had a stroke or heart attack, so obviously it was no accident."

"So then you did do something. Oh, Jordie!"

"Jesus, Jen, I didn't say that I did anything. I just said that it couldn't have been an accident, and we don't want the police to get suspicious. I don't really care who did it. It could have been you or Pete for all I know, but it's a great break for us, and we just don't want a long investigation. So — until the old lady dies and the will is read, I want you to lay off the booze and be very careful what you say. Keep in mind that mommy dearest could linger for a long time. We just might have to help her on her way." He paused here for Jenny's reaction, but she seemed speechless, so he continued. "Why the hell are that damn pushy Cassie and her moronic friend nosing around and even talking to the police. They're stirring everything up. You realize that we've got to stop them — shut them up. We have to scare them somehow so that they'll just let it drop, and if that doesn't work, well, we'll see what might have to be done.

I didn't tell you, but I've finally found the will after a lot of searching. They had it well hidden. Except for the stupid bequests to all their charities, plus a million bucks to Uncle Blake — (Jenny gasped at this revelation) — everything else goes to us. You get the cottage, I get this house, and all that sweet, wonderful money is ours to split."

"Jordie, we can go anywhere and start all over" crowed Jenny, caught up in the thought of all those millions almost within reach.

"Yah, well just lay off the booze, keep your mouth shut, and keep telling yourself that it was an accident. Look at me Jenny. I swear I'll kill you if you do anything to mess up now."

To her own surprise, Jennifer reached up and slapped Jordan hard across the face. "Don't talk to me like that" she started to cry. "I'm not as dumb or as weak, or even as drunk as you think. How the hell are we supposed to keep Aunt Cassie quiet? You scare me when you act so mean, but just remember, I know a whole lot about you that I could tell."

Jenny had never before made this threat to her big brother, and she scared herself when she heard the words jumping out of her mouth.

Before Jordan could reply, Victoria heard another voice. She was stunned, and holding her breath at what she had just heard.

"Oh, there you are, you poor dears. I just came to say good-bye. I'm so very sorry for your loss. It was a lovely funeral though. Such a shame your mother couldn't be here. We're all praying for her, you know."

The garrulous woman seemed unable to stop, so Jordan cut in smoothly.

"Thanks so much, Mrs. Johnston, you are very kind. Jenny and I have been so distraught — we were just comforting each other."

Oh what a crock that was, thought Vickie.

At this, Jenny's sobbing and hiccupping grew louder.

What an actress, thought Vickie. Those must be crocodile tears, judging by the way she turned them on so fast.

"Come on, we'll see you to the door."

There was silence then, and a very shaken Victoria curled up even smaller in her chair, wondering whether they had really left. In spite of being frightened and feeling a bit queasy, she could also see the black humour in her situation. She had watched this scene, or a reasonable facsimile thereof in countless movies. Someone hidden in a high-backed chair overhears a murder plot, or a confession, and either solves a mystery, or stops a murderer, or is killed herself. Damnation, Vickie wondered. Would he really try to kill us to shut us up? We don't know anything. We should never have pretended to be talking to the police. This was no longer fun. In fact it was just plain scary. It was one thing to be talking bravely about solving a mystery, but it was quite another to be smack in the middle of one. She knew without a doubt that Jordan and Jenny would not be happy to discover that she had overheard their conversation.

After an eternity of silence, she raised her head enough to peek around the arm of the chair. There was no one there.

Hurriedly she stood up, and letting the forgotten book fall to the floor, she rushed to the door. Very cautiously she peered out into the hall — no one. Breathing a sigh of relief, she walked down the hall with an air of insouciance, and into the large living room. As she entered, she saw Jordan giving her a quizzical look. Damn, her heart nearly gave out on her. Did he know she had overheard them? She reasoned that she could have been coming from the kitchen or the den, so how could he know for sure? She had to find Cassie and get out of here.

On the way home Victoria was unusually quiet.

"What's wrong" queried Cassandra, momentarily taking her eyes off the busy highway.

"Nothing really. I was just thinking about Jordan. What does he do for a living?"

"Honestly Vic, I don't know. He toils not, neither doth he spin" she chuckled. "Actually I think he dabbled in stocks at one time like his dad, but he got into some kind of trouble."

"Well, he seems, I don't know, too smooth on the surface, but that's all it is, just surface. His eyes give me the creeps. They're like two burnt holes in a blanket. There's nothing behind them."

"I know. He seems soulless somehow. There's nothing behind the façade."

"That's it" agreed her friend. "You look into those black eyes and they're bottomless. Sorry to say it, Cass, but there's something wrong with him. He's evil."

Cassandra drove in silence for a few minutes, and Victoria was afraid that she had hurt her friend's feelings. She had decided not to tell her about overhearing the conversation in the den, until they got back safely to Niagara. Cass had enough on her mind just now, what with Elena and all her bits and pieces of so-called proof. Vickie was still sceptical about her story. Anyway she needed to sit down quietly and try to remember exactly what she had heard before she laid anything else on Cass.

"Did you hear any more about how the accident happened? Do the authorities think that Matt fell asleep at the wheel or what?"

"No, I didn't really hear anything. Everyone has an opinion and no one really knows a damn thing. Jordan made some mean comment about his dad being a really fast driver, and that it was surprising he hadn't killed himself long before now. I thought that was pretty ridiculous, especially since Matt was allegedly an excellent and careful driver. Basically all I know is what Joanne told me. They came down that steep hill on the old highway, and there's a sharp curve to the left between a huge rock cut. They missed the curve and smacked right into the rocks. It makes me shiver to think of it."

Vickie shivered too, and looked around at the relatively flat ground on both sides of the highway. Good, no rock cuts to be seen.

"They were all at the cottage for a barbecue, Blake and Gloria and their kids, and Pru and Matt and Jordan and Jenny. Oh, I wonder whether Elena was there. No one mentioned her. Apparently everyone left before Matt and Pru did. According to Joanne, they took their usual evening boat cruise before packing up for home."

Vickie's ears pricked up at this. Anyone could have cut the brakes while they were out boating, or maybe they put sugar in the gas tank. Would that cause the car to go out of control? She didn't have any idea.

The car seemed to purr contentedly as it turned into the driveway. Even it seemed to be happy to be off the highway after all the talk about the crash. As usual, the house was lit up like a cruise ship.

"You can tell the cat sitter's a little nervous at night" laughed Cass. "She turns on every light in the house. My hydro bill is worse than the cat-sitting bill, but you know how she loves Sugar and Muff."

Vickie thought it was a bit ridiculous that Cassie had the sitter come over when they were only gone one full day, but she knew how careful Cassie was with her cats. Besides, the cat sitter loved to come over and play with them, so it was really none of Vickie's business. Actually, come to think of it, she was just as silly and protective with her dogs.

After talking to the sitter for a few minutes, Vickie said, "I'm going to change and wash up. I'll be down to make us a cup of tea in a few minutes. It's been a long day."

As soon as she got to her room, she closed the door, threw her purse on the bed, and plunked herself down in the rocking chair. Before telling Cass anything she had to remember what she had heard that had scared her. Ears could play tricks on you, and so could memory. Closing her eyes, she tried to wish herself back in that high-backed chair in the den. What had set her nerves tingling? Oh yes, of course. That awful guy had said that he and Jenny might have to help Pru on her way if she took too long to die. She couldn't believe it, this guy talked so calmly about killing his mother. The really scary thing was that he had said they had to shut up nosy Cassie and her moronic friend Vickie. Did "shut up" mean "kill?" Vickie didn't appreciate being called moronic, and she certainly wasn't happy about maybe being on Jordan's hit list. He had even threatened to kill Jenny if she screwed things up. Maybe he was just all talk, but how could they be sure?

She stopped rocking and stared off into space. She was certain now that the so-called accident had been nothing of the kind. It had been a well planned and calculated scheme to kill Matt and Pru. But why? Unfortunately neither Jordan nor Jenny had admitted to being involved. In a way the entire conversation had been innocuous. There had been no blatant confession of wrong-doing. There was nothing substantial to take to the police. What was the point of worrying Cassie tonight? They couldn't do anything, and it would just keep her awake. Tomorrow would be time enough to tell what she had heard.

As Victoria rocked and pondered, she began to wish that she was back in her own safe house with Brian and her books and her dogs. Hell and damnation, what was she doing here? Should she make some excuse and go home? Of course not. Cassie needed her.Besides she had wanted some excitement this summer. She would stay and they would see it through together.

"Just keep telling yourself that you're having fun Vickie old girl" she muttered grimly as she stared at herself in the mirror. Then, pasting on a somewhat lopsided grin, she headed downstairs to join Cassie and the cats.

CHAPTER 13

▼

The next few nights after the funeral, neither woman slept well. Cassie in particular did a lot of tossing and turning. Her comfortable, orderly world had suddenly become alien. In Cassie's world people weren't victims of murder plots. They weren't snuffed out on a whim. At three in the morning, however, almost anything seemed possible.

The ceiling fan was going in a desultory fashion, sulkily moving the hot air around. Muffy didn't care how hot it was. He was snuggled up beside Cass in a cosy, heat-producing ball of fur. She was reluctant to disturb him in order to get up and crank the fan into high gear.

It was probably the heat which was causing her imagination to run amok. She had read far too many mysteries with bizarre plots and devious twists, and now in the wee small hours, every murder plot she had ever read was coming back to haunt her. When she started thinking that maybe Pru had an insane twin brother who had just escaped from the asylum to seek revenge on the family, she knew that she was on the edge. Grinning at her foolishness, she told herself that things would look better in the light of day.

The morning sunshine should have wiped away all Cassie's wild night time imaginings, but something happened to get her riled up again.

She was making tea while Vickie wandered around the back yard. Cass warmed the old brown teapot with hot water while she waited for the tea kettle to boil. Gazing out the kitchen window, she tried to concentrate on pleasant, everyday things. She idly pondered the different ways they enjoyed their tea. Vickie took hers on the weak side, cooled down with lots of milk. Cassie enjoyed hers black and piping hot. This led her to the intricacies and complexities of friendship. How could two women so different in so many ways be such kindred spirits? It must be because we think alike on all the important issues, she thought, as she poured the boiling water into the teapot and covered it with a tea cosy. And maybe it's because we both get scared at the same things, she thought wryly. Setting the timer, and adding a plate of toasted bagels, she carried the tea tray into the sunroom.

Niagara Falls in the morning can be a glorious place, and this morning was no exception. The sun was shining in all its splendour, and the sky was a radiant, cheerful blue. There were absolutely no clouds to be seen, but there was a gentle breeze blowing from the west. It might bring clouds like little cotton balls later in the day.

Sugar Plum was doing a "cat in the hat" trick. Victoria had left her broad brimmed sun hat upside down on the footstool after coming in from the garden. Sugar was curled up in it, although she didn't quite fit. Her tail hung out one side, and one paw stuck out the other. Still, uncomfortable as she was, she somehow knew that this would get her some attention. She squeezed her eyes shut in delight as the two women told her that she was adorable.

Muffy jumped into Cassie's lap, and curled himself into a ball as soon as she sat down. All was well in his little cat world. Cassandra and Victoria, however, couldn't say the same about theirs.

The last few days had been weird to say the least. Vic, of course, had told Cassie everything she had overheard at the funeral. That was scary enough. There was the fact that Jordan had said they had to be silenced. Add to this his threat to kill his mother if she took too long to die. Then there was his threat to kill Jenny if she screwed up before they got the money. Now both women suspected that someone was stalking them.

First there had been a couple of calls with no one on the other end. The caller kept hanging up as soon as the phone was answered. They really didn't think much about it, other than to be annoyed. Then Vickie answered the phone and heard a gruff voice say "the only good snoop is a dead snoop. Take the hint, ladies, and lay off." At first they had laughed uproariously at this idiotic attempt to scare them. Trying to make light of the phone call, both women hid their secret misgivings. It was so juvenile. It had to be someone from the funeral, but who? Jordan had said that they had to be scared off, but this seemed beneath him somehow. It seemed more the type of thing that Pete, Jenny's dumb boyfriend whom they had met at the funeral, might do. Still, why would he bother to try scaring them? He didn't seem either subtle enough or sophisticated enough to do any planned stalking. And what motive would he have for scaring or harassing them? They didn't even know him.

Cass had a bit of a temper which she usually kept well under control. That day, however, after Vickie got the threatening call, she had been so infuriated, that she had rushed up to her bedroom and had begun digging around in an old jewellery box. Eventually she came back downstairs, clutching a whistle on a chain.

"We're going to leave this right by the phone, and if this guy calls again, just blow the whistle as loud as you can. Give him such a blast with it that he won't be able to hear himself take a pee. It may not scare him too much, but at least he'll think twice about calling us again."

Vickie laughed at the idea, and said that she would likely get too flustered to remember, but Cassie wouldn't be discouraged. "It's either some total fool who thinks he's being funny, or we stirred up something at the funeral with our stupid remarks about investigating the crash."

The really upsetting part had been this morning. When they came downstairs they noticed something lying just inside the front door. It was a picture of the cats sitting in the bay window of the little library. It was a close-up, and it had been taken in the past two days. Cass knew this for sure, because in the picture you could see a vase of fresh cut flowers from the garden, which Vickie had placed there two days ago. Someone had been right outside that window. Someone was showing them in a not so subtle way, just how easily they could get at the cats or the women. The awful thing which had sent cold chills right down Cassie's spine, was that there was a big black "X" right across the picture of the two little pets. After Cassie's wild imaginings of the previous night, this was the last straw.

They sat down and racked their brains to try to remember exactly who had been standing under the trees when they had made their silly remarks about the police being suspicious, and about hiring a private eye. It had to be one of those people who had taken the picture. Jordan and Jenny were there, and so was Pete. Blake and Gloria and Elena were also there, but where were Carol and Jim Sinclair? Had they been close enough to hear what was being said? There was the old man who had chased the bee, but surely he couldn't be considered a suspect. How about Joanne Bailey? Could she have had any reason to want to harm Matt and Pru? Could any of these people be making phone calls and taking pictures of the cats?

The police had to be called, but they had to get their facts straight first. The trouble was that they really had no facts. Obviously they had scared someone enough at the funeral to make him or her feel threatened. The question was just which of the funeral guests was doing this. Neither woman could seriously believe that anyone would want to kill them, but Cassie was concerned about the cats. Would anyone be cruel enough to hurt her beloved pets in order to shut her up?

She realized now that she should never have said anything at the funeral. All that business about hiring a private detective was so ridiculous, but at the time it had seemed both witty and clever. Now she and Vickie wished fervently they had kept their noses out of the entire mess.

Vickie was an inveterate list maker. Even when they were kids, Cassie used to tease her about her little scraps of paper with lists on them. She was sitting now with her trusty notepad and pen, and was making a list of all the possible suspects. "Let's start with the least likely. How about Blake? He stands to inherit a million dollars. That's not exactly chump change."

"Yes, that's really strange" agreed Cass. "I wonder why Matt would do that? They didn't even get along. Why would his brother leave him that kind of money, and does Blake even know about it? That would certainly give him a motive, but did he have the opportunity? He was at the barbecue that day, but would he even know how to tamper with a car? Damn, I like him. I don't want him to be a suspect. He's a flirt and a bit of a bon vivant, but he seems awfully nice."

"Is he a lot different from his brother?" asked Vickie, as she nibbled on a bagel loaded with cream cheese.

"You can say that again. Matt was an idiot. He was a 'superior than thou', 'I'm right and you're wrong' sort of person. The few times I met him he was always talking about people being 'lower drawer,' and 'beyond contempt.' He was full of himself and looked down on everyone else. I could never understand what Pru saw in him, except that he was great at making money. He had the real "Midas" touch. Blake is a hundred percent more decent than that arrogant s.o.b."

Vickie was full of ideas this morning. "What if Blake's in love with Pru and wanted his brother out of the way?"

Cass thought a moment. "That's interesting, Vic, but. there's not one scintilla of proof. Remember, Pru was almost killed too."

"Maybe he didn't know that Pru was going in the car that night" replied Vickie, trying to justify her idea. "What if he thought it was just Matthew driving back to Toronto. I'll bet Pru often stayed up there by herself."

"Not likely. If he was in love with her, he wouldn't have taken a chance like that. He couldn't have known for sure whether Pru would be in the car or not."

"Okay" sighed Vickie, undaunted, but putting a big question mark beside Blake's name. Let's get to Jordan and Jenny. Certainly they both had motives. Jordan found the will, so he knew that they would inherit virtually everything."

"Yes, but did he know that before the accident, and did Jenny know about it before Jordan told her at the funeral? If they didn't know for sure that they were in the will it would have been stupid to plan the accident." Cass was now twiddling her hair in a distracted way.

"True" agreed Vickie, absently picking cat hair off her navy slacks. "Well, they were the only children, so they must have known or at least expected that they would inherit everything. There's so darn much money involved that it would be terribly tempting, especially when they didn't really get along that well with their parents."

"Can you really see Jenny doing anything bad like that? She seems so helpless and fragile. She's adorable in spite of being a boozer."

"Maybe her boyfriend, Mr. Tattoo Man, helped. He's apparently a mechanic, although the way he acts I suspect he's been lobotomized. The guy's a cretin. All together now, can we say 'asshole'?" she asked in a Mr. Rogers tone. They both giggled.

"You know, maybe we're outsmarting ourselves here. Just because the guy's a moron doesn't mean that he can't be dangerous. Stupidity is always dangerous."

"I must admit, the fact that he's a mechanic is intriguing. He could certainly have done any number of things to damage the car provided he had the opportunity. But did he have any motive?"

"I doubt it, Sherlock" replied Cassandra, shaking her head. "From something Jenny said, I don't think they were even together at the time of the crash. They had broken up over something or other. What motive would he have had to kill her parents if he wasn't even going with her at the time?"

"Shit, that brings us back to Jordan" laughed Vickie. She was scribbling furiously now. Cass wondered what she could possibly be writing so extensively. "He's the logical choice I think. He looks pathologically cunning, he had the opportunity, and he certainly had the motive. Besides, I heard Jenny asking him if he had done it. I think that she thinks he did. She's either really smart, trying to shift the blame away from herself, or she's totally innocent. Oh, and don't forget. Jordan said that they might have to help Pru along if she takes too long to die, so I think that he's capable of anything."

Cassie shook her head. "I would hate to think that it was one of her own kids." She was absently stroking Muffy's head as she spoke. "Jordan couldn't have been serious. No one talks so cavalierly about killing his or her own mother."

"Oh Cass, get real. The world is full of creeps and assholes. You know that as well as I do. All kinds of people murder their parents for all kinds of reasons."

Cass sighed and shook her head. "I guess it's just too close to home. How could anyone in my family — distant as they may be — be a killer? It just doesn't compute in my simple brain. I guess I just don't want any killers as relatives."

"Well I understand that, of course, but it's really nothing to do with you. You haven't been close to these people your entire life, and you certainly aren't responsible for their actions. Anyway, maybe we're totally off the mark" soothed Vickie.

After a moment's silence, during which they stared at each other, thinking their own thoughts, Cass said, "I wonder whether Pru and Matt could have had a lot of enemies we just don't know about. What if they owed someone a lot of money?"

"Now that's absurd! I'm sure that with all the money they had, they were quite able to pay their debts."

"You never know about people" Cass said stubbornly. "I wonder whether it was merely coincidental that Pru called me just before the crash. Remember I told you that she said I was going to find out some very surprising news, and at the hospital she whispered something about an important secret. Maybe it was that they were in financial trouble, or maybe that they had enemies chasing them. Who knows? Perhaps that's why they were heading to California. Maybe it wasn't just to get Matt away from his girlfriend. Possibly it was to save him from the irate husband."

"Sure, that could be" agreed Vickie, adding Jim Sinclair's name to her growing list of suspects. As for the surprise, I imagine she just meant the arrival of Elena on the scene. You did say, though, that she sounded sad. Could she have been scared or worried?"

"I wish I could remember. What a pair of detectives we are! We couldn't detect our way out of the women's washroom. We're like a couple of old 'Dudley-Do-Rights'. We really don't have a damn clue, do we?"

Vickie grinned in agreement. "We can't discount Elena and her part in all of this. I'm writing her name on the list too. The timing just seems too odd. She suddenly shows up in Toronto out of the blue, just a couple of weeks before the crash."

"Oh, for God's sake, let up on Elena. I don't like her any better than you do, but it appears that she is indeed my half-sister, and how the hell could she have been involved?" Cass said this more sharply than she intended, but she was getting fed up with Vickie's suspicions. "Actually I'd rather think that it was Jim

Sinclair than any of the others. He certainly had motive. I guess he hated Matt. Wonder if he knows anything about cars?"

"We're getting nowhere fast, friend. We might as well put Matt's lover Carol on the list too. Maybe she killed him because he was dumping her. Anyway, it's time to call the police and tell them about the phone calls and the cat picture. Even if there was no murder, I do think that we may have a stalker. It will give us the chance to tell them about all this, and get their reactions. I'm so confused now that I don't know what's going on."

Cassie suddenly jumped up and began pacing the way Muffy always did when he could smell a turkey cooking. "Sit there, Vic, while I run this scenario by you" she said excitedly.

Vickie looked intrigued. "Let's have it. It's got to be better than what we've thought of so far."

"Well," started Cassie slowly, thinking as she went along. "What if Pru was so distraught when she discovered Matt's infidelity, that she just wanted to die? No — don't interrupt. Just let me work this out." Vickie was already looking doubtful.

"What if Pru was suicidal, but she was too angry at Matt to leave him free to be with his little dolly. Maybe she decided to kill him and then kill herself, make it a murder-suicide. She probably didn't have a gun, so shooting wasn't likely. A knife would be too 'up close and personal,' and then how would she have killed herself? It must be awfully hard to actually stab yourself with enough force to do yourself in. Poison might have been a good choice, but Matt could have tasted it and become suspicious."

Vickie was looking fascinated by now, so Cassie continued her ruminations. "What if, in her disturbed state, she decided on a car crash, fast and deadly. She knew the perfect place for it to happen. The road is so straight and flat from their cottage to that hill and rock cut, that Matt wouldn't have realized the brakes were gone until it was too late. She probably had the opportunity, and she certainly had the motive. He had been cheating on her, and maybe she just didn't want to live any more. I like it, what do you think?"

Vickie liked it too. In fact, she was sorry that she hadn't thought of it first. She stared at Cass for a second, then shook her head doubtfully. "Remember you told me that on the phone she went on about the car being all checked out and in perfect condition for the long trip to California. Why would she have said that if she was planning to do something to cause the crash? The car was more likely to crash if it wasn't in good shape."

"Aw shit, you're right. And anyway, if it was Pru who did it, then who the hell is stalking us?"

They were both totally deflated and disconsolate. There was no way they could ever prove anything. Why were they even trying? "You realize that we've got sweet diddly at this point, don't you?" asked Cass ruefully.

"More like 'sweet f — -all'" replied Vickie, frowning at her friend.

"Woo ha!" exclaimed Cass. "Such language from a lady!"

"Hey, remember I worked in the penitentiary for a few years. You wouldn't believe the language I heard, and when I have to, I can dredge up a few meaningful words."

"I just bet you can. You'll have to enlighten me some night."

"Okay, give me a few glasses of wine, and I'll recite my entire repertoire. Anyway, back to business. I think our next step is to call the police."

CHAPTER 14

▼

Detective Jack Willinger was returning to Niagara Falls after a short trip to the nearby city of St. Catharines. Since this was his day off, and since he was in no hurry, the detective had opted for the back roads through the fruit lands of the peninsula. He was thinking about Darla as he drove along. If only they'd been able to have a baby, maybe things would have been different.

The ditches on both sides of this back road were full of the usual detritus, litter thrown from cars, soggy, rotting leaves, weeds fighting for survival. Momentarily he pondered the irony of weeds, which were so hardy and aggressive, while cherished flowers had to be babied and nurtured so patiently. The inevitable analogy sprang to mind. The crooks and perverts were the tenacious, strong-willed weeds of humanity. They sprang from the worst, most sour soil, the tenements, outlying shacks, welfare tracts — the edges or ditches of society. The good people, however, the gentle, clean-living, caring souls were the flowers of the human race. They were the frail, easily wounded ones. Jack laughed at his little flights of fancy as he drove along enjoying the colours of the wild tiger lilies, iris and invasive purple loosestrife.

Thinking again about Darla, he glanced casually in the rear view mirror, and was startled to realize that a shabby blue car had been following him for some time. On a subconscious level he knew that he had seen this same car several times recently. What the hell? he thought, as he looked for a place to get off the road.

Ah, there it was, a long private driveway. Jack wheeled the car onto the winding asphalt driveway leading up to a big red brick farmhouse sitting on a knoll. It was surrounded by giant blue spruce whose spreading bottom branches looked like ante-bellum hoop skirts. With his practised detective's eye, Jack took all this in without any conscious effort. The road to the house was lined with maple trees, so that Jack's car was almost hidden from Willy as he approached from the west.

Ironically, Jack wasn't the only one who was thinking about his wife Darla on this perfect summer day. Willy the Weasel, following along at what he considered a safe distance, was also thinking about Darla. Since he was going to kill her anyway, he wouldn't have to wear a mask when he raped her. That excited him enormously, and as he slobbered over his erotic flights of fancy, he almost lost sight of his prey.

Willy sped up frantically as soon as he realized that Jack had disappeared. Where the hell was he? Then he caught sight of the cop's car, but it was too late. He was too close to it. He had to keep right on going and hope that Willinger hadn't recognized him.

He wondered vaguely why things never seemed to go smoothly for him these days. Had he lost his touch since being in the pen? "Oh shit, oh shit" thought Willy, as he saw with dismay that the detective was pulling out and coming after him. Now what? He didn't even know where this road went. Maybe Willinger would just pass him and keep on going. Maybe this hadn't been such a good idea. Willy started to sweat and to suck his teeth.

Jack sped up and easily closed the distance between them. Who the hell was in the wreck of a car, and why had he been following Jack? He tailed along for a short distance, then pulled out and forced the car onto the shoulder. Once it had stopped, the detective got out of his car in a carefully controlled manner.

Willy was shaking badly. He was sucking his teeth so hard that the slobber was running down his chin. This is it, he thought. I have to knife him now. Fingering his knife to calm himself, he tried to think. It wasn't easy. This wasn't the way he had planned it, but he could do it, hell, he had to do it. He had to take Willinger by surprise. He would move in fast and cut him before he had a chance to react. Yes, that was it. Willy heaved a nervous sigh. It would be all over in a minute, but it wasn't the way he had planned it. Sheeit! Things never seemed to go right any more. He would just stick Willinger and then maybe he'd have to head out to Vancouver right away. He'd have to forget Darla and Bud Lang and just take off. No fuckin' way. He was going to screw that hot Darla if it was the last thing he did. These thoughts were bouncing in Willy's head like bingo balls. The more he tried to think, the more he sucked his teeth.

Willinger was motioning Willy to get out of the car. As he opened the door and stepped outside, his heart sank. Shit, shit, shit. Willinger didn't play fair. He had a fucking gun in his hand. He wasn't pointing it at Willy, not yet anyway. He was just holding it casually down along his pant leg as if it was an extension of his arm. Willy's knees turned to jelly as he leaned on the car door for support. When it came to dealing with women, the Weasel was fearless. They were easy victims. This big detective, however, was a different matter.

Jack had recognized the Weasel right away. He hadn't known that Willy was out and running free again. This was not a pleasant surprise. "Well, well, if it isn't William Thomas Burton" he drawled, with a grin on his face. "Now what would you be doing tailing me, Willy? Let me guess, you just wanted to say hello, or to ask about my scar." As he said this, he turned his face slightly and ran a finger of his left hand along the scar so Willy could see his handiwork.

Willy didn't mean to whine, but that's how it came out. "C-can't a guy take a little drive in the backwoods without being chased by a cop? It's a free c-country" he added in an aggrieved tone.

"You've been following me for days" growled Jack, suddenly realizing that this was true. He had just had so much else on his mind that it hadn't registered. Some detective, he chided himself. "What are you up to, you little twerp?"

"Nothing, I swear. I was just d-driving around. I was just sight-seeing" Willy replied plaintively. "I don't want no trouble — no sir" he added. He was grovelling now, wondering how he could get close enough to slice Willinger before the gun could blast a hole in him. He was fidgeting in his pocket, clasping and unclasping the knife.

Jack picked up on the movement. "Empty your pockets, Willy," he commanded.

"Wh-what?" squeaked Willy.

"You heard me. Empty your pockets, you sorry piece of dog shit."

Willy reluctantly produced a tattered wallet, some loose change, a toothless comb, the key to his motel room, and a filthy tissue.

"Come on, come on, don't make me empty them for you" snarled the detective, losing patience. "I know you never go anywhere without your knife. Throw it down — carefully" he added.

Willy had no choice. Reluctantly he pulled out his knife and dropped it at his feet.

"Kick it over here. Now pull up your pant legs — both of them."

Willy felt hopeless and helpless. Gazing right and left, as if expecting help from some unknown source, he slowly pulled up his pants, exposing a second knife strapped to his skinny white leg.

"You haven't learned much, shit for brains," said Jack, shaking his head. "Kick it here, and do it in slow mo."

Picking up both knives, the detective pocketed them. After looking through the wallet, which was virtually empty, he handed it back to Willy and said "you weren't planning on cutting me up a bit, were you Willy boy — maybe finishing what you started years ago?"

"No, I swear. I was just out drivin' around" cried Willy, feeling totally naked now without his two best friends — the knife in his pocket and the knife on his leg. He thanked himself for leaving the picture of Darla in the motel instead of putting it in his wallet. The thought of this tall detective finding his wife's picture in Willy's wallet made him start shaking convulsively. Fuckin' cop likely would have shot him right here on this back road and nobody would ever know. "I don't want no trouble, — I'm a free man. I done my time, you can't hassle me. I ain't done nothing. I changed my ways, I'm straight now."

"You bet you're straight now, straight back into the pen" laughed Willinger. "Well, Willy, just a word of advice for you. You get your worthless little self back into that car, and get the hell out of my sight. Go back to your motel" — here he glanced at the key to read the name, "and pack up your junk. I want you out of town by tonight. Consider yourself lucky that I'm in a good mood today, otherwise you wouldn't be able to tell your asshole from your ears. I don't like being followed. If I catch you anywhere near me or my family or my partner, you'll be back in that joint so fast that you won't have time to take a piss. Oh, and Willy-boy," Jack added as if it were an after thought, — "just be sure you keep that pathetic little pecker in your pants. You know what'll happen if we so much as hear of any rape or attempted rape anywhere in the peninsula. I'll cut your dick off myself, and stuff it up your nose. Got it?"

Willy could only nod his head foolishly, and frantically suck on his teeth. All thoughts of stabbing Willinger were momentarily forgotten. He had to get out of here and make new plans. Willy wasn't very good at planning things. He performed more on impulse and inexplicable needs. With his burnt out brain, his feeble plans never really made sense. Willy, of course, didn't understand that. He just had a vaguely frustrated feeling that things weren't working out the way he wanted.

Jack watched him drive off down the road. He would have to warn Bud and Darla. He wasn't happy about the idea that Willy was out of the pen, and tailing him. What was he up to? Hopefully he had scared him enough that the Weasel would rethink any ill considered plans for revenge. Jack, however, wasn't taking any chances. He and Bud would have to keep a close eye on little Willy.

Meanwhile, little Willy was having a hissy fit. How come that Willinger asshole always got the best of him? He had taken both his knives and Willy hadn't even had a chance at stabbing or cutting him. How was that possible? Willy had planned his revenge for so long. Well, all was not lost, he told himself as he drove along, sucking on his teeth and slapping himself on his left leg. He would now kidnap Darla and keep her his prisoner — his love prisoner — for a long time. He would use her as he wanted before killing her. Of course it didn't occur to him that he had no place to hide her. One room in a cheesy motel wasn't going to cut it, but the Weasel wasn't able to think that far ahead. He had to go back to the motel, pack up and get out. But where would he go? Well, maybe he'd go as far as Grimsby or Fort Erie. He'd find another cheap place, have a few drinks, and try to sort this all out. There must be a way. There had to be a way.

CHAPTER 15

▼

Vickie decided to go for a walk to clear her head and get a little exercise. All the goodies she'd been eating were beginning to weigh heavily on her conscience, to say nothing of her hips. She tried to persuade Cass to go with her, but Cass had several things she wanted to do around the house, and she didn't want to admit that her leg was aching a bit. She kept herself busy for a while on non-essentials, then finally flopped down at the kitchen table and made up her mind. If she didn't call the police now she never would. Before she could talk herself out of it again, she picked up the phone and dialled.

After being grilled by the dispatcher, she was told that a detective would be there within the hour. Cass and Vickie had watched too many old movies from the forties, and she laughed to herself as she pictured a detective wearing a fedora and pin-striped suit, a cigarette dangling from his mouth. His cold accusing eyes would bore right into her, and he would question her mercilessly for hours. She smiled at this ridiculous picture, but was still having second thoughts about her impulsive act. She should have waited till Vickie returned before calling. Damn! They needed to talk it over some more. Actually they should have left well enough alone and kept their noses out of it. Still, too many things pointed to it being a deliberate attempt to kill Pru and Matt. That couldn't be ignored. Were the Toronto police doing a thorough investigation? How could they find out if not through the Niagara Police?

Standing in her navy short shorts and red and white tank top, she was tapping her bare foot on the kitchen tiles and staring into space. She looked to be about sixteen years old. Shoot, why hadn't she just minded her own business? Well, this is my business, she reassured herself as she hurried up the stairs to change into her new peach coloured slacks and matching top. It would give her more credibility than wearing short shorts, and she would look calm and elegant when the detective arrived.

She had barely made it up the stairs when the doorbell rang. Oh good, Vickie's back she muttered as she raced back down and flung open the door. As she opened it, she gasped in shock and disbelief. She was looking into a pair of piercing blue eyes, eyes she had once known very well. "Jack?" she cried tentatively, feeling her face flush and her heart skip a beat.

Jack Willinger looked as startled as Cassie felt. He did a classic double-take, then grasped both her hands. She stared down at them, her small white hands enfolded in his large tanned ones. She saw the short black hairs on the backs of those familiar hands, and she shivered. She had once loved those hands.

"Cass, is it really you?" he asked with that wonderful grin she knew so well. Then she was in his arms, enveloped in the same hug which had always made her knees weak. For a moment in time she simply could not breathe. Everything was swept from her mind as she was transported back to her teens.

Jack Willinger and Cassandra Kiley had gone steady for four years in high school. He had been the love of her life, or so she thought at the time. It was an intense and romantic relationship, full of ups and downs. Cass had been absolutely crazy about Jack, but her mother hated him. He was a wild, mischievous boy, growing up on the same street as Vickie. He was always in trouble, teasing the girls, and getting into fights. By high school, however, he had turned into a real heartthrob. Standing there in his embrace, her fingers mentally traced the contours of that beautiful mouth which she had loved to kiss.

Cassie's mother disliked Jack because he was wild, and because he had no plans for going to university and furthering his education. To Lizzie Kiley, education and social position were everything. Jack, however, wanted to get a job, to travel and see the world, and he wanted Cass to go with him. He had such a "joie de vivre", such an enthusiasm and curiosity about life that it was very contagious. Eventually, however, Cassie's mother won, and they went through a heart-wrenching break-up. Cass and Vickie went off to university, and a broken-hearted Jack set out to see the world. Cass had never seen him again, and had no idea that he had become a detective, let alone that he was living in the same city.

Finally she disentangled herself from his embrace, and after a few awkward moments, during which they simply stared at each other, she regained her composure sufficiently to invite both men in. She hadn't even glanced at the other one, although she was conscious that he was big.

Jack was tall and handsome, with Paul Newman blue eyes, dark wavy hair, and a scar on his jaw line. That was definitely new, thought Cass, wanting to touch it, but he was still gorgeous. He always seemed to have a five o'clock shadow no matter how often he shaved. He exuded a restless energy which Cass remembered all too well. The years had been very kind to Jack.

Eventually she glanced at the other detective who was a real bear of a man. He looked as if he could beat a confession out of anyone, at least he was big enough for the task. His tanned and weather beaten face, however, looked gentle, and somehow his dark brown eyes appeared mischievous. He was not a threatening figure in spite of his size, at least not once you looked into those eyes with the crinkly lines around them. He seemed comfortable in his big body, and he moved with a certain grace.

Pulling himself together, Jack Willinger said, "I'm sorry, Cassie, this is my partner Bud Lang. You called about a stalker, that's why we're here, but I just can't get over finding you after all this time. You look marvellous. How long have you lived in the Falls?" The questions were endless. He obviously wasn't ready to get down to business just yet.

Bud Lang was showing her his shield, but Cassie couldn't focus. She might as well have been looking at a tin badge from a cracker jack box.

Both men glanced casually around as they followed her down the hall to the sunroom. Cass was sure that they didn't miss a thing. She didn't know just how she felt. She didn't know whether she wanted to laugh, faint, or fall into Jack's arms again. This was a situation she had never anticipated, and she didn't know how to react. Her stomach was doing flip-flops. All thoughts of phone calls, cat pictures and the car crash were forgotten. This was Jack — her Jack — sitting here in her home! It just couldn't be. She had a myriad of questions, but didn't know where or how to begin.

Detective Lang looked puzzled and intrigued as he watched this little drama unfolding. Then, trying to gloss over the uncomfortable situation he mumbled, "Very nice house." No one paid any attention to him. Jack and Cassie only had eyes for each other.

After a few uneasy moments, while her heart continued to beat erratically, Cass discovered that Jack had gone to university after all his roaming, and had studied criminal psychology. He had been living in nearby St. Catharines for several years, and had just recently moved to the Falls. It seemed impossible that they had never run into each other.

They were just beginning to relax, when they heard the front door open. Vickie had seen the police car in the driveway, and was royally pissed off that

Cassie had apparently called them while she was out. Why hadn't she waited? Cass knew that Vickie loved anything to do with crimes and mysteries, and had been looking forward to talking to the police. She'd let her know just how she felt as soon as they were alone. Walking into the sunroom, she saw Jack and stopped in amazement.

Jack leaped up when he saw her. "Vickie" he almost shouted in disbelief. "This is amazing. What in the world is going on? Don't tell me that you live here too?"

It took some time to get everything straightened out. There was so much to discuss that the purpose of the meeting was temporarily forgotten. Eventually, however, Jack turned serious. "It's so great to see you two, and to talk about old times, but let's get to the point. You called the station about a possible stalker, Cass. What's going on?"

"Well, we think that there's been a murder" began Cassie. Her heart was still racing, and she couldn't take her eyes off Jack, he looked so good. Hell, he looked marvellous! She felt as if she was seventeen again, but she had to pull herself together and convince these detectives that something was definitely wrong.

"Let me start at the beginning, but I warn you it's a bit confusing." With that, she began to explain about the car crash, the death of her brother-in-law, her sister's serious condition, the millions involved, and all their suspicions. She told of trying to stir things up at the funeral, and the subsequent phone calls. She finished with the picture of the cats put under her door that morning. She didn't bother to tell the men about the various wild scenarios she and Vickie had conjured up. In the light of day they all seemed pretty silly.

As she got into the story, she told it with clarity and confidence. When she finished, there was total silence. As the detectives looked at each other, Cass suddenly realized that she was wearing her short shorts and tank top. She moaned inwardly. She looked so good in the new peach coloured slacks and top. If only she'd had time to change. Just her darn luck to be caught looking like a twelve year old in bare feet. Then she smiled at her foolishness. Grow up, peanut brain, she told herself. We're here to discuss a possible murder plot. Who cares what Jack thinks about how you look? But she realized to her surprise that she cared very much.

"Well that's quite an intriguing tale" said Jack, stretching his long legs and leaning back in the chair. "Do you have any idea about a suspect?"

He still had that deep, rich voice which she remembered so well. She noticed idly that his shoes looked scuffed. Didn't his wife look after him? She couldn't seem to harness her thoughts, and she had a wild impulse to run her fingers along that scar. She wondered how it had happened. Jack could have been killed and she would never have known. She shivered again as she tried to regain her composure. Somehow it was important that Jack see she was a mature woman now, not some flighty teenager still getting into mischief with her friend. She looked over at Vickie who was perched on the edge of her seat, and Cass rolled her eyes. They both grinned, but then immediately put on their serious faces.

Vickie suggested, "We thought that you could tap the phones or something to catch the guy who's harassing us. He's got to be the murderer. We also thought you could talk to the Toronto police and find out if they are really carrying on any kind of investigation, or whether they just think that it was an accident." She knew it all sounded flimsy and stupid when put into words.

Jack looked at her with a bit of a smile on his face. "You always did love a mystery, Vickie." She had been a big influence over Cassie in high school, and he wondered how much of this was pure imagination. "You must know that there's very little we can do about the supposed murder. Toronto is way beyond our jurisdiction."

"Don't give me that, Jack. You're a detective, for heaven's sake. Police departments are supposed to share info aren't they? What about computers? You can at least talk to the guys in Toronto just to see what, if anything, they're doing. You could say you got an anonymous tip that it was no accident. There must be all kinds of things you could do. And certainly the phone calls and whoever took the picture of the cats from right outside the window would fall into your jurisdiction." She was disappointed that Jack didn't seem too impressed with what she and Cass had told him.

Just then Muffin sauntered into the room. He surveyed the scene, stretched one hind leg and then the other, then wandered over to sniff at the shoes of both men. With an air of insouciance, he leaped into the lap of Detective Lang, made three small clockwise circles, and settled down, apparently for an extended nap. The detective laughed and looked pleased. "Nice little fellow" he mumbled, patting Muffy's head, which disappeared totally under the huge hand.

"You know, we thought at first that it was Jordan, but the calls and the picture seem more like something that moron Pete would do. Of course it could be Pete and Jenny together, or even Blake, and then there's the irate husband Jim Sinclair" They were both talking at the same time, and realized that they likely sounded silly. Bud Lang wasn't saying anything. He just sat there quietly petting Muffy and listening intently.

Victoria then went on to relate just what she had overheard at the funeral. She also mentioned Elena's sudden appearance, and pretended not to notice Cassie's frown.

"It stands to reason," interrupted Cassie, "that with all those Wainwright millions, there could be a lot of people who wanted them dead. It just seems likely that it's one of the family."

"Well, you're family too, Cass", Jack pointed out, grinning.

She gave him her "go screw yourself" look, and said "Very funny. Right now, I'm most concerned about whoever took this picture. I don't want anything to happen to the cats, or to us either. You've got to help us, please."

The detectives looked at each other before Jack stood up. Cassie didn't want them to leave yet, so belatedly she offered to make coffee. They both declined. After cautioning the women to keep the house and windows locked at all times, they added that they would see about a phone tap, but they seemed very non-committal.

Detective Lang seemed unwilling to disturb Muffy, but as he finally stood up, Cass was dismayed to see that the entire front of his black slacks was covered with orange fur! They all laughed, even Bud, as he tried in vain to brush off the cat hair.

Jack paused at the door, then put his arms around Cass and gave her another hug. "It's great to see you again, Cassie. You look terrific. You too Vickie" he added. "We'll be in touch, and meantime, be careful, stay alert, and keep out of trouble. Don't go playing detective, leave that job to us, but do call if anything happens to scare you."

As the detectives drove away, the friends noticed a small dented blue car start up and follow them at a distance. As it drove slowly past the house, they got a good look at the ugly driver, because he was taking a good look at them!

"Yikes, who's he?" queried Vickie as they shut the door. "He doesn't look as if he belongs in this neighbourhood."

"Brother, I hope not. It was almost as if he was following Jack and Detective Lang. I wonder if they noticed him?"

"I'm sure they did. After all, they are detectives."

Cass suddenly began to do a little bump and grind down the hall and into the kitchen. She was grinning widely as she grabbed Vickie and twirled her around. "This is so damn fantastic" she cried. "Jack was here — my Jack! I can't believe it. Doesn't he look wonderful? He's better looking than ever, and did you see that scar? I wonder where he got that?"

They were both still reeling from Jack's sudden appearance. He was like a ghost from the past.

"What do you think? Did they believe us? Did they take us seriously, or does Jack think we're still a couple of ditzy-doodles?"

"I think they believed us. I think they were more interested than they let on. Detectives always have poker faces, you know. At least they always do in books. They'll follow it up, I'm sure of it."

"Poor Detective Lang with his pants all covered in fur. What an impression we made — two lonely women with two cats, just looking for some excitement. Jack knows how ditzy we were in high school. Maybe he thinks we haven't changed."

"Well, have we?" grinned Vickie.

"Maybe not" sighed Cassandra, running her fingers through her hair "But, Vic, it was such a shock to see him again. To tell you the truth, I'm ashamed of myself. When I saw him standing there it was as if I was back in school. So many emotions rolled right over me. I felt as if I was standing on the beach, and the sand was shifting beneath my feet. It was unnerving. You know, to me Jack was always ice cream on a stick. I was so crazy about him that I came pretty close to running away with him. I'm just realizing that there may be some unfinished business between us." Here Cassie sighed and bit her lower lip, a habit she had when she was nervous. "He's still as gorgeous as ever isn't he? If I were his wife I'd never let him out the door. God I hope she's fat and has yellow teeth!"

They both laughed at that. Cass couldn't seem to stop babbling. Vic had never been able to see the charms of Jack Willinger, and he in turn had never cared much for Vickie. Nevertheless, she sympathised with Cassie.

"Vic, don't get me wrong. You know that I love Dave. He's my whole life along with the kids and the cats. I wouldn't change things for anything. Still, I'm just going to lust a little in my heart like Jimmy Carter."

Her friend just shook her head in understanding. Cass had always been a bit crazy when it came to Jack. This new development could prove very interesting.

Cass just couldn't let it go. "Jack and I have a history, and obviously there's still something there — some spark, some little frisson of chemistry. Don't you think so? I mean, he seemed really happy to see me didn't he? Oh hell, what am I talking about? He was just being friendly, and besides we're both married." She shook her head with disbelief at her own foolishness.

Vickie just let her friend prattle away. When it came to Jack Willinger, Vickie had always felt that it was some incurable virus which Cassie had caught. It certainly couldn't have been his charms. As far as Vickie was concerned, he never had any.

They were still mulling things over when the doorbell rang. Cass opened the door and was handed a parcel by a delivery man.

"This must be something from Dave" she said, frowning and shaking it. "I'll bet he ordered some nice little gift for me to cheer me up. I know I sounded depressed the other night when he called." She felt a twinge of guilt. Dave had been momentarily forgotten in her excitement at seeing Jack.

While Cass got the scissors to open the package, Vickie opened the frig to get a bottle of water. She had her back turned when Cass let out a choking sound and backed away from the table. There in the box lay a dead rat.

"Oh no" cried Vickie, staring in disgust. Cass seemed speechless.

"Who the hell would do such an awful thing," wondered Vickie as she peered into the box. There might be a note or some clue as to the sender.

"Whatever weirdo did this is really sick and dangerous. What in the heck are we mixed up in here?" asked Cass, looking at Vickie in dismay. "It's so childish and cruel, but it does have shock value."

"You're right. It was no brain surgeon who thought this up" agreed Vickie, "but it certainly gets the point across."

"Is anyone really dumb enough to think that this would scare us off and make us shut up about the crash?"

"Well, a moron might" said Vickie, still smarting about being called moronic by Jordan at the funeral.

"Maybe it was that ugly guy in the blue car," gasped Cassie. "He could have sent it and was waiting around to see it delivered."

Vickie pondered this possibility, then said, "But he drove away right after Jack and the other detective. He didn't wait around."

"What if he just drove around the block and came back?"

With this thought, both women raced to the front door and peered up and down the street as far as they could see. There was no sign of the blue car or its weird driver.

"Look, we mustn't touch anything in case there are fingerprints," said Cass as they returned to the kitchen and the unwelcome parcel. "Damn, I wish this had arrived while the guys were here. What rotten timing. This would have been proof that we weren't making it all up." They didn't want to touch the rat, but they couldn't leave it lying there on the kitchen table.

"I hate to call Jack. He'll think I'm chasing him. He might think I've still got the hots for him" Cassie said a bit sheepishly.

"Well?" teased Vickie. "You were looking pretty hot and bothered there for a while, kiddo. Anyway, I'll call him. He knows for sure that I don't have the hots for him. I think we really yanked someone's chain at the funeral" she added, heading for the phone.

CHAPTER 16

▼

As the two detectives left the house and settled into the car, Bud said, "Well, shit, partner, what was that all about? Looked like a little blast from the past."

Jack sighed, and fingered the scar on his jaw. "I wouldn't know where to start, Bud. I grew up on the same street as Vickie, and she and Cass and I all went to high school together. Cass and I went steady for four years, and it was really hot and heavy. I wanted to marry her, but she was determined to go to university. I wanted to travel and see the world first before even thinking about more education. Actually, I thought that travel would be a real education in itself, but I couldn't make her see that. Besides, her mother hated me, she thought I wasn't good enough for her little girl. Anyway, we eventually had a big break-up which nearly killed me. I really loved her, and thought I'd never get over it. I didn't for a long, long time, but, of course, I finally met Darla."

As he said this, he was wheeling the car into the parking lot of the nearest Tim Horton's. There was no need to discuss whether or not they were going to stop for a coffee. It was just a normal routine. They didn't say anything more as they ordered their black coffee and jelly filled donuts. It was only after they were seated quietly at a corner table that Jack continued his story.

Sighing again, he took a big sip of his steaming coffee and stared at Bud as he said, "I have to tell you, it took me a hell of a long time to get over Cassandra Kiley. I thought my life was finished when we split up. I drank and screwed my way right across France and Italy and Spain." Here he shook his head and took an angry bite of his donut. "Every girl I met was a substitute for Cass, but not one of them lived up to my expectations. Eventually I realized that I had to go home and go to university. I had something to prove to her. She might never know, but I would know. So, that's how I got a higher education and became a lowly cop." Here he shrugged his shoulders, and laughed a rueful laugh, as he brushed the sugar from his hands. That gesture seemed to indicate the end of the story, but Jack wasn't quite finished yet, and Bud was a very good listener.

"It was so damn strange running into her. I can't believe she's been here all these years and we never bumped into each other in a restaurant or anything. Guess we just travel in different circles. Anyway, it's all ancient history now." Again he heaved a big sigh, and shook his head as if trying to erase the picture of Cassie standing at the door, looking up at him with those big blue eyes he had always loved. "Man, it was so weird to see her like that. I felt that I could easily have taken her in my arms and kissed her. For a moment there I forgot all about Darla. Aw hell, we were just crazy kids then. It probably never would have lasted."

Bud knew his partner well enough to realize that there would be no more said on the subject, so, without comment, he proceeded to the next problem. "Well, what do you think of their story?"

"I'm not sure, but there's definitely something going on. Those two were the smartest girls in high school, so we're certainly not dealing with dummies. The problem is that Victoria was always coming up with wild, crazy schemes, and leading Cass astray. If I didn't know Cass so well, I'd be inclined to think that they were just two lonely women looking for a little excitement — you know, husbands out of town and nothing much to do. I think that they're on the level though. Their instincts are probably good. I don't like this stalker business. Anyone who would go so far as to take a picture of the cats just to scare them, could be dangerous. You know as well as I do that any stalker is a potential powder keg ready to blow. They shouldn't take this lightly. We've got to get onto it right away, and then look into this car crash. I suspect that the two are somehow connected."

"Sounds like a plan" replied the far from loquacious Bud. He was a man of few words, but he was a good detective. Bud Lang was a thinker, not a talker. He was a perfect partner for Jack, who had the gift of gab, and could charm anyone when it suited him.

The handsome policeman appeared taller than his six feet, because he carried himself in such an erect, shoulders back, head up sort of way. He had that stiff backed, somewhat arrogant stride so common to detectives who've seen it all, and who feel in control in any situation. Jack wasn't arrogant, but he was very self-assured. The scar ran from his left ear right across his jaw line, but it didn't detract from his good looks. In fact, women seemed to be drawn to it. That knife attack had been the one and only time a criminal had managed to get the best of him.

He had only been on the job a few months, and was still young and enthusiastic. He had been trying to get the cuffs on the creep who had been breaking into houses and raping women. He had taken Willy's knife, but as he was trying to cuff him, the young rapist had turned like a monkey, and from nowhere it seemed, he had produced a second knife. He caught Jack just behind the ear, and had ripped across his face before Jack could wrestle him to the ground. Bud was around the back to be sure the perp didn't get out that way, and when he heard Jack yell, he came running. Bud was big, but he could move pretty fast when he had to. He had cuffed Willy to the radiator, and then he and Nora, the undercover gal, had raced off to the hospital with Jack, leaving Willy there till other cops could pick him up.

Luckily no arteries or tendons had been severed, and Jack recovered nicely, with a long scar as a badge of honour. It had been a tough lesson to learn, but he never again underestimated a perp. He always just assumed that they carried two or three weapons, and acted accordingly.

Today Jack had a much more serious problem on his mind. Not only had running into Cassie stirred up a whole host of memories and feelings, but he was pretty sure, hell, he knew, that his wife Darla was having an affair, and it was eating him up inside. He felt as if there was a porcupine turning somersaults in his stomach. If he didn't have an ulcer yet, he soon would have.

His suspicions had started about three weeks ago. He was planning to surprise Darla with cruise tickets for their anniversary. She had seemed so unhappy and restless lately that he wanted to do something nice to cheer her up. Searching in her desk for their passports, he suddenly remembered that Darla kept them hidden in her underwear drawer.

Digging to the bottom of the drawer, he found a lacy, fireman red teddy. He took it out gingerly and stared at it in disbelief. In all their married life, Darla had never worn anything this sexy or brazen. Maybe she had bought it as a surprise for their anniversary. No, with sinking heart he realized that it had been worn already. One of the five tiny buttons was missing, and the lace was torn. Oh God, Darla had never worn this for him, but then who, and why, and when?

He had sat there for a long time, thinking back on their marriage and its ups and downs. They both wanted children, but Darla in particular was desperate to have a baby. She had experienced three bad miscarriages, and after the third one she had changed. She became depressed and lethargic. The old spark, that tinkling laugh, those beautiful hazel eyes, now seemed dull and closed down, like the amusement park when the lights go out.

He decided not to say anything yet about the red lacy abomination. He would have loved it if she had bought it to wear for him, but now it was just trash. He wanted to rip it to shreds, but instead, he carefully replaced it at the bottom of her drawer. He would wait and watch, while his heart slowly shrivelled and died. After all, he was a detective, and he needed more evidence before he made any decisions.

He got the evidence sooner than he expected. Just a few days after finding the lingerie, some guy with a deep, sexy voice had called asking for Darla. When he asked who was calling, the guy hung up. Because they had an unlisted number, he immediately associated the caller with the red merry-widow. Darla must have given him the number. This was no call from someone selling light bulbs!

Then came the next blow. The paper boy had come collecting. Darla was away at her part-time job at the mall. Jack was two dollars short, so rather than going upstairs for the money, he looked in his jacket pocket in the hall closet. Finding no money there, he felt in Darla's blazer pocket. There was no money there either. What there was, however, was a key for a motel way out on Lundy's Lane.

Jack had stared at that odious key, the little paper boy totally forgotten. It was a cheap, tawdry motel, the kind used for quickie afternoon assignations. Jack had used it himself once a long time ago. What irony! Darla was screwing some loverboy in the same damn motel where he had done the same damn thing! Was it coincidence, or had she known all along about his brief and stupid affair?

Cops don't believe in coincidence. There is almost always a pattern, or a reason, or a rationale behind events. Could Darla have known about his meaningless dalliance with the girl who looked so much like Cassie that it made his chest hurt? The big blue eyes and reddish gold hair, the long legs, had simply done him in. God he hoped Darla had never known. If that was the case, however, and if that was what had driven her to be unfaithful, then he had brought it on himself. How could he blame her for something he had done first? He couldn't believe he was caught up in such a dirty little cliché. It was so common, so ordinary.

Instead of wanting to kill her, or kill the guy, or even kill himself, he sat there wondering how to handle it. He knew he was at fault, so he couldn't be too angry with Darla, disappointed, yes, disillusioned, yes, but angry? No. He hadn't been sympathetic enough when she miscarried that third time. He hadn't really listened when she tried to tell him how lonely she was. He had hardly noticed how withdrawn and quiet she had become.

Yes, it was definitely his fault. He loved her, and he wasn't going to lose her to some sexy voiced bastard with sweaty hands and a big pecker. This was how Jack pictured her unknown motel mate. It was an untenable situation, and he had to do something, but what?

Well, he was a detective wasn't he? He could follow her and get a look at this guy, and then decide what to do. Shit, he could have the whole damn police force tail her, but of course he wouldn't. This was his problem, his secret. He couldn't even let Bud know.

Just as all detectives seem to be, Jack was a bit jaded. He had seen too much, and heard too much. He certainly was no longer the innocent, irresponsible boy Cassie had loved. He had seen the darker underbelly of human nature too many times. He knew that people, ordinary people, were capable of cheating, stealing, killing and committing adultery, but not his Darla, never Darla. It had been such a shock learning of her possible infidelity, that he didn't know how to deal with it.

Because he was so caught up in his problems, he hadn't noticed the small blue car tailing them to Cassie's home, and to the donut shop. He had actually forgotten all about Willy being in town, and Willy, who couldn't concentrate on anything for too long at a time, had gone back to his motel room to make his fuzzy plans.

CHAPTER 17

▼

Darla Willinger was finishing up the last hour of her shift in the dress shop at the mall. Her pudgy customer had tried on five long dresses so far, and was marching relentlessly back into the dressing room with four more slung carelessly over her arm. Everything she tried on made her look like a stuffed sausage, thought Darla savagely. She was usually very patient, but today she felt like tying a plastic bag over fatty's head, and shoving her out into the mall. Let someone else deal with her.

Darla's heart was heavy. The mantle of guilt was killing her. She had done a terribly stupid thing, and now she felt worse than a murderer. She may have killed her marriage. It had all started as a bit of a lark. Dan was a fireman who had come to the house one sunny morning to check the smoke alarms. It was a crusade the department started after a young family had perished in an old house with no alarms.

Dan was too good looking to be true. He had a deep, sexy voice, and a "melt your heart and turn your knees to jelly" kind of smile. Seeing him in that uniform, any woman who wasn't totally dead from the eyebrows down, would have felt her pulse quicken.

She had opened the door in her shortie nightie, thinking that it was Jack returning for some forgotten item. She really wasn't aware of just how enticing she looked, and she had been truly embarrassed, but Dan just grinned and put her at ease.

After quickly donning a pair of jeans and a tank top, and applying some lipstick, she gave him a tour of the smoke alarms. They talked a bit, and somehow she found herself offering him a cup of coffee. She didn't know what the hell she was doing, but her heart was beating very fast, and she felt alive for the first time in weeks. This guy was actually looking at her, and he obviously liked what he saw. It made her feel terrific. It seemed a long time since Jack had looked at her that way.

When he left, he said he would call her sometime. She had laughed, and flirtatiously pointed out that she was married. To her own surprise, however, she had not said "no". When he did call her three days later, she agreed to meet him for coffee. She told herself that she was being a total fool, and she wanted to back out of this impromptu rendezvous, but she didn't. They couldn't go to a donut shop, because Jack or any of his buddies on the force could be there. The old joke about cops spending all their time in the donut shops was all too true. Since it was a beautiful day, they ended up driving to Niagara-on-the-Lake, and sitting at a picnic table by the water's edge. She spent almost three hours with him that afternoon, and they had talked and laughed, and flirted outrageously.

It was as if she was coming out of a very black chapter in an ever-so-boring book. Jack was so involved with his work that he was barely aware of her these days. She loved him, but she resented him too. His first love seemed to be police work, no doubt about that. He had never told her much about his work. He always said that it was much safer for her that way, but it made her feel left out and lonely. She wanted to be part of his life, but she felt that she was just a pretty adjunct, and after the miscarriages she had felt like a total failure. She was restless and edgy, and very vulnerable, and after meeting Dan she felt like a school girl with her first crush. He was gorgeous, he flattered her shamelessly, and he was funny. He could make her laugh, which hadn't happened in a long time.

Somehow, before she realized what she was doing, she had donned dark glasses and a big hat — just like in the movies, she thought ruefully, and was buying the red merry-widow at the Naughty Lady shop. She wondered why she had never bought anything like this to wear for Jack, and it made her feel sad and ashamed all at the same time. She also felt excited and daring, and couldn't have turned back even if common sense had prevailed.

The "fireman red" was so apropos. Dan had loved it, but he had torn it a bit that sultry afternoon they met in the Paradise Motel. The name was so sleazy that she had almost turned and fled, but she hadn't. Instead she watched herself as if from a distance. It felt as if she were floating near the ceiling, looking down. She had been so nervous. She felt foolish and cheap, and she was desperate to leave the moment he started undressing her. The imagining of a romantic dalliance had been one thing, the reality was something totally different.

It had been awful — a real disaster. She was like a zombie — pretending, just pretending, and wanting to be anywhere but there. She kept imagining Jack bursting through the door, gun drawn, anger and disgust on his beloved face. What was she doing here? Was she crazy? Had she flipped out? She wasn't a tramp. She wasn't the type who slept around in sleazy motels. Why had she led Dan on? He was a nice guy, but he wasn't for her. She had never meant for things to go this far, and being a novice, she didn't know how to extricate herself from this embarrassing and potentially dangerous situation.

At first Dan didn't realize that anything was wrong. He was having a good time nuzzling and petting her. When she started to cry, he was puzzled and concerned. What was wrong? There were more tears and sobs as she shook her head, unable to verbalize her emotions. "Oh Christ, you're feeling guilty" he had said accusingly, "and we haven't even done anything."

Yes, you cretin, she thought. I'm feeling guilty because I am guilty, and so are you. I have a wonderful husband. What in hell am I doing here? If I can just get home safely without Jack suspecting, I'll never look at another man. I'll be the perfect wife.

These were the thoughts racing through her head as she shoved Dan aside, and quickly dressed. Covering up the disgustingly crude merry-widow, she ran for the door, all the time sobbing out, "I'm so sorry, please forgive me." Was she talking to Dan or to Jack? She wasn't sure. The last thing she saw was Dan sitting on the bed looking disgusted and angry.

He had called several times since then, but she always hung up after begging him to leave her alone. Twice he called when Jack was there, and she pretended it was a wrong number. She had no idea that he had called once when Jack had answered. She prayed that Danny would get the message before Jack caught on.

The offending red lingerie was hidden in her drawer — a guilty reminder of her very near fall from grace. Technically she had not cheated on Jack, but she had come too close for comfort. Today she was trying to make up her mind whether she would feel better or worse if she told him.

She had been preoccupied now for days, and as she drove to work, she had no reason to notice the wreck of a car which had followed her several times lately. Twice, however, she did notice a ferret faced man peering in the store window. He looked a bit the way Jack had described Willy the Weasel, but that idea didn't really register with her. She was too caught up in her private dilemma.

The chubby customer finally left the store without buying anything, and Darla was busying herself hanging up all the dresses which were lying in rejected heaps in the dressing room. She was alone in the store right now, but the other salesgirl was due back any minute.

When the skinny little guy finally entered the store, he asked to see some black lace panties — "the same size you would wear" — he had added with a leer. Darla still didn't make the connection with Willy the Weasel, even though Jack had warned her about him.

This customer was ugly to say the least. He was small and wiry, and was making weird sucking noises with his lips. His nose had a dreadful bend in it, and she couldn't help glancing surreptitiously at it.

As she led him toward the lingerie section, he walked very close behind her — too close for comfort. Darla was in no mood for someone invading her space today. His breath smelled like the bottom of a diaper pail, and there was a gagging miasma of odour emanating from him.

When she bent to open a lingerie drawer, she felt him standing right behind her — his vile breath on her neck. As she stood up, she couldn't resist the opportunity to come down hard on his instep with her spiked heel. He howled, and she apologized with great innocence. As he limped hurriedly out the door, she laughed to herself. "What a weasel" she thought. That was her clue! "Oh God, it is the Weasel" she whimpered as she watched him hurrying away. What should she do? She was here alone and couldn't leave the shop. By the time Darla had rushed to the door and peered anxiously out into the crowded mall, he was nowhere in sight. Where were the damn security guards? They were never around when you needed them. Finally, sighing in frustration, she ran back into the store to call Jack.

Willy was enraged at the way Darla had treated him. He had no doubt that it had been intentional. Limping slightly, and still smarting from her attack, he headed to his car. He was looking for some action. He would deal with Darla later — yes indeedy. God she had smelled good though. His nose twitched at the recollection.

Willy headed to the big mall in St Catharines, fifteen minutes away. Parking the car, he wandered inside. As he passed a trendy jeans shop, he caught sight of two great looking girls. They were young, just the way he liked them, maybe fifteen or sixteen. The taller one had black hair in a long braid, and she had great tits. Her face wasn't much though — too plain for Willy. The other — a natural blond he was sure, wore skin tight jeans over a sweet little ass. She had on high black boots and a black turtleneck sweater. Her face was pale and innocent. Willy was getting hot just looking at her. His sore foot was forgotten. He followed the girls from store to store, trying to work out a plan. He had to have a go at Blondie!

He raged with disappointment when the girls met up with two big football types at the music shop. He had lost his chance. Shit!!! This just wasn't his day, and somehow in his mind, it was all Darla's fault. That bitch had deliberately stomped on his foot, and he would make her pay.

Meanwhile, Bud Lang slowly guided the car into his driveway, which presented the usual obstacle course. He could see a bicycle, a tricycle, and a doll carriage, all lying in his way. He also saw what looked like a headless doll, legs askew, lying in a gaily coloured pink and purple wagon.

Bud was a gentle, slow moving, imperturbable type, slow to anger, always ready to give a second chance. He had a rugged, craggy face full of honesty and decency. It was tanned and weather-beaten. His dark curly hair was tinged with silver, and it was receding rapidly. He had chocolate brown eyes which always looked mischievous when his wife and kids were around. He was a huge man, solid muscle without an ounce of fat. He was known around the station as the "gentle giant," and everyone liked and respected Bud.

Amanda Lang hurried out to greet him with a kiss and a hug. She was average height and size, but looked tiny beside Bud. She had an open, freckled face, and a disarming smile.

"Hello, you big bear, how was your day?" she greeted him, entwining her arm with his, and silently uttering a prayer of thanks that he was home safely once again.

"Not too bad, kiddo" he answered lovingly, giving her a bit of a kiss on the top of her head, and a pat on her fanny. "How was your day? Did you manage to survive the midget mafia?"

Just then three giggling little girls raced to meet him. He picked up each one in turn, hugged her, kissed her, and whispered a secret in her ear. They clung to him in spasms of joy, rumpling his hair, kissing his face, and clinging to his legs.

"Now away you go, you little hooligans" laughed Amanda. "Let Daddy have some quiet time before dinner. He's tired from working so hard all day to feed you three little monsters."

This speech, or something similar, always seemed to impress the young girls at least momentarily, as they gazed at their father adoringly, then ran off giggling, happy to get back to their mischief.

As they sat and had a cool beer on the back porch where they could keep an eye on the girls, he told her of his visit to Cassie's place, and of little Muffin sleeping on his lap and leaving a layer of orange fur on his pants. He also told her how worried he was about his partner, Jack, but he didn't mention that Cassie was Jack's old sweetheart. Some things partners kept to themselves, and Bud was very loyal.

"There's something bugging him, Mandy. He's not himself. I'm going to give him a couple more days, then I'll have to ask him what's up. He's no good to anyone the way he is." Here Bud frowned and smoothed his hair back in an old familiar gesture.

"Why don't we have him and Darla for a barbecue Saturday night? That way we can watch them, and see how they are together. Maybe they're having problems since her last miscarriage. I'll get her talking in the kitchen and see what I can find out," suggested Amanda as she got up to put finishing touches on their dinner.

"Good idea, darlin.' You'd make a better detective than I've ever been" remarked Bud as they called the girls and went inside. He'd made it through another day of creeps and perverts and pathetic losers, and he was happy to surround himself with his normal, healthy family. He could relax for a few hours and leave the troubles of the city behind him.

CHAPTER 18

▼

In the Toronto hospital, Prudence had been experiencing some strange, drug-induced adventures. For what seemed an eternity, she had suffered the indignities of a multitude of tubes invading her beleaguered body. Saline solutions, blood, morphine drips, oxygen, had all been looming above her head. Drainage tubes snaked their way over the bedside. The entire room seemed to throb and pulsate to the rhythm of the monitoring machines. She had been pinioned like a dead butterfly.

While she was coming in and out of her morphine hallucinations, she was assaulted by fragmented images of her past. In a way it was as if her entire life was flashing before her. In her monumental efforts to free herself from the collage of pictures, reflections and portraits, Prudence rose to the surface of consciousness, then floated back down. Her father and mother, as well as her husband and children, all drifted in and out and around her like phantoms on sticks. Somehow she was reliving her entire life in those encapsulated visions.

Her engineering father, J.J. Kiley, had worked six months of every year in the exotic jungles of Brazil. Pru briefly relived the romance and excitement of her one visit to that strange but beautiful paradise. Then she was back at university, where she had met Matthew after dating his brother Blake. She should have married Blake. He was a far gentler, kinder, more affectionate man than Matt, who was brusque, rough, snobbish, and too used to the good life. He was spoiled and peevish, but she had loved him. She didn't seem to have very good judgement when it came to men.

Their troubles began when they adopted the four year old Jordan. As Pru's battered mind floated towards the enchanting but strange little boy who had been such an enigma, and who had become the focus of her life, her heart began pounding, and beads of sweat appeared on her face. Jordan, with those black, bottomless eyes, was a sociopath or worse. She couldn't bring herself to say or think the dreaded word "pedophile", but it hovered in and around her thoughts like an invasive stinging insect. It was always there, threatening her with its obscene possibilities. She had always loved Jordan so foolishly and devotedly, even though in her innermost being she knew that he was evil. She had felt that somehow if she just loved him enough she could make him whole. She and Matt had worked so hard to keep him out of jail. His reptilian stare frightened everyone except Jenny. Poor little Jenny, seven years younger, had loved him unconditionally. At least he never hurt her the way he did animals and other children. Jenny kept his secrets and often took the blame for his deeds. When Jordan disappeared, Jenny ran away.

If a nurse had been in the room at this point, she would have seen the anguished tears trickling down Pru's bruised face. Memories were bombarding her now, and she squirmed fretfully in the hospital bed. She felt that she was being pulled back into a life she wanted to forget.

Having lost their children in theory at least, Pru and Matt turned more and more to each other, but sadly, Matt also turned to other women. They filled their time with charity work and travel. Then they won the twenty million dollars! It wasn't long after this windfall that the prodigal son and daughter both reappeared. Matt couldn't forgive them, while Pru just wanted to start all over. She wanted to lavish money on them, but Matt was adamant. They wouldn't get a penny while he was alive.

As Pru moaned weakly, and tried to waken up from this phantasmagoria, a nurse walked into the room, and began gently soothing her forehead until she drifted back into the darkness.

When she finally awoke, there was sunshine in the room, and warm blankets were tucked comfortingly around her as she lay in the high hospital bed.

"Well, Mrs. Wainwright, no more morphine for you. You were having terrible nightmares and hallucinations. It took three nurses and an intern to stop you last night as you tottered down the corridor. I don't know how you managed to get out of bed with the bars up and the intravenous pole attached." Bunny seemed wide-eyed and amazed at Pru's hallucinatory escapades.

"Thank heavens I don't remember much about it" murmured Pru. "I think I do remember ropes holding me back and strange hands grabbing at me from all sides. Did I really go down the hall with the pole attached?" She was weakly incredulous.

"Morphine can do strange things, but you're fine now. We've just taken you off the IV. No more tubes and poles for you. You'll be out of here before you know it." Bunny gave her one of her dimpled smiles.

Prudence realized with surprise that she felt amazingly good. She was alert, and very hopeful. She had made it through another troubled night. Maybe her lurching down the hall, dragging that pole had snapped her body into action. At least this morning she seemed to be holding the pain at bay. This was a good sign.

She was making a miraculous recovery according to Dr. Taylor and the nurses. Even the roly-poly Dr. Martha Sutton had said that she was amazing. Everyone seemed so pleased with her progress. When some of the young Toronto university med students had been in to learn about her case, she felt a bit like a side show, maybe even a freak show, with all those eager faces staring at her as if she were an exhibit under glass. Still, it was wonderful to be improving every day. She could actually feel the changes in her body.

Yesterday the nurses had her up, taking a few halting steps. She must have really astonished them with her marathon run last night!

She was thinking clearly this morning, and she was sifting the dreams and hallucinations from reality. She knew that someone had tried to kill her and Matt, and she feared that it was Jordan. It couldn't have been her darling Jenny, although that Neanderthal Pete could have done it. But why? There was also Blake. He and Gloria and the kids had been at the cottage that last day. He had been in to see her several times too, and seemed very solicitous. Was he worried about her, or the bequest? Was he anxious to see her die in order to get his hands on the money Matt had left him? And then, of course, there was Elena, who had suddenly appeared two weeks before the crash. There was also Jim Sinclair. He was a brute, and had a fiery temper. Did he hate Matt enough to kill him?

Prudence realized that she would have to talk to the police, but she had to get things straight in her mind first. She knew that they had been in to try to question her a couple of times, but she always feigned sleep, and the nurses got rid of them. They were very protective of her. The police would likely attribute her suspicions to drug-induced hallucinations, especially after last night's fiasco, she thought wryly. She couldn't accuse anyone without proof, but what could she do from a hospital bed? She could certainly tell them that the brakes had been cut. That would be a good start. Of course they likely knew that already.

Before she did anything, she needed to talk to Cassandra. She vaguely remembered that Cass had come to see her earlier on. She had been so groggy! She usually played possum when Jordan and Jenny came, which wasn't too often. Thank God for small mercies. Until her head was clearer, she mustn't let them know that she had heard them talking that first day. So far, they talked in front of her as if she wasn't there. Well, maybe she wasn't totally yet, but she was definitely improving, and until she figured out what Matt would have wanted her to do, she was playing dumb. She could learn a lot more that way. She hugged her extra pillow as she lay thinking.

When Christina Marshall finally came on duty, Pru opened her eyes and smiled.

"Hi there. I hear you had quite a night. How do you feel?"

"Actually I feel really good. I don't remember much about last night, but I guess I scared everyone. I'm sorry to be such trouble."

"Nonsense, don't feel that way. You are doing remarkably well. I notice, though, that you pretend to be asleep when your family comes. Would you prefer to have no visitors? We can arrange that, you know. It's just that we thought visitors would cheer you up and speed your recovery."

"Well, to tell you the truth, my children make me nervous. Neither Jordan nor Jenny likes hospitals, so I always pretend to be asleep so they won't have to stay long." This wasn't the total truth, but Pru didn't think Tina would know the difference. "Actually, I need to see Cassandra — my sister — , and I definitely need to see my lawyer, Douglas Bannon. Maybe tomorrow would be a good time."

"Oh, I don't think so. You're still a sick lady, Mrs. Wainwright. You mustn't try to rush things. There'll be plenty of time to see your lawyer next week. First we have to get you back on your feet and looking more like your elegant self again."

"Please be honest with me. Am I really going to recover and walk out of here?" She almost said "out of this hell hole", but she restrained herself. She liked Tina, and didn't want to offend her.

"Absolutely. The worst is behind you. Lots of rest, good food and therapy is what you need now" assured Christina, plumping the pillows and taking her pulse.

"That's good," sighed Prudence. "I have a lot of thinking to do today, and tomorrow I'll make my decisions." With that, she closed her eyes, and left Tina wondering what she meant.

CHAPTER 19

▼

Cass and Vickie had been invited to lunch at the home of one of Cassie's friends. Since she lived only three blocks away, and since it was a gloriously golden day, they decided to walk.

Getting out of her jeans and shirt, Cassie had a quick shower and put on a pair of brown and gold silk slacks, with a plain gold summer sweater to match. As she applied mascara, she stared at herself in the mirror, and went over the events of the past weeks. Things had a habit of going wrong when you least expected them to, and it was second nature for Cass to expect the worst. She sometimes wondered whether she made bad things happen just by dwelling on them too much. She was toying with this idea as she did her eyes.

"Well look at classy Cassie. Aren't you splendiferous" exclaimed Vickie, standing in the bathroom doorway.

Cass laughed. "I feel that I need all the help I can get these days. You look very fetching" she said, admiring Vickie's moss green sweater and slacks. "You clean up pretty good, gal," she drawled.

"What a couple of babes" laughed Vickie, taking one last look in the mirror.

"More like a couple of old broads" grinned Cassie.

The phone rang just as they were leaving.

"Hello" said Vickie, while Cassie looked for her purse.

"What?" she exclaimed, wide-eyed. As her eyes grew bigger and bigger, she shouted "Grow up, you pervert", and slammed down the phone. "Cass, that was another threatening call. Whoever it was had more to say this time. It was something about 'you'd better stop your snooping or you'll be deader than the rat, and being dead is such a lasting condition.' Then he whispered, 'It would be so easy to push someone under a bus or over the falls, and then, of course, there's always poison.'" Vickie was frowning as she tried to repeat the call verbatim. "That's when I hung up on him. I guess I shouldn't have. He probably wasn't on long enough for them to be able to trace it, that is if Jack ever did arrange to have the phone bugged. I keep wondering whether he just said that to make us feel good." Vickie was speaking very quickly now, her thoughts all running together in a jumble.

Cass didn't like her insinuations about Jack.

"Come on Vic, that's not fair. I'm sure that Jack would do as he said. Anyway, this is getting ridiculous. It's so damn infantile. Good for you calling him a pervert and then slamming down the receiver. Hope you didn't break it" she added with a grin. "Still, I wish you had blown the whistle in his ear. It was right there." She pointed at the shiny whistle lying beside the phone. "Was it Pete? Did you recognize the voice?"

"Oh shit, I'm sorry about the whistle. I forgot the damn thing. I couldn't tell who it was, and I wouldn't recognize Pete's voice anyway. It wasn't a clear connection, and whoever it was, spoke very low. Cass, who could be doing this? They must know that we're no danger to anyone. This really frightens me."

"Me too. I guess we really rattled someone's cage at the funeral, and they're determined to scare us off. Don't they realize that they're just reinforcing our suspicions? I suppose that Blake or Jordan could be smart enough to do it, thinking that we would automatically suspect Pete."

"That's right. Now Cass, don't get mad, but we can't totally forget about Elena. She could have an accomplice, you know."

Cass sighed. "Okay, it's possible, but just remember it could also be Blake's wife Gloria. Maybe she's been putting one of her boys up to it. That's the kind of thing that would appeal to a kid. Then of course there's Jim Sinclair. We would never recognize his voice."

"Bummer! This is getting too complicated. Let's go, we can talk on the way."

They wanted to downplay the call, but it was a bit unsettling. Could someone just be joking with them, teasing them in a sick way, or was there actually a killer out there whose threats were real? They mulled it over as they walked along. Suddenly stopping, Cass pushed her sunglasses up on her head and grasped Vickie's arm. Her blue eyes were troubled as she said, "Please don't mention anything about Elena or the calls or all this garbage to my friends. I don't want to talk about it anymore, and I don't want to spoil this lovely day."

"You got it. I won't say a word."

It was after four by the time they waddled home, and they were quite happy to sink onto the comfy love seats in the sunroom, and close their eyes.

"That shortcake did me in," groaned Vickie, who was now regretting her second helping.

"We should be out walking a few more blocks to work off this lunch, you know" muttered Cassie.

"Just do me a favour, and don't even mention dinner."

They were watching a movie later that evening when the phone rang. Muffy flew off Cassie's lap, and Sugar stalked haughtily out of the room. She would just saunter into the kitchen and see if there were any snacks available.

"I'll get it in case it's the stalker. You tell me everything that I miss in the movie. I won't be long," said Cassie, as she headed out the door and into the kitchen. Removing a heavy gold earring, she picked up the receiver.

"Cassandra, it's Jack."

Cassie's heart gave a little leap.

"Hi there. What's up?" She wanted to be as casual as possible. Thank goodness he couldn't see how flustered she felt. She was ashamed of her earlier lusting after him. That chapter in her life was closed permanently. She had Dave, and he was all she needed. Still, her heart was thumping a little more energetically than usual at the sound of his voice.

"Well, Bud and I have been making some inquiries" he said slowly, and I wanted to let you know that your suspicions were right. It was no accident. The brakes were cut."

"Oh no" was all that she could manage.

Jack continued, "Cass, I want you to be really careful. Till this is all resolved, you could be in danger. Don't let Vickie talk you into any sleuthing or something stupid like that. Just leave it to the police."

Before she could answer, Jack continued. "Have you had any more strange or threatening phone calls?"

"Well, if our phone is tapped, you must have heard that call this afternoon."

There was silence on the line.

"Jack" gasped Cassie in surprise and anger. "Vickie was right. There is no phone tap is there? Dammit Jack, we trusted you, and all the while you thought we were just making it all up." She was angry and hurt, and was about to say things she knew she'd regret.

"Cass, calm down. The phone tap thing didn't work out. Up to now there really hasn't been enough evidence to show cause."

Cassandra was a bit disappointed, and a lot irritated to hear that there was no tap on the phone. She bit her tongue, however, and simply told Jack about the latest threats.

After hanging up, she told Vickie, "You were right, Vic. They never put a tap on the phone." She stared at her friend in dismay and anger.

"We should have known. I think to put a tap on they have to come into the house and unscrew the phones or something, don't they?"

"I just thought that they tapped into the line which comes into the house, and I guess I thought that there were some cops sitting in a van somewhere nearby listening and recording all the calls. That's how they do it in the movies anyway," Cass ended a bit sheepishly.

By the time Cass had told Vickie that the brake lines really had been cut, and that Matt's death was no accident, they felt elated at being proven correct, and scared about what it meant. Cass was angry to think that someone had tried to kill her sister. Like a tenacious little terrier, she wasn't going to give up until that someone was caught.

CHAPTER 20

▼

The large Muskoka cottage had been beautiful in its heyday. It was like a grand old duchess who had seen better days, but who could still stand proud and dignified in her former glory. She had endured two face lifts, and the eclectic mix of Muskoka cut stone, vinyl siding and cedar decking, seemed to enhance rather than detract from the overall impression of old money.

The "old dame," as Matt and Prudence fondly called her, stood in solitary splendour atop a slight rise on a lonely promontory jutting out into the lake. They owned one thousand feet of shoreline — something almost unheard of on the very costly Muskoka Lakes. This afforded the rambling cottage complete privacy, plus a fantastic view out into the main body of the water. There were no cottages nearby on either side.

Three of the five bedrooms faced the lake, and shared a cedar deck which ran across the face of the cottage. While the front rooms overlooked the splendour of the navy blue water, the back bedrooms had their own engaging view.

There was a narrow road which wound its way through granite outcroppings, and areas of tall birch, maple and evergreens. Some of the trees seemed to be growing right out of the rock. They looked as if they were forever trying to escape their granite boots. They swayed and sighed and whispered to each other in the gentle breezes, their only hope of escape, the woodsman's axe, or a bolt of lightning.

In the spring, both sides of the road were alive with the joyful faces of the trillium, Ontario's official provincial flower, which danced in shades of purple, mauve, and creamy white.

Overnight guests in the back bedrooms were treated to early mornings filled with the exuberant calls of chickadees and cardinals, and the strident bossiness of the blue jays. These sounds were often accompanied by the insistent rat-a-tat of the woodpeckers, busily drilling for their breakfast bugs in the old trees.

Jordan and Jenny were having an afternoon cruise. They had come back to the cottage right after their father's funeral. It was always a safe haven of peace and tranquility.

It was one of those perfect days found only in cottage country. The water was calm, the sky was blue, with only a few whipped cream clouds floating here and there. The gentle breeze softened and tamed the oppressive heat.

They had stopped the boat in the middle of the lake, and were just floating. This was a throwback to their childhood. As kids they took their books and snacks, and headed out to get away from everyone. They would sometimes stay out there all day, floating, talking, sunning themselves and thinking up mischief. When they began to feel totally baked and soporific in the relentless sun, they would dive into the cold blue lake. Then, revived, laughing, at peace with themselves and the world, at least for a short while, they would climb back out like two water nymphs, bodies glistening, hair slicked back.

On this perfect afternoon the occasional water skier flew past, churning up the dark blue water, and sending minor shock waves toward the handsome red and white boat named "Plaything". Other than these minor interruptions, it was relaxing and peaceful. It was also conducive to confidences and revelations.

Jenny's feelings about Jordan had always been very complicated. There was a certain symbiosis there. She loved him fiercely, but part of her hated him for her perception that he had stolen their parents' time and love. She also feared him, because she knew well that he was capable of anything. She had covered for him so many times over the years. Jordan, in turn, depended on her in many ways, and he could be aloof or loving. She never quite knew where she stood with him, but her adoration rarely faltered.

Fear, resentment, and love, it was a mixed brew of emotions she carried with her like an overflowing jug. She would have been hard pressed to articulate this mishmash of feelings. They were irrational and perverse, but the bottom line was always that Jenny loved Jordan, and visualized an eventual life with him and the millions.

They drifted in silence, both lost in their own memories. The gentle lapping of the water against the boat had a soothing, dreamlike quality. In his red bathing suit, Jordan leaned back, eyes closed, legs outstretched. Jenny drank in his beauty, and of course, he was fully aware of her admiration. He had broad shoulders tapering to a slim waist. She loved the way the sun seemed to caress his beautiful body just as her eyes did. He had a deep tan, and curly black hair on his chest. How different from Pete's smooth, hairless body, she thought. Jordan was her idea of a Greek God.

Strangely, neither brother nor sister seemed to spare any thoughts for the father who had just been buried, or for the mother, lying helpless in hospital.

Knowing she shouldn't break the spell, but with too many conflicting emotions bubbling up inside her, Jenny took a deep breath and forged ahead.

"Jordie, could I ask you something without you flying off the handle?" she queried tentatively.

"Maybe," he replied warily, trailing his hand in the water.

"First put some lotion on my back please. It's hot as Hades out here."

As he rubbed the lotion on her shoulders and back, Jenny closed her eyes with pleasure. She would have been shocked and hurt if she had seen the smug look on her brother's face as he gently caressed her. Eventually she broke the spell by saying, "You were always in so much trouble when you were little, and then it got even worse when you were a teenager. God you were bad! You drove the folks crazy. Grandma Lizzy was the only one who seemed to understand you, except for me of course. It's a good thing I loved you so much, but even so I sometimes hated you just a little bit. No one had time for me, they were always worrying about you and your latest escapades. I guess my wildness was a cry for attention. Shit, looking back on it now, I can see why dad came to hate us, and wanted us out of his life. We're quite a pair, Jordie."

Her brother didn't answer. He just sat staring off into space, a grim look on his face, the lotion tube still in his hand.

Jenny couldn't let it go now that she had started. "Why the hell were you so bad, anyway, Jordie? You acted as if you hated the entire world. You never had any real friends except for me, and then you weren't always too nice. It was as if you were driven by some inner devil."

Jenny was in an introspective mood, and although she knew it was risky, she really wanted to get Jordan to open up to her. Somehow it was important, but she wasn't sure why.

He had stopped rubbing her back, and was twisting the cap on the tube of lotion. Staring off into the distance, he said very quietly, "I guess I acted that way because I do have a devil inside me. And you're right, I do hate the world. It's nothing but a slimy, festering puss ball. No one cares a shit about anyone else. It's every man for himself, and do unto others before they can do unto you."

He was gazing at the calm deep water as he added, "When they adopted me from that last foster home, I was only four and a bit, so I don't remember much, but I know I was always scared when I lived there. That bastard used to whip me, and play mind games with me. It's a wonder I'm as sane as I am." He laughed bitterly. "There were other things he did too — very interesting things. I didn't understand then, but I do now. It was stuff I never told a living soul, even you."

Jordan snorted in disgust at this point, and Jenny interrupted. "Tell me. You know you can trust me. Tell me what kind of things." She was looking at him in fascination, already guessing what he was talking about. She had never heard this before, and wondered whether he was just making it up to tease her.

"Oh no. Some of it is too gross for your delicate ears. I will tell you this, though. There was a cupboard under the stairs in the basement, no air, no light. After he'd finish with me he'd whip me for being a bad boy and then lock me in that hellhole for hours. There was nothing in there except some old jars of mouldy peaches. And, I don't know whether there were bugs or not, but I imagined that there were, which was just as bad for a four year old. I used to cry and beat my fists against the door. I'd promise to be good and never do anything bad again, but, of course, I hadn't done anything bad. The crazy thing is that I really was a good little kid then. I wanted so much for them to love me and be good to me."

Jenny was frowning in disbelief at this tale. Could this possibly be true. Had he been sexually abused and beaten and locked in a dark closet? If so, it explained everything about Jordie's behaviour over the years. But how could she not have known about it? She and Jordan had always been so close.

Jordan kept right on talking now, as if he had forgotten that Jenny was there. "Sometimes his wife would stand outside and try to comfort me. She would cry right along with me, but she didn't have the key, and she was scared of him too. I think she knew what he was doing to me when he crept into my room at night, but she was weak and he was brutal. He was always hitting her, and I remember seeing him knock her down the stairs once. She broke her arm that time. Let's just say the guy was the mother of all shit heads. Imagine letting him be a foster parent! That's the world we live in, Jen." Here he slapped viciously at a deer fly which had landed on his leg. Then he glared at Jenny as if she had been the cause of all his troubles.

She remained perfectly still, not wanting to break the spell, not wanting him to stop with the old memories. As close as they had always been, she had never heard these revelations. This was info for which she was unprepared. She stared at Jordan in amazement, and something akin to fear. This was so bizarre, but it explained so much. Nodding sympathetically, she murmured, "Go on, Jordie, tell me everything."

Removing his sunglasses, he stared at her with those black, empty eyes. "Well, I wasn't even five yet and I'd been in several foster homes. I was just a messed up little kid. I learned to hate him and in turn to hate the whole world because no one came to help me. Now I'm in control of my life. I make things happen. I don't wait to be the victim. You might even say that I've learned the fine art of victimizing." This last was uttered with a derisive smile.

Restlessly putting the sunglasses back on, he continued, all wound up now. The awful hidden memories were pouring out like dirty water into a bucket.

"It must have been around that time that our illustrious parents adopted me. 'Free to a good home', that was little Jordan" he added sarcastically. "I thought they were my real parents who had finally come to rescue me. I couldn't understand why they had left me with that mean bastard for so long. When I eventually realized that they weren't my real folks, I was so disappointed that I talked myself into hating them. It was easier than loving them and then being sent to another foster home. Then they adopted you, all blond and cuddly, and I just hated everyone." He laughed sardonically, and splashed some water at her. "Nothing seemed right in my life. There didn't seem to be a safe place for me anywhere."

"Jordie, you should have told them. They could have got help for you. You should have told about the whippings, and whatever else he did to you." Jenny looked close to tears at this point.

"Jesus, Jen, what was the use? You know what the old man was like. I tried once, but he didn't pay any attention. He never listened to anyone except his darling wife. He just said how lucky I was that he had adopted me. They got me a pet right away, but I was terrified of it. I thought if I lost it, or it disappeared, the beatings would start again. I just kicked it and ran like hell. I wouldn't go down to the basement for years, because I was so sure that there would be a cupboard under the stairs. Finally they stopped getting pets for me. As for the other stuff, well, the less said about that, the better. Anyway, he never wanted to adopt me. I heard them arguing one day. He wanted to send me back!" Here Jordan glared as if his father was there in the boat with them. Jenny could see clearly for the first time the actual hatred he harboured towards their father. Actually when she thought about it, it was surprising that he hadn't tried to kill Matt long before this.

He was now crushing the sun lotion tube in his hand, and staring off at some hurtful memory which only he could see. His face looked almost purple, and there was sweat on his forehead.

Jenny tried to put her arms around him, but he pushed her away roughly. He wasn't finished. Now that he had opened the door to the past, he couldn't seem to close it.

"I got even, though, Jen. I really got even."

"What do you mean? How could you get even? Get even with whom?"

"With that bastard in the foster family. Just before we left Vancouver I picked the lock on that metal box where mom and dad used to keep all their special papers. All the info about my different foster homes, names, addresses, everything was there. I paid a little visit to dear old foster dad."

"Jordie, you didn't." Her eyes were bright with excitement and disbelief.

"Like hell I didn't. He was living all alone in the same shitty place. His wife was dead, I guess he killed her. I beat him to a pulp and it felt so good. I just couldn't stop hitting that ugly face of his. But you know what? He didn't even remember who I was. I guess I was just one of many little kids he had abused, and he couldn't tell one from another. How's that for our foster care system?" He didn't wait for a reply, but forged ahead with his tale. "Guess what I did then?"

"I don't know" Jenny cried, shaking her head. All thoughts of the beautiful day were long gone. She felt sick to her stomach, but strangely excited at this story.

"Yes you do, Jen. Think about it. What would be the best retribution?"

"Well, the worst thing you could have done was to put him in that closet in the basement, I guess" she said doubtfully. "I think that's what I would have done."

"Bingo" he laughed. "After I beat him and told him who I was, I dragged him down the stairs just like he used to do to me, and I threw him into that black, stinking hole. I think the same rotten jars of peaches were still sitting on the shelves. I just locked the door and left. You have no idea how good it felt. We moved to Toronto two days later. He's probably still there," he laughed grimly.

Jenny simply stared. She couldn't think of a thing to say.

As they sat looking at each other, three seadoos went hurtling by, making a huge noise, and rocking the boat with the turbulence. Neither brother nor sister noticed.

"I thought I knew everything about you, Jordie" she mused.

"Not bloody likely" he scoffed. "You only know what I've let you know. But I will admit that you know more than any other living soul. I've always felt that I could trust you."

Then, taking off his sunglasses, and staring at her with those black pits for eyes, he seemed to regret his confidences. In a lightning change of mood he said,

"Let's go back. I need a drink." He slapped her on the knee then, perhaps much harder than he had intended. "Come on, let's get the hell out of here."

Starting up the boat and hurtling across the water at full speed, he glanced at Jenny and scowled, "You better forget all that garbage I just spewed out. I just made it up" he said fiercely, stabbing her with his piercing eyes. He was obviously regretting his awful revelations. It was as if he had let her peek through a crack into the dark, viscous bag of his mind.

They were both silent as they headed back to shore, the lovely afternoon completely spoiled. Jenny wondered, not for the first time, whether Jordan might be insane.

CHAPTER 21

▼

Later that same day, after a quick and uneasy dinner, they took their drinks down to the weather-beaten dock to enjoy the setting sun, which incongruously looked like a huge red party balloon hanging in the sky. Even when Jordan was in one of his moods, this was such a ritual at the cottage, that it was just the normal thing to do.

Jenny was adorable in her hot pink track suit with black collar and cuffs. Her curly blond mane was freshly washed, and the unruly curls bounced and flounced with every move of her head. As the light slowly faded, it was difficult to see the dark circles under her eyes. In this crepuscular light she looked young and innocent, and very beautiful.

Jordan appeared tense in his jeans and rust coloured sweater. No further mention had been made of his startling revelations in the boat. In the twilight where no one could see the bottomless black of his eyes, he was a handsome fellow. Together they made a spectacularly attractive couple.

Since the disastrous face slap at the funeral, there had been strained feelings between them, and Jenny was doing her best to patch things up and bring about a détente. The afternoon boat cruise had helped, at least until Jordan spewed out all those secrets, and now he was withdrawn again.

She was upset by what he had told her, but it made things clearer, and strangely, she loved him as much as ever. She had often wondered whether Jordan could be capable of murder. Now she knew. Instead of being appalled or sickened, the knowledge seemed to excite her. Maybe they were both crazy she thought.

There was something she wanted to say to him, but she didn't know how to get started. She had been thinking about it forever it seemed, and she had to screw up her courage. This was the right time. It was now or never. Her entire future depended on what she said, yet perversely, she felt like rubbing him the wrong way — just a bit — just to see what would happen. She knew what would happen, but she got belligerent when she drank, and she had been drinking all afternoon. She felt so confused, loving him, fearing him, and resenting him all at the same time.

As a chipmunk ran across the dock, intent on some private errand before disappearing into his little home for the night, Jordan made a desultory kick at him.

"Cut it out" she snapped angrily. "Leave it alone. It's not hurting you. You can be so darn mean for no reason."

Jordan started to interrupt, but Jenny was getting all steamed up. It was the booze talking. "Don't you realize that we're on the verge of a whole new life? We have to stay focused. We'll have more money than we ever dreamed possible. Let's just leave all the baggage behind us — everything bad that we've ever done. Let's just wipe the slate clean and turn a new page," she said, mixing her metaphors. "We can do it, can't we Jordie? We can be totally different people. Besides, those little chippies are so cute" she added with a grin.

"God, you're getting on my nerves. "Oh, they're so cute" he mimicked in a high falsetto. "You know how I feel about animals. The world would be a better place without them." Each word was spit out harshly like a snake spitting venom.

Jenny sighed. She knew she should keep quiet, but she felt herself on the verge of a precipitous fall. Besides, the vodka had loosened her tongue. "I don't know why I've loved you all these years." She grimaced. "It sounds like a song title doesn't it?" Maybe if she could just make him laugh — even at her expense — they could work things out. "You really don't know how to love, but I understand now, and I know I can help you. We can help each other — we need each other." She looked hopefully into his face as he digested this last remark.

"That's right, baby sister" he sneered. "I don't know how to love. Use them and lose them — that's my motto. I love no one and no one loves me, oh, except you of course" he added sarcastically. "There's no one to hold me back, least of all a little twerp who can't get her own life in shape. By the way, excuse the non sequitur, but I was surprised to see good old Pete at the funeral. Why the hell did you two get back together after the way he treated you? Beating you up and stealing your money, and then buggering off wasn't very nice. I didn't realize you were so forgiving. You must have something up your sleeve. You should dump him for good before you get your hot little hands on your share of the money. He'll go through that faster than shit through a goose."

Sipping her drink, Jennifer made no reply, but she winced at his cruelty and his crudeness. She and Pete had been together for several months. He was just the latest in a long string of losers, but she had to admit to herself that he was near the bottom of the pack. He was a "wannabe" who had "never be" tattooed right across his forehead. He had taken every penny she had, which wasn't a lot, and was always after her to beg money from her parents. Jennifer had wheedled a couple of thousand out of her mother, but Pete lost that in one night at the races. Between drugs, booze and gambling, (and don't forget the women) she reminded herself, he was a walking disaster. The strange thing was that when he wasn't drinking or snorting coke, he was a lot of fun. He was great in bed, just thinking of him made her squirm. She always closed her eyes and pretended he was Jordan. That night he smacked her and walked out, he had shouted something about getting money out of her parents himself if she couldn't do it. Pete was a mechanic. He would certainly know how to tamper with brakes to cause an accident. Maybe it hadn't been Jordan after all.

She took a big gulp of her drink and shivered as she stared at the black water. The haunting call of the loons echoed across the bay. She thought morosely that the loons were as lonely as she was. Idly she slapped at a mosquito — those tiny vampires of the Muskoka night. Taking a breath, she said, "Jordie, I don't want to talk about Pete tonight. Let's talk about us and the money. That night we were drinking after Pete left, you said that the folks were mean enough to live forever, and we might have to help them along. You were just kidding, right?"

Jordan stared at her intently, and shaking his head, he hissed "Are you on about that crap again? I won't talk about it anymore. As far as I know it was an accident, unless you killed the old man."

"Don't be stupid, you know I didn't. Please let's not fight. We have important stuff to discuss." She was close to tears as always these days. Her hard shell seemed to be cracking, and she desperately wanted someone to love her. No, not "someone", just Jordan, she reminded herself. She knew when Jordan was in one of his black moods, she should leave him alone, but she couldn't seem to stop herself. She was on a collision course with disaster, and there was no turning back. Her life had become surreal. In the past weeks the death of her father, her mother in a coma, the fight with Jordan at the funeral, Pete walking out and then coming back, the appearance of Elena, and now the disclosures which Jordan had made that very afternoon — it was all just too much. She was on emotional overload. She could see everything now with terrifying clarity. She was heading down a one way road, and there wasn't much hope of redemption at the end, except, of course, for the money — all that beautiful pile of money which could solve all her problems.

Sighing, she said, "Where did it all go down the tubes, Jordie?"

"What do you mean?" he queried with a frown.

"Oh, you know," she shrugged. "I was fairly happy as a kid even though you got all mom and dad's attention. Remember how we used to fly out here from Vancouver every summer? Vacations here in Muskoka at Gramma Lizzy's were wonderful. Those were happy times," she reiterated.

"Speak for yourself. I was never happy. I'm not sure I know what 'happy' means. That's just a word for kids."

"You're nuts. We did have fun. Remember all the water-skiing? Gramma Lizzy used to drag us around the lake for hours, and take all our friends too. She loved to drive that boat."

"You forget, dear sister, I never had any friends."

"What about Billy?" she scoffed. "He was your friend, at least until the accident."

"No, he just hung around me because mother was so good to him. She was the one he liked, and I think she felt safer with him than she ever did with me." He grinned wryly at this observation.

"I wonder where he is now" mused Jenny. "You know, I never could really understand how that accident happened, and mom and dad would never discuss it. The whole subject was verboten, but wasn't that when they sent you off to military camp?" she asked innocently. She knew she shouldn't be bringing this up. It was like picking at a scab, but she couldn't seem to stop herself. She was in a strange mood tonight.

"You should never have been out in the boat alone, pulling a skier without a watcher. You got such heck from Dad over that. How could you have run over Billy's foot with the propeller?"

"Jen, I've told you and the whole damn frigging world. He fell while he was skiing, and when I came back to pick him up, the rope caught in the propeller and I couldn't steer. The boat ran over his foot before I could shut off the motor. It was an accident." He rhymed this off as if it were a mantra which he had repeated many times. It sounded mechanical and rehearsed, and it never had made any sense to Jenny.

"Oh, but it was so awful for him to lose his foot." Jenny couldn't help goading him. What had got into her tonight? "I wonder where he is now" she mused.

"Who cares" he growled. "Mr. Billy-one-foot can go to hell. I never liked him anyway. He told on me when I threw paint on his dad's car. I never thought he'd tell" he muttered, as if still surprised at the betrayal.

Oh oh, I've gone too far, time to change the subject, she thought, sipping her drink, and watching her brother's eyes.

"Jordie, remember the times we would sneak out early and go canoeing? The water was always like glass at that hour, and everything was so peaceful. It was as if you and I were the only two people in the world. Mom used to say something about the Godlike aura of tranquility which was Muskoka in the morning. There were three things she always talked about, the mirror-still water, the gently rising mist, and the sun just a promise on the horizon. She was pretty poetic you know. She always said that morning in Muskoka was good for the soul. She was right too. Jordie, let's get up early tomorrow and take the canoe out" she suggested hopefully. "You were always so different when it was just the two of us, and I always felt safe with you."

Jordan snorted derisively at that. "You were always a gullible kid. I could make you believe anything."

"I don't care" she replied, seemingly impervious to his insults. "Those were wonderful times. Why did we ever have to grow up."

They sat there in silence for a few minutes while Jenny pondered what a mess her life had become. The only good news was the money she was about to inherit, and of course, the secret plans she had for Jordan and herself. She could do it. She could turn everything around. It was now or never.

Plunging ahead like some demented long distance swimmer diving into the turbulent waters without much hope of coming out alive on the other side, she said, "Jordan, no matter how the accident came about, when we get the money, do you think — ah — how would you feel about going somewhere far away together?" She hesitated, and then pleaded softly, "we could live as husband and wife." There, she had said it at last.

A disagreeable guffaw came from Jordan. "Why you wicked little temptress" he chortled. "It's finally out in the open. You've been wanting to get me into your bed for years" he exclaimed with a leer. "Now you're finally admitting it. You've got more guts than I thought."

A mirthless chuckle escaped his lips. The sound chilled Jenny. She shivered as she felt her world tilt. He was laughing at her! Her heart seemed to crack. She had pinned all her hopes and dreams on Jordan for so many years, and he was laughing and making fun of her. She had confided an innermost dream, and he was reacting as if she were ludicrous, as if she were an absurd, comical nitwit.

Jumping out of her chair, Jenny put her arms around his neck from behind, as he continued to laugh. "Jordie, we aren't really and truly brother and sister, you know that. There's nothing wrong with it. We aren't related at all except for some stupid piece of paper. Nobody would know, nobody would care. We'd go far away. I love you so, Jordan. I've loved you all my life. I've waited so long." She was pleading now, and the words were tumbling out. "You must love me, you know you do. Things would be so different if we were together. No one knows you the way I do."

"Wow there, baby doll," he exclaimed, unwinding her arms from around his neck, and standing up to face her. "If I had wanted to screw you I would have done it a long time ago. You don't know how lucky you are that I didn't. Don't you know that I go for the juicy little girls? You're not my type, sister dearest, you're way too old. You've got no place in my life once we get that money. As the old song says, 'my bags are packed and I'm ready to go'. Sorry sweet buns, but that's the way it is. You'll have to go back to Pete, or get yourself someone else." He declared these hurtful words as he stared at her with those impenetrable eyes, and a deadpan look on his face.

Something snapped in Jenny's head. She sprang at him, wrapping her arms around him and pressing her lips to his. As he tried to pull away in obvious disgust, she bit him hard on the lower lip, and began beating him with her fists on his face and head, all the time screeching and sobbing.

Jordan let out a surprised grunt, and slapped her hard on the side of her head. Then, grabbing her arms, he screamed into her face, blood dripping down his chin, "you little bitch, I should drown you right now, and no one would be the wiser."

Stunned, Jenny wept in terror and remorse. Things had gone all wrong. This wasn't the way she had planned it. "Jordie, please, I'm sorry, I didn't mean it."

"Get the hell away from me. I have to think, and I can't concentrate with you around. You've turned into a real little hellcat. Look what you've done to my face. I'm bleeding for crissakes."

"Here, let me — "

"No, you've done enough. Go up to the cottage and get out of my sight. You'd better lock yourself in your room, because right now I could kill you," he uttered in a malevolent tone, dabbing at his lip with his handkerchief.

Jenny let out a little moan. Grabbing her glass and her jacket, she ran up the stairs to the cottage. She needed another drink. She needed many drinks, but little shards of terror told her to get out of Jordan's way. There was no time to grab the vodka bottle.

Racing into her bedroom, she glanced quickly over her shoulder to be sure that he wasn't following her. She locked the door and braced a chair under the doorknob. She knew with terrible certainty that if Jordan wanted to get at her, he would. Nothing could save her. "Well, just let him kill me if he wants to. I might as well be dead as the way I am ." She didn't realize that she had spoken out loud as she lay down on the bed and stared at the ceiling till dawn. Sometime during that long night Jennifer Wainwright experienced a sort of epiphany, and by morning she had worked out many things.

All her hopes and plans had floated away like soap bubbles in a breeze. Plan A had involved Jordan and all the money. Plan B wasn't nearly as good, but Jenny was adaptable. She was a bit of a chameleon. She would have to rely on Pete, he was a necessary evil now. Yes, she would have to add Pete to the equation. She could handle him, though — good old Pete.

She couldn't believe that Jordan had laughed at her — had shattered her dreams like a kid smashing a fragile Christmas ornament. Her heart, which had been so full of love for him all these years, was now full of hate. At this moment she despised him for knowing how she felt. She was humiliated that she had bared her soul for him and he had stomped on it. He had known all along that she loved him, all those wasted years of covering for him, of taking the blame for some of the bad things he did, and all along he was just using her. "I love him, I hate him, I love him, I hate him." The mantra went on for hours.

Suddenly she sat up and stared into space. Jordan liked little girls. He had admitted as much to her. There was that little girl who had lived next door to them — oh what was her name? Sarah Jane McCracken — yes that was it. She had disappeared and it was two weeks before they found her body buried in a shallow grave in the woods close to where they lived. Jenny had been about seven, and Sarah Jane was close to the same age, maybe a little older. Jordan would have been fourteen. Police had come to their home more than once interrogating her parents and Jordan. Sarah Jane was sexually molested and strangled, and her murderer had never been found. Jenny vaguely remembered lying for Jordan that time, although she couldn't quite recall what he had made her say to the police. Had she given him an alibi? Had Jordan killed Sarah Jane?

Jenny felt sick and she was sweating. Yes, she was sure of it. Jordan had killed the little girl and used Jenny somehow for his alibi. Oh the vile, disgusting pervert. She hated him. How could she have forgotten all that stuff? No wonder her parents spent all their time with Jordan. They likely knew or suspected that he had killed Sarah Jane, and they were trying to protect him from the police and also keep him from hurting anyone else.

She felt that she would explode with frustration. She was consumed by a rage so intense that she felt nauseated. How could she have been so stupid? Well, that was the end. She would never love or trust anyone again. She would use people the way she had been used. From now on little Miss Jenny was in charge. She would get away from Jordan till he cooled off. He could be dangerous. It was as if a veil had been lifted from her eyes. Oh Jordan you vile creature. You're going to be so sorry. Even as she thought it, however, she knew deep in her heart that she would always love him. It was so confusing. Still, she had to pay him back for hurting her this way.

Her decisions made, Jenny quietly packed her things, and slipped out of the cottage before dawn. Thank God she had driven up in her own car, and Jordan was nowhere in sight. She had many things to do.

CHAPTER 22

▼

"Vickie, I feel badly about going out and leaving you alone tonight, but I promise I'll be back as soon as I can. I wish you'd change your mind and come with me." Cassie had a worried frown on her face as she and Vickie loaded the dishwasher and tidied the kitchen.

"No kidding, Cass, I'm looking forward to a little time to myself. We've talked so much lately that my tongue's swollen! It'll be great to be quiet for a while. I'll shower and wash my hair, and then I want to finish my book. Don't worry, the beasties will be good company. Just go and have fun. We'll be fine."

"Well, I do have to make an appearance at this little soirée, but I'll hurry back. You know that you're welcome to come with me, but if you are determined to stay home, just be sure you lock yourself in and leave all the lights on. Here's the number where I'll be."

"Yes, mother" Vickie grinned as she wiped the counter. Both friends had been unexpectedly nervous since the episode of the rat. So far the police hadn't been able to track down the sender, at least Cass and Vickie assumed this was the case since they hadn't heard from them.

Once Cass had left, (Vickie had to practically push her out the door), she locked up carefully, pulled all the drapes and blinds, and poured herself a generous glass of wine. She also got out a few treats for the cats. "Don't you dare tell on me" she admonished them as they happily dove into the two plates of delicious tidbits. While they were occupied with this unexpected feast, Vickie headed upstairs.

Cassandra was on edge at the get-together. It was a birthday party for her friend Sophie's mother who was visiting from Charlottetown, and who was 93 years old today. Cassie had known Mrs. Sheridan years ago before she had moved to the east coast, and she felt obliged to at least make an appearance, and drop off her gift. Ordinarily Cass would have been delighted to see her old friend again, but tonight she was antsy. She couldn't put her finger on it, but her scalp was prickly, always a bad sign. She simply could not relax and enjoy the festivities.

Meanwhile, Vickie had carefully laid out her nightgown and old housecoat on the chaise lounge, along with her book. She was luxuriating in the opportunity to have some quiet time to herself. She loved this charming, comfortable house. It was a two story family style dwelling, but Cass and Dave had made many interesting changes and additions. The colours were all peaceful and warm, and the furniture and pictures seemed friendly and welcoming. Vickie felt totally at home here, and she and Cass were having such a good time. She felt so fortunate that their friendship had endured over all these years. They had both come a long way since those kindergarten days. She must treat Cass to a lavish dinner in some extravagant restaurant this week just to say thank you for all the fun and excitement. She didn't want to think about the stalker and the scary times.

A few minutes later, she was singing happily and lustily as she lathered up her hair. Her voice wasn't good, but it was loud. What she lacked in quality, she was making up in volume. After her shower she would dry her hair and curl it, then snuggle on the comfy chaise in her room, and finish the latest James Patterson book.

With the water running, and her voice resounding, she had no way of hearing the tinkle of breaking glass in the kitchen. Stepping out of the shower, however, and opening the bathroom door to let the steam escape, she was startled to hear the high pitched yowling of the cats. "Come on you guys" she called. "I know my voice isn't so good, but you don't need to express your displeasure so rudely." The felines were nowhere in sight, but the caterwauling continued.

Quickly wrapping a towel around her hair, and one around her body, she walked into the bedroom, and realized with a start that the lights were out. She had definitely left the bedside lamp on. The awful thing was that she smelled him before he actually grabbed her harshly from behind. She was too surprised to even squeak, and with a numbing terror, she felt the cold steel blade of a knife pressed to her neck. She also smelled the nauseating odour of stale sweat and rancid breath, an odious combination.

"Don't make a sound or your head comes off" warned a strangely high-pitched voice.

Paralyzed with fear, she thought of the rat and the calls and the x'd out picture of the cats. Was there a connection? Was this the stalker?

He dragged her backwards to the bed, and pushed her down roughly, quickly straddling her, the knife tip now pressed against her bare chest. The towels had fallen off as soon as he grabbed her. In those first terrible moments she gasped like a dying fish. By the light of the hall she could see that he was wearing a mask, pantyhose or something, and he was making a disgusting sucking noise with his teeth.

"Oh God, don't let him kiss me" she thought crazily. In her terror Vickie felt that she would rather be killed than raped by this nightmarish creature. Her mind was flying every which way. Her terrified thoughts were twisting and colliding like bumper cars at a midway. There was nothing she could use for a weapon, nothing within reach. The knife was touching her right between her breasts. He was tracing it up and down and around in circles, toying with her, getting himself all excited, all the time giggling and sucking. Vickie was now writhing from side to side, unmindful of the knife. She was clawing at his mask, trying to jab at his eyes. If she could only knee the bastard, but he was crouching over her, and her legs were pinned beneath him.

"No, please no" she kept crying in a frenzied voice. "Please wait, let's talk." She thought she might throw up. God, she would choke on her own vomit if he kept her pinned down like this. Maybe she could spew it out right into his face and eyes. Would it soak through the mask?

"I'm sick" she pleaded. "I have a disease. You don't want to do this."

He giggled insanely at that. "Shut up, girlie. I've got a disease too."

With heart sinking clarity, she felt the sting of the knife as it scraped and jabbed whenever she moved. She couldn't breathe, she couldn't swallow. Moistening her lips, she tried again. "Please don't."

"Shut up I said. You fucking bitches are all the same. You think you're so smart, so bossy and mean, but you all beg and whine like babies when I get you down. You're all useless as shit. I'm gonna give you just what you deserve. Just stop fighting and enjoy it or I'll have to slice and dice." He giggled again at his humour.

Vickie struggled with renewed strength, but he was strong, too strong. Even with the mask on, she could see that his eyes looked crazed. The light from the hall was reflecting off the little slits through which his eyes peered. Her heart was pounding so hard that she could feel it in her temples and her fingertips. Good, maybe she'd have a stroke and never know what he was doing to her. Her tears were blinding her as she put up a valiant fight.

Somehow she managed to get one good dig at his eye. She ground her finger in as far as she could and twisted it. He yelped and loosened his hold. "You bitch, you fucking bitch" he screamed, as Vickie rolled away to the other side of the bed. He was too quick though. He grabbed her leg and yanked it so hard that she thought it had come out of its socket. He dragged her back and put his knife arm across her throat.

"You hurt me, you bitch" he cried in surprise and frustration as he held her, choking her with his arm, while he struggled to pull down his track pants. Vickie knew that Cass wouldn't be home for hours. There was no hope of rescue. She needed a miracle, and her prayers were answered, but the miracle came from an unexpected source. Jerking her head sidewise, she let out two horrendous screams before all hell broke loose.

Suddenly her attacker dropped the knife and scrambled off the bed, as two furry missiles with claws landed on his back, shrieking like banshees. Vickie rolled out of the way and stared in amazement as he twirled in circles, adding his cries to those of the cats, trying desperately to dislodge his clawing, biting and kicking assailants.

Muffy's claws were digging right through the pantyhose mask on the attacker's head. The rapist looked as if he was wearing a bizarre Carmen Miranda hat. Sugar was howling and biting the shirt on his back, while her legs were going like little pistons raking rows of skin off his bare bottom.

He tried to pull Muffy off his head, but Muff bit him savagely on the hand. Little Muffin, the gentlest of creatures, had become a biting, clawing, scratching machine. He was crazed with fear and excitement. The more Sugar howled, the more Muffy clawed and bit. The would-be rapist was definitely getting the worst of the attack. Then Sugar was around at his belly, where she was doing serious damage to his not-so-private parts with her stubby little hind legs. Willy was now howling louder than the cats.

While Vickie looked around desperately for a weapon before this monster hurt her rescuers, the sudden sound of the front door slamming shut caused a momentary pause in the frenetic dance. "Vickie I'm home, and I've brought two gorgeous guys with me," called Cassie gaily. "Get down here girl, it's party time."

At the welcome sound of Cassie's voice, both cats flew off their victim, and out the door. For one shocked moment Willy stood stupidly staring after them, then, pulling up the track pants which were still around his ankles, he fled.

"Cassie" screamed Victoria, trying to warn her friend, as her shaky legs suddenly gave out on her.

Cassie's eyes barely had time to register the rapist flying down the stairs. He gave her a vicious shove, knocking her legs out from under her, as he ran past her, and out the front door.

Cass got herself up, and took the stairs two at a time, terrified of what she might find. Vickie was sitting on the edge of the bed, rocking back and forth, arms clutched tightly around herself. She was naked, and her still wet auburn hair stuck out in all directions. Blood was oozing from a multitude of small cuts. She was crying, and she clutched Cassie like a child clinging to a parent.

"Vickie, look at me. Did he, did he hurt you?" cried Cass desperately, unable to say the dreaded word 'rape'.

"No, no, the cats s-s-stopped him, and then you sh-shouted. He was j-just pulling down his pants when they flew at him." Here Vickie took a huge sobbing breath and tried to continue her hysterical account. "Cass, they were wonderful. They were like wild things. Muffy was on his head, raking him with his claws, and Sugar was clinging to his back, biting him. Then somehow she was at his belly and she was kicking his dick." Here she started to laugh and shake uncontrollably as Cassie hugged her tightly.

Eventually Cass got a washcloth to wipe off the blood. She was relieved to see that they weren't deep cuts, but there were a lot of them, and they were all oozing and dripping.

"Oh damn, we've got to call 911" cried Cass, realizing that they were wasting precious moments while the would-be rapist got away. After making the call, and attending to Vickie, she suddenly cried "where are the cats?"

"Cass, those dear little souls saved my life. They were howling when I came out of the shower, and then they just came out of nowhere and leaped on his back." Vickie was talking non-stop now. Words were pouring out of her like water from a faucet. "They were incredible. He could have killed them with his knife, but he dropped it when they flew at him."

Suddenly staring at each other, they realized that the knife must still be on the bed, and sure enough, there it was, half hidden in the tangled bedclothes. They knew enough not to touch it. It would be evidence against the attacker.

"But where are they?" Cass was alarmed now. Had they gotten out with the rapist? Oh God, had he hurt them? Running to the bedroom door, she called out, "Sugar Plum, Muffin, where are you?"

A slight noise made her look up. In the hall was a beautiful seven foot cherry wood armoire which had belonged to Dave's grandmother. Cassie cherished it, and laughed in relief when she saw two worried little faces peering down at her.

"How did you two ever get up there?" she cried in amazement. It was a jump which Muffy could have made easily with his long legs and lithe body. Sugie, on the other hand, with her short legs and flubby tummy, must have had an almost impossible task to make that leap. Only sheer terror could have inspired her.

Cass was so shaken that she felt as if she was coming apart. She needed Dave desperately, but since Dave was an ocean away, she fervently hoped that Jack would answer the call. Her legs were trembling, but she had to stay calm for Vickie. She leaned against the wall for a moment, closing her eyes and taking deep breaths. Her friend had come close to being raped, the cats could have been killed. It was an immobilizing moment of truth. She uttered a silent prayer of thanksgiving as she looked up at her two little companions.

"Come down, you two ninja turtles. You saved Vickie. You're heroes. Come on, it's okay, the bad guy is gone. You can go back to being little wussies again." The cats were still frightened, but Muffy was finally coaxed down. He jumped into Cassie's waiting arms. Sugar Plum, however, was a different story. It appeared that she was there permanently. She didn't remember how she had managed to get up there, and Cass could tell by the look in her eyes that she sure as hell wasn't about to attempt the return trip. Eventually Cass dragged a chair out of her bedroom, stood on it, and lifted a still trembling little cat down to safety. After much hugging and purring they leaped from her arms and began sniffing all around the room and the bed. They wanted to reassure themselves that the malodorous intruder was really gone.

"Oh God, Vic" gasped Cassie, staring at her in horror.

"What now, what is it?" responded Vickie, looking around in renewed terror. Had the attacker come back?

"We've destroyed the evidence. I shouldn't have washed off the blood. The police might have wanted to take pictures. Damn, what have I done?"

"It's okay, Cass. Don't beat yourself up. We've got the knife, and it will have my blood on it." She grimaced at the thought. "Besides, there's no way any cop is getting a free peek at these national treasures! I've always been rather proud of my boobs, but they're not for general display."

They were both laughing in a semi-hysterical way when the doorbell rang, and they heard the welcome words, "Police, open up."

Cass raced downstairs and opened the door to Detective Bud Lang, and a female officer, along with a crime technician and all his paraphernalia. She couldn't help wondering whether they would have received such excellent and immediate attention if they hadn't been personal friends of Bud and Jack. She was disappointed that Jack wasn't here, but she was extremely grateful that she at least knew one of the detectives. Vickie shakily dressed herself and came down too. Before telling the police everything that had occurred, Cassandra poured a generous glass of brandy for her friend. Vickie had never tasted brandy, but she gamely drank it down as if it were bad medicine which had to be endured.

She was able to pull herself together sufficiently to relate the entire experience. Lang seemed to stiffen when she described the pantyhose mask and the knife. When she told of the awful stench and the disgusting sucking sound, he nodded grimly. "I know who it was, and we'll get him, don't you worry."

He laughed delightedly when Victoria told how the two cats had attacked the attacker. "Wonderful" he cried. "It looks good on him. Damn, I would have loved to see that. Poor Willy will never be the same."

"And neither will his willy" giggled Victoria, who was now guzzling the brandy with more enthusiasm.

Bud Lang thought to himself that Willy the Weasel had got more pussy than he bargained for that night. He could hardly wait to tell Jack.

"He'll be badly scratched, Detective Lang. They were both clawing and biting him all over" laughed Vickie. "They were fantastic. Oh, and I got a good dig at his left eye. I think I really hurt him" she added proudly.

When they found the broken window in the back door, Bud began to mutter about the dangers of doors with big windows in them. They were an open invitation to intruders. He went down to the basement with Cassie, and with her help, he found wood, hammer and nails to fix the door till it could be repaired properly. He suggested the two women go to a hotel for the night, but they were disinclined to leave the house and the cats. The female officer, Debra Hailey, offered to stay with them. "I'm fully prepared to stay over" she said. "I always carry an emergency over night kit with me just in case." The friends, however, felt that they would be quite safe. They needed to be by themselves, to talk and to cry, and to reassure each other that everything was fine. Debra seemed disappointed that they didn't want her to stay. She was fascinated by the cats and their bravery. Bud was disappointed too that they wouldn't go to a hotel, but he assured them that a patrol car would go past the house every hour all night. "Willy's long gone by now. He'd never think of coming back. He's a little coward and a sneak, and he's likely licking his wounds in some sleazy motel or rented room. He's probably still trying to figure out what hit him" he laughed.

Bud couldn't have been nicer. He retrieved the knife, and checked every window and door. This was after he called the station and had an all points bulletin put out concerning Willy. The crime technician had been busy gathering blood and skin samples. Willy had lost a lot of both, thanks to the cats. The tech tried to get samples from the cats' claws, but they had already fastidiously cleaned themselves. They both indignantly stomped away and disappeared for a while.

When they were finally alone, the two friends sat in the little library, going over the unbelievable attack.

"You know, Cass, you yelling that you had brought two guys home with you for a party is what scared him off so quickly. He would have eventually got the cats off, and would have finished what he started." Here she gave an involuntary shudder. "Whatever made you say anything so silly?"

"Honestly, I don't know. I was just so happy to be home. I was really nervous at the party. My tingling scalp was driving me crazy. I just couldn't get back here fast enough, but I figured you'd be pissed off that I had come back so early and spoiled your solitude, so I was just being goofy and hoping to make you laugh."

"Well, thank God you did. You saved me, Cass, you and the cats. You know, I kept thinking, if he rapes me I've got no weapons, no way to protect myself. All I could do was try to jab at his eyes, and I thought I could pee on him. That might have turned him off."

"More likely it would have turned him on, the disgusting pervert," said Cassie, downing her second glass of wine. Once again they broke into nervous laughter.

"I really think that I did hurt his eye. He let out an awful yelp when I dug my finger in. I hope I blinded the bastard," Vickie added angrily. "Oh, and Cass, the stink, I've never smelled anything like it. That guy hadn't had a bath in a year, and his breath was loathsome. Honestly, there's no way I can sleep in that room tonight. The bed reeks of him. What'll I do?"

"No problem gal. We'll both sleep in the front room. It's got the two double beds. There's no way anyone is sleeping alone tonight. We'll bring Sugie and Muff in too, and the cell phone of course. We'll barricade the door and make it a party."

Some party, thought Vickie, but she knew what her friend meant. Everything was alright. Nothing bad had happened, except that she had experienced the fright of her life. She was okay now though. She even felt proud of herself. She had put up a pretty good fight. How was she ever going to be able to tell all this to Brian and the kids? Maybe she wouldn't tell the kids. There was no need for them to know just how close she had come to being raped. It still seemed more like a nightmare than a real experience.

After compulsively checking every window and door several times, they eventually took their weary bodies up the stairs, followed by two tired little felines who weren't letting them out of their sight.

CHAPTER 23

▼

Cassie's inclination was to baby Vickie the next few days. She felt guilty that this had happened to her friend in her home while she was out at a party. Vic seemed to be handling it well, but as they sat in the sunroom, and Cass jumped up to make another pot of tea, Vic cried "Jeez Cass, lay off. Relax! You're hovering like an old granny. I feel as if I've got some terminal disease, and you're trying to make my last days happy ones! You're smothering me."

Cass laughed self-consciously. "I know I'm mothering you a bit too much, but, Vic, I feel so guilty. I can't stand the thought of that cockroach touching you. I was out partying while you were being savaged by the creature from the black lagoon."

"Oh shit, it wasn't your fault. You coaxed me to go with you, and it was my choice to stay. You and the beasties saved me. I'll be forever grateful, but enough already with the tea. If you must wait on me, please get me a glass of vino." This was added with a grin.

"Okay, I'll lay off. You can get the wine yourself, how's that? I just don't want you traumatized for life."

"Forget it, it was a non event. Well, maybe that's not exactly true, but honestly I'm in good shape. I just want them to catch the little turd. What I'd really like is to catch him myself and beat him to a pulp, then take a knife to his dick. I feel so angry!" Vickie clenched her fists and grimaced at this point, and Cass wondered again how long it would be before her friend was completely over the scare.

"I'll bet he's been a weenie wagger all his life" suggested Cass, shaking her head.

"Well, I'll tell you, his weenie wasn't wagging by the time Sugar and Muff were finished with him" laughed Vickie.

Once more they rehashed the events of the almost fateful night, studying and picking at every little nuance. They kept dwelling on any humour they could find — that seemed the right approach. It had indeed been scary, but it was no tragedy. Now they just wanted to hear that he had been caught.

The women were extremely disappointed that so far the police apparently had made no headway with their investigations. It appeared that they were floundering. Not only had they not caught the rapist, even though they knew who he was, but they hadn't tried to trace the threatening phone calls, they hadn't found out who sent the rat, and, of course, there was still the question of who had cut the brakes and caused the deadly crash. It would have been laughable if it wasn't so frustrating and disappointing. Cass was dejected that Jack hadn't solved everything by now. Somehow she wanted him to be her hero the way he used to be.

Cass felt guilty that Vickie had become embroiled in all this mess, so reluctantly she suggested, "Vic, if you want to cut your visit short and go home, I'll be terribly disappointed, but you know that I'll understand. You shouldn't have been dragged into this."

"Are you kidding? You can't get rid of me that easily. I'm not letting that creep spoil things for us. This is more excitement than I've had in years. Don't hurt my feelings by trying to send me home like a naughty child. I want to be here when that stinker is caught, and I do mean stinker. God he smelled awful. I think he must have crawled out of somebody's septic tank."

Cass laughed. "That's great. I mean about you staying, not about how he smelled. I was so afraid you might want to bail out on me. Let's put all this craziness behind us and start having some fun." And that was exactly what they did.

They shopped in every quaint little boutique in Niagara-on-the-Lake. They lunched at the beautiful old Oban Inn. One day Cass buried her wariness of bees, and they shared a picnic along the jewel of Ontario parklands — the Niagara River Parkway, which runs for thirty-five miles from Fort Erie to Niagara-on-the-Lake. The lush, verdant parklands border the greenish Niagara River which flows along sullenly, holding so many secrets. It was there, however, that they had a disconcerting experience.

As they were sitting at a picnic table near the gorge, Cassie suddenly poked Vickie on the arm and hissed. "Look over your right shoulder. Isn't that Jim Sinclair standing beside that tree? He's wearing a baseball cap, and he's looking right at us."

Vickie turned quickly and looked toward the tree. There were so many trees that she wasn't sure which one Cassie meant, but then she saw a figure hurrying away. He was wearing a baseball cap. "I didn't see his face, Cass. Darn it. But what in the world would Jim Sinclair be doing in Niagara?"

"Well I can think of one thing," said Cass grimly. "He's probably stalking us. Why else would he be out here?"

"Holy shit, you're right" Vickie exclaimed, wide-eyed. "It isn't Pete, it's Jim Sinclair who's been after us. What should we do?" She was peering around nervously now, trying to spot him. "You know, that fits." She was wagging her finger at Cass. "It really fits. Listen. Carol Sinclair was having an affair with Matt. Her husband found out, and he threatened that he would kill Matt if Matt ever saw Carol again. Now let's say that Carol did see Matt again, maybe just to tell him that it was all off, or maybe to have one more hot tryst with him. Who knows what happened then? Maybe Matt dumped her, told her they were through and that he was going to California with his wife. Maybe Carol was so angry that she got Jim to kill him. Then, when she heard us at the funeral saying that we were going to hire a private eye and get to the bottom of things, she told Jim that he'd have to scare us badly or else kill us. Or maybe it was all Jim's idea. They did say that he has a murderous temper. Oh Cass, it fits perfectly!"

Then she frowned and said, "Are you sure that it was really Jim Sinclair? I mean we only saw him that once at the funeral. Maybe it was just someone who looks like him."

"Well, I'm pretty sure it was Sinclair, but Vic, there are too many 'maybes' in this theory. "Perhaps" — she emphasized the word — "perhaps he's just in town to go to the casino or to visit friends, or perhaps he has legitimate business here, not necessarily murderous business. Perhaps he just came out here to enjoy the tranquility of the park, or perhaps he's meeting a sweetie here. Two can play that game, you know." Cass was now playing devil's advocate.

"Sure, and perhaps I'll win the big one this week" snorted Vic in disgust. "Come on, Cass. It's all too coincidental, and I think my theory fits perfectly if it really was Jim Sinclair."

"I guess you're right. It does seem too coincidental. Let's just pack up and get out of here before he comes back."

They hurriedly packed the remnants of the picnic, looking over their shoulders and staring off into the trees, but they saw no more sign of Jim Sinclair.

Talking it over in the safety of the house, they began to convince themselves that it was unlikely to have been Jim. They told themselves, laughingly, that they were being fools jumping to wild conclusions. They were determined to get back to normal, but for the next few days, each friend, without saying anything to the other, searched the faces in the crowds, wherever they went.

Making an effort to get into a holiday mood, Cassandra began to look at things through Vickie's eyes. She had always felt that Niagara Falls was a tourist trap for the unsuspecting, but she didn't want to spoil her friend's fun. Actually, she began to appreciate many things about the beautiful area which she had always taken for granted.

They toured the Butterfly Conservatory, delighting in the colourful little flyers as they flitted around in the tropical surroundings, occasionally landing on a tourist's head or shoulders.

They rode to the top of the Skylon Tower in the famous "yellow bug" elevators which climb the outside of the tower, offering the intrepid rider a fantastic view of the falls. Vickie treated Cass to dinner in the Skylon's revolving dining room, marvelling at the view of the city, the falls, and the environs. It was such a clear night that they could see the Toronto skyline right across Lake Ontario.

"Honestly Cass, I can't get over the diversity in this area. You can go from the hectic, high octane atmosphere on Clifton Hill, with all the tourist traps, plus the falls themselves, to the absolute tranquility and beauty of the acres of fruit lands and vineyards — all in one little peninsula. It's amazing! There's something here for everyone."

"I guess when you live here you don't appreciate it that much" pondered Cass. "It's true though, it's a great place to raise a family."

CHAPTER 24

▼

Next morning they were reading the papers and having a leisurely breakfast in the sunroom. It was a glorious day, and the cats were taking advantage of the sunshine. Muffy was curled in his usual ball on a chair, with sun beating down on him, turning his lovely orange fur to gold. Sugie was lying on the floor, all four legs in the air, soaking up the rays on her furry underbelly.

Vickie folded the paper and helped carry the dishes back to the kitchen. Sugar, having had enough sun, trotted after them, thinking there might be a second breakfast in her future.

"Get out of here, rodent," laughed Cassie, picking her up and cuddling her. "You'll soon be known as Sugar Plump, Plumper, Plumpest! You are fast losing your svelte little figure."

"Losing it? I think it's long gone," laughed Vickie.

Cass was still giggling when she answered the phone and found that it was Jack calling.

"Cass" he began in that deep sexy voice, "I've been thinking. I really need to talk to you privately. How about meeting me for lunch tomorrow — just the two of us. We can go over all this stuff, and there are a few new ideas I want to discuss. I don't want Vickie there though — just you. How about it?"

Cassie's heart gave a strange little lurch as she groped for an answer. What was this all about? Was he putting the hustle on her, or was it all legit? She was momentarily suspended between an urge to see him and guilt at the thought. Lunch with Jack would be great, but was it a bad idea? Yes, no, maybe. What was the matter with her? After all, she was a married woman with a great husband, even if he was thousands of miles away. Still, there was no harm in an innocent lunch between two old friends. Oh sure, Cass, tell me another one. There could be great harm in it, but what the heck. She was a big girl now. Maybe this was her own little mid-life crisis. Lusting after Jack in her heart wasn't too bad as long as she left it at that. Besides, it served Dave right for leaving her behind, the rat. She had really wanted to go with him on this trip.

What in the world could Jack want to talk about? Maybe he wanted to rehash their tumultuous high school days, but more likely he had something to tell her about the stalker. No, if it was about the stalker, he'd want Vickie there too wouldn't he?

Jack cleared his throat and Cassie had to come up with an answer. Hesitantly she replied, "Sure, I guess that would be fine. Where did you have in mind?" If he suggested a restaurant in one of the big hotels, she would find an excuse to beg off. No sense in putting temptation in their path. Now she knew she was being silly. She would never consider having an affair or a quick afternoon tryst. She just wasn't that kind of person. Still, it was fun to speculate.

"Let's see" he said slowly, with that lovely deep voice of his. "I could pick you up, but then it might be awkward if Vickie was there. I don't want to hurt her feelings. I think it's best if you meet me at the restaurant. How about the Casa D'Oro at one o'clock?"

"That sounds okay, Jack" said Cassie. Was she being a fool, and how was she going to get out without telling Vickie?

"Fine, I'll call Tony and have him save a booth in the back room for us. That way it will be nice and private. You take care, and I'll see you there tomorrow."

Cass hung up and went directly to her bedroom to give herself a few minutes to think. A private booth in the back room? That sounded suspiciously like a romantic rendezvous. On the other hand, if he had stuff to tell her about the crash or the stalker it made sense that he would want privacy. She sighed as she wondered what to tell Vickie. Then she decided that the truth was best. She knew Vic would be pissed off, but she was going to meet Jack tomorrow regardless.

Vickie took the news with equanimity, although inside she was disappointed. If they were going to talk about the stalker and everything else, she wanted to be in on it. The fact that she was excluded, however, made her think that good old Jack was about to make a move on Cassie. She warned her friend not to fall for his charms again, and left it at that.

The next morning little men with taps on their shoes were doing a flamenco in Cassie's stomach. She was excited and nervous all at the same time. Calm down, Cass old girl, she chided herself, as she attacked her hair with the curling iron. It's strictly business. Ya, right! Whether it was business or pleasure, she dressed very carefully in a lime green sleeveless turtle neck top and a long navy and lime skirt. Grinning at herself in the mirror, she acknowledged that she was acting like a schoolgirl. She knew, however, that she looked her very best as she strode non-chalantly into the restaurant and saw Jack rise to meet her.

It was a bit awkward at first. They talked of trivial things until the waitress had taken their order. Jack wanted the lobster sandwich, while Cassie opted for the Caesar salad. As they sipped their wine and munched on Italian bread, Cass kept wondering why she was there. What was Jack up to? Then the errant thought came unbidden to her mind. What if she and Jack had run off and married in high school as they had discussed so many times? Would they be sitting here today, happily gazing at each other over a delicious lunch? Or, would they have divorced long ago, and be carrying scars and baggage from an unhappy alliance?

She tried to picture Jack as her husband, lying in bed beside her, or standing shaving in the bathroom, hot and clean from a shower, a towel draped casually around his waist. Strangely, Dave's face kept interposing itself. Good! She and Jack hadn't married, and it was all for the best. The physical attraction was still there between them, but she was older now and presumably wiser. She had a new life, a really good life. Still, she was barraged with memories and feelings. As she stared into those unforgettable blue eyes, she was seeing the long lean legs, the narrow hips, the dark curly hair, and she felt her face begin to flush. Hopefully he would think it was the wine.

Eventually Jack began asking questions about Dave and their marriage. He eased into it so gradually that Cass didn't mind telling him about her life. She was barely aware that it was a form of interrogation.

"What exactly does he do, Cass?" Jack asked with a casual tone which belied the searching look in his eyes.

"He owns a talent agency — 'Meredith Stars,'" Cass answered with pride, and then remembered that Jack probably already knew all about what her husband did. Hadn't she told him that first time he came to the house with Bud?

"And what's he doing in Europe" Jack queried innocently as he bit into his sandwich.

"He's tracking down some new talent," she said rather shortly. She made her-self stop fiddling with her spoon.

"Didn't you say he was going to be away several weeks? That seems like a long time."

"Well, no, it isn't really," said Cass hurriedly, wondering why she was sud-denly trying to defend Dave. "He's checking out the entertainment scenes there, you know, all the big casinos and hotels. He's looking for good new talent, and that takes time."

"Sounds interesting" mumbled Jack, taking another bite of the lobster. "How come you didn't go with him? It would have been a great trip." Here he looked at her seriously, and Cass became uneasy.

"Well, ah, actually, I wanted to go, but Dave said he'd be working all the time and that I'd be bored. And anyway, there was no one to look after the cats, and," — here her voice trailed off as she realized how lame she sounded. Why hadn't she gone with Dave? She had certainly wanted to. The trip had come up very suddenly, and Dave had really discouraged her from going with him. He had promised that they would go next year when they could relax and enjoy everything without him working all the time. He had told her that he wanted to concentrate on his work without feeling guilty. Putting it into words now, though, it really didn't make much sense.

Jack nodded and looked at her intently for a moment before reaching for her hand and saying, "Cass, as a detective, I have to look at all possible angles, no matter how farfetched they may seem. Sometimes the most implausible and unlikely ideas turn out to be the answer. There are a lot of strange things going on here, and Bud and I are trying our best to make sense of them. Now don't take offence and don't get yourself all riled up. You know I care about you. I'm not trying to scare you, but first of all, does Vickie know Dave?"

"Of course she does. What are you getting at?"

Instead of answering directly, Jack posed another question. "Did this trip come up suddenly or had it been planned for a while?"

"Actually it all came about in a very short period of time" said Cassie slowly. "What is this, Jack?"

"Who suggested that Vickie come to stay with you?" Jack shot back.

"I guess it was Dave who put the idea in my head. He said it would be an opportune time to have a visit with Vickie." Cass laughed nervously and shrugged. "Actually he almost insisted that she come. These questions don't make any sense, Jack. What are you thinking?" Her big blue eyes were troubled as she gazed into the face of this man she had once loved so intensely.

Jack had a very dead pan expression on his face, but he was watching Cassie closely. "Look, Cass, there could be two totally different things going on here. This stalker may not have anything to do with your sister's crash. Is there any chance that your husband could be trying to get rid of you, or could he be mixed up with some other woman, possibly Vickie? Or could he be trying to frighten you for some reason?"

Cass just stared at him, dumbfounded. Eyes wide with disbelief, she shook a finger at him. "Jack, you've been into the magic mushrooms, haven't you? Naughty boy! Are you thinking that this is some plot hatched up by Dave and Vickie to get rid of me so that they can be together? Boy, you've been watching too much television. Who do you think you are, Columbo?" She laughed, but it had a hollow sound, even to her ears.

Jack frowned, but didn't seem to be concerned with her disbelief. "Cass, I've been in this business a long time, and I've seen some unbelievable shit. Look at it this way, and bear with me for a moment. Your husband suddenly announces that he has to be out of the country for several weeks. It all comes up out of the blue. He doesn't want you to go with him even though I think you really wanted to, but he does want you to invite Vickie to come and stay. As soon as she arrives you start getting threatening phone calls — all of which Vickie answers, and someone is stalking you. Your husband is safely thousands of miles away, so he's got a perfect alibi if anything should happen to you, and who would suspect your dearest and most long-time friend of anything? I'm not saying that's what's happening, but I am saying that we have to look at every angle, and there seem to be a lot of coincidences here. I'm sure you know that detectives hate coincidences," he added with a wry grin.

Cass was momentarily silent. She just sat there shaking her head in disbelief.

"Come on, Cass. You're not stupid. In fact I remember just how smart you are. It's a detective's job to be suspicious. Sure I'm wondering about Vickie. I just don't completely trust her. I'm suspicious of your husband. What the hell is he doing in Europe for an extended time without you? I'm even a bit suspicious of you. You could be making this up to get attention. Get the picture? I have to think of different scenarios and try to make them fit." He raised his hands in a gesture which seemed to say "what can I do? This is just the way it is."

He was being very matter of fact, but looking into his eyes, Cassie could see that he was upset. He wanted her to consider the possibilities without getting mad at him for suggesting them. He was really serious! After all these years she could still tell so much about him just by gazing into those gorgeous blue eyes. He was frowning at her now and waiting for her reaction.

Cass didn't know just how she felt. This was the craziest thing she had ever heard, yet somehow there was a weird semblance of truth to it. Could Dave possibly be capable of anything so nefarious? No, absolutely not. She knew him inside and out, and he loved her. There was no doubt of that. Granted, he was a bit of a party animal, ready to boogie at the drop of a hat, but he certainly wasn't a womanizer. Although he could be stubborn and a bit selfish, he had a gentle, caring, insightful side which was perfect for Cassie's more abrupt, and judgemental nature. They were a perfect duo. No way was he interested in Vickie. Still, many a wife thought her marriage was secure, and then found to her dismay that her loving husband had fallen for her best friend.

She knew Vickie almost as well as she knew Dave, and Vickie loved her. She would stake her life on it. They were pals, bosom buddies, kindred spirits. And yet there was something about Jack that was absolutely hypnotizing. He could always convince her of just about anything. Was she stupid, naïve, childlike in her trust of Dave and Vickie? Poisonous doubts started flying around in her mind like clots of pollution. She and Dave had had an argument just before he left. What had it been about? She couldn't remember now. It wasn't anything important though, was it? Oh God, she was so confused. Could Jack be right? Had she lost track of Dave and of their relationship? Could he and Vicky possibly be in some kind of weird satanic partnership trying to get rid of her or to scare her? She wanted to run, to get out of here and think things through, yet she needed to stay and ask Jack more questions. She was momentarily paralyzed with indecision.

"Jack, I understand your concern, and I really do appreciate the fact that you're working hard to get to the bottom of all these happenings, but, you are way off base. Dave is a darling, and our marriage is solid. You have to take my word for it. I'd know if he was tired of me, or if he was having an affair. And as for Vickie, well, she's a loyal, true friend. I trust her completely. She's as upset about all this as I am, and I know she's not faking it. I'm sure that whoever is stalking us and making all these ridiculous calls is somehow connected with Pru's accident. They're amateurs, and they're afraid that Vickie and I might get too close to the truth. That's all it is, I'm sure of it."

She was speaking quickly, and running her fingers through the back of her hair in an agitated way. She had to stay cool. Jack was aware of her discomfort, and he grasped both of her hands in his. "Cass, it's okay. Everything's going to be fine. We just have to cover all the bases. I'm sure that your husband is a great guy, but we have to be certain. I can't let anything happen to you now that I've found you again. Please don't say a word about any of this to Vickie, — just in case." he added hastily as she began to protest, "You can just tell her that the entire luncheon was a ploy to seduce you." He said this with a sly grin as he waggled his eyebrows and made her laugh in spite of herself.

"Oh Jack, you're crazy." Still, she kept hearing him say "now that I've found you again." What did he mean by that? They were both married to different people, had different lives. This was a relationship with absolutely no future. Sipping on her wine, and in an effort to change the subject, she said, "Tell me about your wife. What's she like? Do you have any children?"

Jack seemed surprised at the non sequitur, but he realized what Cassie was doing. She was putting all his suggestions and questions to the back of her mind until she could get home and study them. He knew her so well.

"My wife's name is Darla, and she's beautiful. I'm lucky to have her. She's ten years younger than I am, and at this point we still have no kids. We're trying though, and I'm sure it won't be long. We've only been married a few years so we're way behind you."

Cassie seemed to be listening intently, but part of her mind was still dealing with the possibility of Dave and Vickie having an affair. What an obscene idea! It seemed too ludicrous to give it any credence, yet, Jack had planted the evil seed and now she couldn't ignore it. She had to get away by herself and sort things out before the seed grew into an ugly weed.

More small talk ensued. It seemed that neither one was eager to make the first move toward leaving. Finally Jack leaned over the table and said, "Cass, I have to say this, and then we'll forget it forever. I loved you more than you'll ever know, and in some strange way I still do. You were my first and only love for a long time, and you'll always have a corner of my heart. I can't let anything happen to you. You and Vickie have got to be careful, and you must stay out of this. No amateur sleuthing is allowed! Don't let Vickie talk you into anything. Leave it to the professionals, please. We may seem slow, but we'll get it sorted out. We'll catch Willy, and we'll catch whoever is stalking you. The Toronto police are on top of the crash and they'll find the murderer. So — you and Vickie just relax and enjoy yourselves, but stay on guard. I know you trust her totally, but don't put yourself in a vulnerable position. Promise?"

Cass didn't really know what to say. She still held Jack in one part of her heart, and hoped that they could be friends forever, but she wasn't about to promise to keep her nose out of things. Crossing her ankles, she gave him her sweetest smile and said that she and Vickie would try to wait for the police to solve everything. She knew Jack didn't really believe her, but it was the best she could do.

They eventually finished their coffee and said their good-byes. He enfolded her in his arms and apologized for the questions he had asked. For one giddy moment she thought he was going to kiss her. She felt as if she could have stood there forever in the safety of his embrace, but she pulled herself free. She had the life she wanted, it was secure, steady, easy. She wasn't about to rock the boat, yet she felt that at this moment in time, her boat was indeed rocking perilously. Pulling herself together, she thanked him for lunch and headed to her car. She felt shaky, as if she had just come out of the pool on a cloudy, windy day.

All the way home her thoughts flew like dust particles. Jack was way off base with his silly scenario about Dave and Vickie, and about Dave trying to get rid of her. They certainly weren't singing from the same page on this one. Her emotions were mixed. She felt angry and hurt at his insinuations, and yet she realized and appreciated that he was only trying to protect her. She wished fervently, however, that he had never made such far out suggestions. They would haunt her now till she could prove him wrong.

What was the matter with her anyway? A couple of questions from Jack and she was suddenly doubting her husband and her friend. How could she be so unstable? He could still yank all her chains, push all her buttons, flip all her switches. Why had she loved him so? He was handsome and intelligent, with a gentle side, a side few people ever saw. He was vulnerable and had a little boy quality which had always made her weak and crazy. He was also self-absorbed, and very opinionated. For Jack things had always been black or white. You were either the good guy or the bad guy. She shook her head in frustration as she pulled into the driveway. All she wanted right now was to put her arms around Dave and hug him forever.

Facing Vickie was her next task, and she forced herself to grin at her friend as she entered the house. Vickie knew immediately that something was wrong, but she also intuited that Cass didn't want to talk just now. Part of a good friendship was knowing what not to say and when not to say it, so Vickie went out to the back garden and began vigorously watering the flowers. She felt sure that Jack had tried to rekindle the old romance, and that Cass was upset and confused about it. It had to be that, what else could it possibly be? Well, she would bide her time and get the story out of Cassie tonight after she'd had a couple of glasses of wine. Cass was so open, so uncomplicated. Vickie would soon find out what was going on, and what crazy ideas Jack had been putting in her head. She had a feeling that Jack was trouble, and she didn't know what to do about it.

CHAPTER 25

▼

Their next trip to Toronto was uneventful. As they walked down the long hospital corridor, they noticed how jammed the hall was with wheel chairs, gurneys, and people rushing around. This, of course, was a teaching hospital, and there were a lot of young med students and interns zipping in and out of rooms. This hospital, this microcosm was a strange place. It was one location where virtually nobody wanted to be, except, of course, the really dedicated doctors and nurses, and there were far too few of them.

Walking slowly and somewhat reluctantly down the hall, the friends pondered the dedication, integrity, and endurance it must take to do this job. They suspected that most of the staff viewed it as just a job, no better and no worse than most. Likely on a hot day like this they all longed to be at the beach, or soaking up the sun at their cottages, or shopping in a cool mall. Instead they were here, up to their elbows in broken bones, blood and puke. What a life! The further away from a hospital she could get, the happier Cass was, and she knew that Vickie felt pretty much the same.

On their way past the nursing station, a nurse stopped them. "Mrs. Meredith, you should know that your sister has had a bit of a relapse. It's nothing serious, she was just recovering too quickly and trying to do too much. She's had a couple of bad nights, and she took a little fall yesterday, so she's quite sedated today. She likely won't be able to talk coherently with you."

"Well isn't that just perfect," said Cass dejectedly. She had still not seen her sister awake. How many times had she been here? She didn't even know whether Pru would want to see her, but she felt a guilty obligation to make the effort. Now it appeared that her effort today was useless. Damnation. They'd made that long trip in vain. What a waste of time and gas and energy. She and Vickie could have been doing a thousand other things much more fun. Why hadn't they called first? What a pair of dummies.

Cass had been a bit nervous on the way in, wondering whether Jenny or Jordan would be here. She didn't really want to come face to face with them, although there was nothing they could do to her right here in the hospital. Still, she wished she and Vickie had never said those stupid things at the funeral. She was leery of meeting Elena too. She just had nothing much to say to her. "Shoot, I wish we'd stayed home" she muttered to Vickie as they proceeded down the hall.

Cass looked very attractive in a long turquoise skirt of nubby cotton with matching top. Her only jewellery was a gold locket on a heavy chain, a gift from David many years ago. With her reddish gold hair, big blue eyes, and long legs, she was a good looking woman. She had the lithe, graceful stride of a dancer. Cass knew that her sister had always dressed like a million dollars — more like twenty million actually, and she had wanted to look her best this morning. Vickie had also got herself all "bedoodled up" as she said, in her best mauve pantsuit.

They parted at the waiting room which was becoming all too familiar to Vickie. Upon entering Pru's room, Cass was relieved that there were no other visitors. Approaching the bed, she saw that her sister appeared to be sleeping. So what else is new, she thought crossly. Damn, I've come all this way for nothing.

"I'm here Pru" she whispered, taking one thin hand gently in hers. The other one was still encased in a cast. She wondered idly why people seem to whisper in hospitals. We must all be afraid that the grim reaper will notice we're here, and sneak up on us. She grinned a bit nervously at this ghoulish thought.

Prudence seemed to have good colour in her face. It was not that putty-grey it had been on the first visit. She opened her eyes, focused on Cassandra for a moment, then tried to wet her lips. "Cassie" she croaked, "I'm so glad you've come, but I'm so tired. I have to tell you that things are all mixed up and you need to know the truth — " here she began to cough and gurgle.

"Don't talk, Pru. I'll just sit here for a while" soothed Cassie.

Prudence attempted to sit up, but then sighed and closed her eyes.

Just then an aide waddled in at a snail's pace, carrying a jug of ice water. She slammed it down on the bedside table, removed the old one, and waddled out with a sour look on her moon face.

"Obviously she'd rather be on a desert island with Mel Gibson" Cass muttered to her sister. As she sat gently holding Pru's hand, she began taking stock of the room. She hadn't paid much attention to it on her previous quick visits. It was far superior to any other hospital rooms she had ever seen. It looked like a room for the rich and famous. Some grateful family had furnished and dedicated it in memory of a loved one. There was a small brass plaque attesting to this. A comfortable looking chair sat on one side of the bed, and on the other side was a pretty little rocker in which Cass was sitting. The curtains were light and cheery, and the room was extra large. It needed to be, just to hold all the flowers!

Cass stared in amazement at a small aquarium. She could almost feel her stress level lowering as she watched the colourful tropical fish swimming in desultory fashion. It was delightful and peaceful. What a fantastic idea for a hospital room. She wondered though, who cleaned it and fed the fish. She was sure that it wouldn't be the overworked nurses.

There were, of course, the usual utilitarian accoutrements of a hospital room, but the extra touches took away the starkness. The room was la crème de la crème — no doubt about it. Someone with megabucks had furnished this place!

Letting go of Pru's hand, Cass turned to admire a Robert Bateman print on the east wall. It depicted a male ruby-throated hummingbird proudly perched on a branch. It was done in restful shades of green, with the only colour relief the brilliant ruby throat, and greyish white chest. It was a quiet, soothing painting, very suitable for a hospital room.

A second painting on the wall directly opposite the bed made Cassie gasp, however. It was the famous "Persistence of Memory" by Salvadore Dali. Any patient looking at it would think they were hallucinating, or at the very least, having a dizzy spell. Obviously someone had a sense of humour, or maybe a sadistic streak, she thought glumly, as she studied the three weird melting clocks plus the insanely oversized pocket watch crawling with ants. What a macabre choice for a sick room!

As she sat gazing around at the surroundings, she was vaguely aware of the occasional squeaking of nurses' shoes coming down the hall. There was the ever present clanging of the metal gurneys, and she could even hear the sighing sound of the elevator doors sliding open and closed. How did anyone manage to sleep here without the aid of a pill or a shot, she wondered.

The intrusive loudspeaker was blaring out a call for a Dr. Navinsky, and Prudence stirred restlessly, finally opening her eyes. In a croaking voice she began, "Cassie, I have to tell you, it was no accident, the brakes were gone." Another coughing spell interrupted her. Cass gave her some water with a straw, and Pru continued. "Someone tampered with the car and I know — " but here she began coughing again.

Cass was dismayed at how bad her sister looked, and how groggy she seemed. Her words were slow and somewhat slurred.

"Pru, don't tire yourself. Just relax, there'll be plenty of time for talking."

"No, I've got to tell you" Prudence whispered with a frown and a sense of urgency. Taking a big breath and trying to focus, she tried again. "Please, Cass, listen. I'm all doped up and I can't think clearly, but I know that someone killed Matt and tried to kill me. It was no accident. There's something else too, but it's so complicated. I don't know where to start. It's a secret, but you have to know now. I'm too confused today to explain it all. You have to come back when I'm awake — please." Here Pru sighed and took a sobbing breath.

Just then Bunny Connors bounced in. "Well, look who's awake" she crowed. "Don't you know you're supposed to be sleeping? Be a good girl now and no more talking. I've got something to help you sleep."

If she hadn't been so upset, Cassie would have laughed. Why were nurses either overly officious and intimidating, or they treated all patients of any age as witless children?

Prudence seemed very agitated now, and stared at Cassie helplessly, as if begging her to do something.

Cassie didn't want to talk in front of the nurse, but she had to ask Pru some questions. Did she know who had tampered with the brakes? What was the secret? What could Cass do to help? As these questions whirled around in her head, she watched in dismay as Bunny took a hypodermic from the tray and held it up, squirting a tiny bit to get rid of any air bubbles.

Pru tried weakly to push Bunny's hand away. "Not yet" she pleaded. Then looking at Cass in desperation, "Please come back soon, Cass. We've got to straighten all this out. You need to know, but I don't know where to start, and my mind is all cloudy. I'm so tired." Her voice trailed off.

Cassie touched Bunny's arm. "Please just give us a few minutes alone. It's very important" she begged, "and she doesn't need any more sedative. Look at her, she's almost comatose. Please, let us talk."

"No can do" said Bunny, plunging the hypo into Pru's arm. "She had a very bad night. She got out of bed and fell, and now she needs her sleep. It's just a little setback, she's been doing so well. You just came on a bad day. She needs more rest than she's been getting. She'll be in la-la-land for a few hours now. You can come back tomorrow" she said cheerfully as she swept out the door. She hadn't wasted her dimples on these two. Mrs. Wainwright looked too groggy, and her sister looked too cross.

Cass stayed with Pru for a few minutes, but it was futile. The shot had knocked her out very quickly. Reluctantly she picked up her purse, and with one last glance at her sister, she left the room. She was angry and frustrated as she strode down the hall. There was no way she was coming back to this madhouse until Pru was sitting up, walking around and talking coherently. The intercom was now braying out a code blue for some unfortunate soul, and she saw nurses rushing into a room with a crash cart.

After a quick lunch, they ambled back to the hospital. Cass had little hope that Pru would be awake by now, but she had to try. She was so curious as to what her sister had wanted to tell her. She could cheerfully have wrung Bunny's pretty neck.

The two friends spent some time in the hospital gift shop which was run by the "pink ladies" — volunteers from the community wearing pretty pink smocks. They were just killing time, waiting for Pru to waken.

"I know they're overdosing her, Vic" complained Cassie. "She didn't need another shot, she was so groggy she could hardly talk. It doesn't make sense. And what the hell is this secret she's talking about? It's driving me crazy."

Finally they made their way back up to room 707. This time Victoria chose to go in with Cassie. She had read all the stale magazines in the boring waiting room, and she was now very interested in seeing Prudence and in hearing what she had to say. If it was some big family secret she would leave them to talk privately. She was hoping, however, that Pru was going to tell them who had cut the brakes.

Cassie warned her that the room smelled like a funeral parlour, and it was no exaggeration. There were baskets and vases of flowers everywhere. It was really obscene. Obviously Prudence had many friends and admirers, but the effect was unfortunate. The cloying sweet perfume was too pervasive. Cass felt like Dorothy in the field of poppies. It was hypnotic. No wonder Pru was so groggy. Maybe she could get the nurses to remove some of the arrangements and share them with other patients. Maybe they could open a window.

They had stopped first at the nursing station, and Cassie asked whether Jordan and Jenny had been visiting Pru regularly. She hated the idea of her sister lying there with no visitors while she was home in Niagara Falls.

The nurse's lips tightened into a disapproving line. "They've been in a few times" was the terse reply. "Apparently they have more pressing business up north at their cottage," she frowned. Then with a smile she added "The brother-in-law, Mr. Blake Wainwright has been in almost every day. He slips in and out quite often. What a nice man. And, of course, Mrs. Santa Cruz comes too."

This nurse, Susan Carmody, certainly seemed to be keeping track of all Pru's visitors. That was probably a good idea. Cass and Vickie were surprised to hear that Blake was visiting every day. Whatever for? Had he and Pru been much closer than anyone knew, or was he just being nice to his brother's widow?

Although they sat hopefully at Pru's bedside for another hour, she made no sign of wakening. Finally Cassie sighed in exasperation. "We might as well go. She's not going to waken up today. Damn, I'd like to punch that little twitzy nurse right in her dimples! It's ridiculous, but now I feel as if I'm abandoning her. She actually seemed glad to see me. I wonder what she wanted to tell me?"

"I'm sure that whatever it was, it will keep. Next time we come, she'll certainly be alert and coherent, and we'll definitely call first" As the two friends made their way to the car, and headed back to Niagara Falls, they wondered whether things would ever get sorted out.

CHAPTER 26

▼

Pete Hoblonski had been doing some sober, objective planning. Marriage was certainly a last resort, but visions of his name in large letters on that Florida marina of his dreams, fuelled his desperation. Marriage was his only guarantee of success. He was taking Jen out that very night to wine her, dine her, and propose. He choked on the very word, but he knew that women fell for all that phony baloney, and he was becoming restless and determined. He just wanted out of his "going nowhere" life, and Jenny was his ticket.

He reflected gloomily that she was an awful screwball, but he felt he could handle her. Shit, business was business, and he needed Jen. They had made up after the bad way he had treated her, and he had gone to her father's funeral with her. Jenny had been glad to make up with Pete for her own reasons. He was easy to lead around, he was fun most of the time, and most of all, she needed him now for Plan B.

For this special dinner date on which Pete planned to ask Jenny to marry him, and on which Jenny planned to wind Pete tightly around her little finger, she wore her favourite black mini dress with no back and a plunging neckline. She wore beautiful diamond earrings — a gift from her mother — and no other jewellery. She didn't want anything to detract from her blond curls and curvaceous body. Her four inch spiked sandals added an extra dimension. Every man in the place envied Pete as Jenny waltzed in twenty minutes late. Pete was so relieved to see her that he forgot to be angry.

He tried to be his most charming at dinner. It was difficult because Pete was not a charming person. Nevertheless he made the effort, and after swilling a few gin and tonics, Jenny gaily agreed to go with him in the morning to obtain a marriage license at City Hall. Pete was playing right into her hands perfectly. The poor fool thought he was orchestrating things, but drunk or sober, Jenny knew exactly what she was doing.

"We should have Aunt Cassie at the reception" she pleaded, looking at him in a forlorn sort of way, "and of course her friend Vickie. We should have Elena too I guess, since my mother can't be there." This last was said with a pathetic little catch in her voice. Actually she wanted Cassie and Vickie there to keep an eye on them, and to find out whether the two women still seemed interested in the crash and in who or what had caused it.

"Sure, babe" a magnanimous Pete agreed. He was getting caught up in the excitement now too. Those millions were almost within reach. Jenny had never appeared that close to her mother, but if she wanted Cassie and Elena as replacements, that was okay with Pete. "We'll invite your Uncle Blake and Gloria and that daughter of theirs too." Here Pete stopped as he recalled that Lindsay was quite a fox. He had to stay focused though, no time for thinking about foxy babes. A quick and legal marriage was his main purpose now. He mustn't do anything to queer the deal.

Jenny giggled to herself. Being married to Pete would serve her purposes very well right now. It was her first marriage, but undoubtedly it would not be her last. Pete was just a necessary cog in the big wheel of life, she thought philosophically. Besides, it would open Jordan's eyes and show him that she wasn't pining away for him — the creep.

Next morning Jenny made a quick and stressful trip to the hospital. She owed her mother the courtesy of telling her about the impending wedding, but she dreaded it. She knew exactly what her mother would think about it. She would probably have a relapse from shock.

As Jenny suspected, Prudence was not amused. "You are what?" she moaned at her daughter in disbelief, raising her head from the pillow. "Jen are you drunk?"

"No I'm not drunk" replied Jenny, seemingly offended at the suggestion. "Pete's a laugh and we have fun together."

"Oh, Jen, that's not the basis for a marriage. Besides, your father has just been buried. Have you no respect, no consideration? Imagine what people will think."

"Why should I care?" cried Jenny defensively. "He never forgave me for running away. He never even understood that he was the one who drove me away. He never loved me anyway."

"Oh child, you are so wrong" wept Pru. "He loved you dearly, and you broke his heart. He certainly didn't like or trust this Pete character. He's just after your money — you must be smart enough to know that."

"What money?" Jenny asked innocently. "I have no money as you well know. Anyway, it's too late now. Pete and I are getting married in three days, and there's nothing you can do about it. Sorry you can't be there, but we just don't want to wait."

Her mother was openly crying now, and reaching for a tissue to blow her nose. Jenny grabbed the opportunity. "Look, I have to go. I'll talk to you in a few days. Maybe you'll feel better then." In an uncharacteristically gentle gesture, she kissed her mother on the forehead, patted her hand, and ran like hell. She couldn't get away fast enough.

Prudence turned her face to the wall and wept as though she would never stop. "Matt," she cried, "where are you when I need you so?"

The three days passed quickly, and for this first wedding — that was how Jenny thought of it — she chose a long white cotton dress, high necked, short sleeved. It was demure and virginal — just the look she wanted. With daisies in her hair, and carrying yellow roses to match her yellow curls, she looked sweet and innocent, and very young. She was neither sweet nor innocent, but nobody knew that.

Jenny had managed to keep her wild past fairly secret. Certainly her Aunt Cass who was too damned nosy, would never know that she was anything but what she appeared. Uncle Blake and Gloria and Lindsay probably didn't know either. She always felt ill at ease around her cousin Lindsay. She was just too good looking, too smart, and definitely too goody-goody. She was going to be a doctor for heaven's sake! Blah! Jenny didn't know just what to make of Elena yet. She was an unknown factor in this family equation.

Jenny had treated herself to a few sips of vodka, well, quite a few actually, just to calm herself. Vodka was good because you couldn't smell it the way you could with gin. Besides, it made her feel all warm and safe. It should be Jordan standing beside her today, she thought sadly, but she would be like Scarlett, and think about that tomorrow.

They had obtained the marriage license from an uninterested woman with a glossy beehive hairdo which had been popular back in the dark ages. Although it was something of an engineering marvel, it seemed on the verge of disintegration. Pete had objected to the $75.00 fee, but calmed himself by thinking that he would soon be rolling in the green stuff. Jenny's mother couldn't last much longer, she had been so badly hurt, and then it would be party time.

The wedding was at City Hall with just two clerks as witnesses. It was going to be a great reception though. Jenny seemed to have invited a lot of her parent's friends, but strangely, neither Pete nor Jenny had any friends of their own to invite.

"You may now kiss your bride" smiled the benign justice of the peace, patting Jenny on the arm. He was quite taken with this little brown-eyed doll, and would have liked to pat her on the fanny, but he wasn't about to risk anything with the big blond galoot standing there.

Jenny was in a teary hung-over daze as Pete gave her a big kiss. She kept thinking that it should be her beloved Jordan standing beside her instead of this moron. Then she remembered that she was supposed to hate Jordan now, and she gave her new husband a sweet smile.

Meanwhile Cassie and Victoria were once more heading to Toronto for the reception. "I could travel this route blindfolded" thought Vickie a bit sourly, as they sped along. They had both been absolutely stunned to hear that Jenny was marrying the tattooed wonder. "It seems so uncaring" complained Cass. "Her father's just been buried, her mother's in the hospital, and she's racing into marriage with Bozo the Clown. What's wrong with that girl? I'd rather stick needles in my eyes than marry that idiot."

Vickie was really intrigued with this strange family. She had the advantage of distance, after all they weren't her relatives — thank goodness! She wondered for the millionth time how Cass had turned out to be such a relatively normal person.

Cass was thinking that this wedding had come at an opportune time in one respect. It would help take their minds off the would-be rapist. Where the heck was he, and why hadn't the police caught him by now? They claimed that they knew who he was, so it should have been easy to find him. It galled them to think that the malodorous swamp creature was still running loose, maybe attacking some other poor unsuspecting victim.

Some time later, Vickie was looking around at the gathering. She thought it was strange that so recently they had been here munching tiny sandwiches and supposedly mourning Matt's death, and now they were here celebrating a wedding. Except, aside from Pete, no one seemed to be very celebratory. The rate at which Jenny was consuming champagne seemed more like desperation than celebration.

The small group gradually made their way out through the French doors and under the latticed archway covered with pink and white roses. The garden was ablaze with colours from the flowers, balloons and streamers. The linen covered tables were laden with delectable food. There were heavy silver trays loaded with tiny hot sausage rolls, bite-size cheese puffs, crackers with salmon paté, tiny sandwiches and platters of shrimp. Magnums of champagne were chilling in silver ice buckets, and on the bridal table sat a four tiered wedding cake. Gloria and the caterers had done a magnificent job on such short notice.

Pete glowed proudly. This was some fancy wedding reception. Then an awful thought struck him. Who was going to pay for all this fancy stuff? He certainly couldn't or wouldn't, he thought belligerently. What had he got himself into here? What if Jenny didn't inherit any money? Suddenly Pete felt like a drowning man who sees that the shore is too far away.

It was certainly a perfect day for a wedding reception, but Jenny didn't appreciate it. She was desperately trying not to look at Jordan and his date — more like Jordan and his baby-bimbo, she thought sourly. How could he have ruined her wedding reception by bringing that young girl?

The young girl in question was attractive, no doubt about it, but she looked to be about fourteen. Where had he found her? Her lustrous mane of blue-black hair cascaded down her back. Her lipstick was too red, her black skirt too short, her peekaboo red blouse was too damn peekaboo, and her black boot-encased legs were too damn long. She looked cheap and somehow pathetic — a little girl playing dress-up — but every man in the place was eyeing her. Even Uncle Blake was having a good look.

Jenny was seething. She knew Jordan so well. She knew that he had brought this kid just to spite her — to keep her from being the centre of attention on her own wedding day. Even Pete was making goo goo eyes at her. She thought how sorry Jordan was going to be as Plan B unfolded. He would never know what he had missed by scorning her so cruelly.

In contrast to Jordan's luscious "jail bate", Jenny looked like a wispy angel with her white dress and yellow curls. She played the part perfectly. No one could have guessed the many schemes floating around in her pretty golden head. She was just waiting for the right moment for plan B to start unfolding.

As Vickie and Cassie circulated amongst the guests, they stopped to speak to Gloria and Lindsay who were standing by the food table. They congratulated Gloria on the wonderful job she had done, and then met Lindsay's date, a gorgeous hunk of a fellow named Jonathan, who looked like the Marlboro man without the cigarette. He was teasing Lindsay.

"I never thought I'd be dating a mechanic" he laughed, "and such a beautiful one into the bargain."

Lindsay and Gloria laughed too. "Honestly, we've had such fun taking that course" said Gloria with a grin.

"But whatever prompted it?" asked Lindsay's friend.

"Well, Blake plans to buy a car for Lindsay for university, and he just felt that she should know enough about cars so that some smart-ass mechanic can't rip her off. You know what some of them are like with women. So, I decided that I would go too to keep her company, and we enrolled in the community college mechanic's course." Here Gloria reached over to help herself to a tiny sausage roll.

"And" continued Lindsay proudly, "we both passed, but Mom was top of the class. She's a natural. We can fix a car now as well as anyone, well, maybe not that well, but we are pretty good."

Cassandra and Victoria looked at each other, eyebrows raised. Now Gloria and Lindsay would have to be added to the list of possible perpetrators. This was getting complicated, there were just too many suspects.

This wedding reception was so strange. There seemed to be a forced gaiety mostly brought on by the champagne. Jenny looked desperately sad, or maybe angry, as she kept her eyes on Jordan and his date. Pete was drinking way too much and trying to flirt with Lindsay. Cassie kept thinking of her sister in the hospital, and how she would have hated this whole farce. Poor Pru. She had lost her husband to death, now she was losing her daughter to this tattooed Neanderthal, possibly a fate worse than death! How would it all end? Who had killed Matt and started this odious snowball rolling?

To her great amusement, Vickie noticed that Pete had removed his shirt, and was demonstrating to Lindsay how his boats floated and moved on the tattooed waves as he flexed his muscles. His gauche behaviour was offensive. Lindsay looked embarrassed, and Jenny looked at Pete as if he was something stuck to the bottom of her shoe. He was making a fool of himself, and Jordan was putting his arm around the bimbo in an intimate way. Jenny was seething, and she realized the time had almost come.

As soon as she had finished cutting the wedding cake, and had jammed a piece of it into Pete's mouth with a little too much enthusiasm, she walked over to Jordan and began to wail. "Oh Jordan, how could you? How could you have done it? I wanted my mom and dad here at my wedding. Why did you have to kill them? No amount of money was worth that. Dad is dead, and Mother is going to die too, I know she is, and you did it, you loathsome creature. You did something to cause that crash and I'll never forgive you. I can't keep any more secrets for you. You have to pay for what you've done. Our parents should have been here on my wedding day" she sobbed. Little Jenny was just getting warmed up. She could hardly keep from laughing at the bewildered look on Jordan's face. His date looked scared.

Jordan appeared to be paralysed. He was absolutely dumbfounded. Everyone was looking at him, and there was total silence. He stared at her in disbelief. Then, seeming to regain a semblance of control, he took a big breath and reached out his hands to her in a placating fashion. "Jenny, little sister, you've had too much to drink again. Remember what the doctor told you about all this excessive drinking. Let me take you inside and you can lie down."

"No, don't touch me, you murderer. You're a killer. I know you did it. I have proof" she wailed. "They'd both be here today if it wasn't for you and your greed."

Pete tried to calm her, but she shrugged him off too. Jenny loved an audience, and she had one now. This was going even better than she had hoped. She had the attention of every single person in that garden. They were all standing around in embarrassed and confused silence. No one was paying attention to Jordan's date now, she realized with satisfaction. She had really got back at Jordan for his cruelty, and this was only the beginning.

After she finally allowed herself to be led inside by Pete and Gloria, a pall seemed to settle over the guests. No one knew what to say, or where to look. Gradually they all drifted away, and the reception was over. Jenny had won this round.

CHAPTER 27

▼

As Cass and Victoria said their good-byes and headed for the car, they looked at each other and shook their heads in disbelief. What a mess! Thank God poor Pru hadn't been there. They couldn't decide whether Jenny was sincere or whether she had staged the entire production. She certainly had blind-sided Jordan. He looked like a man whose legs had been kicked out from under him. Cass was intrigued, and Vickie thought she hadn't had so much fun and excitement in years.

Everything was happening so fast. Pru was in hospital, Matt was in his grave, Jenny had just leaped off the precipice into some kind of marital maelstrom. Was she clever and devious or was she just crazy? There was no way she could actually love that tattooed twit. And then there was Jordan. Had he really caused the crash, or was Jenny trying to take the heat off herself?

Cass could barely wait to get into the car to tell her friend the latest. "Vic, I overheard Blake asking Jordan to come over to his home tonight, and Jordan agreed. I'm sure he'll go, because he'll need to convince everyone that Jenny was either drunk or hallucinating. He'll be doing damage control. That means the house will be empty!" She rolled her eyes mischievously and grinned. "We could get in and look around. Maybe we'll find the will, or, I don't know, maybe he's got books on car mechanics with a bookmark on the page telling how to cut the brakes." She laughed "This is the chance we've been waiting for."

When Vickie didn't respond right away, Cass urged, "Come on, Vic. You know it's a great opportunity."

"You're right, Sherlock, but how will we get in? Can you pick a lock?"

"Probably not, but we can give it a try. Anyway, maybe all the doors won't be locked, or we could get lucky and find a window open."

Vickie sighed and shook her head doubtfully. "This is one of your dumbest ideas, but I guess we could give it a try."

As they put in the time till Jordan left the house, Cassie exclaimed, "Great, there's the chip wagon. Come on Vic, I'll treat you. I didn't eat much at the reception, and I'm starved."

"Cass, I can't. French fries are just cholesterol and fat disguised as a delectable, mouth-watering enticement. My gluteus maximus is expanding just thinking about them."

Patting her friend on the derrière, Cass laughed, "Your gluteus maximus is just fine. I really need some fries. Don't you remember those wonderful little cone-shaped holders of chips we used to get at Bell Park? We'd load them with salt and vinegar and then stroll around looking at the guys and hoping that the guys were looking at us."

"I remember" sighed Vickie. "Were we ever really that young and that thin?"

"It's so darn long ago I can't remember. Come on now, it's time for our daily fat fix. We'll live on bread and water tomorrow." Cassie grabbed her friend by the elbow and propelled her across the street to the chip wagon.

Later, as they drove back to Rosedale, they felt guiltily full. "Those chips were marvellous" said Vickie, closing her eyes and stretching. "I just hope we don't fall asleep now while we wait for Jordan to leave."

They sat quietly, each thinking of things which could go wrong with this little break-in. They should probably be heading right back to Niagara, but this was a golden opportunity. They parked as far down the street as they could, and still be able to see the big house. It was so beautiful with its columned portico and circular driveway. It was old Rosedale at its finest. They knew Jordan would have to turn right to go to Blake's house, so they parked down the street to the left.

Just as they had convinced themselves that maybe it wasn't such a good idea, Jordan's car came driving out and turned right. They both experienced such an adrenalin rush that they could barely swallow.

Suddenly Vickie asked glumly, "Cass, is my face green?"

"No more than usual" grinned her friend. "Why"?

"Because I feel absolutely sick with fear. I don't think we're doing the right thing here. What if he comes home and catches us?"

"No way. We'll be in and out in just a few minutes" Cass didn't feel nearly as confident as she tried to sound. "Come on, let's go. We can't turn back now."

Gaining entrance seemed almost too easy. There was a small pantry window on the back wall sitting open about six inches. After pushing it up as high as it would go, Cassie wormed her way in. She wished that she was wearing her jeans instead of her wedding finery. She hurried across the kitchen and opened the back door for Vickie. She was relieved that her friend hadn't retreated to the car, leaving her alone in the big, empty house.

They had purchased flashlights once they made up their minds to break in. Neither wanted to be alone in this cavernous place, so they worked side by side. They wondered why Pru and Matt had ever wanted to live in such a huge house. It was beautiful, though, in the dwindling light.

They started with the den which seemed the only logical downstairs room where any documents or papers might be hidden. That brought no results, so they headed up the gracious curved staircase which looked like something out of the movies. There were several bedrooms upstairs, so they knew they had to hurry to cover them all. They had no way of knowing how long Jordan would be gone.

"Who knows what we'll find upstairs" whispered Cassie. It just seemed important to whisper even though they were quite sure that they were alone. "There could be some old demented drooling family member chained to the wall."

"More likely Jordan has a stable of luscious blonds stashed in the closets" retorted Vickie. "We don't want to end up the 'victims du jour'. He might want to add us to his collections."

They finally found the bedroom which Jordan seemed to be using. It was a large corner one at the front of the house. "Well at least he's had the good grace not to move into his parent's room," muttered Cassie.

The dresser produced nothing of interest, but one of the night tables held several travel brochures for exotic places such as Greece, Brazil and Argentina.

"Looks like our friend is planning a trip. Maybe he's going to grab his inheritance and skip the country."

"Shoot, he couldn't do that until Pru dies, and I really don't think she's going to. She's getting better every day. Do you think he's really planning to kill her?"

"Who knows? Maybe he just likes looking at brochures" suggested Vickie without much conviction. "It's more likely that he would want to kill Jenny after her little performance this afternoon."

The waste basket was empty. In fact, the entire room was extremely tidy, nothing out of place, nothing lying around.

"This is one up-tight guy" remarked Vickie. "Either that, or his mother really taught him well about keeping a neat room."

"Ya" said Cassie, heading for the desk. "Would you call him anal retentive?"

"Possibly, but maybe he's just good at covering his tracks." Then as Vickie pulled some magazines out of the bottom drawer of the bedside table, she exclaimed, "Cass, look at this garbage. It's kiddie porn."

"Oh no, don't say that."

As they looked at the pictures, they felt embarrassed and sick. Cassie felt weak, then hot. Her face flushed as she stared in disbelief at the ugly, pathetic pages. This creep was her sister's son. She couldn't stand to think that she was related to such a psycho. She could feel the French fries roiling around in her stomach.

"Look, he's even written comments on some of them. He's got 'luscious' under this wee girl's picture, and what's this scrawl — it says 'juicy' with three exclamation marks. This freak is a total pervert. We should report him."

They kept staring, both fascinated and repulsed by the sickening pictures. Then, dropping the offensive magazines back into the drawer, Cass said, "Come on, let's see what else we can find. This may be disgusting, but it doesn't prove much of anything. Maybe he just gets off looking at dirty pictures."

The friends were grimly silent as they continued the search, still unsure of what they hoped to find. They simply knew that it hadn't been kiddie porn they were looking for. As they rummaged through the large desk, Cass let out a little shriek of triumph. "Yes, here's the will. Oh look, it's dated over a year ago. It must have been drawn up right after they won the lottery."

Plunking themselves down on the bed, they avidly perused the document. "Look at this. It says that Blake gets a million dollars after Pru dies," exclaimed Cass. "Jordan was right about that. It certainly gives Blake a motive, but I wonder if he even knows about it."

"Don't forget Gloria. She took that mechanic's course. She could have meddled with the brakes if she knew that Blake was going to inherit all that money."

"Well, Jordan and Jenny are the main beneficiaries, except for a lot of charities. Nothing too surprising there."

Cass went back to the desk and started rustling through the papers. Her scalp was tingling and she felt the need to hurry. "Vickie, here's an insurance policy on Matt. This could be important." She almost sat on Vickie's lap as they both tried to read the small print.

"Wow. It's for two million dollars. Oh, and it's got a double indemnity clause, only they call it 'accidental death'. Look, if Matt dies in an accidental death it pays four million."

"All that money, and they didn't even need it. Let's see who's the beneficiary. I suppose it's Pru, or is it Jordan and Jenny?"

"Here, look. It says the beneficiary is Prudence Wainwright — if living — otherwise the beneficiary is Blake Wainwright!"

"Whew, we're talking big bucks here. I wonder if Blake knew about the will and the insurance policy. If he did, it really gave him a whopper of a motive to kill them both together and make it look like an accident," cried Cassie in disappointment. "Damn, I didn't want Blake to be a suspect. You'd better add him to your list."

"You know, Cass," said Victoria slowly, trying to think things through, "really, if Jordan and Jenny knew about this will, they wouldn't have tried to kill their parents in an accident, because the four million would have gone to Blake, not them."

"True, but they still get all the rest of the money in the will. It's just that now we know that Blake had a huge motive as well as Jordan and Jenny. I guess the big question is, who knew about this insurance policy? This makes things more complicated. Who knew what and when? Do you suppose Gloria knew about the policy and she fixed the brakes? Four million in insurance plus another million in the will would be awfully tempting, especially with all those kids to get through university."

"The fact that Jordan has the policy here in the desk along with the will doesn't really tell us anything, does it? He could have gone looking for all the important documents after the crash, and they could have been a surprise to him too."

The two friends were trying to connect the dots to get a picture which would make sense, but it seemed at this point that there were just too many dots. The picture was nothing but a jumble. It was a mosaic of bits and pieces, all of which could possibly fit together to form a pattern of murder, but at this point only formed a crazed jigsaw puzzle. Nothing really seemed indicative of anything too sinister.

"Shoot, I feel like Don Quijote tilting at windmills. Are we maybe trying to fit square pegs into round holes? We're no further ahead, are we?"

As they sat there trying to make sense of the will, the insurance policy, the travel brochures and the porno pictures, they lost track of time. It was spooky sitting in the dark, using their flashlights, but it was so intriguing. Suddenly they both lifted their heads. What was that noise?

Racing to the window, Victoria moaned "Oh no, it's Jordan, he's back."

CHAPTER 28

▼

"Quick, put these papers back right where they were. I'll smooth the bed."

Panicked now, the friends raced around as quickly as they could in the dark. They were afraid to use the flashlights in case Jordan looked up at his window.

"We've got to get out now. He left by the front door, so he'll likely come in that way. Let's use the back stairs."

Thankful that they had noticed the narrow back stairs which led to the kitchen, they descended as quickly as they could with minimum use of the flashlights. Reaching the bottom, Cassie raced to open the back door. Behind her, Vickie twisted her ankle on the last step, and let out a loud groan.

"Shh" said Cass, not realizing that Vickie had hurt herself. Then, rushing back to help her, she picked up the flashlight which had dropped with a loud clatter.

Putting her arm around Vickie's waist, she pleaded with her to hurry. As they hobbled toward the open door, however, the lights suddenly snapped on, momentarily blinding them. Two hearts plummeted as they saw Jordan carefully shutting the door behind him and turning to glower at them.

He could kill us both, Cassie told herself, as she stared with loathing at this evil man. She couldn't get the dirty pictures out of her mind.

"Well, well" said Jordan in a slow, menacing drawl. "To what do I owe this dubious pleasure? Have you come looking for bodies?" He didn't move, but stood at the door like a sentinel, blocking their only avenue of escape, and slowly tossing his keys from hand to hand. He was in a foul mood after Jenny's little performance, which had really taken him by surprise.

"Oh shit, we're toast" Vickie thought.

"Come on, spit it out. What in hell are you doing here in my house?" His hostility was palpable, and Cass noticed that he was calling it 'his house,' not his mother's house. He must already be picturing her dead. It was ironic that he had used the phrase "spit it out," because right now Vickie's tongue was stuck to the roof of her mouth. She couldn't conjure up any spit if her life depended on it, and maybe it did.

Remembering that the best defence is a good offence, and since she had no reasonable answer, Cassie gulped and said, "Jordan, thank heavens you're here. Please help me get Vickie out to our car. She's twisted her ankle and it's the leg which she broke before. I'd like to get her to the hospital." She heard the frightened, squeaky voice, and realized with surprise that it was hers.

Jordan looked disbelieving as he stared first at Victoria, and then down at her feet. She managed to put on a pained expression. She hadn't twisted her ankle badly, and she had never had a broken leg, but it might be their salvation. If they could only get to the car they would be safe. They could lock themselves in and honk the horn if Jordan tried to hurt them.

"And just how did you twist your ankle?" asked Jordan in a sceptical tone.

"Jordan, please help us to the car and we'll explain everything. Take Vickie's other side." Cass wasn't going to let this bully scare her. Well, not too much, anyway.

"No, I think we'll all stay right here until you tell me what the hell is going on." Jordan's death ray look was boring into them, and the two friends were desperately trying to come up with a plausible explanation. Why hadn't they thought of this possibility ahead of time? Fine sleuths they were! They should have stayed home with the cats!

Cass suddenly had a wisp of an idea. "We called home and told our cat sitter exactly where we were going so she wouldn't worry." He wouldn't dare hurt them now if he understood that people in Niagara Falls knew they were coming here. As she was thinking this, she and Vickie were moving closer to Jordan and to the only escape route which he was so cleverly blocking.

Her second bright idea was even better. It came from a mystery book she had read. "Jordan, we were looking for Vickie's beautiful sapphire ring. She lost it here this afternoon at the reception."

I did? thought Vickie in surprise. I just wish I owned a beautiful sapphire ring. Picking up the cue, however, she quickly added, "Yes, when Cass and I were being a bit nosy this afternoon, and looking upstairs at this magnificent house, I went into the bathroom to wash my hands. I took my ring off and laid it on the counter beside the basin," continued Vickie, warming up to her story. "We heard someone coming up the stairs and we felt so embarrassed at being caught snooping. I dried my hands and raced out of there, and forgot all about my ring."

"We know we shouldn't have gone upstairs this afternoon, Jordan, and we are so sorry for being nosy," said Cassie in a placating tone. "It's just that this is my sister's home, and it's ironic that I had never seen the upstairs. Now please open the door and help us to the car."

Jordan looked from one to the other as if weighing what they had told him so far. "Well, did you find the ring?" he asked accusingly.

"No, one of the guests or the caterers must have picked it up," answered Vickie quickly. "Oh, I do feel very woozy, I think I need some air."

Jordan reluctantly started to open the door, then stopped and asked, "What are you doing with flashlights? Why didn't you have the lights on, and how the hell did you get in?"

"Jordan, please" said Cassie more forcefully. "Help us to the car and we'll explain on the way." With this she gave her friend a little shove in his direction, forcing him to step sideways. She was then able to grab the doorknob and turn it, opening the door wide.

As Jordan made a move to stop them, Vickie said plaintively, "Please, Jordan, help me. I feel faint."

He hesitantly took Vickie's other side, and slowly they made their way to the car, Vickie hanging her head low in what she hoped looked like a fainting mode.

"To answer your question, Jordan, we did have the lights on. We had just turned them off to leave when you drove up. I guess you didn't see them." Her fingers were crossed behind her back at this whopper.

"Why the flashlights?" he asked accusingly.

"Well, you see," — — Cass was totally stuck for a logical explanation, but Vickie jumped in, trying to distract Jordan. "Oh, I feel woozy" she moaned as they reached the car.

They jumped into the vehicle as quickly as possible, but Jordan grabbed the driver's door, and kept Cassie from closing it.

"You still haven't explained how you got in" he growled.

"Why, the back door was unlocked. The caterers must have left it that way," said Cassie, thanking their good sense in having closed the pantry window once they got inside. She was hoping that Jordan wouldn't have bothered checking the back door before he left by the front.

He stood staring at the two women. Their crazy explanation was somewhat plausible, and they were flaky enough to have come back looking for a ring. Was there more to it than that?

He was in a foul mood. The last thing he needed was these two nosy women sniffing around. Fortunately there was nothing in the house for them to find. He was pretty sure that they were harmless, annoying — yes, obnoxious — yes, but dangerous — no. Right now he had more important things on his mind. Jenny had become a major problem. He could no longer trust her, she was too volatile. Something had to be done, the sooner the better. He couldn't worry about these two at the moment. He just wanted them out of here.

"Are you sure you two fools aren't playing Inspector Clouseau, snooping around my house for clues to some non-existent crime? I'm surprised you're not wearing false noses." Glaring at them, he continued. "Well, I'll keep my eyes open for the ring, and in future, I suggest that you not go barging into houses without an invitation. I could have you charged with break and entry."

"Oh for goodness sakes, Jordan, lighten up. We're truly sorry for going in when you weren't there. It was inexcusable, but we were frantic about Vickie's expensive ring and we had no idea how long it would be before you got home." Cassie thought that at least that part was the truth. If they'd known he'd be back so soon they would have been long gone.

"My husband gave it to me for an anniversary," piped up Vickie sadly. "I don't know how I'll ever be able to tell him that I've lost it."

"If it's as valuable as you say, you can claim it on your insurance" he pointed out sourly.

"But that's not the same as having the ring" retorted Vickie, almost convinced now that there really was a ring. "Please, you must call us if you find it."

"Well, if you want, you can come back into the house now and we'll have a good look. I don't want you coming back again," he said ungraciously.

"Oh no, thank you Jordan, but I have to get Vickie's ankle looked at right away. She couldn't make it up those stairs again. We'll trust you to look for it." said Cassie hastily. The last thing they would ever do was go back into that house with Jordan!

Finally they managed to get the door closed and the engine started. As they backed out of the driveway, Jordan stood staring after them with a bemused expression on his face. The entire day had been a nightmare. He had never believed that Jenny would really marry that idiot, and then her histrionics at the reception had caught him off guard. He was astonished that little gullible Jen would ever do that to him. He should have let her down more gently at the cottage. Actually, he should have drowned her right then, but she had always put up with him no matter what he did, so he hadn't realized how upset his refusal would make her. She was crazy now. He had tried to laugh it off with Blake and

Gloria tonight, but he wasn't sure that he had convinced them of his innocence. And now these two ridiculous busybodies! What next?

Pulling into the first Tim Horton's they could find, the two friends stared at each other.

"How's the ankle?"

"It's fine. I barely twisted it at all, but it was great to take his mind off why we were there. I was scared to death there when he had us trapped in the kitchen."

"Me too. Do you think he believed us?"

"Who knows, but I think we were pretty convincing. Hell, even I believed us! Now I'm sad because of a non-existent sapphire ring!" Vickie shook her head and laughed giddily. Cass joined her. They laughed till tears rolled down their cheeks, and other patrons of the donut shop were staring at them. It was such a relief to be away from Jordan and that big empty house.

As they drove back to Niagara Falls, Vickie sighed. "I suppose it really was a bit of a debacle. We didn't accomplish much."

"Oh, I don't know. I think we were pretty good. At least we left Jordan totally confused. If he is guilty of anything he'll be sweating now, wondering what we were doing there and what we found. If he's innocent, which I doubt, he's just thinking that we're a couple of harmless twits looking for your ring."

"You're right I guess. We'll know more if the stalking and threatening calls continue or get worse. We really didn't find out much that's useful though, did we?"

"Hey, at least we know for certain that Blake is to inherit a million dollars from the will, and two million from the insurance policy, with the possibility of doubling that to four million if it appears to be an accident. That definitely gives him a motive, and Gloria too, but the big question is — did he even know that he was in the will or on the policy. Anyway, in retrospect, I guess we were pretty foolhardy. If Jordan is the one who tried to kill his parents, he wouldn't have hesitated to kill us if he thought we had found anything damaging."

"Yes, it was stupid. No one knew we were going there. Only the cat sitter would have missed us. People would have assumed that we just disappeared somewhere on the highway. They would probably have speculated that we had car trouble, and some highway stalker got us. No one would ever have reason to suspect Jordan."

"Oh, I'm sure that Jack would have been on it pretty fast. He knows some-one's been harassing us, so Jordan and Jenny and Pete would have been the first suspects. If Jordan had killed us, he would have hidden our car, but what would he have done with our bodies?"

"Who knows? Maybe we should just back off and leave the whole thing to the police."

They were silent for a moment, digesting this possibility, then shook their heads simultaneously. "Nah," said Vickie. "We're just as smart as they are. Let's just see what happens."

CHAPTER 29

▼

Ever since her lunch with Jack, Cass had been wrestling with the seeds of suspicion which he had planted. The question was, had he done it deliberately to be mean, to throw a little snake into her garden of Eden? She knew that was a possibility, because she remembered so well that Jack did have a jealous nature. He used to go crazy if he saw her talking or laughing with other guys. But why would he try to throw clumps of doubt on her marriage? He was happily married himself, at least he said he was. What would be the point of trying to hurt her? No, she was sure that he had no ulterior motive. He was a smart and apparently dedicated detective, and he was just covering all the angles.

The questions and various scenarios went round and round in her head, flitting and flying like twittering birds. When she went to bed at night she stared into the darkness, trying to picture Dave and Vickie together. That was ludicrous and always made her laugh. They were so different in so many ways that they just wouldn't be good together. Or would they? Opposites attract, she told herself glumly. Looking at it calmly though, when could they ever have found the time and the opportunity for an affair? And, even if by the remotest chance they had fallen in love, they wouldn't want to kill her or terrify her. They were reasonable, mature adults, and they both loved her. She couldn't be that far off in her perceptions. If they were having an affair, they would be worried about hurting her, not trying to do away with her.

Still, those seeds of doubt were determined to sprout, and had to be pulled out, one by one. In her night time fantasies Cass began to wonder whether Dave and Elena had ever met. Now that was an intriguing thought. Could those two be having an affair? Maybe the plan was for Elena to kill Matt and Pru and get her hands on some of their money, then she and Dave would get rid of Cass and live happily ever after. No, that was absurd. Dave wasn't having an affair with anyone. Damn Jack for putting such garbage in her head. Just in case, however, she began calling Dave every couple of nights, just to hear his voice and to try to determine whether he sounded different in any way. Thankfully he seemed to be the same loving, funny guy. She did have a few uneasy moments during one call, however, when he began asking a lot of questions about Vickie, how was she, what was she doing, were they getting along, etc. Was he taking an inordinate interest in her?

She finally convinced herself that they were all crazy suspicions born in the mind of an over zealous detective, and she succeeded pretty well in burying the odious thoughts.

She soon had other things to worry about. It was only two days after the "sapphire affair" when she was surprised to receive a phone call from Jordan.

"Hello Aunt Cassandra" came his sonorous but somewhat oily voice.

"Jordan?" she exclaimed in amazement. What in the world would he want? "Is something wrong? Is Pru okay?"

"Everything's fine. I just wanted to talk to you about a couple of things. Actually I'm here in Niagara, and would like to come over now. Is that suitable?"

Cass was so taken aback that she didn't know what to say. Her thoughts tumbled like clothes in a dryer. "Have you found Vickie's ring?" she asked while trying to regain her composure.

There was a moment's silence, then — "No, I'm sorry I haven't. I need to talk to you though."

Curiosity had always been Cassie's close companion. After having seen the disgusting and pitiful kiddie porn pictures in his bedroom, she had nothing but loathing for this debauched pervert, yet she recognized a golden opportunity in his call. Cass had no doubt that Jordan could be capable of murder, but she was pretty sure that even if he was the stalker, he was too clever to come to the house to kill her. He would have something more devious in mind.

"Well, certainly Jordan," she said, cautiously. "That would be fine. Let me give you directions."

"No need for that. I know where you live. I'll be there in half an hour. See you then." Abruptly the line went dead, and Cass was left holding the receiver with a startled look on her face.

How or why did Jordan know where she lived? That didn't sound good. What possible interest could he have in knowing where her home was? Well, maybe he just looked up the address and checked out a map. Then again, it did lend credence to the idea that he could be the stalker. The thought was unnerving, and she tried to remain cool as she told Vickie about the call.

"This is a great chance to talk to him," she exclaimed, hoping that Vickie wouldn't think she was nuts letting him into her home.

Vickie agreed that it was a good opportunity to find out more about the strange Jordan. Maybe he would let something slip. "Cass, don't let him know that I'm here. I'll hide with the cell phone in hand, and if I hear him getting threatening at all, I'll call 911." Her brown eyes were bright with anticipation.

"Vickie that's brilliant. If I bring him into the library, you can hide in the little powder room. Let's see whether you can hear voices clearly from there."

Vickie hurried to the bathroom and Cassie talked in the library in a normal voice.

"I can hear you, but it's a strain. What if I try the old glass to the wall trick and see if that helps?"

Cass giggled. She and Vickie had often used a glass to the ear, with the other end against the wall, when they were kids playing out their mystery stories. "I don't think we need to go quite that far" she grinned. "You can hear well enough. Just call 911 if he gets really threatening, and for goodness sakes, don't sneeze or cough!"

Before settling herself in her hiding place, Vickie raced upstairs and put on a bulky cardigan with big side pockets. She put a pair of scissors in one pocket, and grabbed the fireplace poker to keep beside her.

"Good grief, he won't stand a chance against you" laughed Cassie. "Remember, if he sounds as if he's getting violent or threatening, call 911 first before you come bounding to my rescue. I'm going to tell him that you're out, so don't make a sound."

"Don't worry, I'll be quiet" she muttered, as she settled herself in the pretty little lavender powder room. Then a worrisome thought occurred to her. From this vantage point she wouldn't be able to hear what was going on at the front door, which was down the hall and around the corner. What if Jordan had come to kill Cass? She swallowed hard as she realized that he would undoubtedly want to kill her too, if he suspected she was in the house. It would be the old "take no prisoners, leave no witnesses" scam. No doubt he would strike quickly like a hit and run artist. He could stab Cassie, or throw acid in her face, or even strangle her without Vickie hearing a thing. Then he would come looking for her. This was not a good idea, she had to warn Cassie not to open the door to him.

She jumped up quickly and reached for the doorknob. Then she heard the voices. Too late. They were already in the library! Okay, he hadn't killed Cass, and likely wasn't planning to. Slipping silently into her chair, she left the door slightly ajar. She felt like a private eye in an old 40's movie. If her family could only see her now what would they think? They saw her as calm and efficient, always well in control. She smiled at that. Her family really didn't know her at all. Sometimes she didn't know herself.

"Aunt Cassandra," intoned Jordan, in an unexpectedly friendly way. "You're looking lovely as always, and I just don't feel right calling you "aunt". You're much too young and attractive to be anyone's auntie. Please, may I just call you "Cassandra"?

Jordan was being as charming as an oil slick, and Cass wondered what he was up to. As he had followed her down the hall to the library, she felt his cold eyes boring into the back of her head. What the hell did he want? She should have let him walk ahead of her, it would have been safer.

She kept reminding herself to speak in a louder than normal voice, and wondered whether he would notice. After pouring two mugs of coffee, she settled back in her chair. As she waited for him to make the first move, she searched his face, and kept seeing the disturbing pictures of the beautiful little girls in sexual positions with grown men. It was disgusting, and she wondered how anyone could become that twisted. What early experiences had shaped this monster sitting here in her home? She couldn't imagine Pru's pain at adopting a beautiful little boy and having him turn out like this. It boggled the mind and bruised the senses. Perhaps it wasn't his fault that he was such a pervert, but she couldn't find any compassion in her heart for him, and she wasn't about to try.

He started with compliments about the small library in which they were sitting, then quickly changed the subject. "Cassandra, I must apologize for the despicable way in which I treated you and your friend at my home after the wedding. I was devastated at Jennie's accusations, and I'm so worried about her heavy drinking. It was no excuse for my rudeness though. I'm sorry I haven't found the ring, and I do hope that Victoria's ankle is better. Did you take her directly to the hospital?"

Cass almost choked on her coffee at this point. She had forgotten all about the ankle incident. She felt that Jordan knew it too. He was staring at her with a smirk on his face, and those black eyes were hypnotic. She wondered whether he could read her mind. His eyes seemed to be penetrating her head.

The small talk didn't last long. Leaning forward in his chair, Jordan came right to the point. "Cassandra, what you said at my father's funeral was terribly upsetting. My parents were in a dreadful accident, and that's all there was to it. I do hope you haven't been talking to the police or any private investigator. It would kill my mother to hear any rumours of murder plots. She's sick enough as it is. It would be insulting and devastating for her to have to deal with such lies. She's your sister, and I know you wouldn't want to do anything to cause a relapse".

This got Cass's dander up. What a phoney! "Jordan, you're her son. Surely you want to get to the bottom of this. You must be anxious to find out who wanted your parents dead, and why."

He frowned in anger and slammed his cup down on the side table. "There's no one who wanted them dead, Cassandra. Are you thick headed? It was an accident, pure and simple. It was your ill-advised and foolish remarks at the funeral which gave Jennie her crazy ideas. She would never have said such things if you hadn't put them into her head." Pausing momentarily, he continued in a lower, more menacing tone. "Actually I've spoken to the police myself, and they just laughed at the idea. They thought it was ludicrous. They've written it off as an accident and that's the end of it. I advise you to forget all about it and get on with your life. I'd hate to have to bring a lawsuit for slander." These last words were squeezed out slowly like paste from a tube. His eyes were two thumbtacks pinning her in place.

Obviously he was lying. Jack had told her that there was no mistake. The brakes had been cut deliberately. Had Jordan really talked to the police? She doubted it. Why wouldn't they have told him that someone had tampered with the brakes, unless, of course, they were setting a trap for him. Then again, maybe he was totally innocent and really believed that it was just a bad accident. What if she and Vickie were on the wrong track suspecting him? Shoot, now she was all confused. She mustn't let him con her. She was sure he was a master at the art.

"Are you threatening me, Jordan?" The way he kept calling her "Cassandra" was beginning to bug her. Somehow he made it sound almost derogatory. "Because if you are threatening me" she continued, "it will just encourage me to delve further into the situation. Your mother doesn't need to know anything about this yet. Leave her alone and let her get well. I do, however, have every intention of pursuing it with the police. Someone's been stalking us, and making ugly threats, and if it's you, you had better stop. The police are aware of it, and are giving us protection, so you can just forget about your stupid phone calls and cat pictures and dead rats."

She noticed with interest that Jordan looked surprised at this. Was he acting or was he really innocent? Well, okay, maybe he wasn't the stalker. He was dangerous though, of that she was convinced. Just being near the sick pervert made her scalp tingle.

"I don't know what you're talking about. You're loonier than that friend of yours." Cass thought she heard a snort from the bathroom at this remark, but she quickly cleared her throat to cover it. She also had to smother a grin. She could picture Vickie seething at hearing herself called 'loony'.

Jordan continued, "Why would I be stalking you? Excuse me Cassandra, but you sound as if you're going a bit strange." This was said with a sneering tone, and Cassie thought how satisfactory it would be to punch him right in that thick-lipped mouth.

"I really don't think there's anything else to say, Jordan. Unfortunately you've only reinforced my suspicions." She didn't think it would be wise to let him know that she knew for sure it had been murder. "I hope for your sake that I'm wrong in suspecting that you had something to do with it." She could make threats as well as anyone, she told herself, standing up to indicate that their little meeting was finished. She had her coffee cup ready to throw in his face if he made any sudden moves.

Jordan hesitated a moment, then stood. He pushed past her and glided down the hall to the front door. It was as if he moved on wheels, he was so smooth. Turning to her, he uttered in a low menacing voice, "I'm very sorry that we've had this misunderstanding Cassandra." He drew the name out as if it had about five syllables. Somehow it seemed like a put-down, as if he was making fun of her. "I sincerely hope that you'll take my advice and keep your nose out of something that's none of your business. I think it would be wise if you didn't make any more visits to the hospital. Your sister needs complete rest, and from now on she won't be allowed visitors." With that he rudely turned his back on her and fumbled for his keys, before calmly and deliberately walking down the few stairs and out to his car.

Cass could barely restrain herself from giving him a swift kick right in his obnoxious butt. She was thoughtful as she slammed the door and walked slowly back to the library.

Vickie was returning the poker to the hearth, and Cassie asked ruefully, "Well, who do you think won that pissing contest?"

"Seems to me it was a draw" said her friend dryly.

"I'll tell you one thing," said Cass, shaking her head and flopping down in a chair. "I doubt that we accomplished anything, but it certainly was interesting, and I do know for sure that I've made a real enemy. I wish you could have seen the look he gave me as he swept out of here. He's not likely to let it drop. We may have bitten off a lot more than we can chew, old pal" she said, raising her eyebrows.

"Nah, we've got good teeth. We can chew anything that psycho throws at us." She wasn't sure whether she was trying to reassure Cassie or bolster her own flagging spirits.

CHAPTER 30

▼

Prudence was so much better now. Her broken left arm was still in a cast, of course, but there seemed to be no permanent head trauma, and she was finally off the heavy pain killers. She was stronger every day, and as her mind emerged from the shadows, she had faced the fact that Matt was not coming back, and that Jenny was throwing her life away on Pete. There were other things she suspected, and now she was motivated to find out who had killed Matt, and to exact some form of revenge. As she lay mulling over these thoughts, Bunny came bouncing in.

"Hi there, sweetie. How are we feeling this morning?" She was taking a proprietary interest in Prudence. She was fascinated at the thought of all the money this woman had, and yet she was so quiet and charming, and just like ordinary people! It amazed Bunny. How could you possibly have all that money and still be so down to earth?

She was working what they called a split shift today. Most nurses hated it, and complained bitterly. Bunny, however, was quite philosophical about it. She was so happy to be a real nurse that she rarely complained about working conditions. Today she was off at 3pm and back for the midnight shift. This was what they called the "killer shift" because it took its toll, but Bunny could handle it. Her friend Jimmy was away for a few days, so she had nothing to do but go home, grab a bite to eat, sleep for a few hours, and get back here to the hospital which had become her second home.

"I'm fine, thank you. I feel really good, but my arm is itching in this cast. I need a knitting needle to reach down inside and give it a good scratch. More importantly, though, I need a phone right away. Could you arrange it for me? I have several calls to make, including one to my lawyer."

"My goodness, that sounds serious. You should only be thinking happy thoughts" bubbled Bunny. "There'll be plenty of time for lawyers later." She said this as she was busily checking Pru's blood pressure and temperature.

"No, you don't understand, I have to change my will, and there's a very important letter I must write," confided Pru nervously. She was immediately sorry she had told something so private to this talkative little bundle of energy.

"Calm down, now" soothed Bunny. "Let me look after you properly, and then I'll see what I can do. You're sending your blood pressure sky high" she scolded, forgetting what this unfortunate information might do to the patient.

Bunny loved this bright and cheery room, so she always took as long as she dared completing her nursing duties. She kept up a steady stream of trivial conversation in a kind attempt to calm and entertain. This morning, however, Prudence was barely able to tolerate her well meant cheerfulness. Frustrated, she helplessly watched Bunny bounce and jiggle her way out the door. She hadn't been able to get a word in. She knew Bunny was kind hearted, and meant well, and was probably a good nurse in her own way, but Pru could feel her heart thumping and she was uptight and on edge. She had a sense of urgency about what had to be done.

Thinking of Matt brought unwanted tears to her eyes, and this morning she didn't even have the luxury of privacy to weep in peace. She heard the rattling of the cart, and looked up through bleary eyes to see the technician coming to take more blood. She thought of these techs as hospital vampires, and winced at the thought of more needles.

When Christina Marshall took a look at Pru's chart she noticed that her blood pressure and pulse rate were up. "How did she seem, Bunny?" she asked with concern. Pru had become a favourite of everyone on the floor.

"Oh you know, she's obviously still weak, but she's wanting a phone now. She wants to call her lawyer and change her will. I wonder if she's going to write her kids out. Wouldn't that be something. Then again, maybe she's going to put us into it! I like that idea!"

"Don't hold your breath" laughed Tina. "It is intriguing though. It would be great if she left something to the hospital. God, could we ever use it around this place. I'm going down to check on her."

Just then a bit of a commotion caught her attention. "Oh, Lordie," she laughed resignedly. "Here comes Luscious Lana in all her faded glory!"

"Luscious Lana" had been the stage name of 85 year old Bertha Roberts. She had been a headline stripper down at the Victory Burlesque House for many years, until Bill Roberts, an accountant with a penchant for strippers, had married her and taken her away from it all.

Now suffering from Alzheimer's Disease as well as cancer, Luscious Lana was in for surgery. Twice she had managed to take off her hospital johnny, and had sashayed down the corridor as if she were back on the runway at the Victory. She had been a knock-out in her day, but now at 85, her once magnificent boobs were making a valiant effort to say hello to her bellybutton, and her once luscious derrière now looked like play dough punched full of little holes.

She, however, had such a "joie de vivre", and seemed to be enjoying herself so much, that people in the corridor, especially the med students, laughed and cheered as she stumbled her way down the hall, totally in sync with some long ago music which only she could hear. Two nurses quickly caught up with her and wrapped her in a blanket as they led her back to her room.

Poor Lana was facing surgery the next day, so this was possibly her last performance. Tina hoped not. She loved the old gal's spirit.

When she finally got around to checking on Prudence, she found her staring at the ceiling, tears running down her cheeks. "What's wrong" she asked in a quiet and sympathetic tone. With a tissue, she gently wiped away the tears and took Pru's hand.

"I'm just feeling sorry for myself because it's so lonely without Matt. He was my whole life" sobbed Pru, embarrassed at having a stranger see her weep in this unladylike fashion.

Tina plugged in the phone, and stood for a few moments talking and comforting this patient she had come to like and respect.

After Prudence had regained her composure she said "Thank you for the phone. I have to talk to my lawyer today, so could you please look up his number for me."

"Sure. Give me his name and I'll do the rest. In the meantime you just relax and save your strength. You mustn't overdo things or I'll get in trouble for not taking good care of you. Promise?"

"Yes, thank you Christina. I do appreciate your kindness. By the way, I must look awful. I haven't had the heart to peek at a mirror — too scared to I guess. Do I look really bad?"

"Not at all. You were lucky in that regard. There are no facial scars. Actually, you know, Bunny's been fluffing your hair every day whether you were awake or not, and it does look a bit wild," laughed Tina. "It's a sure sign that you're getting better when you start worrying about your appearance."

"Matt would be ashamed of me if I let myself go. I'll need some lipstick for starters, and maybe a curling iron. I don't want to scare poor Douglas when he comes," she laughed.

"Okay, shall do. Just tell me what colour and brand of lipstick you want, and what size curling iron, and I'll get them for you on my lunch hour," said Tina obligingly, wondering why this woman's own daughter wasn't around to look after her mom's needs.

As she left Pru's room, one of the volunteers entered, carrying an azalea plant. "I've never seen a room with so many flowers" she commented, looking hopelessly around for a place to put the latest addition.

"Could you do me a huge favour" asked Pru, smiling at her. "Please just give me the enclosure card, and then take the flowers to someone who doesn't have any. In fact, you could come back and take several of the arrangements to other rooms. It would be so kind of you," she added graciously.

"Oh how generous of you" gushed the pink lady as she gathered up a few plants and took off.

While Pru and the volunteer were dealing with the flowers, Jenny was just arriving at the hospital. After her wedding reception, when she so boldly accused Jordan, and subsequent to that awful night at the cottage when she had attacked him, and he had become so angry with her, Jenny had been careful to keep out of his way. She only planned to see him if there were other people around. She believed in "safety in numbers." She had attempted an apology, saying that she had been drunk and distraught. Playing innocent and regretful, she couldn't tell just how Jordan really felt. He was playing his cards very close to his chest, and she was afraid of him now for the first time in her life.

This morning Jenny's heart sank as they happened to arrive at the hospital simultaneously. Still, she had plan B she assured herself. As they walked from their cars and approached the hospital doors, Jordan gave her one of his cold enigmatic smiles. Jenny was relieved. Obviously he wanted to keep up appearances. It wouldn't look good if they seemed to be feuding. There was no point in drawing unwanted attention or suspicion to themselves.

Before they could talk, however, Jenny said, "Look, there's Uncle Blake. What's he doing here?"

"I would hazard a wild guess and say that he's here for the same reason we are" Jordan said dryly. In the old days Jenny would have giggled and punched him lovingly on the arm. Today, however, she simply grimaced and turned away.

"Hi, Uncle Blake" she said sweetly, approaching him from behind. He was an awfully good looking man, Jenny thought. He looked very much like her father, except that he was taller and had that adorable cleft in his chin. Today he was wearing casual cream slacks with a light cranberry coloured shirt. He was certainly aging gracefully.

Blake looked startled, but then smiled. "Why, hello you two. Come to visit your mother?"

"That's right" said Jordan coldly. "How about you?"

"Oh, I just thought I should check in on her, see how she's doing, you know" he replied vaguely. "She certainly is coming along well."

Jennifer and Jordan refrained from looking at each other, as all three walked into the hospital together.

As they approached the nursing station, Jordan spotted Bunny Connors bent over the bottom drawer of a filing cabinet. It was a sight to behold. She had perfect legs, and a classically rounded derrière.

"Good morning, gorgeous" whispered Jordan, leaning over the desk. This was said more to annoy Jenny than to flirt with Bunny.

"Well, hello, tall, dark and deadly. You startled me." replied Bunny, straightening up and smoothing her skirt. She gave him her best dimpled smile. She knew she wasn't being very professional, and hoped that none of the other nurses had heard her.

"How's my mother this morning?" asked Jordan as if he really cared.

"She's wonderful" replied Bunny eagerly. She wanted to keep this good-looking guy talking. Maybe he would ask her out for a coffee. "Your mother is feeling so well today that she wants to see her lawyer and change her will."

As soon as the words were spoken, Bunny experienced a dagger of guilt. She shouldn't be talking about her patient. Seeing the look on Jordan's face, she continued. "Oh, but, she hasn't been able to contact him yet. He's out of town I guess. She should leave it for another day when she's stronger," she stammered, only making things worse. Oh why had she said anything? She was such a blabber mouth. Blake and Jenny were staring at her, but Jordan's face seemed contorted with anger or surprise. She definitely shouldn't have blurted that out.

Tina Marshall, returning to the desk, heard the last part of Bunny's statement. Frowning she said, "Bunny, I need you in the supply room."

Bunny knew she was in trouble now. She had been reprimanded before for not behaving in a professional manner, but sometimes she just couldn't help herself. With a big sigh, and giving Jordan a plaintive smile, she reluctantly followed Tina.

CHAPTER 31

▼

Jordan was utterly shocked at what he had heard from Bunny. His mother changing her will at this late date did not bode well for him. He liked the will just the way it was. She had to be stopped, and quickly, but how? He strode down the hall slowly, thinking about this potentially bad turn of events. Jenny and Blake went ahead.

As he entered room 707, he saw that Jenny was standing on one side of the bed, and Uncle Blake on the other. Their mother was sitting up and talking in a low voice. She appeared to focus on him for a moment, then she closed her eyes.

"Well, Mother" he began in an oleaginous tone. "You're looking a little better today. I understand, though, that you've been bothering the nurses and they're getting fed up with you."

Pru opened her eyes wide at this surprising statement, and stared at him in disbelief, then her frightened eyes darted to Jenny and Blake, and back to Jordan. She looked like the proverbial deer caught in the headlights. Before she could say anything, Jordan continued.

"You mustn't bother the nurses or your lawyer" he said less smoothly. "He's out of town anyway, he'll be gone for days. There'll be plenty of time for talking to Mr. Bannon when you are up and about. You must promise not to bother those poor overworked nurses anymore. They have more important things to do than to cater to the whims of a selfish person. You don't want to get the reputation of a trouble-maker. They can make things awfully hard for you if they don't like you," he cautioned, or perhaps threatened, taking her hand in his and pressing much too firmly against the frail, bruised skin. "I think we'll have the phone removed for your own good. I'll be glad to make any calls for you." He smiled pleasantly at her as she turned her head away from him. "Also," he continued, "I think we'll limit your visitors to just Jenny and myself. It's just too tiring for you. I'll arrange it with the nurses."

Jenny looked surprised, but nodded in agreement. What was Jordan up to? Blake looked bemused. He wasn't sure why Pru would want to talk to her lawyer unless it was to change her will, and that brought up an interesting question. If Matt had left him a million dollars as promised, could Pru countermand that bequest? He wasn't sure, but it didn't sound too good. Well, there likely wasn't a bequest anyway. It was more likely a hopeless, pathetic dream, the delusions of a sucker. Why had he ever believed Matt? Blake did know one thing for sure, though. He did not like the way Jordan was talking to his mother. It was almost as if he was threatening her, and Pru really looked frightened. Why was Jordan trying to isolate her, cut her off from family and friends? He would talk to the nurses himself. There was no way that he trusted this psycho.

Just then Christina came hurrying in. Sizing up the situation, she told them that her patient needed rest, and asked them to go. Prudence looked relieved as all three left the room. At the door Jordan turned and gave his mother a semi-glower. "Don't forget what we talked about, Mother, and don't try using the phone. You're still much too weak. You definitely will not get better if you overdo it." Again, this last remark sounded like a threat. He stared at her for a moment before giving Tina an icy glance and heading out the door.

Once they were gone, Prudence clutched Christina's hand. "Please give me the phone and let me try Douglas again. There's no time left. I have to speak to him today." She seemed quite frantic as she stared up at the nurse with a pleading look.

Later that afternoon, Douglas Bannon received the urgent message, and hurried to the hospital. He was an elderly gentleman, well into his seventies, but he had been a close friend of Matt and Prudence Wainwright for years. His two law partners had both died, and Douglas had been carrying on the practice partly for his old clients, and partly because he didn't know what else to do. He was becoming a bit doddery though, and he was all too aware of his shortcomings.

He was shocked to see his old friend. She had always been so charming, so elegant. Now she looked tiny and frail, and much older than he remembered. He realized that she must have been to hell and back these past weeks, as he hugged her gently, and sat down in the rocker beside the bed.

They talked for at least an hour, and old Douglas was startled at what he heard. Pru was weak but determined, and her mind seemed totally clear. When the revised will and the surprising letter were finished, they needed two witnesses.

Douglas Bannon toddled down to the nursing station, and returned with Dr. Taylor and Bunny.

Dr. Mitchell Taylor was the most popular doctor on staff. Well over six feet, with dark hair, hazel eyes and an impish grin, he just missed being handsome, but he set hearts fluttering wherever he went. He was a brilliant surgeon who had come to Toronto from Australia by way of England.

Mitch was an inveterate tease. He laughed and flirted with every nurse on staff, paying special attention to the unlovely, unlovable ones. He had the knack of making people feel a little better after he had passed by. Even patients facing serious surgery seemed willing to put themselves in his talented hands. He exuded confidence and gentle caring without manifesting the "God complex" which afflicts so many surgeons.

Pru had met him several years ago when she had an emergency appendectomy. He knew what a charming, likeable lady she was, and had been shocked when he learned of the accident. He had been caring for her after having to remove her spleen. He was pleased now to be a witness to her will, but he was quite confident that she was not about to die. She was a survivor, and she was doing amazingly well. He told her so, as he signed his name below Bunny's.

Pru's hand was weak, but she seemed to have gathered inner strength from this effort, and she painstakingly signed her name to the will and the letter.

Sometime later at the nursing station, Bunny Connors answered the phone.

"Hello, this is Judge Graham" said the slightly muffled voice. "I'm looking for Douglas Bannon. It's urgent that I find him right away. I think that he was scheduled to see Mrs. Wainwright this afternoon to work on her will. Has he been there yet?"

The voice was somehow muted, as if there was a hand or a hanky over the speaker, but Bunny recognized it. Judge Graham my ass, she thought. She was positive that it was Jordan Wainwright. What kind of a game was he playing? How dumb did he think she was? Bunny did not like anyone trying to make a fool of her. She felt very guilty about having told Jordan that his mother was planning to change her will. It had just slipped out, but Tina had really given her heck about it. There was such a thing as patient-nurse confidentiality. Christina had pointed out that she felt their patient was scared of Jordan, and that she likely didn't want him to know that she was changing her will. Bunny had done an unforgivable thing.

Bunny felt really badly about what she had done, and this was a chance to make up for her earlier blunder. "I'm sorry, Judge Graham" she said sweetly, crossing her fingers like a child. "Mr. Bannon has definitely not been here today, and we don't expect him. I think he's out of town."

"You're absolutely sure that he hasn't been there?"

"That's right" she said, putting a little trill in her voice. This was fun.

After a slight pause, the muffled voice said "Thank you so much" and hung up.

Bunny laughed at her own cleverness, and hoped she had done the right thing by putting Jordan off the track. She was very fond of Mrs. Wainwright, and if she was scared of her own son, then Bunny didn't like him either.

Back in Niagara Falls that same afternoon, Cassie answered the phone.

"Hello, Cassandra?" said a small anxious voice. "This is Pru."

"Prudence?" exclaimed Cassie in surprise. "My goodness, how are you? You must be doing very well to be able to use the phone."

"I am doing well, thank you. Cassie, I simply have to talk to you — the sooner the better. I know that this is a huge imposition, but could you possibly drive over to see me tomorrow? You'll understand once I explain everything. It's very important."

Cassie was momentarily stunned. She absolutely hated the thought of another trip to Toronto. It seemed that she and Vickie had been spending most of their time on the highway. Still, this was her sister, and how could she possibly refuse. "What is it, Pru? What's wrong?"

"I can't tell you over the phone. I've got to see you face to face. It's rather complicated, Cassandra, and I must beg you to come. Please. You won't be sorry, I promise."

Cass couldn't understand the pleading tone in her sister's voice. What in hell was going on? She could do nothing but agree to make the trip, but how was she going to break it to Vickie that they would be on the road again?

"Alright, Pru, I'll come over in the morning. I should be there by about ten o'clock. Will that be okay?"

"Oh thank you so much, Cass. I'll be waiting for you, and Cassie," here Prudence seemed to take a sobbing breath, "please be very careful." There was a slight pause, and then the line went dead.

Cass and Vickie were puzzled and worried by the strange call. What now, they wondered. And why had Pru warned Cassie to be careful? Careful of what — driving on the highway? — the stalker? — the hospital food? The call made no sense, and if it had been from someone else Cassie would have suspected that it was a joke. One thing she did know about her sister, however, was that she was not a jokester.

"Well, we wanted a mystery, and it seems we've got more than we can handle now," said Vickie ruefully as they made their plans for tomorrow's trip.

CHAPTER 32

▼

Douglas Bannon left the hospital slowly. He was depressed after seeing his old friend. She looked pretty bad, but at least her spirits were good. He felt old and defeated, and wondered again whether he should be packing it all in. He had seen and heard so much over the years, and now he wasn't sure whether he could still cope, or whether he even wanted to.

He knew that he was becoming forgetful, and at times he could see with perfect clarity that he had become an anachronism — a gentle, caring man of integrity and wit, lost in a litigious society full of rapists, killers, incomprehensible DNA evidence, and threatening, all-knowing computers. He had been a hot-shot lawyer in his day, but his time had come and gone.

He would go back to his empty, lonely home, and heat some dinner in the microwave. He would have a drink or two, read a bit, then shuffle off to bed. Tomorrow would be time enough to take the new will and the strange letter to the safety of his office.

At home he wearily showered, and in bathrobe and slippers, he cooked himself some cardboard tasting dinner. Funny how they all tasted the same. His Ruth had been a wonderful cook. They never ate microwave dinners when she was alive. It had been five years now, five years of tasteless dinners, lonely evenings, and a somewhat meaningless existence.

He did have a few good friends left of course. They played chess and bridge a couple of times a week, but he was still so damn lonely. He had just returned from a visit with his daughter Sarah who lived in British Columbia. Actually he had been out there when Pru's terrible accident happened.

Sarah was a good girl who loved her dad and wanted him to come and live with her. Fat chance! Her husband Sam was another story. His weak attempts at enthusiasm for the idea would have been funny if they hadn't been so hurtful. There was no way he wanted the old man around full time, and Douglas knew it. He could see through Sam as easily as looking through a cracked window. His two grandsons were wild, and he couldn't stand them for more than half an hour at a time. No, there was no way that Douglas could ever pack up and move to his daughter's, no matter how much he loved her. Besides, he could never tear himself away from this home where he and Ruth had been so happy. It was full of the memories of a lifetime.

Douglas had contemplated suicide on more than one occasion, but that was the coward's way out, and Douglas Bannon was no coward. True, after a few drinks he might take the "idea" out, turn it, twist it and polish it, then return it to his mind's shelf, and get on with things. It was like worrying at a sore tooth. He couldn't resist thinking about it, but he wasn't ready for such extreme measures. He also knew that Ruth would have been horrified at the thought of such a cowardly act. No, he could never face Ruth in the after-life if he did anything so drastic. He knew that she was waiting for him, and she would wait patiently until his time came.

Berating himself for his self-pity, he took his second glass of rye and ginger, and sat in his comfortable old lounger in the den. It was like an old friend, and it enveloped him in its familiarity. He took out the new will written by Prudence, along with the surprising letter, and read them both again. Everything was in order, but they would certainly make some waves when the time came. Funny the twists and turns people's lives took. Everyone had secrets.

Finally finished with the documents, he laid them on the table beside his lounger, and casually perused a couple of recent magazines. He was so bored and tired, however, that he couldn't concentrate. Carelessly he laid the magazines on the now forgotten legal papers, and made his way up to bed. Tonight he forgot to check that all the doors and windows were locked. He also forgot to put the will and the letter back in his briefcase, which was sitting beside his desk.

Douglas said goodnight to the picture of Ruth, which sat on his bedside table, and with a troubled heart he turned out the light. Tomorrow his housekeeper Maureen Delaney came to clean. Undoubtedly she would bring him some of her home baked goodies. This was what his life had become, he thought bitterly — looking forward to treats from his cleaning lady!

Shortly after Douglas got himself into bed, a person dressed all in black, picked the lock on his downtown office door and warily stepped inside. Using a small flashlight, and making sure that the blinds were drawn, the intruder did a thorough search of the office. There didn't appear to be a safe, but there were several metal filing cabinets, all locked.

It took the figure in black some time to pick the lock on the drawer labelled "W to Z." Finding the folder marked "Wainwright, Matthew and Prudence," the trespasser quickly ascertained that there was no new will. The existing one dated a year ago, was exactly the same as the one which Jordan had found at the house.

So, there definitely was no new will. The burglar sighed with relief. Then an ugly thought occurred. What if there was a new will and the old fool had taken it home with him in his briefcase? Shi-it. That was a distinct possibility. Now what??? Sighing as the folder was put back, the interloper silently left the office, making sure to lock the door on the way out.

Some time later, Douglas Bannon wakened with a start. What was that, he wondered. What had he heard? He sat at the edge of the bed for a moment before standing up. He had learned from past experience that standing up too quickly nowadays would leave him feeling faint and dizzy. He was shaking, but he knew he had to take his time and give the blood a chance to make it to his head.

Quietly reaching under the bed, he grasped his old Louisville slugger. The bat had been with him for a long time. It was an old friend. Douglas didn't believe in guns. He had seen too many tragedies, been in too many trials where guns were involved. Ruth had always laughed at the bat under the bed, and thankfully he had never had occasion to use it. Hopefully he wouldn't need it now either. Heart pumping like car pistons, he tiptoed to the bedroom door and listened. Silence. Good. He must have been dreaming.

With a sigh of relief — his hands were shaking pretty badly — he turned to go back to bed. There it was again. It was a thud, as if someone had closed a drawer too energetically.

Lord, there really was someone in the house! Now what? Closing the bedroom door as quietly as possible, he tiptoed across the deep pile carpet to the bedside phone. Dialling 911, he gave his address, and told the matter-of-fact dispatcher that there was an intruder in his home.

"Please speak up, sir, I can't hear you."

In a slightly louder whisper Douglas repeated his message.

"Sir, you'll have to speak louder."

Sweating now, and feeling queasy, Douglas tried again. This time the dispatcher must have taken the wax out of her ears, for she finally understood what he was saying.

"Where are you, sir?" she inquired.

"In the bedroom upstairs" replied Douglas as quietly as he could, staring all the time at the door in case it should fly open, and the attacker suddenly appear. He wiped one sweaty hand on his pyjama bottoms, then transferred the phone to that hand while he wiped the other one. At this rate he'd lose ten pounds before he ever got off the phone!

"Good. Stay right there. Do not go downstairs. A police car is on its way. Don't go down till you hear them at the door."

Douglas hung up the phone, and sat down again on the edge of the bed. The dispatcher had told him to keep the line open, but in his frightened state he had mistakenly hung up. Should he call back? No, the police were on their way. He couldn't just sit here and do nothing though. Some intruder had broken into his home. Probably some drugged out kid looking for money or something to fence. His heart leaped again as he realized that they might be stealing all Ruth's cherished figurines, or the priceless jade collection gathered over a lifetime, or even the treasured family pictures in their heavy silver frames. He couldn't sit here like a dummy and let that happen. Douglas Bannon was no coward!

Clutching his beloved bat, he tiptoed again across the carpet, and slowly opened the door. There were more soft noises, barely discernible above the pounding of his heart. Silently and slowly he made his way down the carpeted stairs, clutching the bat so that it wouldn't bang against the wall or the banister. His poor old heart was pounding like a jackhammer. Beads of sweat were glistening on his ashen face, and he felt decidedly light headed. Don't let me faint or fall down these goddamned stairs, he silently pleaded. His eyes gradually adjusted to the darkness, and moonlight was coming in through the fan-shaped window over the front door.

The sounds were clearer now. They were coming from his den. Douglas moved as stealthily as a cat. Where were the damn police? He felt as if it had been hours since he called them. Had they stopped for donuts and coffee on the way?

Peeking into the den, he could barely make out the dark figure bending over his desk. He was using a flashlight, and was riffling through the papers on the desktop. Suddenly Douglas was very angry. How dare anyone come into his home like this? How dare he look through Douglas's private papers? Forgetting his fears, and with something akin to a roar, he lunged into the room, bat held high.

The interloper jumped and looked up in surprise. Douglas couldn't see his face because the light from the flashlight was blinding him.

Grabbing the briefcase beside the desk, the intruder rushed out the French doors which opened onto the back garden. The doors had been standing partially open. This was obviously the point of entry.

"Well, damn it all to hell" cried Douglas, who often talked to himself in the big empty house. "I likely didn't even have those doors locked. I might as well have left a written invitation" he muttered in disgust as he flopped into a chair. He could hear the sirens approaching now. Fat lot of good they would do, a day late and a dollar short, that's our finest, he thought angrily. The guy, who might have been wearing a mask, Douglas couldn't be sure, would be long gone. Damnation. His beloved old briefcase, the one Ruth had given him so many years ago, was gone too.

When Douglas unlocked the front door, bat still in hand, the police were actually very nice, once they realized he wasn't going to attack them. Excitedly explaining that the burglar had fled into the back garden, Douglas watched and waited while the two cops made a thorough search of the grounds and neighbouring yards. When they returned empty handed, they all sat down, and he told them the whole story.

He laughed ruefully when they cautioned him not to touch anything because there might be fingerprints. It's a bit late to be telling me that, he thought in disgust. Anyway, he thought he remembered seeing gloves on the intruder, but he couldn't be sure. It had all happened so quickly.

The police seemed to be rookies, and were very solicitous. They told him that he was very lucky the burglar had simply run away, and hadn't stayed to kill him first. They appeared surprised and somewhat impressed with his trusty bat, and the fact that he had actually routed the intruder with it. They wanted to take him to the hospital to make sure that his heart was fine. After all, that was quite a bit of excitement for an old gentleman. Douglas, however, declined. He was beginning to feel rather proud of himself. He had acted in a foolhardy but courageous manner. "There's a bit of life in the old boy yet" he muttered with grim satisfaction. Ruth would have been proud of him.

As the officers accompanied him around the house, Douglas was baffled that nothing seemed to be missing. All the silver was there, and Ruth's Royal Doulton collection was all intact. The jade pieces were still there. For what, then, had the intruder been looking, — drugs, cash?

By the time the two young policemen were finished checking for fingerprints and footprints — a totally unproductive search — old Douglas was ready for bed. Saying goodnight, and locking the doors carefully, he slowly made his way upstairs, his old friend the slugger once more clutched in his weary hands.

There was something not making any sense about this break-in, but he couldn't put his finger on it. He was much too tired tonight, he would figure it out tomorrow.

CHAPTER 33

▼

The same evening that Douglas was having his encounter with the black clad intruder, Prudence was feeling quite euphoric. She had done it! She had changed her will and she had called Cassie. Tomorrow, if all went well, they would have a heart to heart and clear up everything. She regretted now that she had written the letter. Tomorrow after her talk with Cass, she would call Douglas and have him destroy it. It would be so much better to say what had to be said in person. Now the next step was to get well enough to check herself out of this damn creepy hospital.

She had walked down the hall unsteadily several times now, with the nurses helping her. It felt great, but those long corridors were like highways with unpleasant stops along the way. Never mind, she was getting stronger every day.

Pru was thinking about tomorrow. She had things to do, people to see. There was no way Jordan was going to cut off all her visitors. What a nerve! Why would he try to isolate her? She couldn't help the maverick thought which had come to her so often over the years. Why had they ever adopted him? He had been nothing but trouble from the very start. She had loved him so much, and had been so protective of him no matter what he did. She realized now what a mistake that had been.

Heaving a sigh, she forced herself to think of more immediate concerns. She knew she looked dreadful. Poor Douglas had nearly fainted when he saw her. Christina had been so kind getting her the curling iron and the lipstick, and Bunny had wanted to do her hair, but she needed a perm and a cut. Up to this point she hadn't had any interest in looking at herself, but now that she knew she was recovering, she had to smarten up. With all her money, they could bring in a hairdresser for her. She could call Maisie herself. What a marvellous idea! Having all the money a person could ever need was a novel experience, and she was just beginning to realize the power it gave her. She and Matt had invested it immediately till they got used to the idea that they were multi-millionaires. They really hadn't had any fun from it.

She regretted now that they hadn't indulged themselves wildly. Why had they been so careful, so parsimonious? She was going to spend whatever it took to get herself well and out of here. She had to find out who was responsible for Matt's death, and then she would get her revenge, even if it took every penny. Even if it meant accusing one or both of her children, she would do it. She owed them nothing. She owed Matt a lot, even though he had broken her heart when she learned of his latest affair. She wouldn't think about that right now though. She had to focus all her energy on finding his killer.

Pru wished her dad could be here to help her. He would know exactly what to do. Unfortunately J.J. had died in his small plane in his beloved Brazilian forests. The plane crashed in thick, uninhabitable jungle, and it had been ten long days before they found him, or what was left of him. After that her mother had withered like an unpicked peach. Within six months Lizzie was dead from a broken heart. Her mom would have been a great help to her now. She always had an answer. No one ever got the best of Lizzie, except Jordan, of course.

Thinking of her mother and dad reminded her of Elena. When Elena had first contacted her, Prudence was shocked and disappointed at what her father had done. How could he have been so crass, so heartless? Then she thought about those six months he spent in Brazil every year away from his family. He must have been so lonely.

As Pru lay contemplating what had happened in the past weeks, she marvelled and despaired at how inevitably her life had changed. Staring at the Bateman print of the proud little hummingbird, her mind strayed to the cottage. It had belonged to her parents, but it had been their sanctuary, a haven for her and Matt. When the children had been small, they had delighted in it too, even Jordan to some small extent. Her heart thumped crazily when she thought of Jordan. Again she asked herself why she ever forced Matt to adopt him A montage of memorable events, some good, but mostly bad, crowded into her mind.

She remembered grimly that awful quarrel Jordan and Matt had that last day at the cottage. It was about money as usual, and Matt had exploded. He said some dreadful, unforgivable things to Jordan — unfortunately they were all true. Jordan had just laughed and sneered with that terrifying way he had. Then she and Matt had started arguing again about Matt's latest girlfriend. It had all been disgusting.

Staring at the Salvador Dali print, she realized with a shudder, that it looked like what might be inside Jordan's head. All those melting, shape-shifting time pieces could very well be the convoluted cells of his brain. His thoughts and emotions seemed to flow like that. And those angry ants — ugh. She could picture them scurrying and clicking in his head, changing him, eating at him, making him cruel and uncaring. She knew in her heart that Jordan was capable of murder, she had to accept that irrefutable fact.

Pru realized that she hated the odious painting. She wanted it out of here now. When she had been suffering from those morphine-induced hallucinations, she had felt as if she were being sucked into that nebulous, amorphous world. The picture had to go. If she had been strong enough she would have taken it down herself. She would buy the hospital a new one, but as of now, that painting was history. As a matter of fact, why not donate and furnish an entire room just as nice as this one, maybe even nicer. What a marvellous idea! She had to start a list right away.

Forcing her eyes away from the offending painting, she gazed again at the little hummingbird, and her mind turned to Jenny, her dear lovely Jenny. She had always been wilful, and now she was bent on a self-destructive course. They should have pulled the plug on Pete long ago. He'd been brain dead for years. There was no way that Jenny could love him. She had something up her sleeve, because she wasn't stupid. What was she planning? Jenny was a schemer, no doubt of that. Pru knew deep within her heart that Jenny had always had an unhealthy love for Jordan, maybe obsession was a more accurate term. She had tried to head it off, tried to diffuse the alarming situation, but as usual, she had failed.

Well, she wasn't going to fail this time. If either Jordan or Jenny had murdered their father, she would make them pay. She would hire a private detective to investigate the crash. She could at least do that much for Matt. She didn't know how she could go on without him, but she would deal with that later. Now all her energy would be spent on finding his killer. It could have been Jim Sinclair. Pru was there when he had threatened to kill Matt if he didn't leave his wife alone. Selfishly she hoped that it was Jim or even Blake. It would be easier to deal with an irate husband or a jealous brother-in-law than to deal with her own children. Still, she hoped that Blake wasn't the one. They had dated briefly before she met Matt. He was much nicer than Matt, more fun, more caring, more gentle, but there was something which had attracted her to the older brother. Matt was so intense, so sure of himself and his ability to succeed and make money. That had been very important to Prudence in those days. Her mom had always repeated the old bromide about it being just as easy to love a rich man as a poor man. Pru had grown up believing that social position and wealth were essentials for happiness. She sighed now thinking of how foolish she had been.

Anyway, the bottom line was that she had always had a soft spot in her heart for Blake, and she didn't want him to be the murderer. She was glad that Matt had left the million dollar bequest to him. He was a nice guy who had made a few dumb mistakes, but then, who hadn't? He had a really nice family, a lovely wife and four good kids. Hopefully the money would bring him a lot of happiness.

Pru remembered so well the day they realized that they had won the lottery, all that money, it had somehow seemed obscene. She and Matt had been grocery shopping, and she had checked the numbers at the courtesy desk, while Matt paid the cashier. She saw that the numbers were the same, but wouldn't let herself believe that it could be possible. She didn't say a word on the way home, just sat in stunned silence. Matt was listening to an afternoon ballgame, so he didn't notice. She shakily put the groceries away before she sat down quietly, took out her ticket, and compared it number for number with the print-out. She checked and re-checked the date. When she couldn't find anything else to check, she went to find Matt on the patio.

The rest of the day was dreamlike. Because it was still early afternoon, they called Douglas Bannon and told him that it was an emergency. Poor Douglas arrived expecting to hear that someone had committed a murder and needed a good lawyer. They had all gone to the lottery office together. They wanted it kept quiet, but the reporters had been camping out, waiting for the winner to show up. Twenty million was a big jackpot. It was news!

All three of them were in shock as they were handed the cheque. Unfortunately their pictures appeared in the paper, and they had to have their phone number changed right away. People came out of the woodwork asking for handouts, coming up with crazy schemes which needed financing, or just plain threatening them!

She and Matt were in a daze for weeks. That first night, however, they did buy two bottles of Dom Perignon, and got laughing, weeping, hysterically drunk. What fun it had been, like something out of a movie.

Seeing Douglas today had been a treat. It made her feel somehow that Matt would be walking through the door any minute. Pru's happiness, however, was diminished somewhat after dinner when something strange happened. A swarthy hospital worker pushing a waxing machine, had come into her room around

8:30. That struck Pru as rather odd. Surely they didn't polish the floors here at night, or did they? She wasn't really sure, because she had been in such a drug-induced stupor most of the time. She was clear headed now, though, and this guy looked mean and menacing as he pushed the machine around in a lethargic manner. He kept glancing at her slyly, and once made an obscene gesture towards his crotch!

Pru knew that she should push her call button, but she hesitated. She didn't want to give him the satisfaction of knowing that he had scared her. Also, she kept thinking of Jordan's remarks about how the nurses were getting fed up with her. Finally, after several leering glances her way, he sauntered off down the hall, pushing the polisher. He was probably just a dirty old man, but for a few moments there she had panicked, suddenly wondering with a heart-stopping gasp whether he had been sent to kill her. Tomorrow she would arrange for a rent-a-cop. This place was very intimidating, and she felt so helpless with her left arm in a cast and the sides up on her bed. If she could just get through tonight she would be fine, she told herself nervously as she tried to settle down.

CHAPTER 34

▼

At 4:30 am the entire hospital appeared to be asleep. There seemed to be a deathly stillness to the corridors. With all the cutbacks by the provincial government, they were so understaffed at night that there was just a skeleton crew. Pru had never thought about what a frightening term that was — "skeleton crew". It made her shudder. She listened intently for any sound, good or bad, but there was nothing. Was everyone asleep, were they all dead? Had they evacuated the hospital and forgotten about her?

Her pulse quickened. She lay as rigid as a corpse as she considered all these possibilities. Of course they were just the paranoid, delusional ramblings of a frightened, traumatized woman, and yet — — She had to get out of that bed. She had to make it to the nursing station which at this hour would be an oasis in a field of dimness. The lights over the nursing station were always bright.

She lay there plotting her escape. Could she climb over the end of the bed? Of course she could. She had done it one night with her IV pole still attached. Still, she should just lie there and try to calm down.

She sighed as she thought of how different things were during the day. The hospital was a hustling, bustling city. It really was a microcosm, a little city unto itself. People could be born here, die here, shop, eat, work and pray here. Cooks cooked, cleaners cleaned, nurses nursed, and patients lay patiently waiting to hear their fate. There was even a rooftop lounging area with potted plants and patio chairs, a place for smokers to gradually kill themselves while enjoying the panoramic view of the city.

Pru knew from her determined shuffles down the long hall, that during the day there was an almost constant traffic jam. The medical students, interns, residents, doctors, nurses, aides, lab technicians, ward clerks, visitors, pink ladies, and ambulatory patients, filled the halls with a noisy fervour which was both exciting and reassuring. As long as there were people walking, talking and laughing, there seemed hope that there was a normal world out there. At night, however, it was an entirely different situation. It was too quiet, too deadly calm. Every whisper and breath took on new meaning.

Prudence was so desperate for company tonight, that she would have been happy to see fat George, the irrepressible med student appear at her door. He had been in to see her three or four times, and always made her laugh. He was so young and earnest, and he was always humming happy little tunes as he looked at her chart and patted her hand. He would undoubtedly be a good doctor some day, and right now Pru would have been thrilled to see his moon shaped face and big grin. She would even be happy to see Bunny, the chatty Barbie doll, so eager, so enthusiastic. Pru didn't care whether or not she was a good nurse. She just knew that Bunny would be good company to help get her through this spooky night. Right now the entire hospital seemed so threatening. There was an eerie quality to the air and Pru felt so alone.

The extra pillow was at the foot of the bed, forgotten by the overworked nurse or nurse's aide. She could feel it when she moved her feet. Hopefully tomorrow she wouldn't need that extra pillow. Cassie was coming, and Pru would be sitting in the rocker all day. Maybe they would even walk down the hall together. She would accompany Cassandra to the elevator and they would hug goodbye. This thought brought a small smile to Pru's lips.

Mood swings were to be expected with all the medication she had been given these past weeks, and Pru was swinging between hope for tomorrow and fear for tonight. She wished desperately for the morning light. At night the sights, sounds and smells of a hospital all combine to trigger atavistic fears long buried in the subconscious. When darkness sets in and visitors go home, the fears multiply. The hospital becomes a place of potential evil, of torture and terror. It becomes everyman's nightmare. The fear of the unknown bangs against the awareness of reality, and all combine to create a heart pounding, pulse quickening desperation, and longing to escape. It is the original twilight zone of terror. At least this was how it appeared to Pru with her overactive imagination.

Sleep seemed an impossible dream. She was too excited about the day's happenings, and about what she planned for tomorrow. "Tomorrow, tomorrow," she hummed fretfully. Damn, it was already tomorrow, and she had to get some sleep. The night nurse had checked her about half an hour ago, and wasn't likely to be back for ages. She knew that the nursing station was far down the hall. She also knew that there was an exit and stairwell close to her room. She didn't like that at all. Anyone could sneak in undetected. Anxiety washed over her like a huge wave.

Tomorrow she would arrange to have someone stay with her all night. She had the money, she could hire a special duty nurse. Why hadn't she thought of that earlier? She could hire a nurse and a cop. Heck, they could have an all night party! But that was tomorrow night, and this was tonight. How she wished that she had someone with her right now. She couldn't stop twisting and turning in the uncomfortable bed.

When the nurse did eventually come back to check on her, she would ask her to put on all the lights. She wasn't sure where the switch was, or she would do it herself. Why hadn't she asked when the nurse came in to check her a while ago? It was because she was ashamed to admit how frightened she felt. The sides were up on the bed so that she couldn't fall out and sue the hospital, but it also meant that she couldn't get up and do anything for herself. Where was that darn nurse? She didn't want to use the call button. Jordan had frightened her when he said that the nurses were getting annoyed with her. She never used the call button, and she wasn't going to start now.

The only light available was from the small aquarium. If she squinted, she could see the fish swimming lazily. Didn't they ever sleep? Maybe they were nervous at night too. She tried to shut her eyes and keep them shut, but they kept popping open. There were so many questions hurtling around in her head. Tomorrow she would get some answers. Cassie would be here, and they could talk. Tomorrow would be a whole new beginning.

She had been so busy worrying about Matt's killer that it just hadn't occurred to her until tonight that if someone wanted Matt dead, maybe they had wanted her to die too. She had been in that cursed car. Maybe she had been the prime target. No, she had no enemies, did she? Would they try again? No, they would have tried something by now while she was still so helpless. They, whoever "they" were, could have killed her while she was in the coma. They wouldn't wait till now, would they? Somehow the niggling doubt kept crawling around in her head like a caterpillar on a leaf. Was it Jordan who had killed his father? Surely he wasn't that evil. She tried to dismiss the ugly thought. Still, Matt must have been killed for the money, and in that case it would have been Jordan, and he would need to get rid of her too. Of course, if Matt was killed by Jim Sinclair, it had nothing to do with money. Oh, it was so complicated. Her head was beginning to ache.

Earlier in the evening, Pru had looked up to see a man's face peeking around the door at her. For one heart stopping moment she thought it was Jim Sinclair. She had only seen him that one time when he came to their home and attacked Matt, threatening to kill him. Would she recognize him again? He was big and surly looking. Did he want to kill her too? Surely he didn't think that she condoned Matt's affair with his wife. He would have no reason to kill her. No one had a reason to hurt her. Why was she being so paranoid? Still, the man peeking into her room had definitely looked like Sinclair, but he had disappeared too quickly for her to be sure. She tried to tell herself that it was likely a visitor looking for a certain patient and he had the wrong room. Or, was it Jim Sinclair come to finish the job he had started with Matt?

Pru's adrenalin was pumping through her body, and she felt terribly vulnerable. She had to get out of here and get help. She was working herself up into a full blown panic attack. She should have taken the sleeping pill the nurse offered. If only she could get out of this confining bed and make her way down the hall. She didn't want to be alone. Panic made her weak and sweaty. To heck with what Jordan had said. She was going to use her call bell and get the nurse in here. Where the heck was it? It should be pinned to her pillow, but it wasn't there. Great! The one time she decided to use it, it wasn't there. This hospital was the pits. Her beautiful, safe home loomed in her mind's eye. It was only a few city blocks from here, yet it might as well have been across the continent. Would she ever see it again?

She tried to calm herself by thinking of what she would do for all the medical people who had been so good to her. What kind of gift could she give each and every one of them? Good, this should keep her mind occupied for a while. There was so much she could do with all that money. It was all invested, and growing at an obscene rate. Darn, she needed a pencil and paper to jot down some ideas. She squirmed in the uncomfortable bed, as ideas spun around in her head like the slot machines in Vegas.

There were only a couple of hours left before daybreak. If she couldn't sleep she would just pass the time making mental lists. She knew it was always darkest before the dawn, but she just had to hang in there a little longer, and then everything would be fine. Once daylight came she would take charge of her life again.

Wait, what was that noise? Eyes wide, she stared into the dark. It was nothing, why was she getting herself so hyper? "Get a grip, Pru" she chided herself in a tiny voice. It sounded strange in the quiet room. "Take some big breaths and calm down. There's no one here but me."

There it was again. It wasn't just her own frantic breathing. It was a soft, shuffling, whispering sort of sound. It was as if someone was trying to walk silently, and holding their breath. Her mouth was an arid desert, and her heart was a drum. She should try to yell, but would anyone hear her? She would feel like such a fool if it was just her imagination. Was it that menacing floor polisher coming back to attack her? Was it Jim Sinclair? Was it anyone at all?

Just as she tried to sit up and crawl over the end of the bed, she felt the pillow at her feet move. Staring in terror, her eyes focused on the figure standing there. There really was someone here in her room. He or she moved quickly, and as the dark apparition stood over her, holding the pillow, she gasped and croaked, "Oh no, not you, oh please no." This cry was filled with terror and resignation. "Why?"she cried into the pillow.

As she struggled weakly to fight off this deadly, silent killer, her flailing arm knocked over the plastic water jug from the bedside table. It bounced and clattered loudly, leaving a pool of water on the floor. Her hairbrush skittered away, and the wheeled table flew halfway across the room as she fought to sit up, fought to fend off the suffocating pillow, fought to stay alive.

The noise could have and should have alerted the nurses, but apparently no one heard. No one came running. No lights came on, no sirens blared. There was just the silent struggle between Pru and her killer. She had come too far to give up easily, so she put up a good fight, but she was no match for her assailant. It felt as if fire was racing through her blood. She felt tingly and heavy all at the same time.

With her one arm in a cast, she was at a serious disadvantage. She tried to use it as a club, but her attacker easily fended it off. She tried to scream, but the pillow muffled her pitiful efforts. She fought with every ounce of strength she had, but the attacker was able to wait her out. The pillow was as deadly as a gun would have been.

Prudence Wainwright put up a courageous fight, but her killer was determined. It was over quickly, although to Pru it seemed she struggled for a very long time. Eventually, however, her flailing arms lay quiet, her legs ceased to kick, and she fell reluctantly back into the frightening blackness.

CHAPTER 35

▼

Bunny Connors happened to look up from the nursing station just as the black clad figure emerged from room 707. It was somewhere around 4:45 in the morning, — certainly no time for visitors!

"What the heck" she exclaimed, standing up so quickly that her chair toppled over. The noise of the chair, along with her voice, echoed down the long silent corridor. The intruder paused and stared at her momentarily before disappearing down the stairwell. Because there was always a light in the stairwell, Bunny saw the face quite clearly.

"Laura" said Bunny in amazement, to a nurse just returning to the desk. "You'll never believe who I just saw coming out of Mrs. Wainwright's room. It was — — "

At that exact moment fate stepped in, and there was a loud crash from the room across the hall from the nursing station. Both Bunny and Laura Stephens raced into the room where Mr. Sanchez was supposedly sleeping. His roommate was looking frightened and bewildered, while Mr. Sanchez lay unconscious on the floor. Several items from his bedside table were scattered around him. A small pool of blood was beginning to seep from under his prone figure.

"Poor old bugger's broken his nose, I bet" said Bunny. Laura ran to put in a call for the doctor, while Bunny took his vitals and covered him with a blanket until the orderlies arrived to lift him. All thoughts of the black clad intruder had flown from her mind.

It was a good half hour before Mr. Sanchez was carted off to ICU, probably with a head trauma, and Laura and Bunny were just returning to the station when the call board began buzzing. Sighing in exasperation, Bunny noted that it was Mrs. Jackson. Hurrying down the hall in the opposite direction from Pru Wainwright's room, Bunny silently prayed that Mrs. Jackson hadn't thrown up again. Unfortunately her prayers went unanswered. During the day, a nurse's aide would have had the job of cleaning her up, but in the middle of the night, Bunny was stuck with the dirty task.

By the time she had Mrs. Jackson into a clean hospital johnny, and had changed the sheets, she was in a bad mood. This was not why she had become a nurse. There was nothing glamorous about cleaning up barf in the middle of the night. Suddenly she remembered the dark clad figure whom she was sure she had recognized. Oh shit, that must have been at least an hour ago, she thought in panic. I have to check her right now. Damn Mrs. Jackson and her barfing, and why did that old fool Mr. Sanchez have to try climbing out of bed over the high side bars?

Bunny had an uneasy, sick feeling in the pit of her stomach. The more she thought of that dark clad figure, the more nervous she became. As she raced down the hall, and saw that the door to room 707 was closed, she knew with heart stopping certainty that something dreadful had happened. Mrs. Wainwright's door was always open.

She gingerly pushed the door, and shone her flashlight into the dark room. Immediately she was aware of the signs of a struggle. The water pitcher, a plastic cup and straw, two magazines and a hair brush were scattered on the floor, along with a pool of water. The portable hospital table, designed to fit across the bed, thus providing a flat surface on which the patient could have his or her meals, play cards with visitors or apply make-up, was pushed helter-skelter halfway to the window.

Bunny noticed all these things subconsciously before she could bring herself to the bedside. Stepping carefully, she pocketed her flashlight, and turned on the light over the bed. She stifled a gasp, and put her hand to her mouth in horror at what she saw.

Pru Wainwright was lying flat on her back, her hair dishevelled and wild. Both hands lay on the pillow, palms up on either side of her head as if in supplication. The cast on the left arm looked awkward and heavy. Her lips were cyanotic, and her bulging eyes showed signs of petechial hemorrhaging, a sure indication of strangling or smothering. Her cheeks were a mottled, purplish blue. Bunny noticed that the patient's call button on a cord was hanging uselessly behind the bed, totally out of reach.

Strangely, the bed clothes seemed to have been carefully straightened and pulled up to the patient's chin. One foot, however, had escaped the sheets, and was sticking out at an angle. It looked small and pathetically white, as if it had been making a desperate effort to escape whatever mayhem had occurred.

In the small aquarium, the cardinal tetras, sea horses and fire clownfish swam unconcerned, keeping their secrets. They would never tell what they had seen.

Bunny's instinct was to take the patient's pulse and to check for signs of breathing, but she knew she mustn't touch anything. Anyway it was all too apparent that Prudence Wainwright was very dead. In that moment Bunny forgot everything she knew about being a professional, supposedly calm and cool at all times. She panicked. Mrs. Wainwright had obviously been murdered, and Bunny didn't know what she was supposed to do, so she backed out of the room, somehow afraid to turn her back on the frightening body, and she ran.

She was nearly hysterical as she bolted down that long corridor back to the nursing station. Laura was walking from the other direction, and Shannon Armstrong was at the desk looking at charts.

"She's dead" sobbed Bunny, unable to control herself. "Mrs. Wainwright is dead. She's been murdered."

Laura and Shannon stared at her stupidly. "Bunny, get hold of yourself. You must be mistaken. Go wash your face and calm down and I'll check on her." Laura took off at a run while Bunny gladly obeyed.

She spent a good fifteen minutes in the washroom trying to get her wildly pumping heart and her leaking eyes under control. She couldn't think straight, but she knew that there was no logical reason for the black clad intruder to be at the hospital at this hour except with the purpose of killing Mrs. Wainwright. Oh, why hadn't she checked as soon as she saw the person coming out of the room? Was she going to be in trouble? Maybe she could have saved the patient. She might not have been dead at that point. Should she say anything, should she tell anyone? She didn't want to lose her job. Was she at fault?

Bunny realized with terror that she had seen the face of the killer, and more importantly, the killer had seen her. It was the first snowflake in an absolute avalanche of fear which promised to bury her. In a moment of total paranoia she looked in every stall. Logic told her that there was no way the killer could be hiding there, but she looked anyway. This was no time for common sense.

By the time a still frightened Bunny came back to the nursing station, Laura had been busy making important calls. She had contacted Mrs. Wainwright's personal physician, Dr. Jennifer MacDonald. She had paged the attending resident, Dr. Phil Martin. She had contacted Dr. Mitch Taylor, and of course, she had immediately called the coroner, Dr. Solly Jalnek, an old family friend. Laura was covering all the bases and doing everything by the book. Because of who Prudence Wainwright was, this was going to be a very high profile investigation, and Laura was leaving nothing to chance.

Pru's body had to be left exactly as it was found. They could touch nothing, they couldn't even close her eyes or cover her face. Some important trace evidence might be destroyed. Until the coroner and the police had investigated, room 707 was off limits. Pru's body would remain right where it was until the coroner and police were finished, and possibly as a courtesy, until her next of kin could see her and say their good-byes. Then, because she was a murder victim, she would be taken to the forensic lab for the autopsy done by a forensic pathologist. There was to be no going softly into that dark night for Prudence.

"Laura, my shift is over in fifteen minutes, but I feel so sick. I have to get home. I'm, leaving right now."

Laura Stephens looked incredulously at Bunny. "Are you crazy? Prudence Wainwright has just been murdered. The police are on their way. They'll want to talk to all of us. Shit, we'll be their prime suspects. All hell is going to break loose. There's no way you can leave, Bunny, not till the police say so."

"But, Laura, I've got the flu I think," Bunny lied quickly. "I threw up in the bathroom. I shouldn't be around the patients."

"You don't have to be around the patients, Bunny," Laura said crossly. She was terribly upset and frightened by what had happened. A murder had taken place while she was on duty. Could she in any way be found responsible, or maybe irresponsible? "You can just sit here and wait with the rest of us."

"Oh no. I'm going to be sick again," cried Bunny as she raced back to the washroom.

Shaking her head, Laura turned and began talking with Shannon, who seemed to be in a catatonic trance. Neither she nor Shannon noticed Bunny slip quietly out of the bathroom and down the hall to the stairs.

CHAPTER 36

▼

Bunny took off like a scared rabbit. The more she thought about it, the more she realized that she was in danger. The intruder, make that murderer, had looked right at her. Logically Bunny could or would be the next victim.

Her hands were shaking so much that she could barely get the key into the car lock. She had to try three times, all the while looking over her shoulder in case someone attacked from behind. Then it took her three more times to fit the key into the ignition. Finally she sat there in her locked car, taking big gulping breaths as she twisted her head this way and that, looking for the murderer.

On the short drive home she was vaguely aware that it was going to be a hot day . Even with the air conditioner going, her skin was clammy. Was that from the heat or just from fear? She tried to tell herself that nothing bad could happen in Toronto on a beautiful summer morning, but she didn't believe it. Maybe she was being totally paranoid, but she had to think, and to do that she had to be safely locked inside her apartment. It was her little "safe house," her oasis in the craziness which was Toronto. She couldn't get there fast enough. She didn't care if she got a speeding ticket. Actually she would welcome a policeman with open arms.

She assured herself that only good things could happen on this perfect Toronto morning. She was a silly fool getting all worked up over nothing. She should go back to the hospital right now and talk to the police. After all, she was the only one who could tell them the killer's name. She was an important player in this little drama. The longer she waited, the worse it would appear. Oh, damn, damn, damn. Why had she looked up just as the killer was leaving? What awful little twist of fate had caused her to look into the startled face of the killer? She had to turn around right now. No, she was past the point of no return, closer to her apartment than to the hospital.

Glancing in the rear view mirror, she reassured herself that no one was following her, but then, how would she know? She couldn't tell one car from another. Oh, if only Jimmy hadn't gone away yesterday. Why didn't she have a key to his apartment? No one would find her there. Shoot, she was just being stupid, imagining crazy things. She had to calm down. She would get into her own safe little apartment, all fixed up the way she liked it, and she would call the police. She would lock herself in until they got there.

Reaching the apartment parking lot, she peered around anxiously. How would she even know if there was someone waiting there for her? Well, she might not be able to distinguish car makes, but she could distinguish people, and she knew who the killer was. Taking a calming breath, she opened the car door and jumped out, tearing her panty hose in her haste. Racing for the apartment building, she made it inside safely.

The building had been erected in the late 40's, just after the war. The owner had made his fortune in a gold mine in Northern Ontario. He had built four six-story apartment buildings in Toronto, and had left one to each of his four children. The daughter who owned Bunny's building had more money than she could spend. She travelled most of the time, and kept the rents surprisingly low so that the apartments would always be full, and people wouldn't be moving in and out all the time.

Bunny's lucky day came when she began nursing the old lady who lived in the particular apartment which was now Bunny's. The old woman had died in hospital. Her son lived in California, and when he flew to Toronto and realized that his mother was dying, he had asked Bunny if she knew anyone who would like to rent a large two bedroom apartment only four blocks from the hospital. At that time, Bunny was living in a tiny one bedroom in a high-rise at Eglinton and Yonge. She had been paying more for it than what she eventually paid for her large two bedroom. She furnished it slowly and carefully, haunting the second hand shops and watching for bargains. Bunny had very good taste, and soon there were elegant prints on the walls, several pieces of Italian pottery scattered about, and her precious animal collection.

The apartment was bright and cheery, with two bedrooms, a large living-dining area, a good-sized kitchen with lots of cupboards, and a very nice balcony. It was Bunny's haven, and she knew that if she could just get there and lock herself in, she would be safe. As she raced across the parking lot, however, she wished fervently that she was still in the high rise with the snooty doorman who kept everyone out if they didn't have a good reason for being there. Anyone could get into this old building at any time. Not even stopping to catch her breath, she plunged across the lobby to the elevators. Should she take them or try to run up the four floors? She was safer in the elevators, someone could be hiding in the stairwell.

"Oh please, I'll be such a good nurse. I'll take extra good care of all the patients. I'll never flirt with a doctor again, at least not the married ones. She had to add that little caveat. I promise I'll call my parents three times a week. I'll take piles of food to the animal shelter every month. I'll even be kind to fat George, and I'll ignore the pimple on his chin. Please just let me make it safely into my apartment." Bunny was whimpering and whispering as she rode the elevator to the fourth floor. She wasn't exactly bargaining with God because she knew that was wrong. She was just grasping at any lifeline and hoping for the best.

Why had she ever volunteered for night duty? She could have been safely sleeping in her pretty little bedroom instead of seeing the face of evil. Her thoughts and fears were racing aimlessly like the beetles she had once seen at a science fair. They hurried and scurried, but got nowhere.

Bunny kept going over the events in her mind. It was murder, no doubt about it. She had to tell the police, even if she did get in trouble for not checking on Mrs. Wainwright right away. She couldn't stay quiet about it because Laura knew how upset she had been, and she had even started to tell Laura about the killer. Besides, she liked Mrs. Wainwright, and wasn't going to let anyone get away with killing her. The truth shall set you free, she thought grimly. Seeing poor old Mr. Sanchez lying out cold on the floor had really knocked all other thoughts from her mind, and then she'd had to clean up Mrs. Jackson and her mess. She couldn't conceivably get in trouble for doing her duty. Telling the truth was best. She would call the police the minute she was safely locked inside.

Diving out of the elevator, she ran down the hall toward her apartment, the end one right beside the exit. She had always felt so safe being by the stairwell in case of fire. She didn't realize that she was making a considerable racket as she flew down the hall. With her purse flapping on her shoulder, and the little moans of terror coming from her in bursts, it was surprising that no one heard.

Didn't anyone get up at this hour? The long hall was like a tomb except for the panicked race. She wondered fleetingly if she should pound on someone's door, but she didn't really know anyone in the building except for Jimmy who wasn't there. In her mind the killer could be lurking behind any door. She knew that there were two dear old retired folk in the apartment next to hers, but they likely slept till noon. What could they do anyway to protect her? She was being totally hysterical now as she prayed to get safely inside.

Finally, after an eternity, which in reality was less than a minute, she was at her door. In her haste, her shaky fingers dropped the keys. Bending to pick them up, her purse fell off her shoulder, regurgitating the myriad of necessities which Bunny always carried with her. Crying now, and hyperventilating, she ignored the spilled items. She could get them later.

Because of her own sobbing, she didn't hear the fire door open behind her. Before she could get the key into the lock, however, something made her turn her head and glance over her shoulder. The movement was so swift that she didn't really see it. She just felt the incredibly hot, piercing pain in her neck. As she sank slowly to her knees, eyes wide with terror and surprise, she put her hand to her neck and saw with distant amazement that it was covered with blood. The blood in fact, was spurting everywhere. It was a gusher, as if the killer had struck oil. Opening her mouth to scream, she felt another stabbing pain, and then another.

As little Bunny Connors, so pretty, so carefree, fell to her knees, she thought regretfully of her new uniform which had looked so good on her, and which was now ruined. Then as she took her last breath, she wished she had told someone the name of the killer.

The apartment next to Bunny was occupied by Claire and Donald Simpson. Donald loved to sleep late in the mornings, but Claire was always up early. A couple of times a week she dressed quietly and slipped out. She always walked slowly down the street to the Tim Horton's on the corner, and bought two coffee and two croissants. It was a little treat they both enjoyed.

This warm, sunny Toronto morning, as eighty-three year old Claire Simpson toddled out of her apartment, she saw what appeared to be a heap of bloody clothes lying in front of the next door. When curious Claire went to have a closer look and realized what the heap was, she couldn't stop screaming.

CHAPTER 37

▼

That morning Douglas Bannon — defender of the innocent — (himself in this case), slept late. When Maureen Delaney arrived, she was surprised to find him still in bed. After checking to be sure that he was still breathing, she went about her chores.

Maureen had looked after the Bannons for more years than she could count. She and Ruth Bannon had often worked side by side, cleaning closets, polishing silver, even washing windows. Her friend Ruth had been a lovely woman. She never put on airs in spite of living in this beautiful big old house. After Ruth died, however, things changed dramatically. The life and sparkle had gone out of the house and out of Douglas too.

Maureen felt so sorry for the lonely old soul that she started bringing date squares and home baked muffins and the occasional casserole for him. They had developed a companionable friendship, and although they only saw each other for a short time each week, they were comfortable together. Their fond memories of Ruth gave them a certain bond. Today Maureen put a chicken pot pie in the freezer, and fresh muffins on the counter, then got down to work.

It was easy to clean this old house because it seemed that Mr. Bannon only used a few rooms. Actually it was way too big for him now. The kitchen didn't get very dirty, because all he used was the microwave, and he was good about putting his few dishes in the dishwasher. His bedroom was always neat and tidy. All she had to do was change the linens, dust and vacuum. His ensuite bathroom was easy. This was a very tidy man. Ruth had trained him well. It was actually only the den which required much work. That was where Douglas really lived. There were always papers and magazines scattered everywhere, usually along with a few forgotten glasses. He did like his little bedtime drinks.

When Douglas finally wakened and heard noises in the house, he thought for one terrified moment that the intruder was back. Then he realized with a laugh that it was the vacuum he heard. Maureen was here! Shaking his head at his foolishness, he showered and shaved, and dressed in his favourite navy blue suit. He still took pride in his appearance, and was always nattily attired. Ruth had seen to that.

Going down to the kitchen, he told Maureen of the night's adventures. He tried not to make himself out as too heroic. Harrison Ford he wasn't! Still, he was quite proud of the way he had attacked the intruder and chased him off. Maureen was suitably impressed.

Douglas ate one of the delicious home baked carrot muffins, and had a glass of juice. He would have his tea when he got to the office. This was one of the days when his secretary, legal assistant, and all round girl Friday worked. Sheridan Winslow came in three days a week, and when she was there they shared many a pot of tea during the course of the day.

Douglas headed to the office without turning on the car radio. He therefore had no idea of the dreadful events which had taken place during the night and early morning. Without his briefcase he felt lost and angry, and he tried to remember what important papers it contained. With all the excitement he had totally forgotten that the will and letter were still sitting on the table in the den.

Maureen thought that the den this morning was unusually messy. Newspapers and law reviews were strewn all over the carpet. The intruder must have been in quite a hurry. She was always exceptionally careful not to throw anything out except for the week's supply of scattered newspapers. She had Douglas's permission to bundle those up for recycling.

This bright sunny morning she hummed happily to herself as she picked up the papers on the floor, then turned to his desk. She carefully straightened a pile of letters and documents, and placed them in the centre of the desk. Then smiling, she added his interesting paperweight which was an onyx cube. She often kidded him that it looked like a lump of coal, and should be pitched. Douglas always replied that he would use it to hit her on the head if she ever disturbed or lost any of his important papers.

Next Maureen turned to the messy pile of magazines on the table beside the lounger. She was thinking about Douglas attacking the intruder last night. It had been a foolhardy thing to do, he could have been killed. She understood, though, that it had made him feel really good about himself. Strange that the thief hadn't stolen anything but the briefcase. Maybe he just hadn't had time before Douglas heard him and came charging into the room. She would have loved to see that! Douglas and that old bat were funny. She always had to move it when she vacuumed under the bed. She and Ruth had laughed about it more than once, but now Douglas had had the last laugh. Well, good for him.

Tidying the magazines into a neat pile, she added them to the collection on the shelf under the table. She didn't notice the will and the letter which were now unintentionally hidden between the magazines.

When the doorbell rang, Maureen expected that it was probably some religious group peddling their monthly bulletin, or possibly someone canvassing for a local charity. The strange looking person at the door seemed startled when she opened it. It was as if he or she, Maureen couldn't be sure, hadn't expected anyone to be home. Before she could really register this odd fact in her mind, she was given a mighty shove, and knocked back against the solid Deacon's bench.

"Where's the old guy?"

"He's at the office" replied a badly frightened Maureen in a trembling voice. Maybe she shouldn't have said that. She should have pretended that Mr. Bannon was upstairs, then possibly the intruder would have run away. She was sure that this was the same person from last night.

"There's no money here" she began in a placating tone. "Mr. Bannon doesn't keep any money in the house."

"I don't want money. Does he have a safe? Where does he keep his important papers?"

"I don't know" stammered Maureen. "I don't think there's a safe. I've never seen one." She felt that if she were polite and reasonable, this scary person might leave without hurting her.

"Well, lady, it's too bad you had to be here. You're going to take a short vacation in a closet. If you promise not to scream I won't gag you, but if you let out so much as a whimper I won't hesitate to kill you. I'm not in the mood for fooling around."

Maureen tried to fight back as she was dragged and shoved along the hall. There was a closet with a lock on it, and the intruder stuffed her inside. Maureen was terrified. She was making weird little mewing sounds, and her breath was coming in tiny puffs as if she were trying to blow out a candle. She needed Mr. Bannon's baseball bat!

She couldn't see this person's face clearly, but she was sure now that it was a man. The big slouch hat and upturned collar and glasses made identification impossible. She would never be able to finger this clod in the future, if in fact there was going to be a future for her. She calmed down enough to realize that if he was going to kill her he would have done so right away. As long as she didn't stare at his face or appear to recognize him she was likely okay. She had resisted the impulse to tear off his hat and dark glasses, and now she was thankful. That may have saved her life.

The closet was full of jackets and coats, with a few pair of boots and shoes on the floor. There was barely room to stand, and there seemed to be no air. She felt as if she was suffocating, but she didn't dare yell.

Maureen waited in silence, her wiry little body shivering and shaking, first in terror, then gradually in anger. How dare anyone break into Mr. Bannon's home and threaten her? What was this guy after? She would listen for the front door to close and then she would start yelling.

Unfortunately Maureen's hearing wasn't the best, and she couldn't hear any sounds from the den. Had he gone upstairs? Where was he? She strained to hear the front door close. She would only feel safe once she knew that this bully was gone. With a sigh, she realized that she was stuck here in the closet till Douglas returned.

Pushing boots and a box of odds and ends to one side of the cramped little closet, she gingerly lowered herself to a sitting position, and tried to breathe slowly so as not to use up all the oxygen. There was a slight crack under the door through which a mere sliver of light entered, so she was pretty sure now that she wouldn't suffocate, but she continued to make herself breathe slowly and calmly. She had read somewhere that the brain uses up less oxygen when the eyes are closed. It didn't make a lot of sense, but she was willing to try it. Sitting in the dark closet, eyes closed, breathing slowly, she raged at this intruder, this monster defiling Mr. Bannon's home.

The ringing of the telephone provided a frustrating interlude, since it rang at least twelve times before the caller hung up. She prayed it was Douglas, and that he would rush right home to rescue her.

Meanwhile at the office, Douglas was discussing the night's adventures with Sheridan. He kept asking himself what the intruder could have been after. Suddenly he thumped his mug down on the desk. It was as obvious as the pimple on a teenager's chin. The masked man hadn't taken anything of value, except his beloved old briefcase. He or she was looking for something. Of course! It had to be the will. Oh no, where was the will?

Staring blindly at Sheridan, and frantically replaying last evening in his mind, he picked up the phone and called Maureen. The phone rang and rang, but she didn't answer.

At this point Douglas was still totally unaware that his old friend Prudence Wainwright was dead. It was only when he made a second call, this one to the police, to tell them about the will and about his suspicions concerning the identity of the intruder, that he discovered the horrible news about Prudence and the pretty little nurse who had witnessed the will. He realized then that Maureen could be in danger, and he asked the police to meet him at his house.

They reached his home just moments before Douglas did. It was a good thing that they hadn't seen how fast he was driving. He had never driven that fast in his life, and he was shaking as he hurried up his front steps, fearful of what he might find. He pictured poor Maureen dead on the floor, her head caved in with his onyx paperweight. Then his mind's eye saw her gagged and bound to a chair. When his imagination carried him to a naked Maureen spread-eagled and tied to the bedposts, he shook his head in horror and embarrassment to shatter the visions. It was a great relief to find her unharmed in the closet, and mad as a little hornet at the indignity of it all. Douglas, who was a very shy man, found himself hugging her warmly, as they freed her from the dark enclosure.

The police questioned her while Douglas hurried to the den to retrieve the will and letter. The intruder had made a dreadful mess of the place. There were papers and books everywhere. He wondered idly whether Maureen had already tidied the room before being thrown into the closet. All that work for nothing. Judging by the way things were scattered every which way, he guessed that the intruder had been in a mindless rage as he searched for the will and letter. He tried to figure who would have known about the will. Surely the doctor hadn't done this. Had Pru told her family about changing her will? That seemed highly unlikely. It was all too confusing for Douglas. He would let the police figure it out. They were now admonishing him not to touch anything, but it was a bit late for that. With a sigh of relief, he saw that the little pile of magazines remained untouched on the lower table shelf. Maureen had inadvertently found the perfect hiding place for the documents.

CHAPTER 38

▼

It was almost daylight when Vickie struggled awake. Why had she set the alarm for this ungodly hour? They were going over to Toronto to see Pru today and find out what was so urgent, and what the big secret was, but this seemed to be the middle of the night. Oh shit, it's the phone, she realized in panic. There was no way it could be anything but bad news at this time of the morning. Suddenly it stopped. Cassie had either answered it, or the person calling had hung up. Maybe it was the stalker again, just trying to harass and annoy them. She lay there for a minute wondering who it could be, then she grabbed the old plaid housecoat which was actually Brian's. It wasn't fashionable, but it was cosy, and she felt safe in it. She hadn't really been missing Brian, she was used to him being away a lot. At this moment in time, however, she felt a chill as she huddled into its warm familiarity and hurried down the hall to Cassie's room. Just wearing his old robe brought him closer.

The door was open as always so that Sugar and Muffy could come and go as they pleased. She reached the room just as Cassie was hanging up the receiver. "What's up Cass? Is anything wrong?" Even as the words left her mouth she realized that something was indeed very wrong. She could tell by the look on Cassie's face.

"Sit here beside me, Vic." Cassie patted the mattress and Vickie dutifully sat down. She saw that Cassie's blue eyes seemed the size of saucers, and she was beginning to tremble.

"Pru's dead" she cried in a quiet and disbelieving tone. "She's dead."

Vickie let out an unbelieving squeak as she put one arm around her friend. She sat in silence for a stunned moment, trying to comprehend the magnitude of this news. "It can't be. You must have dreamt it or misunderstood. We've both been stressed out. It was just a bad dream." Although she was saying these comforting words, she realized that she had definitely heard the phone ringing. "Maybe it was a crank call. Probably it was someone mean like our stalker friend, just trying to cause trouble and scare you." This last was offered doubtfully, because Vickie knew that it wasn't likely.

"No, it's true, Vic. That was the nurse at the hospital. The doctor's been there and confirmed it. They don't know, or aren't saying what the cause of death was — not yet anyway." Cassie put her hand up to her mouth as if to stop the flow of sad and unbelievable words pouring forth. "I can't accept it. Pru is dead." She said this very slowly, as if trying to understand the foreign words. "It makes no sense. She was doing really well, everyone said so. She called me last night, for goodness sake. The nurse was very evasive and upset when I tried to get details. Vickie, you know what I think has happened?" There was absolute horror in her eyes as she looked at her friend.

Before Vickie could answer, Cassie continued. "She was murdered. I know it. You don't just die in the hospital when you are on the mend. They were monitoring her, so they would have known if she suddenly had a stroke or a blood clot, wouldn't they? Besides, something else is really strange." She was now twisting a piece of hair in her fingers in an absent minded, nervous fashion. "The nurse said that they were contacting me first because this week Pru had asked them to change the records to show that I was her next of kin. She had them remove Jordan and Jenny and put me on!"

"That's bizarre. She must have been really mad at them, or maybe she just felt that you are more stable than those two flakes. I can see her thinking that." Vickie was feeling more and more like Alice at the tea party. Something was weird about all this. Could Cassie be right? Could it have been murder? "You know, maybe it was just a whim. She's been doped up a lot of the time and she may have been hallucinating."

"Well, it makes no sense, and anyway I don't want to be her next of kin after all the years she ignored me. I'm just her kid sister — not close at all. Like it or not, she had two kids and they should have been on the records to be notified first. I don't want any part of it. Oh, I wish Dave were here. He'd know what to do."

Cassie phoned the hospital while Vickie went to make some tea. She was hoping that it was all some dreadful mistake. It was no mistake, however, and this call proved to be as frustrating as the first one. The nurse with whom she spoke was very guarded and unresponsive. She couldn't or wouldn't answer any of Cassie's questions.

Cass bounded into the kitchen and announced. "Vic, we've got to get going right away. It's a good thing we were heading over this morning anyway. Apparently being listed as next of kin means that I have to sign something to allow them to do the autopsy. This is just beyond belief! We seem to be involved whether we want to be or not. I'll call Peggy to stay with the cats because we may end up staying over night. We really got our mystery in spades didn't we?" she grimaced as she went back to the phone.

She wondered whether it was her responsibility to call Jordan and Jenny, but her efforts to contact them failed. Perhaps they were already at the hospital. She did manage to get Blake, who seemed badly shaken at the news. Actually he seemed devastated. Cass wondered again whether he might have been in love with Pru. Her last call was to Elena, who sounded surprised but not overly upset. Cass couldn't really tell what her reaction was.

Vickie drove this time and they talked non-stop.

"She was doing so well. Who the hell did this, and why?" Cass sighed as they sped along the highway.

"We don't really know that anyone did anything, do we?" Vickie was trying half-heartedly to be rational. She, however, was strangely excited to be caught up in the middle of this mystery, and she was sure in her heart that Cassie was correct. Pru may very well have been murdered.

"Oh Vic, I'm sure that whoever killed Matt, just finished the job with Pru. But why would they have waited so long? Why not kill her when she was still in the coma? That would have been easier and less suspicious wouldn't it? And, her phone call yesterday asking me to come over this morning, what did that have to do with anything? Was that just coincidental, or did someone overhear her and try to shut her up before she could tell me "the secret"?"

Eventually they switched on the radio in hopes of finding some soothing music. Instead they got the hourly newscast, which, as usual, was full of violence and crime. "A brutal stabbing of a young nurse occurred in a downtown Toronto apartment building early this morning" blared the newscaster. "The lifeless body of Bunny Connors — aged twenty-two — was found in a hallway by a neighbour. Police have no leads at this time, but a full investigation is promised."

"Bunny Connors" shrieked Cassandra. "She was one of Pru's nurses. She was the good looking little Barbie doll."

"Dear Lord, what could the connection be? She must have seen whoever killed Pru, so the murderer had to chase her down and kill her too." Vickie's eyes were round with excitement as she made her deductions.

Stepping off the elevator onto the 7th floor, the two friends walked into a chaotic scene. Ambulatory patients were peeking out their doors, looking both scared and interested. Several reporters and a cameraman were already becoming nuisances. Looking down the hall towards Pru's room, their hearts began thumping as they saw the yellow crime scene tape across the door. Two uniformed cops were standing nearby chatting. As Cass and Vickie approached the nursing station, they saw two detectives questioning one of the nurses. They knew with certainty that their fears and suspicions were correct. Pru must have been murdered.

"I'll get the doctor" said a very solicitous nurse when she realized who Cassie was. She ushered them into a rather drab little room and told them to wait till the doctor or the detectives came.

"We heard on the car radio about Bunny Connors" said Vickie before the nurse could escape.

"It's just so unthinkable" she answered, pausing at the door. "We're all in shock. Nothing like this has ever happened before. Bunny was a nice friendly person and the patients all seemed to love her. Everybody loved Bunny" she added generously. But apparently there was someone out there who hadn't loved Bunny.

As they waited in the grim little room, Cassandra realized just how much she was missing Dave. Vickie was a wonderful friend and confidante, but she needed Dave. His gentle strength and comforting quiet manner were exactly what was required to keep her calm. She felt a bit like an old sweater gradually unravelling. The infrequent calls from him were inadequate and frustrating. She hadn't told him much of what was going on. Why worry the poor guy with all her hair-brained suspicions? Now, however, with all these new developments, she could hardly wait to call him. Perhaps he could come home sooner than anticipated. The problem was that she felt like an imposter here. Pru had never given her the time of day till recently. Why should Cass be the one to be representing the family? Where were Jordan and Jenny?

Waiting in that dull little room, both women wondered how many grief-stricken people had sat here over the years. Vickie offered to get a cup of tea from the machine, but Cass just shook her head. She was beyond tea at this point. What they needed was a good stiff drink.

Eventually Dr. Taylor came into the room, quietly closing the door behind him. "I'm very sorry," he said, without wasting a moment. He looked haggard this morning. "We don't know yet just what happened" he began, shaking his head. "There was no sign that she tried to use her call button." He didn't mention that the call button had been totally out of Pru's reach. That would look very bad for the hospital. "No one heard her call out either. Her water jug was knocked on the floor, however, along with other things, so she must have been putting up a good fight."

When he saw the stricken look on Cassie's face he paused, and then continued. "I'm sure it was over very quickly. She wasn't very strong yet you know." He looked at Cass appraisingly, then plunged ahead. "I'm sorry to tell you this, but as the listed next of kin, you must give the permission for the autopsy. Actually it's just a courtesy. By law there has to be an autopsy whether you agree or not." He paused again to see Cassie's reaction.

"Of course" she replied quickly. "We certainly want to know just what happened, but I don't feel that I'm the one to be giving permission — courtesy or not. She has two children. Where are they, and what exactly happened to her, how was she killed?"

He sighed at this and said very quietly, "she was smothered. It would have been quite quick." He knew this wasn't true, but why give the relatives any more grief than necessary. Also, it looked better for the hospital if it had happened very quickly. There would be less questions as to why no nurse heard the struggle and came to help her.

"Smothered!" Both women looked at each other, mouths agape. "You mean, like with a pillow or something?" inquired Vickie.

"Yes, exactly. We're pretty sure that's what happened. There was no plastic bag or anything over her head, and there was an extra pillow on the floor beside the bed." Here Dr. Taylor looked as if he regretted giving this much information, and he headed for the door.

"Are there any suspects?" Cass didn't want him to run away so quickly.

He laughed grimly at that. "Actually I imagine that every person who was here last night will be a suspect, even the other patients. I don't think that the police have a clue."

"Well, what about Bunny? Was she murdered because she saw Pru's killer?" Vickie didn't want him to run away before giving them as much info as possible.

"Oh, I have no idea." He smiled at them both then, and they knew he was putting on the charm. "If you'll wait a few more minutes I'll bring the papers for you to sign."

Just as Dr. Taylor was hurrying from the room, Blake appeared. He looked shocked and dishevelled. Gloria followed on his heels. They all embraced, and then, looking around the tiny room, Blake asked "Where are Jordan and Jenny?"

"I don't know," replied Cass. "I'm not sure whether they've even been contacted yet. I know that I couldn't get in touch with them, although I tried both the Toronto house and the Muskoka cottage, but maybe the hospital has been able to."

Just about now Cassandra felt like crying and stamping her feet. Guilt was setting in. Why hadn't she insisted on protection for her sister? She had distanced herself too much just because she was hurt by Pru's lack of attention over the years. On the other hand, why hadn't Jordan or Jenny insisted on security for their mom, and where the hell were they? Did they know yet that she was dead? Had one of them killed her? Cassie's mind was going like an out of control racer. Her thoughts were flying like petals in the wind. She couldn't hang on to any of them. She felt ashamed of herself, and so angry. She had let Pru down. Like it or not, Prudence had been her sister, and she had done nothing to protect her.

Finally she excused herself and made her way down to the washroom. She needed to put cold water on her face and take a few deep calming breaths. As she passed the nursing station she heard a nurse saying to the detectives, "I know that Bunny saw something that frightened her. She saw someone coming out of Mrs. Wainwright's room, but before she could tell me who it was, we heard a crash. We both took off and found Mr. Sanchez unconscious on the floor. Bunny stayed with him while I got two orderlies. After that things got really busy. It seemed that all the buzzers were going, and Bunny never had a chance to tell me who she saw. Actually we both forgot all about it because Mr. Sanchez was our immediate concern. Bunny was scared, though. I know that now, looking back on it. When she found Mrs. Wainwright dead she became hysterical. Then she claimed that she was sick and had to go home right away. The last time I saw her she was heading for the washroom, but she obviously snuck out on us. She must have been terrified."

Laura paused here, then continued seriously. "I just know that she saw the murderer, and it was definitely someone she either knew or at least recognized. It must have been one of Mrs. Wainwright's family or friends."

"Or possibly another nurse or doctor" growled the cop, who was short and paunchy. He had very little hair to speak of, just a monk's ridge around the edges. He had one eye which seemed to wander independently of the other. "No point in jumping to conclusions. That's not how we work" he added with self importance.

"At this point we are just making inquiries" added the tall, anorexic one with the razor thin lips. "No one has said anything about murder."

Laura gave him a disbelieving look as if to say "who are you trying to kid?" Then she said, "Oh, please, you're not dealing with morons here, detective. We don't usually have yellow crime scene tape strung across a patient's room if they died of natural causes. Give us a little credit." Laura was tired and depressed, and had been answering their idiotic questions for hours it seemed.

Cass continued on down the hall feeling very antsy. Whoever had killed Pru had certainly killed Bunny too. Was anyone else on the murderer's list? More importantly, was she on the murderer's list?

Before leaving the hospital, the friends decided that they would definitely attend the wake for Bunny. They might learn something useful. Who knew — maybe the murderer would show up.

CHAPTER 39

▼

The funeral parlour was not quite what they had expected. It was one of the old fashioned ones popular in the forties, dark and scary. What an unfortunate choice for Bunny's wake. She had been so bright, sunny, and full of life. This place was so dark, drab, and full of death. They were surprised, however, at the number of people there. Bunny must have had a lot of friends. There were also probably a lot of "looky-loos" — nosy people who were attracted to murders and accidents. These ghouls made a hobby of going to funerals and wakes.

Cassie recognized many of the nurses and doctors. Obviously Bunny had been a favourite. There was chubby George, the med student who was always singing. Standing by the coffin they noticed Dr. Taylor. Then they saw Christina Marshall come in with a tall nice looking man. Was this her boyfriend? Vickie was sure that he was a doctor she had seen at the hospital. What if one of these doctors or nurses had killed Pru and Bunny? They all had ample opportunity, but did any of them have a motive? No, it wasn't likely. Whoever killed Pru had surely killed Matt as well. It was just an unfortunate chain of murders and undoubtedly poor Bunny was the innocent victim.

With so many of the staff here, both women wondered who was minding the hospital. They walked slowly across the thick dark red carpet. It reminded Cass of the colour of blood. The drapes were red velvet, and the elaborately carved wall sconces gave off muted lighting which threw strange shadows — all very depressing. There was a large gilt mirror on one wall, and Vickie caught a glimpse of her own pale face as they approached the coffin which lay in a recessed area. The archway was flanked with two enormous jardinières filled with white lilies and trailing greenery. Cass hated white flowers, they were just too funereal.

The lugubrious organ music moaned on until they felt like covering their ears. It was haunting and mournful. It certainly was designed to put one in the right mood, if that mood was meant to be depressed and disconsolate.

"Promise you'll see that I'm cremated and scattered to the winds," muttered Vickie, as they made their way slowly toward the coffin.

"More likely over your favourite restaurant" Cass whispered with a straight face, but Vickie could hear the laughter in her voice.

"After we pay our respects, let's sit right at the back near the door in case we want to leave early" suggested Victoria. "Back there we'll be able to see everyone who comes and goes."

"Sounds like a plan" agreed Cassandra.

They spoke with Bunny's shell-shocked parents, and with her sister and two brothers. They were all baffled at the ugly murder of their darling daughter and sister. None of them seemed to be considering her boyfriend Jimmy Tierney as a possible suspect.

Both women tried to offer comforting words, but to their own ears they sounded like empty platitudes. How could anyone find comfort in such a tragic situation?

As they finally reached the coffin, they gasped when they saw Bunny, or this waxen doll masquerading as Bunny. She was so small and diminished that she looked like a child. Instead of the usual prayer book or beads placed artfully in her hands, there was a large teddy bear tucked in her arms, and two stuffed animals lay beside her. Gone were the dimples, the sparkling eyes, the "joie de vivre."

Her thick red hair looked beautiful on the creamy satin pillow. Her lips were a lovely coral, but her face and hands were so dreadfully white. She looked like a wax dummy instead of the bubbly little nurse. "It's awful, Vickie. Who could have done such a maniacal thing? She was just an innocent young girl. What did she ever do to deserve such a fate? Last week she was alive, vivacious, full of laughter and hope. Today she's dead, just dead." Cass shuddered as she stared into the coffin.

As they stood looking at the unfortunate girl who had been in the wrong place at the wrong time, a pale young man walked up to the coffin beside them and gently patted Bunny's hands. He emitted a low groan which turned into a wail as he leaned over and kissed her on the lips. "Bye-bye my Bunnykins" he sobbed as great tears rolled down his cheeks.

Cass and Victoria quickly moved away. They felt like intruders in this very intimate moment.

"This must be the boyfriend" whispered Vickie.

"Right" answered Cassie. "He's certainly distraught."

"I can't see him killing her, can you?"

"Not likely. He seems sincere, and anyway, what motive could he have had? I'm sure he didn't know Pru, so he wouldn't have killed her, and these two murders are definitely tied together somehow."

When the wake was over and the two friends were leaving, they took one last look around at the gathering. They wondered whether the killer was there, and whether they might even have talked to him or her. They noted that neither Jordan nor Jenny had made an appearance. Was that indicative of guilt or innocence?

"I wonder why her folks picked this place" murmured Vickie as they descended the stairs. "It's so old fashioned and depressing. Everything is dark and heavy, it's like a medieval castle. I thought most funeral parlours today were more light and airy — not that I've been in many, thank God. The only thing worse here would have been if there had been candles burning all around the casket."

"Oh don't remind me. I had to go to a parlour like that when I was a kid, and they really did have candles all around the coffin. Remember that awful parlour down on Ducharme Street? I had nightmares for a long time after that. Hey, look across the street. There are three, no four video cameras pointing right over here. It's either the police or the TV stations."

"I think it's both. I'll bet they're checking out everyone in case the killer shows up. They'll go back and study all the footage and maybe they'll get some clues. Let's get out of here. If they recognize you as Pru's sister they might want to talk to you."

They were staying overnight in Toronto, since Pru's memorial service was to be the next day. It was a relief to get back to the normalcy and excitement of the hotel. They wandered the lobby for a while, people watching, then lingered in the gift shop. Eventually they went into the piano bar and had a drink, while listening to the show tunes being belted out by the big black pianist who looked and sounded like Fats Domino.

In contrast to last night's disheartening experience in that sombre parlour, Pru's memorial service was somehow joyful and uplifting. It was held in the old stone church which she and Matt had attended. The sun shining through the stained glass windows was making a golden glow around the marble urn containing Pru's ashes.

Jordan and Jenny sat in the front row along with Pete. Mercifully his tattoos were covered up with a jacket. Cassie and Victoria, Elena, Blake and Gloria and all their family, sat directly behind them. Jenny sobbed loudly throughout the service, and gently dabbed at her beautiful brown eyes.

The choir sang many of Pru's favourite hymns. The warm and loving eulogies portrayed her as a gentle, caring person who had done much for her community. They told funny anecdotes about her sense of humour, her elegance and her charitable nature. Cass kept hoping that Bunny's funeral in her home town would be as nice. As she heard these eulogies, she regretted more and more that she hadn't known this sister at all, and realized that she had apparently missed a great deal by not knowing her. How sad! Life was so short and so full of missed opportunities. Why hadn't she contacted Pru more often? Why hadn't she cared enough to try to close the gap between them? Funerals were a great time for self-recriminations.

She listened carefully as Pru's cottage neighbour, Joanne Bailey, read the passage from Eccleseastes. "To every thing there is a season — — a time to be born and a time to die, — — a time to weep and a time to laugh." This was finally Cassie's time to weep. She wept for all the lost opportunities, for all the sisterly things they hadn't shared. Drying her eyes, she promised herself that somehow she would find out who had killed Pru and Matt and Bunny. She would work to put them behind bars. She felt that she owed her sister that much. It annoyed her that Elena sat there so stoically, seemingly unmoved by the service.

Meanwhile, beside her, Vickie was thinking uncharitably that if Jenny didn't soon shut up and stop her weeping, she would wash them all right down the aisle! No one could cry that much — could they? She suspected that Jenny's histrionics were all sound and fury — signifying nothing. Either Jenny was totally distraught and broken hearted, which seemed highly unlikely, or she was the best little actress in town.

The spell of peace and hope was shattered as they left the church. There were media people everywhere. Cameramen recorded the mourners, zooming in on the immediate family. Cass noticed with interest that Elena seemed very camera shy. They were like a swarm of killer bees, darting this way and that, and sticking mikes into people's faces. They shoved, they pushed, they stepped on each other's toes. They seemed shameless in their collective attack. They acted just the way they were portrayed in the movies.

She was startled as a mike was shoved into her face. "Mrs. Meredith, why do you think your sister was murdered?" asked one brash blond with oddly pale eyes and eyelashes heavy with mascara. Cass wondered how these people knew that she was Pru's sister. "I have no idea" she replied, trying to keep her cool. "I'm sure the police are working hard to find all the answers."

Vickie grabbed Cassie's arm and pulled her towards the waiting limousine. "Please excuse us" she said, pushing through the crowd.

Undaunted, the news people followed. "Mrs. Meredith, what's the connection between your sister and Bunny Connors?"

"Mrs. Meredith, who do you think caused the car crash? Was it murder?"

"Mrs. Meredith are you expecting to inherit some of the Wainwright money?"

"Do you think you might be next on the killer's list?" shouted someone from the back of the crowd.

The questions seemed endless, and Cass and Vic were relieved to enter the safety and quiet of the funeral limo.

"Whew! Talk about piranhas!" exclaimed Vickie. "They're relentless."

Cass closed her eyes and took a big breath. "I just hope we aren't a sound byte on the six o'clock news!" She didn't want to let Vickie know how upsetting that last question had been. Was she on the killer's list?

"They just don't give up, do they?" complained Vickie, peering out the window at the gang who were now assaulting Blake and his family. "I should have planted a big wet kiss on those flapping lips of that pushy blonde. Wouldn't that have been a salacious tidbit for the news!"

"That obnoxious little bald twerp really pissed me off asking if I was expecting to inherit the Wainwright money. What garbage! I should have jammed that mike right up his old kazoo."

"What about Jenny?" laughed Vickie. "Didn't you think that was quite a performance? Look at her over there, smiling and talking to the newsmen. She doesn't seem too distraught now, does she?"

Cass leaned back and closed her eyes. "Do you know where I wish we were right this very moment?"

"No, and I can't even make a good guess."

"I wish we were in the Bahamas, sitting under a sun umbrella on the beach, sipping piña coladas. Wouldn't that be wonderful?"

"Wowie, you dream in Technicolor, don't you? What a great idea," sighed Vickie as the funeral cars headed down the street.

By the time the reception ended, the two friends were anxious to be on their way back to the Falls. Most of the guests had left, and they weren't eager to be alone in this mausoleum with Jordan and Jenny. Pete and Elena seemed to have disappeared.

They were just gathering their purses when the doorbell rang, and they heard Douglas Bannon apologizing for disturbing everyone after such a long day. As he entered the den behind Jordan, he got right to the point.

"I want to gather the beneficiaries of Pru's will for a reading in my office next week. I was halfway home before I remembered. I'm getting very forgetful in my old age." Here he smiled sadly at no one in particular, and shook his head ruefully at his own failings. "Would next Friday be a convenient time for all three of you?"

"Three of us" queried Jenny in surprise.

"Why, yes, you and Jordan and Mrs. Meredith" answered Douglas quietly.

Cassie was surprised to find herself described as a beneficiary. She looked at Vickie and raised her eyebrows. She and Pru hadn't been close by any stretch, so why would her sister want to leave her anything? She had two greedy children who were expecting to inherit everything. Besides, she and Vickie had seen the will, and she was sure that her name hadn't been mentioned. What was going on now? She didn't like the way Jenny was glowering at her.

"I shall contact the others by phone, and we'll set the date for next Friday afternoon at 3pm" said Douglas firmly as he headed towards the door.

"The others?" repeated Jordan, obviously dismayed at this turn of events. "How many others?"

But Douglas was already on his way out. He pretended he hadn't heard Jordan as he disappeared into the night.

CHAPTER 40

▼

With Pete lying naked beside her, Jennifer gazed around the room appraisingly. She felt a delicious sense of excitement and anticipation. She was like a kid waiting for the birthday party to begin, but this was going to be much more than a birthday party. Everything was coming together beautifully, all her plans were about to reach fruition.

She studied her own nude body with pride and pleasure. Her waist was tiny, her thighs were nicely curved, and even lying on her back, her boobs stood up and looked delectable. She wished her legs were longer, but in spite of that flaw, she thought smugly that she was a treat for any man. Pete didn't have the ghost of an idea of just how lucky he was to have her — even though it wouldn't be for long. And as for Jordan, well there was no point in dwelling on what might have been.

It was early morning in Toronto and already it was hot and humid. Jenny and Pete were using the master bedroom in the big house. It was Jordan's house now, but he was at the cottage, and he didn't even know that they were in it. Jenny couldn't face the room which had been hers as a teenager. It had too many unhappy memories. Besides, this room was something else!

They hadn't gone on a honeymoon, telling people that they just couldn't leave town when her mother was lying in the hospital fighting for her life. Then after her mother was killed, everyone was so sympathetic. Jenny laughed at how easy it was to fool people. She knew she just had to squeeze a few tears into her big brown eyes, a trick she had perfected years ago, let her lips and chin tremble a bit, and people thought she was pathetic and helpless. It was a ploy which had always worked. Men in particular were so stupid. She just had to gaze up at a man trustingly and he would fall all over himself to help her.

Even her beloved Jordan had no idea how smart she really was. It never occurred to him that she could scheme and plot, and devise scenarios which were as tangled as a kitten's ball of wool. To Jordan she had always been the helpless, harmless, gullible kid sister. She was the only one he had ever trusted, and even when they had fights and blow-ups, they always seemed to be drawn together again. This time it had been really bad, but for appearances sake until the will was read, they were still speaking.

All her life Jenny had believed that someday she and Jordan would go away together. She had loved him with a burning intensity, and had protected him whenever she could. In the back of her mind it was always Jordan and Jenny, an indestructible team. None of her boyfriends had meant anything. They had been just pleasant diversions until she and Jordan could be together. In her mind they were together, always. None of his girlfriends had meant anything to him, she knew that for a certainty. He never dated anyone more than two or three times at the most. Until recently Jenny had always thought it was because he was waiting for her and the right time to make his move.

After that awful night at the cottage, however, when he totally broke her heart and shattered all her dreams, something had snapped in Jennifer. She knew now that it would never be Jordan and Jenny. She had wasted all these years on a stupid kid's dream. He wanted no part of her. Actually he probably hated her now because she knew too much about him, and because of the scene she had caused at her wedding. It was his fault that they were now in Plan B.

She still found it difficult to accept that he liked little girls. If that was the case, why had he never touched her? She had been a very accessible little girl. Well, maybe he did have some tiny modicum of integrity, she thought bitterly. The funny thing was that she had always loved him so ferociously that she likely would have been a very willing sexual partner, even when she was just a kid. Now she realized that any of the women he ever dated were just covers for his real propensities. Sick, sick, sick. How could it be that she had never guessed? Had her parents known all along? No wonder they felt obliged to give him all their time and attention just to keep him out of trouble.

She gazed around this peaceful room as she lay quietly beside "the hulk". It gave off a quality of gentility and wealth without being too ostentatious. She promised herself that she would soon have a room as beautiful as this one, only better. Nothing but the best for Jenny from now on. She studied it carefully to discover what made it so restful and elegant. It was all done in shades of rose and burgundy, with touches of pale green. The focal point was the floor to ceiling windows which looked out onto the magnificent back garden. The jacquard wallpaper and the thick pile carpeting were wonderful, but what Jenny liked best was the ensuite with the huge sunken bathtub and the skylight overhead.

She stretched luxuriously as her agile mind went over all her plans once more. She mustn't forget anything. Nothing must tear the fabric of her perfectly woven plan. The will was to be read on Friday. That would be the first day of her new life. Tonight would be the last day of her old life. Hallelujah! The few days in between were just limbo.

She pondered again why Cassandra would be in her mother's will, and who the other beneficiaries might be. Obviously her mother had managed to change her will before she was killed. That was bad news, but it couldn't be too bad. Her mother would never have cut her out, so there was nothing to worry about.

She lay quietly so as not to waken Pete yet. She needed this time to think. Lately he had taken to wearing his longish blond hair in a tiny ponytail. He thought it looked cool, made him look like a mover and a shaker. Jenny thought it looked asinine. Poor Pete, always trying to be cool, to be something that he wasn't. She sighed. She needed him now for Plan B, pigtail or not.

She thought back to the first time she had seen this old Rosedale mansion. They had left Vancouver hastily right after Jordan's latest escapade with the young girl. She had been eleven years old, and Jordan was nineteen. He had got her pregnant, and their parents had pulled a lot of strings and paid a huge price to keep it quiet, and to keep Jordan out of jail. Jen thought happily that money could buy anything, and that her pot of gold was just days away.

She was in an introspective mood as she felt this chapter in her life coming to an end. She had hated leaving Vancouver and all her friends. She had despised her parents for dragging her so far away to Toronto, but strangely she had never blamed Jordan. Looking back now she saw how utterly foolish and selfish she had been — so full of teenage angst and misplaced rage.

Jennifer had always been greedy for more time, more attention, more love, more adventure. It was all more than her parents could give. They were always so distracted by Jordan's latest delinquent actions. Jenny wasn't sure just when she had learned to be such a good little actress, to pretend to be sweet and vulnerable when in fact she was tough and resilient.

At the time of the move from Vancouver, however, she had been a scared little girl, lashing out at her parents. She hung out with the most stupid, rebellious kids at her new school, and she was soon partying and drinking with the worst of them. Eventually her folks threatened to put her into a rehab place, so she had run away and disappeared. It had been scary at first on the streets, but she soon toughened up and learned to take care of herself, or learned how to get men to take care of her.

She remembered the time that her parents had nearly run into her on Yonge street, but luckily she had seen them coming, and had taken off around a corner. That was the closest call she ever had. She knew they were looking for her, but she always managed to keep one step ahead of them. Then one day, glancing at a newspaper, she read that her parents had won twenty million dollars in the lottery!

Jenny's life changed again from that day on. She rehabilitated herself quickly, at least on the surface. She called her mom a few times before she actually went home. She found, however, that her dad was impossible. He might have been glad to see her, but he wasn't forgiving, and he certainly never forgot. He knew that she had just come home to get some of that money, and he wasn't about to give her any. Her mom, however, couldn't do enough for her at first. She lavished her with love and attention, and slipped her money without her dad knowing. Then Jordan showed up and everyone became edgy. It was wonderful to see him, but he was even more strange now. Jenny never found out where he had been all those years. Soon she met Pete, and everything started going downhill again in the Wainwright family.

Jenny sighed as she rolled over and began running her fingers down Pete's back over those stupid tattoos. Pete had no class. What a loser! He was interesting though, in that he had one very unusual talent. Pete could mimic anyone perfectly. He could do their gestures and voices absolutely unerringly after just seeing the person once or twice. If he had the brains to go with the talent, he could probably have made a fortune on television as an entertaining impersonator. Too bad for Pete and lucky for Jenny. She needed him now. He was serving a useful purpose, and he would certainly be surprised when he discovered Jenny's plans. There was no way they were going to Florida to own some stinking little marina. They were getting out of the country the minute the money was in her hot little hands. They would likely go to Greece or Italy and then just keep moving around. She would get rid of him somewhere along the way.

"Waken up, Petie Pie" she coaxed, nibbling on his ear. "It's a gorgeous day, and we're heading to the cottage for a big celebration tonight."

"Let me sleep" groaned Pete, who had a bit of a hangover. "Anyway, Jordan's at the cottage. We don't want to go there."

"Come on, get up. The three of us are going to party tonight. We'll surprise him. I'll shower first while you waken up. It's almost the day they give millions away," she chanted, jumping up gracefully and strolling slowly to the bathroom so that Pete could admire her nude body. She thought she might as well give him a treat. Poor guy didn't know what was in store for him. She knew she looked great in the buff, and she assumed that Pete would be gawking. Glancing provocatively over her shoulder, however, she frowned in exasperation as she saw that Pete, the moron, the quintessential cretin had burrowed his head back under the pillow.

CHAPTER 41

▼

Dressed in red short shorts and matching red sandals, with a white halter top, her golden curls bouncing like a child's, Jenny was well aware of how delicious she looked. She had to look her very best today, it was all part of the plan.

Packing the cooler with steaks, potatoes, fresh asparagus, and a lemon cheesecake, she quickly added paté, Brie, and some fancy crackers. This was going to be a memorable feast for a memorable evening.

"Thanks Petie Pie" she said, as he carried the overloaded cooler to the car. "Just put it in the back seat. The trunk's full of junk."

"De nada señorita" Pete answered proudly.

"I think that should be señora, Pete. I'm a married lady now" she said a bit sourly.

Pete looked crestfallen. He didn't understand the difference, but he knew Jenny was smarter than he was.

The drive to the lake was uneventful. Highway 400 heading north wasn't too busy at this hour.

"Does your brother know we're coming?" asked Pete as they cruised along.

"No, it's a surprise" replied his new wife, laughing to herself at just what a surprise it would be.

"He might not like us barging in on him" said Pete doubtfully. He was afraid of Jordan. When those deep black eyes gave him that contemptuous stare, Pete always wanted to be somewhere else.

"Of course he'll like it" she snapped angrily. "Anyway, the cottage is mine. It says so in the will. Besides, we're on our honeymoon, so what can he do about it?"

Pete was afraid there were a lot of things Jordan could do about it, like running them off the property with a gun, or pushing them off the deep end of the dock. Sighing, he answered "Quién sabe?"

Pete's habit of trying to throw Spanish phrases into the conversation drove Jenny crazy. He was such a moron. Too bad she needed him for her plan.

"Maybe he'll leave as soon as we get there" suggested Pete hopefully. "I don't think he's forgiven you for your little scene at our reception."

"No way. Jordan isn't going to leave, that's for sure. My dear brother is a big part of this celebration tonight. Just think, Pete. This is our last week as paupers. Next week we'll be multi-millionaires! Of course he'll want to celebrate with us." Actually, she wasn't too sure about that, but she pushed the thought from her mind.

Pete didn't understand, but he knew that something about Jenny was very different now. She hadn't been drinking, and she was very intense these days. Suddenly she wasn't his helpless little bird anymore. The realization made him uneasy.

It was blazing hot by the time they arrived in Muskoka, but there was a welcome breeze rippling the navy water. Jenny knew that the dear old cottage had been waiting patiently for her. It never seemed to judge her no matter what she thought or did. She felt safe when she was here. Jordan was out in the boat, so Jenny sent Pete down to the dock with a cooler full of drinks and treats. Meanwhile she made the necessary preparations for the evening. Everything had to go off without a hitch.

There was the usual plethora of water vehicles found at most large Muskoka cottages. The triple boat house was home to a double-engine, gas guzzling cabin cruiser which slept four, a racing sail boat, two seadoos, two sailboards, a canoe, a hundred horsepower water-skiing runabout, and a two hundred horsepower red and white bow rider named "Plaything." This last was Jenny's favourite of all the water toys.

The wonderful smell of gas in the boathouse was so evocative of happier days. They had spent so many fun-filled days here at Gramma Lizzy's cottage, water-skiing, racing the seadoos, diving off the dock into that deep, clear water, sitting around a bonfire at night, singing up a storm. Jenny sighed as she remembered those wonderful days of childhood innocence. She and Jordan had never really needed friends. They had each other, and for Jenny at least, that had always been enough.

Of course, Jordan had always suffered dreadful mood swings. When he was in one of his down periods there was no living with him. He would disappear an entire day at a time, and no one ever knew where he went or what he was up to. It drove their parents and grandparents crazy. When he was in a good mood, however, he was the best companion in the world, — funny, sarcastic, daring, wild, ready to try anything or to talk Jenny into anything.

By the time she spotted the red and white boat skimming across the water and heading for the dock, she was lounging in her drop dead itsy-bitsy pink bikini, and Pete was snoring on his beach towel. White fluffy clouds like an army of Pillsbury Doughboys were just appearing over the horizon.

Jordan seemed neither happy nor angry to see them. He wasn't even surprised. As usual he had on his "I don't give a damn" face.

Jenny hugged him affectionately as if nothing bad had ever transpired between them, and gave him her best disingenuous smile.

"Well, the beaming bride" he smiled scornfully. "What a surprise."

Jenny noticed that he hadn't said "What a nice surprise." She felt that old familiar pang in her heart as she looked at him. He was tall and tanned, and with that thick black hair and his Ray-Bans, he looked like a movie star. With the sunglasses you couldn't see those scary eyes. In comparison, Pete looked like a monstrous joke. With a sigh she thought again of how perfect it could have been for them. What a fool Jordan was.

The lazy afternoon progressed slowly, and by dinner time there had been a lot of drinking. At least that was how it appeared. In actual fact, Jenny had been very circumspect. She had done all the bartending, claiming that she wanted to look after the two men in her life. Her glass was filled with Sprite instead of vodka, and no one had noticed the difference. She needed a clear head for what was to come.

A family of red-headed ducks floated past the dock, bobbing and weaving and searching for food. Jenny always had a box of crackers ready for them. Jordan scowled and closed his eyes as they flapped and squawked, fighting each other in a friendly sort of way for the welcome tidbits. He opened his eyes a few times to be sure that they weren't coming up on the dock. He hated birds, they were so unpredictable.

They stayed to watch the sunset before going up to the cottage to eat. The sun was dropping quickly now, leaving behind a blazing sky.

"What are you going to do with your share of the money, Jordan old boy?" quizzed Pete, in a jovial attempt at closeness with this brother-in-law he feared.

"Well," began Jordan slowly, staring at Pete in a disconcerting way, "I've got many plans, and the first one is to get the hell out of this country."

"And just which country will get the pleasure of your company?" asked Jenny innocently.

"Aha, that my dear sister, is my little secret," said Jordan, shaking his finger at her. "No one will ever have a clue as to where I have gone."

There's more truth than fiction in that, thought Jenny to herself.

The dinner was a great success. Jenny coaxed her brother to cook the steaks while she did last minute things in the kitchen. Pete opened the wine. By the time they had eaten the last of the cheesecake, it was close to midnight.

"Now for the pièce de résistance" said Jenny brightly. "I'm going to make us Spanish coffees, and we are going out together for one last midnight cruise. It's a perfect night."

"No way" said the two men simultaneously. "Bad idea. It's late, and we've all had too much to drink. I'm really sleepy" added Jordan, shaking his head.

"Come on fellas, you have to" pleaded Jenny, pouting prettily. "This could be the last time that we three will ever be together again, if Jordan really goes away and disappears. I've been looking forward to this all day. Besides, this is my honeymoon, and you can't refuse the bride anything so simple as this. Please, please," she begged.

Jordan stared at her for a moment, and as he did so, his glance metamorphosed into a malevolent grin. "It's hard to say no to you, sister dearest. Okay, let's go. Come on Pete."

"Great! You guys get the boat revved up, and I'll make the Spanish coffee. Just give me a few minutes."

After grabbing a jacket, Jenny walked out onto the balcony and gazed into the blackness. Good, there was no moon tonight. It was blacker than the inside of a witch's pocket. Muskoka at night could be terribly romantic, or it could be downright scary. Tonight it was scary. Jenny's nerves were all on the outside of her skin, but she knew that Plan B was going to work. She just had to be careful and make no mistakes.

She watched a raccoon investigating the garbage and the bird feeders. They were inveterate climbers, but at least she couldn't spot any bears tonight. Since the garbage dumps had been done away with in the Muskoka region, the bears were coming closer to the cottages in their quest for food. She was delighted to see a flying squirrel — an adorable little creature with big bush-baby eyes, flying from limb to limb.

Jennifer loved the velvet black smoothness of the night, and she sighed sadly as she realized that she might never stand on this deck again. What would happen to the cottage once she was gone? Would the next owners care for it and love it the way she did? Would it be possible for her to come back? She didn't think so. She was about to take another bend in the road, and this time there would be no turning back. There had been so many changes in such a short time. Her parents were dead, she was married to Mr. Brainless. Where had it all gone off the tracks? She blinked away tears as she hastily ran downstairs to prepare the Spanish coffees.

They crawled along at a snail's pace on the inky black water. Jenny was driving the boat, and she hoped they wouldn't notice that the powerful stern light was out. All they had were the two red and green running lights. Neither man was in any condition to realize that she had deliberately loosened the bulb of the too bright stern light, so that the boat would be more difficult to see.

No one spoke as they glided across the water, sipping from their mugs. They passed occasional twinkling lights from cottages along the shore, but Jenny was steering the boat right out into the large open part of the lake.

Suddenly Jordan broke the silence. "Go back, Jen. I don't feel good." His words seemed to slur a little as he tried to get her attention.

"We're just about there, Jordie, right in the middle of the lake where you and I have spent so many happy times. It's two hundred and sixty feet deep here, Pete," she added quietly.

Pete answered "Oh ya?" without much enthusiasm. He'd had too much to drink, and was wishing he was in bed. There was no response from Jordan. Looking at him, Jenny noticed that the mug had dropped from his fingers, and was rolling on the floor of the boat. By a flash of heat lightning she could see fear in Jordan's eyes as he stared at her. For the very first time in her life she was actually seeing fear in her brother's eyes. There was something else too, a mixture of bewilderment and disbelief. "Jen" he mumbled, "what have you done?" He was struggling to stand up, but his legs weren't working.

Jenny watched with interest and a certain dispassionate detachment. Then, not caring that her husband would hear her words, she said sadly, "Jordie, it could have been so perfect for us, but you ruined it all. You've made me do this, I had no choice."

There was real regret in her voice as she looked at her brother, who was now slumping over in his seat. She seemed totally unaware of Pete, who was looking puzzled.

"Don't do this Jen, — loved me, never hurt me. Counted on you. You know all secrets," he said drowsily, once again struggling to stand up. "Just back to cottage. Need — help" — But then his stricken voice trailed off, and there was only the silence of the black night, and the gentle lapping of the water.

Jenny shut off the motor and said quite calmly, "Okay, Pete. This is where you help me now. He's out for the count. I've put seven sleeping pills in his wine and the coffee. Help me tie this anchor around him." She was busily dragging the anchor out from the lower compartment in the floor of the boat.

Pete was pretty mellowed out by all the booze, but he snapped to attention at her words. "What" he cried. "Are you crazy? What the hell are you doing?"

"No, Pete. It's what are WE doing. We're getting rid of Jordan before he gets rid of us. There was no way he was going to share the money with me. He planned to kill me and take everything. He would have had to kill you too. Come on, hurry. We have to dump him before any other boats come along."

Pete thought about this as he fingered the right side of his face, his stubby fingers moving smoothly in and out of the familiar pockmarks. He had always been scared of Jordan, now Jordan was dead, or close to it. Okay, that was one less problem in his life, one less asshole taking up space. Pete shrugged mentally as he began to help Jenny. She was one cool little lady. He didn't really know her at all.

Glancing hastily around to make sure that they were alone, she whispered "Move it, Pete, and be quiet. You know how voices carry on the water. Stop slapping at those mosquitoes. You'll wake the dead." Then she gave a strange little choking sound as she realized what she had said.

"But Jen" argued Pete half-heartedly, "can we get away with it?" He was so shocked and surprised at this turn of events, that he was staring at his flaky little bride, mouth agape. Was this really his helpless little Jenny tying the anchor rope around her brother so casually?

At this point Jordan gave a sigh and seemed to twitch. Pete jumped, and so did Jenny.

"Come on Pete. Let's get this over with."

Pete was freaked out. His world had just tilted badly, but he overcame his doubts and helped her double knot the rope around Jordan's body. There just seemed to be so much killing going on these days!

It was difficult lifting Jordan over the side, Jenny couldn't have done it without Pete. Just as they let him go, there was a flash of heat lightning which lit up the sky. They both flinched, but managed to get him into the water with a minimum of splashing. Neither of them noticed the dark, motionless figure in the small boat, silently watching each time the lightning flashed so brilliantly in the moonless night. Quickly glancing again in all directions into the inky blackness, Jenny started the motor and headed back. Pete tried to make sense out of what had just happened.

Working with total soundlessness, they tied the boat securely inside the boat house.

"Now go to the trunk of the car and get out the big package. It's another anchor and rope. We have to leave them in the boat so that nothing appears to be missing."

"But won't they look too new?" inquired Pete with a flash of common sense.

"They're old ones. I'm not stupid" snapped Jenny, using her flashlight to check out the boat. "Just go get them, and hurry up, and for goodness sake don't make any noise!"

Pete obeyed as if in a trance.

Jenny brought the three coffee mugs to the kitchen, washed them thoroughly and put them back in the cupboard. She did the same with the wine glasses. She then pored Pete a strong black coffee, sat him down and told him the rest of the plan. He looked warily at the coffee, but she laughed and assured him that it wasn't drugged. "I need you Pete, so drink up" she commanded. "You have to drive Jordan's car to the Toronto airport and leave it in the long term parking area. I'll follow along behind in our car. Don't speed! When the police find it, they'll think he's left the country under an assumed name, since his name won't be on the manifest of any flight."

Pete was trying hard to follow all this. He was entirely sober now. "But Jen, no one will believe he left the week before the will was read, and before he got his share of the money. Wouldn't he be stupid to do that?"

"They'll believe it by the time I'm through with them" replied Jenny easily. "I'm going to be very tearful at that will reading. Between sobs, I'll tell them that Jordan has left the country for fear of being arrested. I'll say that he told me he had killed both our parents, and then had to kill the nurse because she saw him. He was afraid that the police were closing in on him." Jenny laughed wryly at this point. "That's when I'll look very ashamed and contrite, and I'll admit that I promised never to tell anyone because he's my brother and I love him. Besides, I'll tell them regretfully that I've always been afraid of him, that the entire family has always feared him. I'll let that sink in a bit, and then I'll say that I just can't keep such a dreadful secret any longer because I can't stand what he did to our parents and that poor nurse. I'll say I realize now that he's a monster and should be put away."

Jenny was drawing strange little circles on the table with her fingers, as she pictured herself at the reading of the will, looking beautiful and tragic, and telling her story to an enthralled audience. "I'll tell them that he plans to contact me in a few months and give me instructions about how to get his share of the money to him. Don't worry, Pete. I've got it all thought out and I can be very convincing. Being a murderer, he won't be able to inherit anything, and it will all come to me." Jenny's eyes were bright with excitement at this point, and Pete felt both scared and amazed at this total stranger who was his wife.

"I'll just bet you'll be convincing" he laughed nervously, shaking his head. "Poor Jordan. He didn't have a chance against you. He trusted you too much. I underestimated you, Jenny babe. I thought I was pretty sneaky, but you take the cake for sure."

"What do you mean?" she asked defensively. "Jordan deserved to die. He really would have killed us you know. He broke into the old lawyer's office and his house, checking for a new will, and if he had found one, he would have killed the old guy and destroyed it. He told me that much, but the old coot chased him off with a baseball bat. He planned the crash that started this whole thing, and — — "

"Wrong, baby buns" laughed Pete. "You still haven't got it right. You aren't as smart as you think you are. He may have killed your mother in the hospital, I don't know anything about that, but I'm the one who cut the brakes on your father's car!"

"You?" cried Jenny in total shock and disbelief. "But how, and why?"

"Simple" he said proudly, apparently anxious now to tell his tale. "I was working up here on Mr. Duncan's boat the night of the crash, and I came over to talk to your dad. I told him that I was going to marry you, and I asked him for half a million dollars to start the marina in Florida. I'd been drinking and we had quite an argument. He said that he would never let you marry me, and that I would never see a penny of his money. He called me a 'tattooed mental midget'. He even said that he would call the police if I ever came near you again. That made me mad, Jen. No one can call me names and treat me that way" he added in an aggrieved tone.

"I pretended to leave, and as soon as he came back up here to the cottage, I slipped around to the driveway and cut the brake line. It was a spur of the moment idea, but it was a good one, wasn't it?" Pete grinned happily at her, waiting for praise. Somehow it was important that Jenny realize Pete could be just as bad as she was. He mustn't appear weak in front of her. She frightened him now, but he admired her strength and cleverness.

Staring at him in disbelief, Jenny had to quickly rethink and reassess the events of the past few weeks. So Jordan hadn't caused the crash which started the entire mess. It had been Pete after all. She'd really been fooled this time. She had underestimated Pete. Had she made any other mistakes? For a moment she felt a nervous tremor in her stomach. She hated loose ends, and she was beginning to unravel just a tiny bit. For once in her life little Jennifer Wainwright was totally speechless.

CHAPTER 42

▼

Jenny was in a state of nervous exhaustion as she set off to hear the long awaited news about the will. As soon as she was out of the house, Pete began skulking around the Wainwright mansion, going through every drawer and closet to see what he could steal. He knew logically that after Jenny inherited the twenty million plus, he would have access to more money than he had ever dreamed possible. Still, Pete was a pragmatist when it came to money. He may not have known what the word meant, but it described him perfectly.

He liked Jenny, maybe he even loved her a little bit. She was usually a lot of laughs, and he knew that she was his meal ticket to a new and fabulous life. Still, there was something about her that scared him. She had so coolly and calmly killed Jordan, that it had amazed and frightened him. He knew that she loved that weird brother of hers, yet she hadn't blinked an eye about drugging him and pitching him into that inky black lake. If she could do that to someone she really loved, what might she do to Pete when she no longer needed him?

He had married her to get his hands on the fortune, thinking that he was the one in control, taking advantage of her. Now, however, he realized that she didn't really need him once she had her inheritance. In fact, here Pete gave a little involuntary shudder, he had become a liability to her. He could tell the police how she had killed Jordan. Of course he would never do that, because then she could tell them about how he had killed her father. It was a bit of a Mexican stand-off. Why had he ever been so stupid boasting about cutting the brakes? He had been trying to show her what a man of action he was. What an idiot! Now she could blow the whistle on him any time she wanted, or she could leave him without a penny. He was between a rock and a hard place for sure. He didn't know who had murdered Pru and the little nurse, but he had just assumed that it was Jordan. Now he wasn't so sure.

It was all too complicated for Pete, and he had decided that just in case Jenny dumped him before he got the benefit of all that new found wealth, he would feather his nest with a few baubles which he could easily fence. He knew that he was lucky to have snagged himself such a soon-to-be rich wife, but he also felt out of his depth. She hadn't been any fun since that night at the cottage. She seemed nervous and jumpy, and she had taken up drinking again with great enthusiasm. Unfortunately she wasn't a happy drunk any more. She seemed serious and disconnected. Pete liked that word. He rolled it around on his tongue. It sounded like a word a smart person would use. Yep, disconnected, that was what Jen was these days, and it worried him. She was scheming about something and he had to get the jump on her.

Prudence Wainwright had owned some very nice jewellery, and Pete had no trouble stuffing his duffel bag. He figured there were some real diamonds and emeralds in the pile, and he knew just where he could get rid of them. Jenny might suspect him, but what could she prove? He laughed happily as he stuffed a gold watch of Matt's into his pocket. He remembered the shouting match he and Matt had at the cottage that last night. Lucky no one heard them. He had almost punched Matt out and thrown him in the lake at that point, but cutting the brakes had been an inspiration. "Who has the last laugh now, Mr. High and Mighty Wainwright?" he asked gleefully as he took one last look around.

While Pete was pilfering, Douglas was getting himself ready for the reading of the will. He had to look his very best and be at his brightest today. He donned a white shirt with a burgundy tie, before putting on the gray suit which Ruth had chosen for him shortly before she died.

"The old boy looks pretty spiffy, Ruthie," he said with a smile, glancing at her picture. Douglas often chatted to Ruth's picture. Just looking at her dear face, he could tell what she would have wanted him to do. Sometimes she almost seemed to frown or to broaden her smile. He knew it was a whimsical notion, but it made him happy, so who did it hurt? No one.

Today as he dressed, he told her of his misgivings about this particular will and letter. "There are going to be fireworks, Ruthie old girl. I may come home with my eyebrows singed! There's no way they'll take this one sitting down." He grinned at her picture as he picked a piece of lint off his cuff and proceeded downstairs.

Back in Muskoka, while Pete was stealing, and Douglas was dressing, the Bracebridge detachment of the OPP received a strange call.

"Hello, I want to speak to a detective" said the hesitant voice. He was put on hold, and waited impatiently for someone to pick up.

"Sergeant Sherwood here, what can I do for you?" came an abrupt and gruff voice.

"Well, Sergeant Sherwood, I think maybe I saw a murder or something bad."

"What do you mean? Who is this?"

"This is Joe Ballantyne, and I own a little cottage here in Muskoka. I was out in my boat in the middle of the lake the other night, out where it's really deep. I was just sitting there listening to the loons. It's a great place to get your head straight, you know. It's so peaceful. Anyway, it was blacker than the devil's heart that night, except there was a lot of heat lightning. Well, I heard a boat coming, and it only had its running lights on, no stern light. I just sat there quietly because I had a bad feeling about that boat. I didn't want anyone to know I was there. I just felt that they weren't up to any good."

Here Joe paused as if to collect his thoughts.

"Go on" came the voice, sounding more interested now.

"I could hear people talking, but I couldn't really make out the words, because they were speaking very quietly. Anyway it started to thunder, and I wanted to head for home, but I couldn't start up the motor on my little outboard or they would have heard me, so I was stuck there. Lucky for me they weren't looking my way, because I saw them drop a heavy bundle — it took two of them to lift it — over the side. There was lightning just then or I wouldn't have been able to see. There was a splash and then the boat took off almost right away. I know which direction they headed, but that's all. I keep thinking about it, and it seems to me that it had to be a body. Why else would they be so sneaky about it? And, anyway, I thought I heard a man's voice saying something about 'You can't do this, you love me.' It was hard to hear, but it sounded as if maybe he was drunk. His voice was slurry and weak."

Joe paused here and cleared his throat. "Well, that's all I've got to say. I just can't get it off my mind, and I thought I should report it."

Sergeant Sherwood was very interested now. "Give me your address, Mr. Ballantyne, and we'll come over to see you. Maybe you could take us for a little boat ride."

On this same day, someone else was preparing for the reading of the will. Elena studied her naked body judiciously in front of the hotel room mirror. She still looked damn good she decided. Her legs were long, but a bit skinny. Her hips were not too rounded, and she still had a waistline. Her breasts were firm and full, and she had a swan-like neck. She had always taken pride in that long graceful neck. Her blue black hair was thick and wavy. She could do anything with her hair, it was her crowning glory.

Next, she stared at the dark purple birthmark on her right hip. It was unique, and Elena had come to terms with it years ago. The mark looked like a scorpion. As a child her father had called her his "little scorpion girl." Her mother, however, had hated it. She rubbed at it constantly as if trying to erase it. It was as if she was insulted by this unsightly blotch on her otherwise perfect child. Elena's mother was very superstitious, and she feared the scorpion mark. Elena, on the other hand, had come to love it. It was her talisman, her good luck charm. As long as she had her scorpion looking after her, nothing could go wrong. She ran her fingers over it gently and smiled to herself.

A careful application of eyeliner and shadow made her eyes seem even bigger and darker than they really were. Still staring into the mirror, she muttered, "Well, Miss Cassandra, are we going to be friends when this is all over and the dust has settled? Probably not, sister dearest. If Pru has left me some money, I'll be long gone. If, however, she didn't remember her new half-sister in her will, then you can expect to see a lot of me in the future." Her image gave her a conspiratorial smile.

She chose her outfit with special care. This was to be a big afternoon in her life. She was actually named in the will, whether for a little or a lot was yet to be seen. Elena's timing had been perfect. Now she could hardly wait to hear what Pru had left to her. She knew that it might be nothing more than a ring or a pin, but she hoped desperately that there was real money involved. After all, that was exactly why she had come looking for Prudence and Cassandra. They had money and she didn't. Nothing could be more simple.

She quickly put on her mid-calf length black skirt, the dusty rose blouse, and the black embroidered vest. It was too hot for her black boots, but she pulled them on anyway. The ensemble made her look very Spanish and aristocratic. It set the perfect tone for this red letter day.

Descending in the elevator, she was haughtily aware of the admiring glances of the two men who got on behind her. She gave them a charming smile as she swept across the busy lobby and hailed a cab.

CHAPTER 43

▼

Sheridan Winslow spent the morning preparing the materials Douglas would need that afternoon for his meeting with the Wainwright estate heirs. So many wills were predictable, even boring, she mused. In this case, however, she could hardly wait to see the heirs. She wished she could hover near the door to the inner conference room in order to hear, or even better, to see the reactions to this startling document. Maybe she would go in and fuss around Douglas's office which adjoined the conference room. Douglas wouldn't care. He knew she was just as intrigued as he was to see the reactions. Actually he had quipped that she might have to rush in with a fire extinguisher once the will was read. There'd be a lot of fires burning after this one!

It had been a happy and busy morning for Sheridan. Her mind was spinning with speculation about the people and events described in Prudence Wainwright's will and letter. She imagined so many possible scenarios. Cassandra might faint or cry, or even rush out. Blake might leap on the desk and do a celebratory dance. He might hug and kiss everyone, including Sheridan. She was sure that Elena would be ecstatic. Then there was Jenny, oh boy, Jenny. What would she do when she found out? Perhaps she would pull out a gun and shoot everyone! No, not likely. Maybe she would try to leap out a window. Sheridan laughed at this foolishness, reminding herself that the office was on the ground floor. Nevertheless her eyes sparkled as she contemplated all these possibilities. One thing was for sure. There would certainly be some very interesting reactions. The only disappointment was that apparently Jordan was not coming.

Sheridan Winslow was wearing a navy "power" suit with red trim. It showed off her platinum blond shoulder length hair. She was an attractive woman who had been an airline stewardess for three unhappy years. She had been married to a handsome, egotistical captain with the morals of a mink. Of course she hadn't known that when she married him. It hadn't taken long, however, to realize that Captain Michael Hale was screwing every dolly from Toronto to Istanbul and back again.

Sheridan finally divorced him and returned to school to become a legal secretary. She had worked for Douglas Bannon now for ten years, and had loved every day of it. Dear old Douglas was an anomaly. He was courteous and kind, the old fashioned family retainer of years long gone. He had once been a well known and respected trial lawyer, but that was before Sheridan had known him. Now he was just a sweet old man putting in his time in a rather bewildered way. She suspected that he might be in the early stages of Alzheimer's disease, and she would stay with him for as long as he needed her. Sheridan was the one who kept him from making mistakes or getting too muddled. She protected him like a mother bear, and it broke her heart to see him gradually getting more doddery as the weeks and months went by.

After her divorce, she had taken back her maiden name, and was living contentedly with a quiet, gentle guy who owned a small bookstore. He was as different from Michael Hale as anyone could be, and she felt safe with him. They were totally compatible, and were talking about marriage, but she would keep on working for Douglas. Sheridan got vicarious pleasure from the day to day dramas of the legal world.

When Cassandra and Victoria arrived, Sheridan buzzed Douglas, who came out of his office to greet them.

"Jennifer should be here any moment" he told them, "but she claims that Jordan has left the country!" He waited for this little bombshell to sink in, and was gratified to see the women look at each other in puzzlement. "We haven't been able to contact him at all" he continued, "but as soon as we know his location we shall simply forward all the information. It seems so bizarre that he would leave town just before the reading of his mother's will. Anyway, it's not essential that he be here for this preliminary reading." Then as an afterthought Douglas added, "Jennifer seemed extraordinarily upset when she called. They've always been so close."

Cass was amazed to hear that Jordan had actually left the country. That made no sense at all. She was in a state of excitement, however, and couldn't help wondering what her sister had left her in the will. It was so unexpected that Pru would leave her anything. Her mother had often told her about Pru's beautiful jewellery. Cass hoped it might be a bracelet or ring waiting for her. Something like that would be a wonderful keepsake.

As Cass thought about what Pru might have left to her, she looked up and saw Elena coming through the door with her elegant and haughty walk. What in the world was she doing here? Surely she wasn't in the will too, she thought resentfully. Pru had just met her two weeks before the accident. She saw Vickie staring at Elena in disgust and then lifting her eyebrows at Cassie. Vickie had the most expressive eyebrows she had ever seen. Without saying a word, Vickie had conveyed the question, "What in hell is she doing here?" Cass had to grin and shrug her shoulders.

Just then Blake came sauntering in. He was casual in beige slacks, a cream open-collared shirt, and a chocolate brown sports jacket. His casual demeanour, however, belied the excited look on his face. Well, no wonder. There was a lot of money on the table.

Jenny arrived, looking very classy in a long cream coloured skirt with a multi-coloured tunic top. Her high-heeled sandals were multi-coloured as well. Although she had obviously dressed carefully, on closer inspection she appeared extremely agitated. There were dark circles around her lovely brown eyes, and she kept twirling the wedding ring on her finger as if it was burning her skin.

Jennifer Louise Wainwright had kept her maiden name when she married Pete. No way was she ever going to be called Mrs. Hoblonski. The very thought made her shudder. "Wainwright" was such an elegant name. It conjured up pictures of beautiful mansions and big cars. She had explained to Pete that it was a complicated legal matter which had to do with the will, and he had believed her. What a dimwit!

On this most important afternoon of her entire life, poor Jennifer had a ball of writhing snakes in her stomach. Since the night at the lake, Jordan had been haunting her. He wouldn't leave her alone. He came to her in the night, staring and menacing. He stood at the foot of her bed, and when she curled up against Pete and peeked over his shoulder into the darkness, there was Jordan, still staring, still sneering, still threatening.

Jordan was dead, Jenny knew that. It had been absolutely necessary to kill him, but somehow he just kept coming back. He wouldn't stay dead. He kept rising from that black cold water. Droplets ran down his face and off his chin. She could see the anchor still attached to him. Those awful unforgiving eyes followed her. He had started coming to her in the dark, but now she had seen him this morning in the light of day, and had freaked right out. She needed a drink badly.

Her hands were shaking, and her eyes kept blinking. She couldn't help herself, she was looking for him in every corner.

All her wonderful plans to act scared and weepy about Jordan leaving the country were totally forgotten. She wouldn't have to act at all. She truly was scared and weepy. She was terrified that his fearsome ghost was going to make an appearance here in front of the others. She had realized this morning with horror and a fatalistic acceptance, that she was more attached to Jordan now than when he had been alive. The irony was unbearable. He was her bête noire. They would be together forever, just as she had always wanted, but not like this, never like this. Wherever Jenny went, wherever her inheritance took her, Jordan would tag along like some loathsome leper, always trying to touch her with those long shrivelled fingers and bleak accusing eyes. They would do a macabre dance throughout her lifetime.

She stifled a sob, and tried to pull herself together as Douglas said "Good, we're all here, well, except, of course for Jordan." Jenny winced at the mention of his name, as if in fear that it would conjure up his ghost. "Please come into my office and make yourselves comfortable."

"I'll wait right here for you Cass," murmured Vickie, giving her friend an encouraging smile, and seating herself comfortably in a chair in the reception area. She considered pressing her ear to the keyhole, but discarded the notion, mainly because there was no keyhole. Anyway, she suspected that the redoubtable Miss Winslow would object. Instead she sat quietly, flipping unseeingly through the latest Reader's Digest, and wondering what her friend was about to inherit. She was getting vicarious pleasure from this latest drama.

The office of Douglas Bannon was probably similar to every lawyer's office, lots of leather and muted lighting, and the comfortable smell of those rows and rows of legal books. Douglas had the requisite family pictures on his desk, and Cassie was just looking at them, when he suggested that they go through to the adjoining conference room which was much bigger. Cass thought it seemed much less friendly.

When they were all seated, Douglas cleared his throat, adjusted his spectacles, and shuffled some papers. He was making a bit of a production out of this extraordinary will, and with something of a flourish, he produced the document. This was his moment in the sun. He was orchestrating everything. He wanted everyone to feel the grandeur and power of the law. It was so disappointing and bewildering that Jordan wasn't here. Something was not quite right, but Douglas didn't have time to waste figuring it out at the moment.

He had performed this business of reading a will so many times over the years, and he loved the solemnity. Glancing around, he assessed the looks on the faces before him. It had been his experience that the expectant faces of beneficiaries usually showed hope, eagerness and plain raw greed. Greed was such a powerful motivator. He felt that Blake looked nervous and hopeful all at the same time. Cassie seemed quite calm and merely interested. Elena looked serene, but her eyes were hungry. Jenny showed the pure unadulterated greed he expected, but there was something else there too. She looked as if she was terrified. She kept squirming in her seat and looking over her shoulder. Well, if she was nervous now, she'd really be a basket case in a minute. This was going to blow the roof off!

He formally repeated the condolences he had already expressed to the family of Prudence Wainwright, widow of the late Matthew Wainwright, late of the city of Toronto — — — blah, blah, blah. Cassie let her mind drift with the rhythmic liturgy of the preamble to the will.

The cottage in Muskoka and all its contents was left to Jennifer, the house in Toronto and all its contents went to Jordan. One million dollars went to Blake, as had been promised to him by his late brother Matthew. He was also the beneficiary of an insurance policy, but Blake didn't even hear that part. He sighed deeply and closed his eyes as if silently thanking his brother for keeping that promise. Good old Matt had come through. He might have been a bastard, but he had kept his word. Blake felt like dancing. He couldn't wait to tell Gloria.

Jenny simply scowled and chewed on a knuckle in an agitated way. She was sitting on the edge of her chair, staring at Douglas, watching his lips move as he slowly and deliberately read every line of the will. Cass wondered what the heck was wrong with her. She knew she'd be getting millions so what was her problem?

When Douglas read "and to my dear new found half-sister Elena Santa Cruz, I leave $500,000," Jenny let out a shriek, and glared at Elena with hatred and disbelief. The imperturbable Elena looked like a cat who has just been given a saucer of cream. She smiled an enigmatic smile which somehow unnerved Cassie. Elena looked too smug, something wasn't right. Had she known she was getting all that money? Had she somehow coerced Pru into putting her into the will? This was certainly not the same will which she and Vickie had found at the house. What was going on?

Various charities were given substantial bequests, and some specific items such as rings and paintings went to special friends. Cassie suddenly sat bolt upright in her chair. What had Douglas just said? His mind must be wandering, or else hers was! "And the entire residue of my estate, I leave to my dear daughter, Cassandra

Meredith — — " he intoned. Then with a start, he stopped reading. "Oh God, what have I done?" he exclaimed in dismay. "I've done this all wrong." The air was electric. Shock waves abounded.

"What is it Mr. Bannon?" Cassie felt that he needed help. Was he having a mini stroke? What nonsense had he just uttered? She should have been paying more attention, but she had been looking at Jenny and wondering what was wrong with her. Cass jumped out of her chair and was around the desk in a flash, laying her hand on his shoulder with concern. She poured him a glass of water from the carafe on his desk. Jenny, Elena, and Blake were all staring at her as if she had suddenly grown a second head.

Douglas began to regain his composure. "The fact is that Mrs. Wainwright, Prudence, left a letter for you, Cassandra. I was supposed to give it to you before the will was read. This business about Jordan not showing up totally threw me off, but I realize that's no excuse. I'm so very sorry, my dear. We'll have a fifteen minute recess to allow you to absorb the contents of this letter in private. When we resume I'll have to read the letter for the benefit of the others. It was Pru's request because it explains so much."

Cassie sat like a statue as Douglas put the sealed envelope into her hand. She wasn't aware of them, as Elena, Blake and Douglas left the room. She was beginning to shake, and knew with certainty that she wasn't going to like what she was about to read. Her scalp had been tingling all morning and she had tried to ignore it. She didn't even realize that Jenny was still in the large conference room, tapping her nails nervously on the table and crossing and uncrossing her legs.

Jenny knew that she couldn't have heard that foolish old man correctly. He was an imbecile. He should be disbarred. Whatever he had said was a mistake. She would fix it, somehow she would make it right. She was breathing rapidly and biting her lip, as she stared at Cassandra. Cass read and then reread the letter. Jenny noticed that Cassie's face had become ashen. What was in it? With a dreadful premonition and total despair, Jenny saw her world crumbling around her feet.

CHAPTER 44

▼

Cassie's hands shook as she reread the letter.

My dearest Cassandra,

The very fact that you are reading this letter means that I am dead. I wish I had been able to talk to you face to face, but I have always been such a coward, and now the opportunity has passed.

I pray that what I am about to tell you will not be too much of a shock. In fact it is my hope that in time you will come to understand, to accept, and finally, to forgive.

The story begins when I was just fifteen years old and discovered that I was pregnant. I had fallen in love with a young man who came to live with our neighbours, while he studied architecture at university.

When my mother found out, she was furious. I was so young, and you know what a temper she had. In those days in our social circumstances, there was still a dreadful stigma attached to anyone who became pregnant without benefit of the golden wedding ring, and, of course, abortion was not yet legal. My mother, ever practical, devised what seemed to be the perfect solution.

She told no one, not even my father. She explained to all her friends that she was taking me to Europe to further my education, and off we went. From Spain she wrote and told everyone that she was pregnant! The timing was perfect because Dad had just been home on his six month Canadian work project, and he was now back in Brazil. Way back then it was easy to bribe any official if you had enough money, so mom was able to obtain a birth certificate which said that she was your mother, when in fact, Cassie, I am your mother!

I hope you can understand the position in which I found myself. I was young, spoiled, vulnerable, and afraid to stand up to my mother. Besides, to be brutally honest, I didn't want the responsibility of a baby. I wanted an education, parties, dates, not diapers, bottles and a crying baby. Anyway my mother gave me no choice. She made me promise never to get too close to you, never to let you get too attached to me. Right or wrong, I went along with the deception. It seemed the easy way out.

I made the fateful promise, and for years it was an easy promise to keep. In my mind you became my baby sister, and I rarely thought about you. Somehow I came to almost convince myself that Lizzy really was your mother instead of your grandmother.

Then, of course, I was caught in a trap of my own making. I had passed the point of no return, and simply couldn't tell you. There was no appropriate time. I had school, I had a boyfriend, then I was married and had children. Because I was terrified of hurting you and of having you reject me, I kept silent. The path of least resistance was to avoid you at all costs.

I convinced myself that you were happy with your life. You had a mother and a father, and you didn't need me. It has only been recently as I have grown older, that I have realized what a dreadful deception we perpetrated on everyone — especially you. Watching you grow, and realizing the fine person you are, I have become filled with self-recriminations and shame. Once mother died, no one else in the world knew the secret, except for me. I never even told Matt, but you, Cassandra, deserve to know the truth.

I have always kept my distance as promised, but it has been a challenge these last years. I had made the decision to tell you face to face as soon as we returned from California, but things haven't worked out that way.

"I'm so sorry Cassandra, (a name I chose), for the shock which this must be. I hope though, that the gift I am leaving you will bring you much joy, and that someday you will forgive me. I have lived with this terrible deceit for so long that it is a great relief to share it with you now. Enjoy this inheritance, my daughter, and remember that I did love you, if only from afar.

By the way, your father was killed in a skiing accident while we were in Spain. I never saw him again, and he never knew about you.

My prayer is that you will have a long and happy life with David and your children (my grandchildren). How strange that sounds! Again, I hope that the loss is all mine and not yours. Remember that Lizzie and J.J. loved you with all their hearts. To them you were always their own child.

Forgive me, Cassie.

Your mother, Prudence

Each of the four heirs who reassembled fifteen minutes later, had undergone a drastic change. Cassie seemed to be in a trance as she tried to assimilate the facts in the letter. Blake was in shock. The news of the million dollar bequest was not a total surprise. He had hoped for it for a long time. He was aghast, however, at the insurance policy for two million. Suddenly all his money problems were over. A huge weight should have been lifted from his shoulders, but instead he felt awful. A mantle of guilt had fallen on him, and he was consumed with shame. At one point he had really wanted Pru dead.

Elena seemed in her own little world. She was oblivious to everyone else, and couldn't seem to get the smug look off her face.

Before Douglas had even finished reading Pru's letter aloud, Jenny was shouting and carrying on in a mad fashion. "It can't be" she screamed. "That fortune is mine. Elena I don't even know who you are. Why did she leave you all that money? I don't believe that you were her sister." Then, shaking her fist at Cassie, she cried, "You'll never get a penny. I'll fight it forever. She was just a crazy old lady. Her head was damaged in the accident, she didn't know what she was doing. The will won't stand up in court. After all I've done for that money, it's mine." At this point she seemed to realize just what she was saying. She had said far too much. Moaning, she sat back down and sobbed hysterically. This time the tears were real.

The others looked at her with blank expressions. They were all too stunned with the magnitude of their inheritances, to realize the significance of her words. Cass, however, stared at Jenny for a moment, then leaned toward her. "I swear I'll use every penny of that money to put you behind bars if what I suspect is true. I think that you killed them all, and I'm going to prove it."

Jennifer stopped sobbing long enough to look up at Cassie and say, "How could you be so cruel? I loved my parents and I loved Jordan most of all. I would never hurt anyone. I'm just so upset. I know that my mother loved me and wanted me to have that money. She told me so. There's been a dreadful mistake. The will must be a forgery."

In the lull that followed that declaration, Douglas cleared his throat and stated unequivocally that this was indeed the last will and testament of Prudence Wainwright. He was extremely indignant at Jenny's claim that it was a forgery. He told them that he would be in touch with all of them after probate. It occurred to him that he couldn't remember a will reading that had been so chaotic and so noisy. It had been as exciting as he had anticipated, but now he desperately needed a cup of tea or something stronger.

Elena left the office quickly, not stopping to speak to anyone. Cassie and Blake both stood talking to Douglas in his office for a few minutes, asking about certain legalities. Cass was in a total fog, and totally unaware of Jenny, who had remained seated in the conference room, staring into space and digging the nails of her right hand into her left palm.

Coming out of the office, Cassie collapsed onto the leather sofa in the reception room. Strangely, she felt as if she was watching this scene from afar. She felt numb, and wondered distantly what this Cassandra person would do next. She put up her hand to fend off Vickie, when her friend solicitously asked what was wrong. Vickie had heard all the shouting, and was desperate to know what had ensued behind the closed door.

Cassie felt hot and sweaty. Her heart was racing as she tried once more to read the incomprehensible letter. It felt as if someone was stabbing at her with a livewire. Little jolts of electricity were sparking in her stomach and her head. She tried to make sense of the totally nonsensical words, tried to absorb their meaning.

Finally, in defeat, she handed the letter to Vickie, who was sitting beside her trying to read her face. Cass sat quietly gazing into space while Vickie read the astonishing letter. For once Victoria Craig couldn't think of a thing to say, as she stared at her friend with an incredulous look.

"We need a drink, Vic. Let's get out of here" Then, realizing that she had left her purse behind, Cassie went back into the conference room. The purse was there, although it didn't seem to be where she had left it. Jenny was gone.

CHAPTER 45

▼

The extraordinary events of the last few weeks had left both women emotionally drained. They were feeling decidedly fuzzy around the edges. The reading of the will and letter was the final bombshell. On the way back to Niagara Falls they talked incessantly. Cassie's mood swings were going from one end of the scale to the other. She was exhilarated and scared about the money, angry and suspicious about Jenny, and devastated and depressed about Prudence — her alleged mother. No way! Pru was no more her mother than Vickie was. What a crock! It was all too surreal to really grasp.

Cassie kept wondering how in the world she was going to cope. What did she know about having that kind of money? It was obscene. She envisioned stultifying hours and hours of sitting with accountants and tax lawyers, listening to mumbo jumbo about tax shelters and wise investments. She shuddered at the thought. Would the money and all its attendant hassles be worth it? You betcha baby, she grinned as they turned into the driveway.

What she was really doing, was trying to keep the intrusive knowledge about her parentage from pounding at her head like a merciless hammer. Her mother was not her mother. Her father was not her father. It made no sense. There was no room in her clouded mind to accept these unbelievable facts. All she could see was her beloved mom and dad suddenly becoming her grandparents! It made her feel nauseous. She wanted to beat her fists on someone's face — preferably Pru's.

Later, as Cass was stepping out of the shower, Vickie came to the bathroom door with a strange look on her face. "Cass, we've had another crank call."

Cass stared in disbelief as she towelled herself. "What next?" she groaned. "What did they say this time?"

"It was mostly like the other calls — very short, but somehow more angry. He just said something about 'You nosy bitches have had it now. You'll never live to spend the money.' Obviously it was someone who was at the will reading, or who has a pipeline to one of the heirs. Who else could possibly know about it? Someone seems to know our business before we do. Who's out there menacing us, and why?"

Vickie was thinking of the incredible fortune which her friend had just inherited, and she feared now that Cass might be kidnapped or murdered. If so, what would happen to herself? Was she going to be a target too just because of her close proximity to Cass? Should she get the hell out of here right away? Her heart was jumping at the vile possibilities. "At least I remembered the whistle this time, and I gave it two good blasts before he hung up. His head will be ringing for a while." She grinned at Cassie. "I just wish that you would get one of these calls. I'm not going to answer the phone any more. It's your turn now. I've had every one of them."

"Okay, that's fair, but somehow I always seem to be in the shower, or doing something else, and you get there first. From now on, I'll answer all calls, and if I'm busy, just let it ring. Anyway, I'm going to call the police again," she said resolutely. "I hate to, but we may be in real danger now. The money has changed everything. It gives someone a real motive. I'll feel more safe once Jack and Bud know the latest."

Vickie plunked herself down on the bed while Cass made the call. She was drawing worried little circles on the fluffy comforter. Muff jumped up beside her, and she began petting him absently, all the while staring at Cass on the phone.

Unfortunately Jack wasn't at the station. Cass hadn't really expected that he would be at this hour. Insisting that it was an emergency, and that she had to talk to Detective Willinger, the dispatcher finally agreed to contact him and have him call Cassie. It was only minutes before the phone rang, but to the two friends it seemed to be forever.

"Oh, Jack, it's Cassie." She started off sounding calm and controlled. "Sorry to bother you, but we've had another threatening call. This time we're taking the threats seriously. Listen, a lot of things have happened since we last talked, and I think we could be in real danger. Honestly I don't know just where to begin."

She could hear herself talking faster and faster. All semblance of calm was gone.

"Cass," he said with concern in his voice, "slow down. What's happened?"

"Well, Vickie answered the phone while I was in the shower, and the call was very short, but to the point. Basically he — I'm assuming that it was a man —

just called us names and said that we'd never live to spend the money." She looked inquiringly at Vickie to see if she had got it correct.

"Did Vickie recognize the voice?"

"No."

"Well, what money is he talking about?"

"Jack, it's very long and involved. I don't want to get into it now, but I've inherited some money from Pru, and there are people in the family who want it I guess."

A slight pause ensued, then, "Cass, are you sure that Vickie isn't making up these calls? Maybe she just wants to scare you, or perhaps she's just looking for some excitement or attention. Could she be jealous of you? You remember some of the crazy schemes she used to come up with in high school. She was always leading you astray."

Cass glanced at her friend sitting on the bed, hands clasped and looking worried. She knew in her heart that Vickie could never do anything so mean or so stupid. She inhaled deeply and smiled at Vic as she replied into the phone, "Not this again, please Jack" Don't waste your time on such an asinine idea. You're way off base," she added crossly.

"Okay, calm down. I had to ask. It's just odd that she seems to be the only one getting the calls. You haven't had one yet have you?"

"No" sighed Cassie wearily, shaking her head, "but that's just coincidence or fate or something."

"Unfortunately there isn't much we can do until this stalker makes a move — frustrating as that may be. Now, tell me what he said, and what this money thing is all about."

Cass felt too tired to go into details, and after a few more words, she hung up with a gnawing ache in her stomach. Things were going all wrong, and Jack might not be able to help them. Maybe she should ask Dave to come home, but she hated to do that.

Later, sitting with her eyes closed, and scratching Muffy between the ears, Cass pondered all the recent shocking events, — the stalker, Jack's reappearance in her life, all the deaths, the funerals, the reading of the will, the letter, the strange Elena, all that money. It was like something out of the movies. She probably did need Dave home with her, but she hated to admit her vulnerability. Neither she nor Vickie knew what to do next, and were disappointed and puzzled that the police weren't jumping all over the case.

Eventually Vickie tried to shake them both out of their gloomy moods by saying, "You're a multi-millionaire, Cass. Can you believe it?" She felt ashamed of herself as the green-eyed monster reared its ugly head. She determinedly batted him down. Still, all that money! Wouldn't it be lovely?

Cass didn't really know how she felt, but at this point the inheritance was an embarrassment since it came from Pru — a person she disliked. It didn't seem right, and anyway, no one deserved to have that much money. She was excited about it, intrigued by it, yet didn't really believe it. It might all be some monstrous joke or colossal mistake.

"When are you going to tell Dave and the kids?"

"I've been thinking about that. I have to tell Dave in person just to see his face. A phone call won't do. And, I don't want to tell the kids till Dave knows, then we can tell them together. I really don't want to ask him to come home early, so, it's just occurred to me that I could fly to Spain and surprise him. It would be smart to get out of the country for a while, and your visit will soon be over, so it seems like a good scenario. What do you think? Once you're out of Niagara Falls you should be safe. I'm sure it's just your proximity to me that has put you in any jeopardy."

"Sounds good to me, although I hate to think of my visit ending. It's been so bizarre, and so wonderful. And I hate like hell to give up on the mystery, but what else can we do?" There was real regret in Vickie's voice. She was scared of the person threatening them, but she loved the excitement. She had wanted a mystery and she got one, so she hated to go home leaving it unsolved. It would drive them both crazy if they never found out who had been harassing them, and who had killed Pru and Matt and Bunny and maybe even Jordan. So many deaths, so many suspects. Jenny, however, seemed to have zoomed to the top of the list.

"Funny about Pru," said Cass, shaking her head. "There's no way in hell that I can ever think of her as my mother. Maybe she did do what was best at the time. An unwed mother and illegitimate child were really ostracized in those days I guess. Lizzie was a good mother to me. She loved me, cherished me and virtually smothered me. She was always so protective and hovering, and now I understand. And my dad, well, I'm still mad at him because of Elena, but he was still my dad. I could never think of them as my grandparents."

Vickie was feeling a bit nervous, because she had done something behind Cassie's back, and was afraid that Cass would find out. She hadn't trusted Elena from the very beginning, and was sure that she was up to no good. She had called Jack a few days ago, and told him of her concerns. Of course that was before the will was read and before she heard that Elena had inherited half a million dollars. Now she was even more distrustful of this woman who had appeared out of nowhere, and had somehow ingratiated herself with Pru in a very short period of time. Jack had listened with interest, and promised to check things out. She knew that Jack thought she was flaky, and she hoped that he would take her seriously. She also devoutly hoped that Cass would never have to know what she had done.

Thinking of Jack, she ventured, "Are you going to tell Bud and Jack what Jenny was saying at the lawyer's? You said she was yelling something about all she had done to get that money. It sounds to me as if it was almost a confession."

"Yes, of course I'm going to tell them. I'm sure that she killed Pru and Bunny, and I'll bet she's killed Jordan too. Sweet little Jenny — who would have guessed? I should have told Jack while I had him on the phone, but it just all seems too much. I'm still reeling from the shock of the megabucks I've supposedly inherited."

CHAPTER 46

▼

The next day Vickie and Cass tried to keep busy. They hadn't slept well, and the money and the threats were filling their heads and making them nervous. Cass suggested that they both go and have their hair done at some fancy salon — her treat. Vickie, however, seemed reluctant. She didn't want Cassie spending money on her as if she was a poor relation. Cass was a bit hurt, but reasoned that she would likely feel the same if their positions were reversed. She would have to tread very lightly with Vickie, who could get some weird ideas in her auburn head, and who was quite sensitive under that wise-cracking façade.

After a quick lunch, they decided to go their separate ways, and then have a cosy dinner together. They told themselves that they weren't going to waste their time being scared and afraid to go about their normal routines. Cass set out for the library, while Vickie stayed home to spend some time on the computer.

Cassie loved the Niagara Falls Public Library, and she spent almost two hours roaming around, browsing through the new fiction, and looking for a few old favourites. She also enjoyed the current display of miniature doll furniture in the large glass cases near the front door.

The trip to the hair salon was a laugh. She had never been in the high priced establishment before, so no one knew her. She wished so much that Vickie had come too. They could have had a lot of fun. As it was, she was cared for by a very nice young man named Bruce. Cass decided it was just as well that Vickie wasn't with her. They would surely have developed the giggles and disgraced themselves, as he minced and pursed his lips and shook his head in horror over her previous haircut. He hummed some jaunty little tune to himself as he fluffed and snipped, and grinned coyly in the mirror from behind her. Then, humming some more, he danced around her, tilting his head this way and that, as he gazed lovingly at his handiwork. Cass wanted to explode with laughter, but managed to contain her giddiness. He was likeable in spite of his prancing and preening.

To her surprise, he actually did know what he was doing, and he performed a miracle with his cutting, shaping, and curling. She felt like a new person — glamorous, carefree, and queen of the world, as she emerged from the salon, two hundred dollars poorer.

Her next stop was the bank, and she giggled to herself as she realized the trauma everyone would suffer when she eventually got her hands on that twenty million, and had to do something with it at the bank. She visualized everyone bowing and scraping, and positively drooling. Most of the clerks and the bank manager knew her by name, and she was sure that they would all become her new best friends when she waltzed in with that obscene pile of money. She pictured herself staggering in with a huge suitcase full of bundles of thousand dollar bills. Actually she didn't have any idea what form it would take, — it was likely all invested in various things foreign to her, but it was fun picturing the bulging suitcase scenario.

By the time she reached the grocery store, her scalp was tingling, and she was feeling nervous. Her euphoric state had passed, and now she was anxious to do her shopping and get home to Vickie and the cats. She had been away too long. Were they okay? Had something happened?

En route to the supermarket, she noticed a big brown van behind her. She never really noticed cars, but this was a big old ugly thing, and somehow she thought she had seen it before. Then she decided that there were likely many big old ugly vans around town, and dismissed it. She had so much on her mind today that it was difficult to focus on anything for too long. That huge inheritance was occupying all her thoughts.

As always, she parked in the back lot, which was never crowded, and which forced her to walk a little further to the store. She tried to park far away wherever she went. It was a self imposed exercise regimen, her own little fight in the battle of the bulge. It was such a habit with her that she didn't have to think about it. The car just went automatically to the farthest reaches of any parking lot. If she had been thinking clearly on this particular day, however, she would have realized the potential danger in parking in a rather isolated area, and instead, would have parked as close to the store as possible. Unfortunately Cass was not thinking clearly. She was picturing herself telling Dave about the inheritance, and about the wonderful celebration they would have. Pru's letter was also on her mind. She had still not come to grips with the fact that Pru had been her mother. It seemed so bizarre.

Cass usually loved to go grocery shopping. She took her time, wandering up and down every aisle, looking for new and interesting products. She rarely went to the store without meeting someone she knew, but today the place was relatively empty. She picked out two delectable looking butterfly pork chops, two baking potatoes, and some fresh asparagus. She rarely ate desserts, but good old Vickie had such a sweet tooth that she didn't dare come home without something, so she picked up a key lime pie and groaned inwardly at the calories it represented. Never forgetting her two little beasties, she went to the deli and got some freshly sliced turkey breast for them.

When she exited the store, she saw to her dismay that it had started to rain quite heavily. Shit, there goes the new hairdo, was her first thought. Carrying two plastic bags of groceries, she hurried to her car, head down, and was annoyed to see a big brown van, or possibly the same big brown van, parked right beside her. There were only four or five cars in the entire back lot, so why had this numbskull parked so close? The sight of the van tweaked a thought in the back of her mind, but it was so amorphous that she couldn't quite grasp it. It flickered like a firefly, then disappeared. She was still thinking of the $200 she had just spent on her hair. Was she crazed? She had never spent that much money on a hairdo in her life. She mustn't become self-indulgent and let all that new-found money go to her head, no pun intended. Switching the bags to her left hand, and shaking the rain from her face, she groped in her purse for the car keys. What a lame-brain, she scolded herself. Why hadn't she fished them out in the store, where she was still dry, and had a cart to hold her groceries.

She was vaguely aware of the van door sliding open, but was totally taken by surprise when the big arm grabbed her from behind, and clamped an evil smelling cloth over her mouth. It was so large that it partially covered her eyes too. Cass let herself go limp, and managed to turn towards the assailant. She had seen this move on a television program about defending yourself from an attacker. Supposedly it gave you a chance to whack him in the crotch or poke him in the eyes. She and Vickie had discussed ways of protecting themselves several times after the attempted rape.

As she turned in his arms, the heavy bag of tinned cat food did what she had planned to do. It hit him in the crotch. She then dropped the bag and rammed her keys right up his nose. He had a mask on, but she knew she had hit the target when he squawked, and dropping the foul smelling cloth, put his hand to his nose.

She had been trying to hold her breath so as not to breathe in the noxious fumes on the rag. As she kneed him, he let out another surprised grunt. She took a huge breath of clean air and screamed at the top of her lungs, all the while struggling to free herself from his grasp.

Everything happened so quickly that it was difficult to understand the sequence. The man held on to her, as he bent to pick up the cloth which had landed in a puddle, and Cassie just kept on screaming and trying to get free. He was having difficulty holding onto Cass, who was struggling so valiantly that she seemed to have eight arms and ten legs. She knew that it was game over if he managed to get her into that van. She was holding her own, pounding, kicking and screaming. The element of surprise was on her side. He hadn't expected the old keys up the nose trick.

The sound of pounding feet and men yelling, gave her renewed strength. Her would-be kidnapper heard them too, because he stood up, and, dropping the cloth, he tried to drag Cassie into the open van.

Now they both heard shouts of "Let her go", and "Stop right there." It was a wonder that they could hear anything other than Cass screaming at fever pitch. The assailant realized that he was in trouble, and letting go of Cass, he gave her a vicious push, and leaped into his van. It shot out of the parking lot like a rocket. Cass fell heavily onto her knees and hands, then pitched forward onto her face, so that she had no chance to see the license plate.

John Carmody and his teenage son Robby had been kneeling on the far side of their car, looking at a tire which seemed rather flat, when the screaming started. That was likely why the would-be kidnapper hadn't seen them. Looking up, they could see a man and a woman struggling between a large van and a car way at the far side of the parking lot. Wasting no time, they yelled as they ran towards the screaming woman.

The van sped away before they could see the plates. Cassie was just lifting her head from the pavement, still on her hands and knees when they reached her. One hand was bleeding from a piece of glass which had pierced her palm. Both knees of her slacks were torn and muddy, and there was a scrape on her cheek from hitting the pavement. They helped her up as she shook her head in frustration and indignation. She did, however, bend down again and pick up the stinking rag which had been left behind. She knew it might be useful evidence.

The older man leaned her against her car and stayed with her while the teenager ran back to his vehicle to call 911. Cass was dizzy from inhaling the fumes on the cloth. It had smelled like ether or chloroform, and it was fortunate that she had only inhaled a few whiffs of it before the bumbler had dropped it. Trembling violently, she thought she was going to be sick, but she just kept taking deep breaths and trying to calm down. She was so grateful to these two rescuers that she could have kissed them both. If they hadn't come running, she would have been lifted into that van, and likely would have been killed and dumped somewhere. Had his motive been kidnapping for ransom, or was he going to kill her? Cass really didn't want to know. She just wanted to go home.

By the time a police car arrived, she had calmed down, and was making futile stabs at her wet hair. The new hairdo was a thing of the past. John Carmody and his son stayed right with her, and gave the police whatever information they could. Unfortunately it wasn't much. Not knowing that Cassie had inherited all that money, they simply assumed that the man was trying to abduct her in order to rape her. The police thought the same thing. Cass was too weary to try setting them straight. She didn't look like an heiress, and she certainly didn't feel like one, and it was unlikely that they would have believed her.

After thanking her rescuers over and over, she got their names and phone number, and promised to be in touch. She already knew in her mind that she would give them a reward — a big reward. They had been brave and fearless, and if they had been parked closer, they likely would have gotten into a struggle with her assailant. It was just unfortunate that they hadn't been able to get a license number.

One policeman took Cassie to the hospital in the squad car, while the other drove behind them in her car. Her hand and knees were bleeding, as was her cheek. On the way, she sat back and closed her eyes, and it was then that she realized where she had seen the brown van before. It was either this one or one just like it which had been at Matt's funeral, and again at the wedding reception. It belonged to someone in the family, but which one? Blake didn't look like the type to drive a van, nor did Jordan. He had been driving a small sports car the night she and Vickie broke into his house. There could have been a van in the garage, though. Again all evidence pointed to Pete. He was a truck or van type for sure. The attacker had been as big as Pete, but then Jordan and Blake were also big men, tall and strong. Jim Sinclair was another possibility. Cassie's head was hurting now, and she couldn't think clearly.

The police couldn't have been nicer, and once she told them that she was a personal friend of Jack Willinger and Bud Lang, they couldn't do enough for her. Unfortunately she was beginning to feel very queasy, as she huddled in a waiting room chair. Every time she thought of that rancid, filthy cloth clamped over her mouth and nose, her stomach lurched.

The younger of the two cops came to sit beside her, and said that she was next. "You'll be right after that poor woman with the bloody towel on her hand," he whispered. "She accidentally whacked her little finger off chopping veggies for a stew. Her husband put it in a bag of ice and rushed her here. Good thinking on his part."

Cass looked over at the unfortunate woman who was crying and moaning while she clutched the bloody towel. She really didn't realize that she was going to throw up until, picturing the bloody finger landing in the stew pot, she gulped and barfed all over the cop's shoes. Then, gasping in horror and embarrassment, she leaped up and raced for the nearest washroom. As she ran down the hall, she thought she heard the loud guffaws of the older officer.

She threw cold water on her face and rinsed her mouth out several times, before looking at herself in the mirror. She gasped as she saw her $200 hair "do". It was now a hair "don't." She looked like something the cats had dragged in and then decided they didn't want. Her cheek was bleeding, her nose looked puffy, and her hair hung limply as if in silent condemnation. "Oh man, what a mess" she giggled, as hysteria and shock set in. "Wait till Vickie sees her raggedy-ass friend. She won't know who I am."

After feebly plucking at her wilted hair, she gave up and turned to more important matters. Wetting some paper towels, she hurried back to the emergency waiting room to apologize, and to clean up the hapless cop's shoes. He, however, was nowhere in sight. Instead, the older policeman grinned at her and explained, "He's in the washroom trying to repair the damage. Don't feel badly though. This is the second time today that someone's barfed on him. The other one was a baby, and she got it all over his shirt. Some days it just doesn't pay to get out of bed." He laughed some more and seemed to think that his partner's misadventures were extremely funny.

Eventually the young policeman returned. Both men waited around at the hospital while Cass was x-rayed and bandaged, and given a tetanus shot. When she was ready to go home, they sat her down and got a complete statement. They were very interested when she mentioned vaguely that she had recently inherited some money, and she was sure that was what the attack had been all about. They promised to give Jack a full report, and then took her home.

Vickie took one look at her friend, and couldn't believe what she saw. Cass had either been in a car accident or had been attacked by a gang. Her face was swollen on the one side, and there was a band-aid on her cheek. Her left hand was bandaged, and her slacks had two huge holes ripped in them. With her hair hanging in sullen strings, she gave new meaning to the term "dishevelled."

"Wow, what does the other guy look like? I thought you were just going out to get your hair done!"

They all stood in the hall as Vickie surveyed the damage.

"I did" moaned Cassie ruefully. "I paid $200 for this disaster." She ran her fingers through the wilted strands.

"Maybe you can get your money back," said Vickie dryly.

"Hey, that was only the beginning of the fiasco. Wait till you hear the rest of the tale."

The two policemen handed Cassie the keys to her car, and suggested that Vickie take good care of her friend. Cass thanked them profusely and waved as they drove away. She had already made up her mind that she was going to buy a pair of expensive new shoes for the quiet young cop. Now, however, she had to tell Vickie about her afternoon misadventures.

CHAPTER 47

▼

Cassie was sore all over from the fall she had taken when her attacker pushed her so viciously. The next day her cheek was black and blue, as well as swollen, and she was quite content to stay hidden in the safety of the cosy library, and the sun porch. She felt depression settle over her like a wet blanket. Would her life ever be back to normal? Would she ever be safe from predators now that she was going to have all that money? Maybe she should just give it all away before she even got it. Huh, fat chance! Her mind was reeling as she and Vickie finished their dinner.

She started to laugh as she ruefully shook her head. "Oh, Vic, we were going to have such a lovely dinner last night. I had even bought you a delicious key lime pie. It's likely still lying out there in the parking lot along with the pork chops and the turkey for the cats. What a waste!"

"I wish I'd been with you, Cass. I just wanted some time to play with the computer, and," here she paused and looked sheepish, "to tell you the truth, I was a bit jealous about your money. I feel so stupid and mean now. I'm sorry, Cass. I'm really happy for you, and my moments of envy are long gone. Forgive me?"

"Oh forget it. You don't have a selfish or jealous bone in your body. It would have been nice, though, to have you beside me. I doubt that he would have tried anything if there'd been two of us. Do you think he'll try again?"

"Who knows? Maybe you should hire a bodyguard until Dave gets home. Maybe Jack could suggest someone."

"I don't think so" laughed Cass. "What I do think though, is that we should just continue on as if nothing was wrong. I mean we'll be careful, but we aren't going to let this guy, whoever he is, spoil our lives. Why don't we get away from it all tomorrow and have a nice picnic down in Queenston Park? We could visit

Brock's monument. Every Canadian should see where Sir Isaac Brock defended Canada against the Americans in 1812 in the Battle of Queenston Heights. Hopefully it will take our minds off everything. We need some time to chill out and regroup. Besides, it's supposed to be a beautiful day tomorrow."

"Okay" said Vickie enthusiastically. "I don't give a rat's patootie about Brock's monument, but you know me, the wild and crazy gal. I'm game for just about anything. We'll forget about everything weird that's happened."

In actual fact, Vickie felt quite uneasy. She missed Brian, so kind, so gentle, so boring. She missed her fun-loving, raucous kids, but mostly she missed her own youth with its laughter, wildness, hopes for the future. The years were rushing by too quickly, and she felt restless and edgy. She figured that she must be in the midst of a full-blown mid-life crisis. All the crazy events of the past few weeks were just adding to her edginess.

Brushing away sudden tears, she impulsively threw her arms around Cassie and hugged her. "I love you, old friend. Just being here this summer has been so good for me. I hadn't realized how restless I was, or how much I needed a change. Thanks for everything, Cass. No matter how things turn out, it's been a fantastic few weeks."

"Oh, Vickie, what would I have done without you?"

They soon retired to their beds, looking forward to the next day. Sometime around 4am Vickie wakened with a start. What had she heard? Muffy was mewing, so he had heard something too. Hurrying to Cassie's room, she was relieved to find her friend awake.

"Did you hear something, Cass?"

"I'm not sure what wakened me. It was likely just Muff making an awful racket. He seems agitated."

"Well, I think I heard a noise, but I don't know what it was."

They stood at the bedroom door, listening intently. Muffy wound himself in and out around their ankles, purring happily. He liked having company in the middle of the night.

"We might as well turn on all the lights and go downstairs, otherwise we'll never get back to sleep."

An entire search of the house turned up nothing. Doors and windows were all intact, and no intruder lurked behind a door or a curtain, waiting to pounce.

"Why did we ever think we would want to get involved in a murder mystery? Now we're imagining noises in the night like a couple of kids, but darn it, I'm sure I heard something."

"Vic, what kind of noise did you think it was?"

"Honestly, I don't know. It wasn't footsteps, it was more like a door closing."

"Maybe Sugar Plum was helping herself to the kitty treats in the cupboard" laughed Cass, as she made them a cup of tea. She wondered whether Vickie had imagined the noise, but then chided herself for doubting her friend. If Vickie said that she had heard a noise, then there was probably something to worry about, but what?

"I just know that it was something that wakened me and put me on the alert" said Vickie defensively, sensing that Cassie was doubtful. "Maybe Muffy heard someone outside, and when we turned on the lights it scared them off."

"Well, there's certainly no one around now. Let's go back to bed and try to get a few hours of sleep."

The next morning was gorgeous, and although Cassie's scalp was tingling again, she was determined to pay no attention. On a lovely day like this it just wasn't possible that any more bad stuff could happen. They weren't going to think about the threatening calls or all the killings, or the kidnapping attempt. This was going to be a completely relaxing and happy day.

A warm breeze from the west lifted their spirits as they set off down Morrison Street. They planned to take the leisurely and scenic route down to the Niagara River and then onto the Parkway right to Queenston Heights. They were cruising happily along, talking non-stop as usual, when Cassie suddenly veered to the left and almost lost control of the car.

"What's that buzzing?" she squeaked, looking frantically around. "Oh my God, there are BEES in here! Get my epi-kit from the glove compartment." She swerved wildly to the accompaniment of blaring horns and squealing brakes.

"Cass, it's not here" cried Vickie. "I'll get the one from your purse." Frantically she dumped the purse contents into her lap, but there was no life-saving epi-kit there either. She grabbed a piece of newspaper off the floor, and began swishing at the bees, which were now swarming all over the front dashboard as well as her legs. This only served to make them more angry. The incessant buzzing was drowning out Cassie's terrified whimpers.

"Ouch" cried Vickie, rubbing her arm. "They're stinging me, Cass. We've got to get out of this car. Pull over" she shouted.

Cass responded with a quick turn of the wheel. There was a bump as they climbed the curb, then a loud crash, as the car came to a sudden stop with a red Canada Post mail box jammed onto the hood. Both women flung open the doors and leaped from the car. They ran down the sidewalk, a few bees still chasing them.

In the car behind, Ross Skinner had been watching the wild manoeuvrings of what he assumed to be a very drunk driver. He had already called 911 on his cell phone. Jack Willinger and Bud Lang were just leaving the station, which was directly around the block from the accident scene. The dispatcher asked them to check it out.

"God, it's Vickie and Cassie," Bud exclaimed, as he stared at the red metal mail box impaled on the hood of their car. "Is this what they mean by 'going postal'?" he laughed.

The women were now standing on the sidewalk half a block up from the car. They were much relieved to see Bud and Jack.

The two detectives stared glumly at the mail spewed all over the sidewalk and road. It was almost time for the morning pick-up, and the box had obviously been full. They would need crowd control quickly, before looters started picking up the mail, which was now blowing around and being stepped on by the curious spectators who had already gathered.

"You should go sit in our car" suggested Bud, while he and Jack tried to control the situation. Cass and Vickie were happy to sit quietly and try to figure out who had plotted this latest bit of harassment.

"This is the last straw. Bees in my car! What next, a poison snake in the shower?" Cass was in turns angry and frightened, as she realized what a close call she had had. Not only could she have been killed by a bee sting, but she might have caused an accident with her wild swerving on the road.

As Bud drove them back to the station, Jack stayed to keep things under control until extra help arrived. No one noticed the small beaten up red car trailing along at a safe distance. Willy the Weasel had been sitting down the street from the police station, trying once again to figure out the schedules of Willinger and Lang. Because he had been drinking all morning, he was having a difficult time concentrating.

Willy had left town after his attempted rape of Vickie. He had been really spooked that night when the cats attacked him, and Cassie had come home unexpectedly. He was covered with some very deep and painful bites and gouges. How could two little cats do such damage? It had felt like two tigers attacking him, and Willy had convinced himself that there were at least four cats tearing at him. The bitch had really hurt his eye too, and he had a patch on it.

He had been hiding in Toronto ever since the fiasco, and now he was anxious to finish the job of killing Willinger and Lang, and raping the good looking wife, before taking off for the safety and anonymity of Vancouver. He had borrowed this old car from the only friend he had, and he was wearing a baseball cap pulled well down over his face. It hadn't occurred to him that a bright red car might be a little obvious, but so far he had been lucky. Everyone was too interested in the mail box caper to notice him.

When the two detectives came out of the station and headed around the corner, so did Willy. Like everyone else, he laughed at the sight of the red mailbox gracing the hood of Cassie's car. He hiccoughed delightedly as he slapped his knees. When he recognized Victoria, he couldn't believe it. A jolt of fury and frustration zipped through him. That bitch and her cats had nearly ruined him. She had almost blinded him digging her finger into his eye. He just might go after her again when he was finished with the cops. She needed to be taught a friggin' lesson.

The realization that someone had deliberately put those bees in the car was a sobering thought for the two women. Someone definitely wanted Cassie dead, and it had to be someone who knew about her allergy to bees. And what about Vickie? Were they after her too?

"Honestly, I feel as if I'm perched on a tree limb, and the man with the chain saw cometh." said Cassie, trying to make light of the situation. Those flying death darts had scared her. Then she realized in amazement that although Vickie had been stung several times, she herself had not been stung. How could that be? She wondered whether it had anything to do with the cologne which Vickie was wearing. Maybe the smell had irritated them, otherwise it made no sense.

"What devious little mind conceived that bee plot? It's ridiculous. Who knows that I'm so allergic to bees? They likely thought that if I died from an allergic reaction, you would just go back to Vancouver and they would be rid of both of us," she mused.

At the station, Bud managed to find some strong coffee (more like battery fluid) he muttered to himself, and a chocolate bar, which he scoffed from one of the secretaries. He felt that the women could use a little pick-me-up. They were grateful for his kindness, and looked around the station with interest. It was probably similar to every police station around the country. Although it was air conditioned, it stank of that ineffable mix of stale coffee, cigarettes, sweat, and the despair and fear of countless parades of drunks, prostitutes, con men, vagrants, and various denizens of the streets.

There were cubicles, swivel chairs, filing cabinets, waste baskets. Everything was utilitarian, and it was all painted an institutional green. Above the talking, laughing and shouting, could be heard the steady clickety-clack of the computers. It was neither a restful nor a friendly environment.

As they drank their bitter coffee, they talked with Bud, and with Jack, who had finally returned from the chaotic scene. "How did the bees get in the car?" wondered Cass again. "And what happened to my two epi-kits? The car is always locked, and my purse is always with me, so how did they do it?"

"Wait a minute, Cass. Remember we were surprised that the car was unlocked this morning. We thought that the policeman who drove it home for you had left it unlocked."

"That's right, Vic" cried Cass, light suddenly dawning in her eyes. "The noise you and Muffy heard, — it could have been someone shutting the car door after putting the bees in."

"Of course" cried Vickie. "I knew I'd heard something." She was happy to be vindicated. "Now who all knows that you're allergic to bees?"

Jack and Bud were sitting there quietly, letting them work things out in their minds. The detectives knew that this was a very effective way of getting to the bottom of things without breaking up the train of thought with a lot of questions.

Cass thought for a moment, and then said, "The funeral, of course. Remember I made an ass of myself flapping around in the yard at Matt's funeral when the bee attacked me. Everyone was there, so it could be any one of them."

"Well, it wouldn't be Blake. He's got his million now, so why would he try to hurt you? It wouldn't do him any good. We don't know where Jordan is, so that leaves Jenny and Pete, and maybe Jim Sinclair. The only reason Jenny would have to kill you is that she was so mad that you got all the money. She couldn't inherit it now even if she did kill you. It would just go to your kids, but she might want you dead just because you threatened her. I guess it has to be the half-sister, the half-brother or the half-wit," Vickie finished with a wry grin. "Oh, and I almost forgot Elena, your half-aunt."

Bud and Jack were now looking at each other in confusion. Although they knew from yesterday's attack, that Cass had inherited some money from Pru, they hadn't heard any details about the will. Cass hadn't had time yet to tell them about Jenny's histrionics in the lawyer's office, and Cassie's warning to her. It took a while before they got everything sorted out. Jack kept looking at Cassie in amazement. He couldn't picture her with twenty million dollars. Like everyone else, he had a momentary twinge of envy at her good fortune.

"But how would Pete or Jenny or Elena or Jim have had access to my purse?" wondered Cass. "And as you say, we don't even know where Jordan is, although I think that Jenny does."

Vickie had a strange little shiver of fear. She had access to Cassie's purse, and to the car. Could anyone possibly suspect her of trying to hurt her friend? She knew that Jack had never really liked her. Hastily she told herself to stop being so paranoid. She'd been reading too many mysteries. Then, with relief, she remembered.

"Of course, at the will reading, remember, you went back into the conference room to get your purse, and you mentioned that it wasn't where you had left it. Jenny was the last to come out. She could have taken the kit then."

Cassie suddenly thought of something. "Why didn't the bees appear right away when we got into the car?"

"I think I know how it happened," said Jack. "They were in a crate under the front seat — right where Vickie was sitting. The top was on loosely, and the motion of the car would have jarred it open just enough to let them out. It was a pretty dumb scheme. It's amazing that you weren't stung though, Cass."

Eventually they drove the friends home. "Don't go anywhere tonight, and keep the doors locked" warned Jack. He had a special, protective feeling towards Cassie. Things were getting more complicated now that she had all this money. "I'll check in on you later tonight" he promised, as he dropped them off. Jack felt embarrassed and frustrated at his lack of success so far. They had been working round the clock, but still hadn't picked up Willy, and didn't know who was making the threatening calls. It was a dismal showing, and he and Bud just had to get a break in the case soon. He was pretty sure now that Cassie's husband wasn't involved. That had been one of his hair-brained ideas. Talk about clutching at straws! Anyway, he fervently wished that Dave would come home now and look after his wife. Didn't he know or care what was going on?

CHAPTER 48

▼

It was a few days after the "bee" incident, and Cassie and Vickie were enjoying some quiet time. They had been on an emotional roller coaster, and they were just chilling out.

"Shouldn't Blake be here by now?" asked Vickie, as they sat down with their usual glass of wine in the sun porch after dinner.

"I wonder if he's lost" said Cass, looking at her watch.

They had decided to invite Blake and Gloria over to Niagara so that they could have a good discussion about everything that had transpired, and to possibly get some ideas about their next step — if any. The police were still diddling around. They hadn't caught the rapist, the stalker, or the "bee" person. In Toronto there seemed to be no leads as to who had killed Pru and Bunny, and Jordan had still not turned up. It was discouraging and frustrating and absolutely ludicrous.

They hadn't had a chance to talk since the will was read, and Blake still hadn't heard anything about the bee attack. Vickie and Cass were now sure that he wasn't involved in any way. Actually they thought he might be a target too, since he had inherited a goodly sum of money. They were zeroing in on Jenny and Pete as the culprits, although Jim Sinclair was still high on their list. Jordan would have been the prime suspect if he hadn't disappeared so mysteriously. Elena was still a wild card too. Unfortunately Gloria couldn't make it, but Blake was on his way.

When the phone rang, Cassie jumped up. "Bet that's Blake now. He's lost for sure."

"Hello, Cass, it's Jack."

"Jack" cried Cassie in surprise. "What's up?"

"Well, I'm in a hurry but I've got great news. We've discovered some evidence about the bees which were put in your car. We know now who's trying to kill you. The special task force is setting a trap, and we really need your help. We're going to get the killer tonight. Do you know where the old Graham farm is on the way to Virgil?"

"Yes" said Cassie hesitantly, "but I'm sorry, I can't hear you very well. We've got a bad connection. What is it you want?" She wasn't interested in the old Graham farm house. It had been haunted for years, or so the locals claimed.

"I'm calling from my car phone. There may be some interference, but I can hear you just fine. Now, what we need is for you to drive to the farm, park your car around back, and don't look for any police. They'll all be hidden. Just go in the back door, which will be unlocked, and go down the hall to the room with the light on. We need you to leave right away, and we'll meet you there. Don't worry — you won't be in any danger."

"Wait a minute, Jack. Slow down and tell me again. Who do you think it is, and why do you need us? Who's going to be in that room?" She was so surprised by Jack's call, that she wasn't really assimilating what he was saying.

"Look, there's no time to talk. Bring Vickie and get out there as fast as you can. I'm on my way now. We've got half the force out, so don't worry, we'll get him, and you'll be perfectly safe. Remember, you won't see us, but we'll be there. Just do exactly as I say. You're the bait, and we need you to spring the trap."

There wasn't the usual warmth in his voice, but Cass realized that he must be very rushed and excited if they were about to catch the killer.

"Okay," she said, doubtfully. "We'll be there as soon as we can. You promise we won't be in any danger?"

"Absolutely not. We'll see you there. Leave right away," and the connection was broken.

"Vickie, that was Jack. He was in a real rush, and he didn't explain things very well. Anyway, they've got new evidence, and they know who's trying to kill us. He was on a cell phone though, and I couldn't hear him clearly. Those things are a pain. Apparently they're setting a trap tonight, and they need us to help. He said to leave right away and to go to the old Graham farmhouse, which is just out by Virgil. It's been deserted for years. I don't know, Vic. What do you think? I hate to go out to that old place at night, but he said that there's absolutely no danger involved. Oh, God, wouldn't that be wonderful if they could catch this guy tonight. What do you say? Should we co-operate?" Even as she spoke, Cassie's doubts were telling her that something wasn't right.

"So good old Jack is coming through after all. I was beginning to think that he's nothing but a pretty face. They've been really dragging their feet, but this is great. They actually need us to help them catch this guy. Perfecto. What are we waiting for?"

"Wait a minute, slow down. Let's think about this. If only we could call him back and get more details, but I don't know his pager number. Damn, I wish he had explained it better. This could be dangerous, but he hung up before I could ask any questions. He didn't give me a chance to say 'no'. Doesn't it seem odd that they would need to use civilians to help them? What's wrong with this picture?"

"Cass, we've got to get out there. They must want us there in place before the killer arrives. It makes sense to me that they would use us as bait. We can't miss this chance to catch him, whoever he is. Come on, get your cell phone and —" This was vintage Vickie, racing into things without thinking them through.

Cassie grabbed her arm and said "Vickie, slow down. Let's not be too hasty. Let me call the station first and see what we can verify. Maybe we could talk to Bud and find out more. I'm as anxious to catch this guy as you are, but let's not go into it like two blind mice."

Vickie reluctantly agreed, but she felt that they were wasting precious time. Moments later Cass hung up in frustration. "They wouldn't tell me anything. They said that they couldn't discuss the special task force, and they couldn't contact Jack. I don't think they even tried. I don't know whether they thought I was a crackpot or they were just being cautious, or they didn't know what the hell I was babbling about," she said with a frown.

"Well, they're not going to blab about the task force to just anyone who calls. That would be stupid. Come on," she half coaxed, half bullied. "This is our big chance. You'll hate yourself if you do nothing, and think how it would look to Jack. You agreed to go, so let's do it. Did you tell the dispatcher where we're going?"

"Yes, but he didn't sound too interested."

"Okay, you've got your phone, and the police know where we're going. We'll call Peggy to come right over to sit with the cats, and she'll be here to welcome Blake when he arrives. What can possibly go wrong?"

Vickie asked this question with such innocence and excitement that Cassie decided she was being too cautious. All she could think of, though, was a lonely country road and a ramshackle old farmhouse. She was also thinking of the gruff voice on the phone. Had it sounded suspicious or was she just being too careful? It had definitely been Jack, or had it? Now she wasn't sure. Dave would hogtie her if he knew she was planning anything so foolhardy, but Dave wasn't here, and Vickie was. She didn't want to let Jack down, so taking a deep breath, she nodded her head and went to get a phone and a couple of flashlights.

Because of the rat incident, along with everything else which had been going on, Cass was reluctant to leave the cats alone in the house at night. Anyway, as Vickie had pointed out, Peggy would be there to greet Blake, make their apologies, and tell him where they had gone.

Peggy came right over. Perhaps if she hadn't been available, Cass and Vic would never have gone to the fateful meeting at the old farmhouse, and everything would have turned out differently. She was available, however, and the two friends set out on their short journey into the unknown. At the last moment Cassie stuck her small tape recorder and her scissors into her jacket pocket.

"Here we go, dumb and dumber, off to another misadventure" exclaimed Vickie with mischief in her eyes. "We should have had Chinese food for dinner. We could have read the fortune cookies. Maybe they would have said "Adventure comes to those who dare."

"More likely 'Misadventure comes to those who are reckless'" countered Cassie. "Or what about 'They who take bull by horns sure to get gored.'"

"How about 'They who play with fire sure to get burned?'"

Neither woman realized just how close to the truth they were.

"I think we're about to give new meaning to the term 'fools rush in'" muttered Cassie, patting her pockets to see that she had everything they needed.

Their nerves were humming like guitar strings by the time they reached the old farmhouse. "What a dark night," whispered Cass as they jolted down the rutted driveway. They could, however, see a dim light in one of the downstairs rooms, and just as Jack had said, there were no police in sight.

Parking around the back as directed, Cass felt her bravado melting like marshmallows in hot chocolate. The humid dark air hovered over them like a sauna, making breathing difficult.

Carefully they climbed the rickety porch stairs. Common sense was now setting in, and it occurred to them both that it was a rather ill conceived plan. It certainly wouldn't stand scrutiny, but neither friend cared to articulate her doubts. Both hoped that a police officer, preferably Jack or Bud would open the door. The silence was broken by the mindless chirping of crickets, and the dissonance of the cicadas. Then a dog howled in a distant field. The sound echoed through the surrounding trees.

"Oh gawd, the hound of the Baskervilles" quipped Vickie. "Not a good sign."

"Maybe we should just get out of here. Let the police do their jobs and catch this guy. They don't need us."

Vickie, however, was on a mission. Her adrenalin was flowing, and she was momentarily fearless. She was putting all her doubts behind her. As they had been told, they tried the door and found it unlocked.

Cassie's mouth was as dry as old parchment. "What a couple of numbskulls we are" she muttered to Vickie, just as a step creaked behind them.

"Whew, that was just the wind" said Vickie, looking over her shoulder in alarm.

There was no one in sight as they tiptoed down the hall, and headed for the door under which a dim light shone. Their resolve was crumbling like old cork, but they were going to see this through.

CHAPTER 49

▼

As they gingerly pushed open the door under which a small light glowed, they each took a deep breath. Had they made a mistake? What if there were no police, just a trap of their own making?

"I've been expecting you. What took you so long?" the petite blond snarled. Her blazing eyes made her look crazy as she grinned at them. The room smelled a bit like a gin mill. Little Jennifer had been into the sauce again. Well, maybe that could work in their favour.

"Jenny?" cried Victoria, full of false bravado, "what's going on?"

"What do you think is going on? I'm going to kill you, that's what's going on."

Cass and Victoria looked at each other with sinking hearts. What if it wasn't Jack who had called? What if it was Pete? If it was Pete, he had done a good job fooling Cassie. What if there was no special task force laying a trap to catch the killer? Maybe it was just Jenny and Pete. The good news was that Jenny didn't appear to have a weapon, unless it was hidden in her pocket. The bad news was that they didn't know where Pete was. Well, the two of them together should be able to outwit Jenny. They could take her down easily. This didn't make sense. She wouldn't have dragged them out here if she had no way of killing them. Pete must be here, but where was he lurking, and what was he up to? Their best hope now was that this was all part of the police plan. Somehow the police knew that Jenny was going to lure them to this forsaken spot, and they needed Cass and Vickie to get her talking and confessing. Then Jack and all his cops would come rushing in to save them. They both knew that was highly unlikely. They were in deep shit.

"Jenny, what's this all about?" asked Cassie, trying to appear calm and confident. She and Vickie would have to talk their way out of this just in case there were no police.

"How many have you invited to this little soirée?" she inquired.

"Just you two. You're the ones who wouldn't stop snooping around, and you are the one who thinks she's getting all my money, sister dearest. Even if I can't have it, I'll never let you get your hands on it, not after all I've been through."

The friends were surreptitiously looking around for something to use as a weapon. Unfortunately this old abandoned house was virtually empty. They noticed the wallpaper hanging in strips. Cracked and filthy linoleum was curling up and peeling back in the corners. Over everything hung the pungent smell of mouse droppings.

Vickie was thinking that they could easily overpower Jenny, and use her as a human shield to get out of here. They would just have to get their timing right. They glanced at each other, trying to communicate. Should they make a move on her, or should they just have faith that the police were hidden all around, listening to every word, and ready to rush to the rescue at the opportune time. Bad idea. They had better rely on themselves just in case there were no police.

"This is all about the money, you know, those beautiful big piles of money which would have changed my life," said Jenny, glaring at Cassie. "You've taken everything from me. You've ruined my life. You've stolen all the money, and you stole my mother too. She was my mother, not yours." She was becoming more feverish as she spoke. "My father, my mother, my brother, they're all dead because of you." Accusations spewed from her lips like venom from a spitting cobra.

Vickie wondered how she could possibly blame Cassie for any of this. Poor Cass had been an innocent bystander. It wasn't her fault that someone had cut the brakes, or that someone had killed Prudence and Bunny. It wasn't her fault that Pru had been her mother and had left her all the money. Jenny was really off the wall, making no sense. This was all great material, though, if, in fact, the police were listening.

"You're going to pay now," Jenny snarled. "You'll never live to spend a cent. After all the other killings, this one will be pure fun." She added this in a strange little sing-song tone. Where was her soft, breathy voice which always sounded so sexy and helpless? This vitriolic diatribe shouldn't have been coming out of that pretty mouth.

"How did all this happen, Jenny?" queried Cass, stalling for time.

"It just snowballed. Pete started it all by killing my dad in that car wreck. I always thought it was Jordie who had done it. Pete was just mad because my father wouldn't give him money for his old marina."

So it had been Pete after all, they thought, glancing at each other.

"Then I had to kill my mother, our mother I guess" she amended grudgingly. "I killed her to stop her from changing her will, but I was too late. She had already changed it and left everything to you, her secret daughter. Next, sister dearest, I had to kill that silly nurse because she saw me coming out of mother's room. That was too bad. I really hadn't planned on that, but she deserved it anyway. She was always flirting with Jordie."

This confession was pouring and tumbling like Niagara Falls. They couldn't have shut her up if they had tried. Obviously the gin had loosened her tongue. "I grabbed the scissors off the floor when mother struggled and knocked everything off her bed table. I just thought they might be handy to stab anyone who tried to stop me on the way out." She stopped momentarily, and then with a sigh she continued. "I hadn't expected her to struggle so much, she just about wore me out."

Jenny continued now, looking extremely pleased with herself. "It was a bummer that the nurse saw me, just a stupid little twist of fate. Why couldn't she have been tying her shoe or looking after some patient when I ran out of the room? Anyway, I knew I'd have to kill her, and I had the scissors in my pocket. It was so easy. I just followed her home." She paused here and looked pensive.

"Next came Jordie, my beautiful Jordie. He wasn't really my brother, you know. He was adopted, and we were going to go away together, at least I thought we were." She stopped and frowned, as if she still didn't understand just what had happened to her plans. "But then he laughed at me you see. He was angry and disgusted. He really didn't love me after all. I knew then that he would kill me and take all the money, so I just beat him to it. What else could I do? He should be swimming with the fishes, but I keep seeing him. He won't stay dead." This was said with a little sob. She looked at them as if expecting sympathy. Then, shaking her head as if to clear away the evil picture of Jordan covered with seaweed and glaring menacingly at her, she said, "Now it's your turn."

Both women intuitively understood that Jenny needed and perhaps craved, admiration and praise. They appealed to that need by acting interested in her tale. Hopefully this would buy them time, but time for what? Oh ya, time for Jack to come riding in on a white horse. Surely the police had heard enough by now. What was taking them so long?

They were still kidding themselves into thinking that the police might be coming to the rescue, although they knew in their hearts that they were on their own.

"The bees, Jenny, how did you manage that?" interrupted Vickie. Anything to keep her talking.

"You know, it was all Pete's fault," scowled Jenny. "What a screw up. He was supposed to grab you and get rid of you, Cass. He was going to chloroform you and throw you in the upper river so that your body would float down over the falls. It would have been days or weeks before they found you, and it would have seemed to be a suicide. People would have thought that you just couldn't handle the news that your sister was really your mother. Somehow he blew it, and those men in the parking lot scared him off. He's such a moron" she added, shaking her head.

"It was his idea, and it really should have worked. It was so simple. Luckily I had a back-up plan which seemed pretty foolproof at the time. I bought the bees from an old coot up in Newmarket. I'd read about him in the paper, and I knew about your allergy, Cassie, from dad's funeral. You were so funny that day, flapping your arms around like a crazy person. I stole the epi-kit from your purse at the lawyer's, and to make things even easier, your car wasn't locked when Pete and I put the bees in it. I took the other epi-kit from the glove compartment. The hardest part was loosening the lid just enough so that the bees couldn't get out till you were driving along, and the motion of the car bounced it loose. Actually Pete got stung a couple of times before we got it set just right."

Jenny carried on with her tale, never taking her eyes from them. "I still don't understand why it didn't work" she muttered. "You should be dead by now if you are so allergic to them. You're harder to kill than a damn cockroach." Then, changing her tone, she added with a laugh, "You almost caught us that night, you know. When Pete shut the car door, it made a noise, and we heard a cat meowing. Then all the lights in the house came on and we had to run."

"Shut up Jenny. Let's just get this over with and get the hell out of here. I've been watching, and they weren't followed." They hadn't heard Pete creep up silently behind them, and their hearts sank at this news. Did it mean that there were no police, and that they had been enticed out here by these two killers? Before they could even think of running or doing anything clever, Pete delivered a vicious blow with his gun butt to the back of Vickie's head. She had been trying stealthily to get the cell phone out of her pocket, but she dropped like a puppet whose strings had been cut. Cass tried to catch her friend. Pete, however, hit

Cassie on the head too. This caused them both to fall in an ignominious heap at his feet.

CHAPTER 50

▼

Vickie wakened with a blinding headache. Her throat was burning, and there was a strange ringing in her ears. Someone was shaking her.

"Waken up, Vic, we have to get out of here." Cass was coughing, and her head seemed stuffed with pain and fog. Tentacles of fear were squeezing her heart. She could smell the smoke which was curling under the door.

"My eyes are stinging" groaned Vickie. "Is that smoke I smell? Oh God, where's the fire?" With her friend's help, she managed to sit up.

"Have you still got your phone?" gasped Cassie hopefully. After a moment's pause and a frantic search of Vickie's pockets, she got the answer she didn't want.

"It's not in my pocket. It must have fallen out when he hit me. It was Pete wasn't it?"

"Yes, he hit you really hard. Are you okay? We're lucky to be alive. I don't know why he didn't shoot us. He hit me too, but I don't think it was as hard as he hit you. I thought he'd cracked your skull. Come on, help me find the door. We've got to get out of here."

A tiny window high up on the wall, let in a minimum of moonlight. The dirty old basement was rapidly filling with smoke, and Vickie went into a long and hurtful paroxysm of coughing.

"It's locked" she wailed, wildly jerking the doorknob. On the periphery of her awareness came a new sound, a crisp crackling. She realized that it was the sound of hungry flames, and they were too close for comfort. Both women coughed and gasped as the smoke and heat seared their throats and lungs. The thought of burning alive was almost incapacitating. It was absolutely knee-buckling. It grabbed them by the throat and wouldn't let go. Their own mortality was suddenly slapping them in the face.

The acrid black smoke was curling under the door more enthusiastically now, caressing their feet and legs like some demented lover, working its way slowly and deliberately up their bodies. The stink of burning wood and linoleum was painful in their chests.

Dying in a fire was not the way Cass intended to go. This thought crackled and sparked in her mind, as she and Vickie kicked and pulled uselessly at the door. Vickie was crying and coughing, and using swear words which Cass had never heard from her friend.

Cassie's nerves were jumping like water droplets on a hot griddle. She forced herself to take a deep calming breath. Mistake! She went into such a virulent coughing spasm that she feared she would shake her lungs loose. Tears streamed from her stinging eyes as she tried to focus. There had to be a way out of this mess. Under no circumstances were she and Vickie going to be roasted like a couple of Cornish hens.

"Vic, could you get on my shoulders and knock out that window with a shoe?"

"Maybe" cried Vickie, wiping her nose with the back of her hand, and peering up at the tiny window through the thickening smoke. "What good would it do, though? Neither one of us could squeeze through it."

"Well, the fresh air would give us a little longer to figure a way out of here. Okay, then how about getting the door off its hinges? Could we unscrew the bolts?"

"Let's try." Vickie attacked the door with renewed strength. The bolts, however, wouldn't budge. They were there for the duration. In her frenzy, she jerked the doorknob right off, and stared at it stupidly before hurling it at the tiny window. It missed by at least a foot.

Determined not to be beaten by a moronic bully like Pete, and a simpering drunk like Jenny, they pounded and yelled to no avail. With lungs seared, throats as thick as melted caramels, and the flames crackling outside the door, it appeared that they were engaged in mission impossible.

Suddenly, above their cries and the snapping and hissing of the flames, they heard a somewhat familiar voice. It was music to their ears.

"Cassie, Vickie, where are you? Are you here?" There was wild alarm in that welcome voice.

It's Blake, they realized, in amazement, buds of hope suddenly sprouting in their hearts.

"Basement" they croaked in unison.

Soon Blake was pounding ferociously on the other side of the door. "There's no key. Stand back, I'm going to kick it in," he yelled.

When the door flew open, the women flew out. Flames were now licking lovingly at the stairs. They had to scramble through them. Vickie's sleeve caught fire, and she frantically tore off her jacket, as they staggered away from the house. They coughed and gasped, and eagerly sucked in that cool, sweet night air, as they followed Blake into a stand of trees beside the farm house. Where were Jenny and Pete? Please God let them be long gone.

When the first bullet rang out, Blake dropped in his tracks. Cass and Vickie let out muffled shrieks, as they knelt beside their rescuer. Pete was upon them in an instant, gun in hand. "Where's Jenny? What have you done with Jenny? She went back into the house."

Vickie was barely able to speak. Her head was throbbing and she was dizzy. Her throat was burning, and she couldn't stop coughing. "We thought she was with you. You left us there to burn" she coughed accusingly. She tried to stand up, but Pete pushed her aside and rushed towards the farmhouse, which was now an inferno.

Meanwhile, Willy the Weasel had been drinking beer all afternoon. Tonight was the night. He would get Willinger first, so that he could have a go at Darla before he got Lang. It had taken him a couple of hours to track down Jack, and he was frustrated and angry. Pounding the steering wheel of the car, he was about to give up, when he saw his prey finally arrive home. The detective had gone into his house, but had hurried back out again before Willy had time to think. He had jumped into his car and taken off, laying some rubber as he went. Willy had to make a quick choice. Should he break in now and rape Darla, or should he go after Jack Willinger first? He decided to get Jack out of the way, then he would come back for Darla.

He had kept within a reasonable distance. Nervously snapping the fingers of his left hand, he wondered how far they were going. It had never occurred to him to fill up the gas tank, and it was more than half empty. Three cups of coffee had sobered him somewhat, but now he had to pee. Dammit! He'd have to take a leak somewhere soon before he actually knifed Willinger. He needed all his concentration. As he finished the last of his coffee, he threw the cup onto the floor along with the rest of the detritus which lay there.

The old farmhouse was already ablaze when Jack arrived. He dashed in, looking frantically for the two women.

What a fool, thought Willy, who jumped out of the car and circled around through the trees to watch and wait. He hoped that Willinger didn't burn up in the old house. He wanted the pleasure of killing him himself.

Willy didn't see Blake lying on the ground, he didn't notice Vickie hunkered down beside Blake, and he certainly didn't spot Cassie, who was now leaning against a tree. He had eyes only for the burning house, watching for the detective to come out. As he waited and watched, and shifted from one foot to the other, he lovingly ran his fingers over his new knife, his beautiful new companion. For the moment his full bladder was forgotten.

"Stop right there" came a commanding voice from the shadows somewhere ahead of Pete. "Police, stop I say." A gunshot rang out, then another, an instant's pause, then one more.

The shots scared the heck out of Willy. In his fuzzy state, he thought that Jack Willinger was shooting at him. In his panic, he peed his pants.

Just then, two piercing screams came from the old farmhouse, as the entire roof fell in on itself. Windows shattered, and the house seemed to be echoing the victim's cries. The sky lit up like a Christmas tree, sparks crackled and popped.

Cassie peered through streaming eyes to see Jack running towards them, gun in hand. At the same time she spotted a man hiding behind a tree, and peeking out. In his right hand he held a wicked looking knife, much like the knife which had been left behind in her home the night of the attack on Vickie. He was making weird sucking noises with his teeth. Cassie understood in a heartbeat who he was and what he was planning to do. He was Vickie's would-be rapist, and he was going to kill Jack!

Suddenly everything coalesced in her mind. She had been attacked by bees, almost kidnapped, hit on the head, dragged down a flight of stairs, locked in a burning building, shot at, and now here was Vickie's assailant waiting to knife Jack. She couldn't let this creep hurt her old friend. She wanted to destroy this tooth sucking scumbag who had attacked Vickie.

She straightened up as if she had just taken a heavy load off her shoulders. Quickly pulling out her sharp scissors, she quietly motioned to Vickie. Poor Vic was in bad shape, but when she saw Willy in that single blistering moment, she recognized him. She remembered with perfect clarity, the sucking teeth sounds, the awful stink, the feel of the knife on her chest. This was the rapist, this was her chance. God was giving her a crack at the monster. Momentarily she felt that her muscles and bones had turned to liquid, then her adrenalin kicked in.

It took a supreme effort. She was weak and hurting, but she was also consumed with hatred. This was the loathsome creature who had tried to rape her.

He had cut her with a knife just like the one he was brandishing now. Somehow she found the last bit of strength in her battered and bruised body. She picked up a rock, and launched herself at Willy with a weird, guttural cry from her seared throat, just as Cassie flew at him with her trusty scissors, shrieking like a banshee.

Willy didn't have a hope against these two. He was so engrossed in watching Jack, who was now running right towards him, but who still had not seen him, that he was unaware of the girls flying at him from behind. Just as he stepped out in front of Jack, his arm raised to strike, Cassie let out another unholy shriek. She plunged the sharp scissors into the Weasel's knife-holding hand. As he yelled and dropped the knife, Vickie brought the rock crashing down on the back of his head. Willy crumpled like a rag doll out for the count. Vickie fell to her knees beside him.

For the next few moments there was total pandemonium, but somehow they got it all straightened out. Jack called for three ambulances plus the fire department, and told the women that he had shot Pete after Pete had taken two shots at him. The screaming must have been Jenny trapped in the house. Why was she there? Had she experienced a change of heart and gone back to rescue Cassie and Victoria? Cass wanted to think so, but they would never know.

"What the hell did you two think you were doing?" growled Jack. His voice was gruff, but he was obviously relieved that they were basically unscathed. He kicked at Willy the Weasel in disgust. The girls had done a good job on him. He was out cold, and his hand and head were bleeding.

A short time later Vickie whispered, "How did you find us?" looking from Blake on the stretcher, to a handcuffed Willy on a second stretcher, and then up at Jack.

"There was a message that you were trying to find me and that you were heading out here. I phoned your house to stop you, but your frantic cat sitter confirmed that you had already left. She told me that Blake had already set out looking for you." He paused and stared at the two sooty faces looking up at him. Both women were still coughing and gasping in the cool night air, and their eyes looked spacey, as if they might be going into shock.

Now they were all looking at Pete, who was swathed in blankets and buckled onto the third stretcher. In the light of the fire which was still burning ferociously, they could see that Pete's face was white and his eyes were closed. The paramedics were busy rigging IV lines and applying oxygen masks to the three patients.

"Is he dead?" asked Vickie, staring at Pete, the one who had started it all.

"Not yet" the paramedic responded curtly as they pushed Pete's stretcher through the yawning doors of the ambulance.

Blake's eyes were open, and he was grimacing in pain.

"You saved our lives, Blake" croaked Cassie with a smile and a gentle pat on his cheek. She felt teary as she looked at this man who had put his own life on the line to rescue them. She couldn't believe that at one time she and Vickie had thought he might be the murderer.

"Glad I got here in time, kid," he managed with a crooked little grin. "Next time you invite me to Niagara Falls, don't arrange anything quite so dramatic." He said this as he was lifted into the ambulance.

Willy had regained consciousness on his stretcher, and was screaming obscenities at everyone within earshot. His ratty little eyes focused on Jack, and he began shouting what he was going to do to Darla as soon as he was loose. Jack had to fight the urge to leap on the stretcher and strangle the loathsome little turd. As the doors closed on the still yelling Willy, Jack turned to Vickie and Cass.

"Get in. I'm taking you two to the hospital. You both need some looking after." He was tired and upset at having shot Pete. He was also angry that these two foolish women had come so close to being killed. Why did civilians love playing detective? He realized grudgingly, however, that he owed them his life. He hadn't seen the Weasel behind that tree, and would most certainly have been stabbed before he could get off a shot. They had done an amazingly brave thing attacking Willy that way. If he had been killed, that little rat would have gone after Darla. Jack couldn't let his mind go down that road just now. All he really wanted to do was to get home to her. He wanted to hold her tightly and tell her how much he loved her. When he thought of her at the mercy of the Weasel, he felt sick. Darla had finally confessed to Jack just how close she had come to having an affair with Dan the fireman. Jack had been appalled at first, but it was so much better than what he had been imagining, that he had no trouble forgiving her. Since then they had been like two newlyweds appreciating what they had almost lost.

The fire trucks were here now, and as Jack helped the two girls into his car, he barely nodded at the good looking fireman named Dan who ran past him toward the burning building. It was just one of fate's little jokes. He would never know that he and Darla's would-be lover had just come face to face.

Cassie's eyes were burning, her throat was raw, and every breath she took felt as if it was being drawn in over broken glass, but she suddenly remembered something. "Jack, I have it all on tape" she croaked, pulling out her trusty little recorder. "Jenny confessed everything just before Pete knocked us out. She seemed really proud of what she had done. She must have been crazy. Listen to this."

As she turned on the recorder and they heard Jenny's words, Jack shook his head. "Good for you. Guess I owe you an apology. I was so angry at you for coming out here, but you were both brave, foolhardy but brave. Actually you're just one step down from a couple of real pains in the ass." He grinned as they flew down the highway, sirens screaming. "You two are really something, taking Willy down with a rock and a pair of scissors. Maybe we'll get you a couple of tin badges." He was trying to keep it light, but actually Jack was very concerned about these two old friends who had saved his life. Neither woman looked to be in very good shape.

CHAPTER 51

▼

The Greater Niagara General Hospital is small compared to the huge Toronto hospital where Pru had been such an unfortunate patient. Because it is smaller, it seems to give off a more calm, less frenetic feeling. Entering by the main door, visitors can smell the wonderfully enticing aromas of various exotic coffees from the small coffee bar right behind the front desk. Entering by the emergency doors, the coffee aroma isn't as strong, but neither are the antiseptic smells which usually accost the hospital visitor.

The emergency waiting room was fairly busy, as Jack and his two tattered looking companions arrived. Fortunately he knew Lucy Roberts, the nurse working in triage. There were definitely some perks to being a cop. He strode directly to Lucy's cubicle and said "Hi, Luce, how's it going?"

"Jack, how are you?" cried Lucy in delight. She had always had a soft spot for this tall good looking man with that dashing scar. He had once helped her younger brother out of a jam, and she thought he was wonderful. Too bad he was married, she mused as she smiled up at him. "What brings you here tonight?"

"I've got two women with me, both smoke inhalation victims. I need you to process them right away. They're important witnesses in a murder investigation," he confided quietly. "Take the red head first, I suspect she may have a concussion."

There was much mumbling and grumbling from the others in the waiting room, but with detective Jack Willinger at their side being as protective as a mother hen, Cass and Vickie were able to ignore them. Actually, Victoria was ignoring pretty well everything at this point. She was trying to stay awake, but her eyes just kept closing.

She had been hit much harder on the head by Pete than Cassie had. When Cass bent over to catch Vickie and to break her fall, the second blow from Pete had glanced off her head. It had been enough to knock her out for a few minutes, but she didn't have a concussion or even a headache. She did feel very bruised and achy from being dragged down the stairs, but she was in better shape than Vickie, who had a large lump on her head, and whose hair was matted with blood. It was a miracle that she had been able to stay on her feet as long as she had.

Thanks to Jack and Lucy, they were both admitted quickly. That was another miracle. Cass barely had time to reflect upon the fact that she had just been here in emergency a few days earlier after the kidnapping attempt. She grimaced as she thought that she had been spending an inordinate amount of time in hospitals and funeral parlours this summer.

She was insistent that they be put in the same room. She wouldn't leave Vickie for a moment, till she knew that she was going to be fine. A head injury can always be serious, and if it hadn't been for Cassie's awful relatives, Vickie never would have been out at the old farmhouse, at the mercy of Pete and Jenny.

Cassie's throat was raw, she was nauseated, and she felt as if she had been worked over by a meat mallet. She was determined, however, that she wouldn't leave her friend's side. She stumbled along beside Vickie's gurney as it was pushed quickly down the hall and into the elevator. Her mind was becoming a little fuzzy, and she was confusing Jack with David. It was David running down the hall on the other side of the gurney, wasn't it? Then her head cleared again and she realized that David was far away. It was Jack who was striding along beside the gurney, and keeping his eyes on Cassie, ready to catch her if she fell. She should have been in a wheelchair, but she had stubbornly refused. She knew, somehow, that Jack would take care of her.

Vickie's eyes fluttered as she stared at the bright ceiling lights. Where was she, and why did her head hurt so much? She tried to talk to Cassie, but was barely coherent. "I don't feel so good, Cass" she mumbled.

"Well, you're not going out on a date tonight, so it's okay," Cass joked, patting her hand.

Once Vickie was settled in her bed, Cass was relieved to hear two nurses saying that her head looked worse than it really was. It was just a small cut which had bled a lot, and although she did have a big lump, it was only a mild concussion. They said, however, that she had to be kept awake for a while. Cass should have been in bed too, but she was reluctant to give up her place beside Vickie.

Taking Vic's hand, she kept talking and joking with her, and squeezing her fingers to keep her awake. "You're one feisty old gal, you know that?" she laughed. "You put a good dent in that little twerp's head with your rock. If you think your head hurts, just imagine how he feels. Remind me never to piss you off."

Vickie acknowledged this with a weak attempt at a grin behind her oxygen mask.

"It's weird, Vic" croaked Cassie. "Remember how we started out to visit the Brock monument and we ended up being attacked by the killer bees? Well, tonight we've ended up here in the Brock unit of this hospital. Isn't that coincidental?" She was just rambling, wheezing along with her smoke-encrusted throat and lungs, but she had to keep Vickie awake.

Vickie, of course, just wanted to sleep, and she wished that Cassie and Jack and those pesky nurses would leave her alone. She knew she was supposed to stay awake, but it was very difficult. All she needed was a good sleep and she would be fine.

Cass continued in her efforts to keep Vickie alert. "Tell me, kiddo, are we having fun yet?"

The irrepressible Vickie's brown eyes opened and stared at her over the oxygen mask. Then, lifting it a bit, she coughed and whispered, "Hell yes, we're having fun. What's next?"

Cass grinned and uttered a little prayer of thanks. Vickie was going to be fine. With this reassuring thought, she let the nurses talk her into bed. The cool hospital sheets felt wonderful on her bruised and aching body. The oxygen mask felt soothing on her burning throat. Knowing that her friend was in good hands, she gave herself up to the arms of Morpheus. As she plunged headlong into the darkness and comfort of oblivion, she smiled at the way the nurses seemed to be putting on a little show for Jack. They obviously found him attractive and wanted to impress him. As long as he hung around, they'd be there too to keep Vickie awake. Jack had said that he would stay for a while, so Cass just shut her eyes and let the world disappear.

Jack stayed, talking to Vickie and keeping an eye on Cassie. He was still amazed at how they had attacked Willy in order to save his life. He owed them so much even though they had been very foolhardy. He was sure that it was Vickie who had dragged Cass out to the old farm. Cassie would always have a special place in his heart, and he felt very protective of her.

Bud Lang had heard of all the excitement, and he showed up at the hospital too. Gloria and her family made the trip from Toronto in record time in the new car which Blake had bought her after the reading of the will. Blake underwent surgery to remove the bullet from his hip, but fortunately no major organs or arteries had been hit. He was a very lucky man.

Jack was exhausted by the time that he and Bud left the hospital around 4am. Pete had died, but not before regaining consciousness and admitting to causing the car crash and helping Jenny with the bee escapade. He seemed embarrassed about the aborted kidnap attempt. He had been the stalker, making the phone calls, sending the rat, and taking the picture of the cats. He seemed proud of his part in Jenny's schemes, and he had helped her set the farmhouse ablaze. When they told him that Jenny had perished in that fire instead of the two intended victims, Pete just stared past them with glazed eyes. Perhaps he was looking for his beautiful golden curled Jenny. Perhaps he was picturing their lives together without all the killings. Maybe he was seeing her dead and burned beyond recognition, or maybe he was thinking of that Florida marina which had been almost within his grasp. In any case, he sighed a deep, throat rattling sigh, then closed his eyes and died.

Jack was at the hospital the next morning to take Cassie home. He was glad that she had come back into his life. Now he could put their romance behind him and close that chapter for good. It would always be a bittersweet memory, nothing more. He had Darla, and he would never do anything to risk losing her.

Cassie's hands were bandaged, and her throat and chest hurt with every breath, but she was going home! There wasn't much wrong with her hands except that they were bruised and skinned, with a couple of torn nails from when they had been tearing at the door to get out. Once she was assured that Vickie was okay, she was happy to say goodbye to this place.

Vickie begged her not to contact her family. She didn't want to alarm them unnecessarily, and she was going to be fine. She was pissed off that the doctors wanted her to stay one more day, but they assured her that she would be sprung tomorrow. Actually this morning she was feeling amazingly well, considering what had occurred. She would have so much to tell her family when she returned to Vancouver. Strange, but at this point in time, Vancouver seemed another lifetime away. Would she ever be able to explain it all? Why hadn't she kept a diary?

Cass was relieved to get out of the hospital and home to the cats. They were excited to see her, rubbing against her legs and sniffing her all over. She obviously had that hospital smell about her. She cuddled and nuzzled them while she thought about all that had happened.

After an hour's rest, she went back to the hospital to spend time with Vickie and to look in on Blake. Jack had arranged for her car to be brought back from the old farm, and it was waiting in the driveway. This was actually Dave's car which she was driving now, and she was anxious to go out and buy a new one to replace the one which had the unfortunate encounter with the red mail box. Oh, there were so many things to be done! It was difficult to grasp that she would soon have all the money in the world at her disposal. She could buy anything and go anywhere she wanted. Right now she just wanted to be home with Dave and the kids, and she wanted Vickie out of the hospital.

By the end of the day, she felt that she knew Gloria and Blake and their family much better, and she liked them all. Lindsay in particular was a truly lovely girl, so different from her cousin Jenny. She was bright and enthusiastic, yet so gentle and caring with her dad. Strangely, no one had heard a word from Elena since the dramatic afternoon when the will was read. Had she left town? Was she out of their lives now? No. She would show up once the will was probated.

Jack and Bud came by the hospital to see how everyone was doing. They mentioned that after Willy's head and hand had been bandaged up, he had been taken right to the Welland Detention Center. It seemed obvious that he would be heading back to prison where he belonged.

Cass was having difficulty accepting the fact that all Pru's family, Matthew, Jordan and Jenny, were dead, as well as Prudence herself. She just couldn't deal with the fact that Pru supposedly had been her mother. That was still some kind of ugly fairy tale. All this psycho-drama was almost too much for her. She had always felt that she was as resilient as the unsinkable Molly Brown, but she was feeling emotionally soggy at this point. Oh well, she told herself with a grin, I'll be like Scarlett and think about all that stuff tomorrow.

CHAPTER 52

The incredible events of the past weeks were finally sinking in. Not only had Cass and Vickie come close to being the victims of two crazed killers, and not only had Cass discovered traumatic news about her parentage, not to mention the near rape of Vickie, but she and Vic had actually saved Jack's life. They were both rather proud, and perhaps a bit surprised at how they had acted under pressure. Then came the real bottom line. She, Cassandra Meredith, had inherited over twenty million dollars! What an unbelievably wonderful turn of events.

She wasn't going to spend any more time being inordinately introspective about Pru and Elena. No more psycho-babble mumbo jumbo. At this point, Pru was still a lump in her throat, a stone in her heart. It would be days, weeks, maybe years before she would be able to understand and accept the shift in relationships.

As for Elena, well, she wasn't worth Cassie's time. She hadn't liked her from the start, and now she understood why. Because of something Jack had told her yesterday, Elena was out of her life for good. Cass knew she would have difficulty forgiving her dad, whom she had always worshipped, and who was now unbelievably her grandfather. She had to smile to herself as she was reminded of the crazy song "I'm My Own Grandpa." It was all a bit nightmarish, and what she planned to do was forget everything except the inheritance. In her mind Lizzie and J.J. were still her parents and Pru was a distant sister. She wanted to leave it like that.

Now she had to come to terms with all that money. She had done what everyone dreams of — she had won the lottery! The enormity of it made her laugh out loud. It was scary though. She was a neophyte at being a multi-millionaire. Were there any guidelines? She sincerely hoped so. Even the minutiae of daily life would be different. The downside would be the responsibility which came with the money. Could she manage it with dignity and discretion and good old common sense? Hopefully. There would probably be endless meetings with lawyers, accountants, bankers. It wasn't as if she could just pop it in a bank account and watch it grow. She hoped that the downside would be far outweighed by the fun she and her family would have, as well as the happiness she could bring to others.

She told herself philosophically that there was no point in feeling guilty about the money. She hadn't asked for it, but it was hers now, and she and Dave and the kids were going to enjoy it. She already knew exactly what her first fun deed would be.

Ever since returning from the hospital, it had been raining. Today the sky was a sulky, sullen gray. Coming out of church that morning, they were accosted by a pack of media people. The news of the fire and of Jenny and her murders had been rehashed ad nauseam in all the newspapers, radio and television. It seemed never-ending. Somehow the media had found out that Cassie was the beneficiary of the Wainwright millions, and they were all agog over the story. They had been hounding her constantly, looking for one more interview, one more salacious tidbit for the six o'clock news.

The friends were now curled up in the library, a rather pretentious name for a cosy little room. All her life Cass had pictured having a house with a library. This room was smaller than the childhood attic where they had spent so many happy hours, but it was a good size, and it was floor to ceiling bookshelves on every available space. There was a stone fireplace for coziness, and an enticing cushioned window seat for enjoying the sunshine. This was one of the cats' favourite places to curl up and contemplate the world. It was where they had been sitting when Pete took their picture. There were comfortable chairs and a lovely little escritoire. The deep pile carpet and pots of greens everywhere gave a feeling of relaxation and safety. Cass adored this room. It housed all the books which she and Dave had collected and enjoyed over the years. It was the perfect hideaway for the true bibliophile.

At this moment they were sitting in the chairs facing the fireplace, and reliving the past weeks. It seemed that events had flown past at a rate too fast to comprehend. Cass had started packing for her surprise trip to Spain. Dave still didn't know that she was coming. Vickie was almost finished packing for her flight home. The kaleidoscopic summer was drawing to a close. Both women felt as if they had been caught in a whirlwind. True, there had been a lot of bad and tragic things happen, but there had also been a lot of fun thrown into the mix.

Today, instead of the usual cups of tea or glasses of wine, they were drinking champagne and munching on potato chips.

"This is absolutely decadent you know, guzzling champagne and eating chips in the middle of the day" giggled Vickie.

"It's worse than decadent, it's hedonistic," replied Cassie, taking another sip from her fluted glass.

"How about sybaritic?" mumbled Vickie, "or obscene or self-indulgent or debauched?"

"It's all of those things and more" laughed Cass as she refilled the glasses.

The news about Jenny and Pete and the murders had spread through Niagara like diaper rash on a baby's bottom. Cassie's little tape recorder had been the clincher. It tied up all the loose ends. They were even dragging the lake for Jordan now, with the help of "Joe" from Muskoka. Because the lake was so deep, however, they might never find him.

Blake had been released from hospital. His wound wasn't nearly as bad as it had appeared. He and Gloria had come to see Cass and Vickie on their way home to Toronto. Even dear old Douglas Bannon had called and spoken with Cass for a long time. He told her how happy Pru was the day she wrote the letter and changed the will. He made Cass feel so much better, as he advised her to enjoy every penny of the money.

Jack and Bud had visited yesterday, and it had turned out to be a day of celebration as well as a day of more shocking news. Vickie had been correct about Elena all along. She was indeed an impostor! Working on Vickie's request, the detectives had made inquiries and contacted the RCMP. They in turn contacted Interpol. It hadn't taken too long to discover that the real Elena who was Pru's half-sister, and Cassie's aunt, had died of meningitis in Spain six months previously. Elena had owned and operated a translating firm in Spain, and Maria Ortega, alias Elena, had been her secretary. Clients often commented on how much alike they were in appearance.

When the real Elena died, Maria saw her chance. She had access to all Elena's important papers, her passport, birth certificate, photo albums etc. Maria decided to become Elena and go to Toronto to find Prudence and Cassandra. She would ingratiate herself with them, and somehow get her hands on some of that lovely fortune. Elena had kept close tabs on Pru and Cassie from afar, and talked about them constantly. Her obsession to find them and become part of their lives became Maria's obsession. While Elena's goal had been to get to know her family, Maria's goal was to get her hands on the money.

Maria was clever and devious. She took her time organizing all the documents. She made certain that there were no pictures of Elena as an adult, except for the passport picture, but those, of course, are always a poor likeness. Pru had been much more gullible than Cassie. She was taken in right from the start. She wasn't really happy about Elena's existence, but she welcomed her into the family. Cass was doubtful, but all the papers and pictures convinced her, and if it hadn't been for Vickie and her "I'm from Missouri" attitude, Maria Ortega would have succeeded in her scheme to become Elena and possibly share in all the Wainwright millions. Instead she had been arrested before she could get her share of the inheritance. All her work had been for nothing — thanks to Vickie and her suspicions.

Today the friends were having a private celebration. "To tell you the truth, being amateur detectives isn't all that wonderful," mused Vickie, holding her champagne glass up to the light to watch the bubbles before taking another sip. "My hands are tender, it hurts to breathe, and I've been scared witless, or should I say shitless, several times lately."

"I know what you mean" agreed Cassie absently, watching the cats performing a familiar ritual. Sugar was on the footstool, Muffin on the floor beside her. She was industriously washing his ears and the top of his head. Muff was purring and staring off into space in a hypnotic trance. Suddenly Sugar Plum swatted his head, and jumping down, she raced from the room. Muffy took after her, his luxurious massage forgotten.

"You know, Vic, we were so wrong about so many things. We both suspected Jordan right from the start, and he certainly was a vile specimen of the human race, but in this particular case he didn't really do anything too bad. He did break into Douglas's house to see if there was a new will, and he did lock poor Maureen in the closet, but he didn't kill anyone. Maybe he planned to, but the point is that he didn't."

"That's right" agreed Vickie, taking another handful of chips, "and although we did suspect Pete of causing the crash, we never really believed that Jenny could be a killer. I still can't take in that she killed her own mother, as well as Bunny and Jordan. She was a real killing machine." Vickie uttered this last remark with a bit of a shudder.

"Not to mention how close she came to killing us" added Cassie. "Those bees were an inspired attempt."

Vickie wondered how she was ever going to be able to tell it all to Brian and the kids. She'd be lucky if they believed even half of it. "Look at Blake, after all our suspicions he turned out to be quite a hero. We would have been toast if it hadn't been for him."

"Bud turned out to be a genuinely nice guy too. I wasn't sure about him the first time we met, but once I saw how he was with Muffy, I knew he was okay. And then, of course, there's Jack." Cass rolled her eyes and grinned. "Honestly Vic, I didn't know just what I felt when I saw him standing at the door that first day. It brought back so many memories, some good and some bad. I was surprised at how many of the old feelings surfaced so quickly. It's a closed chapter now, though. I wouldn't trade Dave for anyone, even Jack, but I must admit, he is still gorgeous. I'd love to see what his wife is like, and I would still like to run my fingers along that sexy scar," she said defiantly.

Vickie put her finger to her mouth and made a gagging gesture. "The wife is likely drop-dead gorgeous and dumb as a post, and you keep your nasty little fingers off that scar. I could never understand what you saw in him, he was such an obnoxious kid."

"I'll never tell," grinned Cassie.

At this point Vickie started laughing. "Here we are, two middle-aged broads, and all we needed was a rock and a pair of scissors to bring down Willie and save Jack."

"That rock was the quintessential coup de grâce," agreed Cass. And, when I think of little Jenny flipping out like that and spilling her guts, I'm still amazed. She seemed so proud of all her killings. Thank heavens the wheels finally fell off her wagon, and all her schemes and dreams went up in smoke, literally."

"Don't mention smoke," shuddered Vickie. "I wish we knew why she went back into that inferno though. That's one mystery that no one will ever solve."

The friends sat for a while in companionable silence. Then Vickie said, "You know, Cass, in spite of everything, or maybe because of everything, this has been the most memorable holiday of my life. These past few weeks, sharing so much with you and the cats have been incredible. It's been the best of times and the worst of times, and I've enjoyed myself immeasurably."

Putting her glass down on the table, she added, "When I came here I was restless and anxious, and wanting some excitement. I felt tired of my family, and I needed a change. Being away for a while has made me realize just how much I love them all. Brian is the dearest guy in the world. He's quiet and a bit shy, but he's really smart, and he's so good to me. He puts up with a lot. I'm proud of my kids. They're just normal teens going through the self-discovery phase, but they're smart and honest and I think they're turning out well. Now I feel totally satisfied. I've had my fun, and I can hardly wait to get back to them. There's something to be said for peace and harmony and a certain amount of boredom. I feel good about myself, and I'm not restless anymore. It will be wonderful to see them and hug them to pieces. I hate to break up this 'ménage à quatre' though, or should I say, 'ménage à cats?'"

Cassie groaned at the pun. "It's not over yet, kiddo. The best is yet to come. I owe you an apology because at one point Jack had me almost convinced that you and Dave were having an affair."

"Whaaaaat?" shrieked Vickie, almost falling off her chair, a potato chip poised half-way to her mouth. "Are you serious?"

"Oh there's more," grinned her friend. "The great detective thought that you two might be plotting to kill me or to scare me to death."

Vickie's eyes were huge as she stared at her friend. "Cassandra Meredith, I don't believe you. Even Jack couldn't be that stupid."

"I know, I know, but with everything else that was going on, it took me a few days of serious thinking before I realized that it was impossible. I finally convinced myself that you two would be a horrible combination. You would be so incompatible."

This said, Cassie stood up and pulled an envelope from her pocket, handing it to Vickie.

"What's this?"

"It's a little something from me to you. I couldn't have managed these past weeks without you. You've been my support, my confidante, my friend. We've been through so much together that this is my way of saying thanks. And you know, it's very rude to refuse a gift, so you must accept it."

Now very curious, Vickie opened the envelope and stared incredulously at a cheque for one million dollars made out to her!

"Cass" she sputtered, "Are you crazed? I can't take this."

"Oh yes you can. Remember it's dreadfully rude to refuse a gift, specially one given with love and affection. I've got more money than Dave and the kids and I could ever possibly need. You've helped me through the worst period of my life, and I want you to have it. If you hadn't come to visit, I'd likely be dead by now." Then, grinning a bit, she added, "Actually this is just a fake cheque till the will is probated, so don't try to cash it yet! We may find out that it was all a hoax."

Vickie simply stared stupefied at her friend, as she tried to comprehend the magnitude of the gift. She knew it was useless to protest. When Cass made up her mind, she could be very determined. Suddenly she laughed. "Cass, guess what's going to be the very first thing I do with this ridiculously generous gift?"

"What?"

"Well, I'm going to buy myself the most beautiful, the biggest, the flashiest sapphire ring you've ever seen" chortled Vickie, her brown eyes flashing with mischief and delight.

"That's perfect," grinned Cass as she refilled their glasses. "It will be a great reminder of this crazy summer."

They had been friends in the past, they were friends in the present, and, God willing, they would be friends long into the future. It was a wonderful feeling.

"Hey, why don't we plan a vacation together to somewhere exotic?"

"Maybe we'll find another mystery to solve" they spoke in unison as they smiled fondly at each other.

The End

978-0-595-38617-8
0-595-38617-2

Printed in the United States
52562LVS00004B/1-9

9 780595 386178